Praise for *The Knight of the Red Beard*

"A strong story of magic and political power plays in a harsh northern land. The warmth of family bonds brings the characters to life and holds your heart with their trials and changes."
—*RT Book Reviews*

"The final volume in the late Grandmaster Norton's Cycle of Oak, Yew, Ash, and Rowan series ends with a rousing climax. . . . Coauthor Miller brings her storytelling talent to this fantasy that will appeal to YA as well as adult readers."
—*Library Journal*

Praise for *To the King a Daughter*

"Veteran SF and fantasy writer Norton combines her formidable storytelling talent with coauthor Miller to create a new series that . . . should appeal to adult and teenage fans of high fantasy."
—*Library Journal*

Praise for *Knight or Knave*

"An engaging saga building up to a future tumultuous climax . . . The hints of magic and destiny are intriguing . . . and promise to be further explored in future novels."
—*RT Book Reviews*

Praise for *A Crown Disowned*

"Enough swashbuckling, poisoning, and intrigue to keep readers turning the pages."
—*Publishers Weekly*

Praise for *Dragon Blade*

"Provides enough twists to hold any reader's interest."
—*Voice of Youth Advocates*

Tor Books by Andre Norton

THE OAK, YEW, ASH, AND ROWAN CYCLE
(WITH SASHA MILLER)

To the King a Daughter
Knight or Knave
A Crown Disowned
Dragon Blade
The Knight of the Red Beard

The Crystal Gryphon
Dare to Go A-Hunting
Flight in Yiktor
Forerunner
Forerunner: The Second Venture
Here Abide Monsters
Moon Called
Moon Mirror
The Prince Commands
Ralestone Luck
Stand and Deliver
Wheel of Stars
Wizards' Worlds
Wraiths of Time

Grandmasters' Choice (EDITOR)
The Jekyll Legacy (WITH ROBERT BLOCH)
Gryphon's Eyrie (WITH A.C. CRISPIN)
Songsmith (WITH A. C. CRISPIN)
Caroline (with Enid Cushing)
Firehand (WITH P. M. GRIFFIN)
Redline the Stars (WITH P. M. GRIFFIN)
Sneeze on Sunday (WITH GRACE ALLEN HOGARTH)
House of Shadows (WITH PHYLLIS MILLER)
Empire of the Eagle (WITH SUSAN SHWARTZ)
Imperial Lady (WITH SUSAN SHWARTZ)

THE SOLAR QUEEN (WITH SHERWOOD SMITH)
Derelict for Trade
A Mind for Trade

THE TIME TRADERS (WITH SHERWOOD SMITH)
Echoes in Time

THE WITCH WORLD (EDITOR)
Four from the Witch World
Tales from the Witch World 1
Tales from the Witch World 2
Tales from the Witch World 3

WITCH WORLD: THE TURNING
I Storms of Victory (WITH P. M. GRIFFIN)
II Flight of Vengeance (WITH P. M. GRIFFIN & MARY SCHAUB)
III On Wings of Magic (WITH PATRICIA MATHEWS & SASHA MILLER)

MAGIC IN ITHKAR (EDITOR, WITH ROBERT ADAMS)
Magic in Ithkar 1
Magic in Ithkar 2
Magic in Ithkar 3
Magic in Ithkar 4

THE HALFBLOOD CHRONICLES (WITH MERCEDES LACKEY)
The Elvenbane
Elvenblood
Elvenborn

CAROLUS REX (WITH ROSEMARY EDGHILL)
The Shadow of Albion

━━━━━━━━━━━━━━

Tor Books by Sasha Miller

Ladylord
On Wings of Magic (WITH ANDRE NORTON & PATRICIA MATHEWS)

The Knight
of the Red
Beard

Andre Norton &
Sasha Miller

TOR®
fantasy

A TOM DOHERTY ASSOCIATES BOOK

NEW YORK

This is a work of fiction. All of the characters, organizations, and events portrayed in this novel are either products of the authors' imagination or are used fictitiously.

THE KNIGHT OF THE RED BEARD

Copyright © 2008 by the Estate of Andre Norton and by Sasha Miller

Map by Ellisa Mitchell

A Tor Book
Published by Tom Doherty Associates, LLC
175 Fifth Avenue
New York, NY 10010

www.tor-forge.com

Tor® is a registered trademark of Tom Doherty Associates, LLC.

ISBN 978-0-7653-4661-2

First Edition: October 2008
First Mass Market Edition: December 2009

Printed in the United States of America

0 9 8 7 6 5 4 3 2 1

To my late collaborator, Andre Norton, whose vision
inspired the NordornLand cycle.

The Knight of the Red Beard

One

*E*leven-year-old **Mikkel was not** studying *The History of the NordornLand* as he had been instructed to do by his tutor. It wasn't his fault; he was distracted by the argument taking place just beyond the door of his outer chamber.

"Please go somewhere else," he called. "I'm trying to read."

Neither his older brother nor his sister deigned to answer. The least they could do, Mikkel thought, was to fight in one of their apartments or even the Great Hall. There were weapons in the Great Hall. Let them take up arms, settle the matter once and for all, and be done with it.

At another time, Mikkel would have been studying at the desk he and his tutor customarily occupied in the outer room, but even if Bjaudin and Elin hadn't chosen that room for their latest battle, he had no real objection to moving to his inner chamber. The room was much cozier and he preferred it for that reason, particularly during the cold months. He just wished it had been his choice.

At the moment, he was sprawled on his bed. He stuffed cotton wool in his ears, and, for good measure, covered them with his hands. He could still hear the two of them going at one another.

Why, he wondered, *do they do that? What have they to complain about?* Bjaudin held the title of NordornPrince; he was next in line to become NordornKing, and, in fact, had assumed many of the duties of kingship. Elin, as NordornPrincess, was next in succession after Bjaudin. His eldest sister Hegrin, whom he seldom saw, was actually a queen! Queen of Rendel she was, and turning out princes and princesses of her own. He, Mikkel, didn't have a title of any kind beyond the one he had been born with. His sole honor was that Father had knighted him last year. He could be called "Sir Mikkel" if he didn't care to be known as a prince. For a moment, he wondered what his title might be, if he had one. Duke of Obscurity, probably.

But there was no chance of even that crumb for him. There wasn't any need for him to be granted a title, other than Extra Prince, the younger son of Gaurin NordornKing and Ashen NordornQueen, the one who had no real prospects other than a life of hanging around the Nordorn Court, playing King's Soldiers and trying to stay out of trouble.

Or, he thought wryly, to cause it. Like Elin was now doing with her clamor to be proclaimed heiress to the Duchy of Iselin.

"Granddam Ysa isn't going to live forever," she was now arguing, forcefully enough that Mikkel could hear her clearly even through the cotton wool. "Iselin is a fair country—or would be, if Granddam would just care for it instead of only for herself—and it deserves to come into caring hands. All it would take is a word from you—"

"I am not the NordornKing," Bjaudin told her, not for the first time. "Such a bestowal is Father's to make, not mine."

Mikkel could almost see his sister's shrug in the dismissive tone of her voice.

"That's only a formality. All you have to do is mention it to him and it will be done."

"I see no reason to," Bjaudin said, again not for the first time.

"Well, I've *told* you," Elin retorted. "Shall I tell you again?"

Oh, no, Mikkel thought. He closed his book. Better to give up now and risk a caning from his tutor than stay and have to listen to the whole argument repeating itself.

He was saved by the arrival of Rols, one of the senior house stewards. The signal bell atop the Water Tower had begun ringing.

"The Sea-Rover ships are entering the fjord, young master," Rols reported. "Your father and mother and others are gathering at the landing to give proper greeting."

"Thank you, Rols," Mikkel said, grateful to have a legitimate excuse to leave his studies. "I thought I heard the warning bell. Have you informed the NordornPrince and the Princess?"

"I did on my way to you."

Rols bowed his way out of Mikkel's inner chamber and, before he closed the door behind him, added, "There are four ships."

Four ships when but two had been expected! Mikkel's day brightened immediately. *Who could the others be carrying?* he wondered. There had been a report at dinner last evening that the newest addition to the Nordorn fleet was being delivered under escort and should very likely arrive today, but nothing had been said about a third vessel, let alone a fourth.

One, three, four, or a dozen, this prospect was infinitely more interesting than listening to another of Bjaudin's and Elin's interminable battles, or even reading the history of the NordornLand and the tale of how Gaurin NordornKing and Ashen Nordorn-Queen had, at great pain to themselves, rid the land of an Ice Dragon that was held to be virtually unkillable.

He swung himself off the bed and dashed out of his bedchamber, tossing the book ungently on his desk, and in the process disturbing the half-grown warkat that had been drowsing on a rug in front of the hearth. The warkat shook its ears vigorously, then got up and followed Mikkel down the stairway leading to the Great Hall, and thence to the cool, clean air outside the Castle of Fire and Ice.

"When did you become interested in ships, Talkin?" Mikkel asked the warkat. "Or were you bored to tears with *them*, like me?" He indicated the area where Bjaudin and Elin had been fighting. "Well, whatever it is, let's go see what we can find."

The young Prince and his companion reached the landing at the top of the stairs that led down the cliff to the quay to find a considerable company already there.

The Castle of Fire and Ice had a sizable population. Not only the NordornKing and NordornQueen and their immediate family lived there, but also Uncle Einaar and Aunt Elibit, the Duke and Duchess of Åsåfin and the NordornLand, even though they had fine estates outside Cyornasberg and a handsome manor house inside the city as well. Mikkel stifled an exclamation of displeasure; Yngvar was with them, dressed in deep blue velvet, pale and slight and a total bore. For a moment, Mikkel regretted that he hadn't changed into better clothing to greet the visitors, but the feeling passed as quickly as it had come.

Admiral-General Count Tordenskjold was, naturally, on the scene to receive his newest addition to the growing Nordorn navy. Count Svarteper of Råttnos, Lord High Marshal and Protector of the NordornLand, stood beside the great Admiral-General, with the Countess Gyda at his side. Tordenskjold's wife, Aud, was absent and Mikkel remembered that she had left Cyornasberg to be with their daughter, Audiline, who was expecting the Admiral-General's first grandchild at any moment.

Svarteper's town residence was a part of the Castle of Fire and Ice, and Tordenskjold had an apartment set aside especially for him when business required his uninterrupted presence.

Other barons and counts came and went as they pleased, though this day it seemed that most of the Nordorn nobility had chosen to attend. Several had joined the crowd to watch the ships make the turn into the fjord. Mikkel recognized Count Baldrian of Westerblad and, a little to his surprise, Mjødulf of Mithlond and his wife, the Countess Ekla. Mjødulf almost never came in to Cyornasberg except on important occasions.

Father leaned on a staff carved with dragons and other fierce creatures, and Mother stood close beside him. Beatha, who had served as nursemaid to Hegrin, then Bjaudin, and so on through the rest of the royal children, hovered in the background. Though the need for a nursemaid had passed, Beatha stayed on. Transparently, she hoped for Bjaudin or Elin to marry and start producing babies for her to care for. In the meantime, she ministered to Father and Mother when they would allow it.

Mikkel's conscience bit him a little; he had just been attempting to read about the wounds his parents had suffered. Their Maimed Majesties, they were called now. Both wore gloves to hide their withered right hands. In addition, Father had suffered a weakened right arm as well as permanent injury to his left knee. It must be painful today for, handsome though his staff was, he disliked using it and did so only at need. Mother also bore the marks of that encounter with the Ice Dragon. Her left hand, where she had gripped the blade of a sword that had been forged from the scales of the Ice Dragon's mate, was badly scarred. Both were old beyond their years, their faces lined with wrinkles. Once Father's hair had been like Elin's, honey gold. Now it was almost pure white. Mother's hair also had lightened from its silver-gilt color until the gilt had melted into silver alone. Looking at the two of them, Mikkel wondered where his bright red hair and ice-blue eyes had come from.

"Greetings, Mother. Greetings, Father," Mikkel said, with a bow.

"And to you, dear son, greetings," his father replied.

"Did you come to watch the ships come in, or are you merely playing truant from your lessons?" Mother asked.

"Not playing truant!" Mikkel protested. No need to tell either of them that Bjaudin and Elin were fighting again. "You know I've always loved to watch ships, and, even better, to go on board one!"

"Well, then," Father said. "This is a brave sight. Find a good place from which to watch."

Arngrim of Rimfaxe, one of the barons, beckoned to Mikkel and he moved over to stand by him. He liked Arngrim, who bred excellent horses at his holding in Rimfaxe. He did not expect to see Gangerolf of Guttorm, who had a well-earned reputation for tardiness, and so was not disappointed.

Three ships had already cleared the headland. One he recognized immediately as *Spume Maiden*, as it was a frequent visitor to Cyornas Fjord. The second could be none other than Earl Royance's yacht, *Silver Burhawk*, with its rakish lines and boldly flying banner. The third was just cobby old single-masted *GorGull*, wallowing along, bobbing in the other ships' wakes, her stern wagging and threatening to throw anybody off the aftercastle.

The fourth ship had to be the newest addition to the Nordorn navy, saved for last to impress the crowd.

"Can you see the banner on that fourth ship?" Arngrim asked, smiling.

"Not yet, sir."

"You will in a minute, and there's a rumor that it's going to be a nice surprise to more than one. That's the new Nordorn ship, *Ice Princess*, and your uncle of New Vold, Rohan, is at the helm. He wouldn't entrust her to anyone but himself. Further, I have had word that he is bringing Obern—he's taking his turn captaining *Spume Maiden*—and young Tjórvi with him. Look to the banner, Prince Mikkel. There's a very special person on the *Ice Princess*."

At that moment, the ship cleared the headland to a gasp of admiration from the waiting crowd. Her design was radically new, crafted along marvelously clean lines. Like *Spume Maiden* she boasted three masts, with sails square-rigged on the foremast and mainmast and lateen-rigged on the stern, but *Ice Princess* was built without the overhanging forecastle that always made sailing to windward almost impossible. With a fair wind at her back, she looked capable of outrunning anything that currently rode the waves. Timing her entrance into Cyornas Fjord to follow awkward old *GorGull* emphasized the improvement. *Ice Princess* sliced through the chop created by the other ships with scarcely a dip of her bow.

The banner—Mithlond's snow-fox on a deep blue ground—flying alongside Uncle Rohan's blue-green with the device of a crashing wave, indicated the presence of one of Count Mjødulf's relatives. It was a mystery Mikkel did not take time to explore. He was too joyful over Arngrim's other news. Tjórvi was coming to

Cyornasberg! Now there would be good times indeed! The royal lad closest to Mikkel in age and station was his cousin Yngvar, and he was a stick. You never could have much fun with Yngvar around. Or, even worse, Mårten of Mithlond, who was nine and thought himself very grown up, much to the annoyance of those who really were. He always wanted to shove in on games of King's Soldiers—a very popular pastime for all castle residents—yet either could not or would not learn the rules.

Count Tordenskjold of Grynet, Admiral-General of the NordornLand and Uncle Rohan's friend and mentor, had been the one for whom Tjórvi had been named, but nobody called him by anything but his nickname. Mikkel and Tjórvi were almost the same age and furthermore, they shared the burden of being younger sons in families where the succession of rulership was already secure. Yngvar was as yet without a rival for his father's rank and estates and furthermore, made no bones about it.

Mikkel rubbed Talkin's ears. "Do you hear that?" he said. "Tjórvi's almost here! Good games of King's Soldiers for a change! And we can go out hunting! You'll like that." Life in the Castle of Fire and Ice, so burdensome just a few moments ago, seemed sweet once more.

"Think you've got the perfect excuse to get out of your lessons, do you?" said Granddam Zazar as she puffed her way onto the landing, followed by the unearthly little creature, Weyse, that went with her everywhere. For once Weyse was unaccompanied by Finola, the oldest female warkat in residence at the Castle of Fire and Ice.

Talkin uttered a sound halfway between a chirp and a purr, and immediately trotted over to Weyse to begin a wrestling match. The two creatures grappled playfully, getting underfoot.

"No, Granddam Zazar!" Mikkel exclaimed with as much innocence as he could muster. "One must show hospitality when visitors come, that's all."

Zazar sniffed audibly. "Well, let them come and then let them be gone again."

"How now, Madame Zazar," Gaurin said, visibly amused. "You will not be pleased to see Rohan? Or others of your grandchildren? Possibly even great-grandchildren. Young Obern is married now, you know."

"No blood kindred," Zazar retorted. "None at all."

"And so the more cherished," Ashen said, a smile hovering around the corners of her mouth as well. "Perhaps he's remembered that one piece of magic he could ever master, and will make you a silken rose."

Zazar just sniffed again. "I don't need any roses, silk or otherwise." She turned to Mikkel. "If you're so concerned about manners, why didn't you bring the NordornPrince and your sister with you? Answer me that!"

"I'll go get them," Mikkel said.

"No need," Zazar told him. "They were arguing over who went through the door first. I informed them on my way here that they'd better put their disagreement aside, at least for the time being, and get out here to greet their guests or risk my wrath. They'll be along presently."

Nobody, Mikkel thought, ever got the better of Granddam Zaz. For all that she had become very stooped with age, her mind—and her tongue—was as sharp as it had ever been.

After Granddam Zazar had scolded them and bade them depart in haste to the landing to greet their Sea-Rover guests, Elin-Alditha, NordornPrincess, scowled at her brother, the Nordorn-Prince. "This conversation is far from over," she told him.

"Oh, I know," he replied. "You won't stop until you get Granddam Ysa's duchy away from her. Or you think that is what is going to happen. But it isn't."

We shall see, Elin thought. She nodded her head, not quite a bow, and a slight frown on Bjaudin's forehead smoothed. *Go ahead and think you've won—for now. I'll have that nice bit of property, never you fear, my dear brother.*

"Anyway," Bjaudin continued, "what makes you think Granddam Ysa would agree to such a scheme as making you her heiress unless she thought of it first?"

In spite of herself, Elin stopped, struck by his words. Of course. Elin had overlooked what should have been obvious. As the implications of what Bjaudin had said sank in, she smiled as another plan unfolded in her mind.

Granddam Ysa had always been one for schemes and plots. She was old now, but surely she hadn't lost all of her cunning. Why not, then, enlist her aid, rather than making her an adversary? All Granddam Ysa really needed was a good excuse.

Elin's smile widened as she contemplated the avenues of speculation that opened up before her. Father and Mother were both in ill health. Father now confined himself to Council meetings only, leaving the administrative work to his brother, Uncle Einaar. It was a precarious situation at best, one open to charges of collusion and even treason.

"Thank you, dear brother," Elin said. "You have convinced me of the foolishness of my request. You will hear no more about it from me, I promise."

He nodded in acknowledgment, though his expression told her he did not fully believe her sudden capitulation.

A bothersome princess, even the NordornPrincess, second in line to succeed to the throne, might find herself married off to the first suitor who seemed likely, and sent away to trouble another land. Her sister had been wed when she was not much older than Elin was now. And that would not do at all.

Right now, there was the tedium of exclaiming over the new ship to get through, and the greeting of whatever guests had taken it into their heads to visit the Castle of Fire and Ice, and the necessity of guarding her tongue every moment and trying to convince everyone that, while high-spirited, she nonetheless was sweet and mild and compliant in her nature.

To that end, she allowed her brother to precede her through the doorway and down through the ward and thence to the landing where, she had to admit, the arrival of the ships was a brave sight. She paid particular attention to the new ship, *Ice Princess*, for she was certain it had been named for her. Therefore, it would, when she had gained enough power, be her own private vessel. She would deck it out in silver and white. The sails would be of snow-thistle silk—

Her reverie was interrupted by the arrival of the first wave of guests. Oh. Nothing to be concerned about. It was only Uncle Rohan and his ill-mannered sons. No sign of his daughter Amilia, with whom she could at least have converse even though she was a rough Sea-Rover maiden, or young Naeve who would be amusing to bully. Elin set her features in the pleasant, noncommittal smile she had practiced often before the mirror in the privacy of her bedchamber. Behind that smile she could think as she pleased, or even doze and dream herself a thousand miles distant.

A sudden burst of laughter, shouting and applause brought her back to the present. She realized that Earl Royance had arrived at the landing, escorting a woman who, though elderly by Elin's standards, was still passably attractive. The waiting crowd was now offering the Earl congratulations and wishes for a long life and—heirs?

It had long been a topic of conversation—oh, call it what it was, gossip—that the old Earl had been smitten with the lady whom he always referred to as "the handsome Mjaurita" and she had accepted his attentions without ever committing herself to any sort of deeper relationship. That explained Mjødulf and Ekla's presence. Mjaurita was Mjødulf's aunt. She had kept Royance dangling for years now, and apparently, had acquiesced at last to be married.

The ignorant might laugh behind their hands and make jokes about heirs, but Elin had long known that "Uncle" Royance was quite hale for a man of his years, and those years fewer than most thought. Royance was simply one of those men who had looked mature when he was young, and elderly when he was mature. He enjoyed looking the part of the seasoned statesman and also being still able to deliver a surprising counter to those who thought to take advantage of his supposed infirmity of age. If there would not be heirs from this union, the fault, if any, would lie with Lady Mjaurita, whose childbearing years must be well past.

Then Elin came fully awake behind her smile. Royance had come to the NordornLand to claim his bride. Such an important wedding demanded the most capable person in the land to organize it, and that would be none other than Granddam Ysa.

Of course she would be recalled to the Nordorn Court. It would be an unforgivable insult not to do so. Then, Elin would volunteer her services to assist. In the cozy intimacy of making wedding plans, she could remind Granddam that she had long been told she was Granddam's favorite. What a pity they had been separated so long. What an excellent opportunity to repair that oversight. Perhaps she could even go to live with Granddam for a while, once the wedding was over.

Later, Elin told herself, *I will go and find that bracelet I once saw in Mother's jewel chest, a bracelet composed, oddly, of nine tiny teeth strung on a thin chain.* She had never seen Mother wear the bracelet and, in fact, it had been hidden under the false bottom of the chest itself. She had found it only by accident—well, by snooping, actually. At first, she had thought it composed of baby teeth shed from her and her brothers and older sister, but the shape wasn't quite right. Anyway, Elin had only three siblings and that would not account for the nine teeth. When she had handled the bracelet, she had felt an odd, almost unsettling vibration as she touched each tooth in its turn. Furthermore, each vibration was subtly different. One tooth, one—person? They did not look like human teeth, not all of them.

Here, she thought, was an article of Power if only one had the means of divining how to use it. Perhaps now was the right time to try to find that means. Granddam Ysa would know. Or, between the two of them, they could find out.

That would be her avenue to begin to explore with Granddam ways she could grow more solidly in her favor and become her heiress in fact and in deed.

Yes, that would work and much better than her original plan. With Granddam Ysa in the forefront—and taking the brunt of the opprobrium and disapproval that would come her way—Elin could work in the background and, in the end, have the Duchy of Iselin and even the entire NordornLand itself!

Elin-Alditha NordornQueen. Now there was a name to be reckoned with.

As quickly as they could manage, Mikkel and Tjórvi slipped away from the crowd now surging toward the Castle of Fire and Ice, bearing with them Earl Royance and the Lady Mjaurita, who, as a prospective bride, had arrived on *Ice Princess* and not Royance's yacht. They also managed to elude Yngvar, who showed signs of wanting to be included in their company.

"Royance and Mjaurita have been all but living together for years," Tjórvi said with a shrug. "I do wonder what he bribed her with, to get her agree to becoming his Countess, though."

"Probably his entire estate of Grattenbor with Åskar thrown in as well."

"She already had those, or as good as. Well, it's a woman's mystery." Tjórvi shrugged again, dismissing the entire matter. "Let's go hunting!"

No sooner said than done. The boys, not bothering to wait to instruct stewards as to the disposition of Tjórvi's belongings in whatever guest apartment had been assigned to him, paid a hasty visit to the armory. A short while later, having avoided Yngvar once more, and now accompanied by the warkat Talkin and equipped with bows and a sheaf of hunting spears, they slipped out the postern gate of the Castle of Fire and Ice.

"They're starting to call this place Cyornas Castle down south," Tjórvi remarked as they made their way out of town and toward a copse of woods where reportedly there was small game to be had. With the approach of winter, conies would have put on their layer of insulating fat.

"Cyornas Castle? Really?"

"Well, you've got Cyornasberg the town, and Cyornas Fjord

already. So why not? Too much of a mouthful, all this Fire and Ice nonsense. Makes people think you have too high an opinion of yourselves, if you get my meaning, and maybe need to be taken down a peg."

"You mean there are people who would go to war over a—a *name?*" Mikkel said incredulously.

"Some people would go to war over the way you wear your hair," Tjórvi retorted. He glanced at Mikkel meaningfully.

Mikkel touched his bright red braids. "It's the Nordorn style," he said defensively. "When I'm older, I'll cut it. Maybe."

Tjórvi shrugged. "I suppose the braids keep the stuff out of your eyes. But I'm saying there are people who would fight you for just such a minor thing." He smoothed his wavy hair, a little more blond than red, cut a noticeable manly inch above his collar and secured with a headband. Unruly locks nevertheless escaped and hung over his forehead. "I have this, too." He showed Mikkel an amulet on a thin silver chain. The amulet was in the shape of an open circle and waves forever crashed inside it. "My da gave it to me on my birthday, for luck."

Mikkel had no such amulet—at least not yet. He decided to change the subject. "Why the fourth ship?" he asked. "Surely Mjaurita could have sailed on *Spume Maiden* or even on *GorGull* if she didn't want to be seen by her new bridegroom." He sniggered, and Tjórvi joined him.

"Well, as to that," he said, "*Ice Princess* is going to have a sea trial. Tordenskjold's going to insist on it, regardless of the trial she's already had, both the sailing up the coast and before then. Da will go back in *Spume Maiden* of course, Royance will be off on his honeymoon in *Silver Burhawk, Ice Princess* has a quick cruise up and down the coast, and even though it's late in the season, *GorGull* is going a-roving." He paused, relishing his next words. "I'm going to be on her."

"No! Truly?"

"Yes, truly!"

A sudden suspicion gripped Mikkel. "Does your father know about this?"

"Not yet." Tjórvi grinned mischievously. "But by the time he finds out, it'll be far too late for him to tell me no. Obern's been set to watch, but I can evade him easy enough."

"I suppose, in all the excitement—" Mikkel thought a moment, and then came to an instant conclusion. "I'm going with you. You think there'll be room for me on the *GorGull*?"

"Always room for one more. Well, maybe not Yngvar."

Both boys sniggered.

"Definitely not that stuck-up little princeling in training. Just you and me?" Mikkel said.

"Just us. I was hoping you'd want to go along. That's the big reason I told you."

"We'll be cabin boys together, or deckhands, or whatever the captain sets us to do," Mikkel exclaimed happily. "Who is the captain?"

"Fritji the Younger. He's grandson to my grandfather Snolli's old Wave Reader. He says he has a portion of his grandfather's gift, too, though I've never seen sign of it. His brother Jens has it more, so he wields the Spirit Drums."

"What do you think he'll say or do once he finds us aboard? Will he take us back home?"

"Not likely. It's the way of the Sea-Rovers. We take ourselves out to sea when we think we're ready, and nobody objects. If we are, we are, and if we're not— Well, it's a weakling gone and not much mourned." Tjórvi grinned again. "Fritji's a fledgling captain. He won't dare take us back. That would mean his first outing as a Sea Rover was a failure. So we're set. In fact, that's why we're on *GorGull*. It's the oldest ship in the fleet, and if it's lost, there's not much to mourn. The keel's already laid for her replacement. It's to be a sister ship to *Ice Princess*, and called *NordornQueen's Own*."

"Never mind that. You're talking about us maybe being lost as well," Mikkel said reprovingly.

Tjórvi threw back his head and laughed aloud. "The keel's been laid for *my* replacement, too!" he said. "Mam's expecting again. Anyway, there's nothing to worry about. Fritji won't go far.

One good raid and we'll be back at home, safe and sound, with stories to tell around the fire all next winter."

Talkin stiffened, and growled low in his throat. He began to move forward at a crouch, eyes intent on something the boys could not yet see. They fell silent immediately, and followed the young warkat. Tjórvi hefted a throwing-spear, while Mikkel nocked an arrow to his bowstring.

What seemed to be an entire nest of young conies erupted from the underbrush, scattering in every direction. Talkin raced after them in furious pursuit. Mikkel let fly one arrow, then another. His aim was better the second time. Tjórvi got one with his spear, picked up a rock and brought down another. A high-pitched squeal from farther in the brush told of Talkin's success.

"He won't bring it back, will he," Tjórvi said. It was not a question.

"Not likely. But he won't be trying to steal ours, either," Mikkel told him. "Let's skin these and take them back. I know a cook who'll prepare them in a pie, just for us. With a pastry crust and tubers and onions and lots of gravy inside."

Tjórvi licked his lips. "I can fair taste them already!"

Neither boy paid much attention to the ruination of their good clothes as they knelt in the dust and yanked the skins off the three rather small but plump conies. Stewed with a few vegetables and then baked in a dish covered with pastry, they would make a very good meal for two hungry boys. Later they could occupy themselves with a game of King's Soldiers, and leave both Yngvar and Mårten to entertain themselves.

The prospect seemed much more inviting than sitting through what was bound to be a boring state dinner that evening, almost certainly with both of them stuck at the same table with Yngvar.

Ashen and Gaurin had retired to the privacy of their own apartment, where they could speak freely as they prepared for the evening's welcoming guest-feast.

"Do you really think they're just out hunting?" Ashen asked Gaurin anxiously.

"Of course they are, my Ashen," he replied. "Don't they always, whenever they are together?"

Ashen had to concede his point. "They should have told us first," she said.

"So they should. But they did not. They are both growing up."

"And I hate to see it. Oh, I'm being silly."

He didn't try to disguise how stiffly he moved; that was reserved for public appearances, when he had to hide the pain. He took her in his arms and put her head on his shoulder, burying his face in her pale hair.

"You always smell so good," he murmured. "Clean."

She had to smile at that. "You never knew me when I was growing up in the Bog. I knew nothing of soap. Also, I was less than clean while I was following you to give you the Dragon Blade," she said.

"And you couldn't wait to bathe." He held her closer. "You are as you are. Let your youngest child be as he is."

"Only if he returns to make his manners with our guests. Just imagine what Ysa would think or, worse, say!"

"Speaking of Ysa," Gaurin said as he released Ashen, "Elin has petitioned that she be allowed to go and give the Duchess her personal invitation to oversee the wedding. She'll be there and back in less than three days. I am inclined to grant her this request."

"It is surprisingly well thought on," Ashen commented. "Ysa has scarcely visited Cyornasberg since I *suggested* she turn her energies to the governance of her duchy."

"As good as exile. It's been a very peaceful several years. But now I recognize that we must welcome her back to our midst for the sake of others. Perhaps she's mellowed."

At that, Ashen laughed out loud. "Never!" she said. "You do bring up the question of what gifts we shall bestow on the newly wedded couple, though."

"I will discuss it with Bjaudin and Einaar."

Then they both took their seats at dressing tables and Ashen rang for Ayfare and Nalren to come and make them ready for the banquet.

Though Ayfare had been Chatelaine and Nalren Seneschal of the Castle of Fire and Ice for many years, neither would dream of giving up the privilege of being personal attendants and body servants to Ashen NordornQueen and Gaurin NordornKing.

They took off their gloves, in preparation for donning fresh ones of white snow-thistle silk. Their Maimed Majesties, Ashen thought, gazing at Gaurin's withered right hand, a match to her own. She picked up a jar of soothing cream prepared by the Court physician, Birger, in collaboration with Zazar. She opened it not without some difficulty, and began applying it to her hands, especially the dry, withered one. Naught but Nordorn-crowned, the saying had gone, could wield sword of dragon spawn. Well, they both had wielded the sword and, though the NordornLand had been saved, both had paid a fearsome price. She handed Gaurin the jar of cream. He applied it to his hands in turn. The cream kept the skin from cracking and bleeding.

"Have you got Rohan's gift ready?" Gaurin asked as Nalren began massaging his face to smooth out the wrinkles.

"I have," Ashen said, "and I think you will be pleased with what I have chosen." Ayfare was ministering similarly to Ashen and as a consequence her words were a little muffled as the Chatelaine massaged a different cream into the skin around her lips. "Ayfare put it in my jewel box for safekeeping." The two women smiled at each other fondly; they had been friends since they were barely out of childhood.

Though Rohan had never made mention or complained of its absence, Ashen knew that Chieftain of the Sea-Rovers had always worn a particular badge of his office. Rohan's grandfather Snolli had been the last to do so. "It's a thumb ring. A special one."

"Ah," Gaurin said, understanding at once.

"All shined and polished, and fit for a Sea-Rover chieftain," Ayfare said with the easy familiarity of long acquaintance. She set aside the jar of skin cream and began brushing Ashen's long silver hair. When it was smoothed to her satisfaction, she would braid it in Nordorn fashion.

"Snolli set great store by his ring. It is still with him, wherever he may be." Gaurin held his head steady for Nalren to begin applying a thin layer of cosmetics, a process he particularly hated. Nonetheless, it would not do for the King to appear pale and wan, so he suffered the tinted lotion and a dusting of rouge without protest.

Ashen likewise was receiving a slightly heavier layer of rouge to her cheeks and lips than usual. She had to admit that they both looked better and healthier with the applications; appearances must be maintained.

"The white silk is laid out," Nalren told them. "Perhaps with red surcoats and mantle?"

"That is well thought on."

As women's styles had changed, so had men's. Though men customarily went clean-shaven, the NordornKing now wore a neatly trimmed beard, a fashion that several in the court emulated. His doublets were padded to hide a certain gauntness, and his collars were high, to conceal the thinness of his neck. When Nalren finished dressing him, only a close eye could detect that he was no longer his hale and robust self.

Rather like me, Ashen thought. *I am too thin.* "Who is overseeing the preparation of the feast?" she asked.

"My assistant, Huldra," Ayfare said.

"You trained her yourself," Ashen commented. "Therefore, she is to be trusted with tonight's important event."

"When you have finished with your lady's hair, would you bring the new Chieftain's ring for my inspection?" Gaurin said.

"Yes, Sir."

Ayfare put a few last touches on the shining looped braids she had arranged on Ashen's head, set the small diadem in place, and went to do Gaurin's bidding.

How clever Ayfare is, Ashen thought. The diadem, one of a

matching pair made for the Nordorn monarchs, settled under the pile of braids as if an integral part of them; the midpoint of the band dipped lightly onto her forehead. A crystal snowflake glittered at the center, and in its heart glowed a fire-stone, one of the handful that remained of the crown of Cyornas NordornKing of reverent memory.

Neither Gaurin nor Ashen wore their own state crowns often these days. The spiked silver columns spangled with crystal snowflakes made for a precarious burden, and the bands encrusted with fire-stones rested on their heads far too heavily. The diadems sufficed.

Ayfare returned with the newly made ring for the Chieftain of the Sea-Rovers and laid it on Gaurin's dressing table. As far as Ashen could tell, and working only from her memory, the goldsmith had duplicated the ring as closely as anyone could. Yet another fire-stone, of a size fit for wearing on the hand, adorned the broad band of the thumb ring. Ashen recalled how the original ring's red stone seemed to flame in whatever light was to be had; perhaps it, too, had been a fire-stone, gleaned ages past from another dragon's hoard. This one had been chosen from among the ones the Mother Ice Dragon had disgorged from her scales when she had been defeated. Rohan would be pleased.

Then Nalren and Ayfare helped Gaurin and Ashen into their festive clothing. Current styles for ladies dictated simply cut dresses with a snug bodice ending just below the bosom. The sleeves were separate items, laced in place, and these were lined with soft wool blended with silk. Over this went a crimson fur-trimmed sleeveless coat. Her dress and Gaurin's doublet were covered with embroidered silver snowflakes and on Gaurin's there was also an embroidered silver snowcat wearing a silver collar—the badge of his house. On her skirt she bore the Ash badge—flame rising from a vessel of pure silver. The silver state necklaces set with the remainder of Cyornas's fire-gems and coats of deep crimson warmed what might otherwise have been too cold an appearance for the two monarchs. Crimson mantles completed their attire.

Nalren placed Gaurin's diadem on his silvery hair and settled it onto his forehead. He and Ashen drew on their gloves, arose from the dressing tables, and Gaurin took up his staff.

To Ashen's secret amusement, both Nalren and Ayfare stepped back a pace, heads cocked appraisingly, so identical in attitude that she nearly smiled.

"Do we pass your muster?" she asked, unable to hold back the words.

"You both look very fine. Now, please do not over-do tonight. You need your rest."

"I hear and obey," Ashen said with a laugh.

Contentedly, Ashen took Gaurin's arm and they left their apartment, there to be met by her ladies and his Court gentlemen. To the sound of welcoming trumpets, they descended into the Great Hall.

Two

Zazar customarily left the Great Hall as soon as she could, once the banquet was finished and the musicians had begun "The Song." This evening, however, she wasn't quick enough, and had actually been asked to dance—twice! And would have been again, had she not made a hasty, undignified exit.

Her bones creaked anew at the thought. But Gaurin himself had requested her to partner him, and Wysen-wyf or no, one did not refuse the NordornKing.

She had thought that would end her ordeal, but then she caught Lady Mjaurita whispering in Earl Royance's ear. The answering mischievous smile on his face told her clearly that he also had in mind a turn around the circle of dancers. Unable to escape, she had acquiesced, thinking that she was surely the butt of many whispered jokes. Then, brooking no further delay, she hurriedly fled the Hall just as Bjaudin NordornPrince started to arise from the table, his intent plain.

Gratefully, she let herself in to her small apartment, located in the northeast tower high up where the great folk would not deign to reside. Her quarters had originally been intended as guard rooms, to be manned with soldiers in time of war. It was, possibly, the coldest of all such installations, though certain improvements such as glazed windows and heavy shutters made it habitable. On the other side of the room from the hearth, one's breath showed plainly in the cold air, making it prudent to keep a hood drawn up over one's head.

Zazar did not mind the cold, though she was grateful for the fire that was always kept going in the grate. And, of course, the garments of new-fangled snow-thistle silk, though she preferred sturdy garments sewn of the coarse variety.

Over the years, she had gradually turned the rooms into almost a replica of her old mud-and-daub hut back in the Bog, where Nayla, the current Wysen-wyf, now held sway. In place of snug mud walls, she had somewhat haphazardly stitched together old blankets and hung them on the chilly stone walls to act as insulation. Zazar had divided the room itself with another curtain made of more old blankets hung from a metal rod fastened to the corbels that supported the tower room's roof. This set aside the area where she slept, also insulated with yet more of the old blankets.

Strings of dried and drying herbs hung from cords strung here and there around the main room, and she had cajoled castle carpenters to build shelves on which she could store jars of ground bones, seeds, dried leaves, the remains of an orb snake, a little box with a few precious threads, castings from the Loom of the Weavers. Another box held divining bones.

On another shelf were arrayed jars and bottles of healing mixtures, herb-enriched salves, potions to dull pain whether from battle wounds or for women in labor, emetics and laxatives, soothers and binders. Here also was her jar of trade-pearls, items hard to come by but another habit even harder to break. Nayla always refused payment for the Web castings, but she would accept a gift of trade-pearls.

Two chairs were drawn up to the fire, and on one of them Weyse was curled up, sound asleep. As she was half again the size of a house cat, she filled the chair entirely. For once, the warkat Finola was not with her. Finola and Weyse had formed a well-nigh unbreakable bond many years ago, during the War of the Four Armies, against the Great Foulness. Nowadays, however, Finola was just as likely to be with her own cub as with Weyse.

Zazar took a twig from a jar on the hearth, touched it to the fire, and then lighted candles on the small table between the chairs, and the larger worktable in the middle of the crowded room. On the worktable stood her kettle, and nearby a basket full of reeds ready for soaking. She still wove reed mats, not because she needed them, but out of habit and for lack of anything better to do. She liked keeping her hands busy but did not care to indulge in the craze for the board game King's Soldiers.

No longer did she need to boil mollusk glue to repair the thatch roof, nor did she need to make her tart lemongrass stew, thick with noodles, except when she had a hankering for it. Nowadays the kettle was used for soaking reeds, brewing potions and—rarely—for invoking the Ritual of Asking, that required a sprinkling of the precious Loom castings.

"It's a soft life you have," Zazar told herself aloud, pretending that she was speaking to Weyse. The unearthly creature drowsily opened her eyes, yawned, and shifted positions a little, asleep again almost before she settled.

A wicker-covered bottle on a shelf beside the fireplace caught her eye. Yes, if ever she had earned the comfort of a dram of that particular potion, it was tonight. Dancing—and at her age, too!

She took a goblet from another shelf and poured herself a generous portion. No tame spirits this; it was *brandewijn* she personally distilled from snowberry juice and used, much reduced in strength, in several of her best potions. This, however, was not diluted. The sharp, fruity aroma filled the little room and warmed her even before she set the rim of the goblet to her lips and took a hearty swallow. This brew was much better than the one she had used to make, back in the Bog, from whatever berries she could find in that inhospitable place, and the results were both tastier and more consistent.

Contentedly, and perhaps already feeling the effects of the *brandewijn* on top of the wine she had drunk at dinner, she took down yet another box from a low shelf, set it on the little table, sat down in the other chair, and began examining the contents.

Spurs. Real knight's spurs. Zazar could still feel the touch of Gaurin NordornKing's sword on her shoulders as, in gratitude for her part in vanquishing the Mother Ice Dragon, he had knighted her and made her a peer of the NordornLand.

Lady Zazar, she thought derisively. *Or, perhaps, Dame Zazar. Sir Knight Zazar?* She snorted and took another sip of *brandewijn*. The liqueur's heat spread through her, vanquishing old, nearly forgotten aches, making her feel almost young again.

"He could have made me a baron, too, or perhaps a count," she told Weyse. "Countess. But what would I do with the title? Fight Tordenskjold or Gangerolf for territory? That would be as useless as these." She tossed the spurs back into the box.

Ashen NordornQueen had taken part in the ceremony as well, presenting her with the spurs. Pure silver they were, and only a fool would try to actually use them if the fool happened to own a horse, which she did not. They were strictly for show.

Ashen. Only when she had drunk a little *brandewijn* would Zazar allow herself to admit how fond she was of the girl—despite the fact that she was now a grandmother several times over, Ashen would always be a *girl* in Zazar's eyes. And she was much too fond of Gaurin as well. No one but Gaurin would ever have been able to coax her out into the center of the Hall to dance.

Zazar had always regretted bitterly that she had no power to stop the relentless withering of Ashen's and Gaurin's right hands, the ones that had wielded the Dragon Blade when at last they had confronted the horrible, well-nigh unconquerable beast. It was a failing on her part and the soothing cream only a palliative. They were known as Their Maimed Majesties these days, and they accepted their titles with public grace and private resignation.

In a moment of self-pity for this failure, fueled by the *brandewijn*, Zazar told herself that they were ungrateful, that they had no real right to still be alive. The Mother Ice Dragon had all but killed Gaurin outright and Ashen had escaped only because something had told her to break the sword rather than try to kill the dragon.

They had both entered into legend.

Zazar hoped their children would live up to their parents' legacy. Bjaudin she had doubts about; he was more the scholar than the warrior his father had been. Elin? There was something, well, unsettling about her. Mikkel was, Zazar thought, still too young to know. He was much more interested in playing that board game or going hunting with that Sea-Rover boy than thinking about his future.

Behind her, the box containing a small ball wound of the Web castings rattled a little on the shelf. Without glancing back, Zazar could see a faint glow reflected on the stones of the fireplace. That generally happened when there was some message for somebody the castings were eager to relate.

"Be quiet," Zazar said firmly. "In my time, not yours."

She finished the contents of the goblet, thought a moment, and then refilled it.

Duke Einaar watched from a window of the room he used as an office as the Duchess Ysa of Iselin came sweeping into the Castle of Fire and Ice much more regally than she had left it. Because her arrival was by land, she had come in her own carriage through Cyornasberg Gate, down Broad Street and through the barbican.

Her ladies would also be accompanying Ysa, though not in her carriage. With an effort, he remembered their names. Gertrude, Ingrid, Grisella, all well past their prime. They rode behind the carriage with Elin's ladies, and behind them, Ysa's House Troops in double file. Bringing up the rear was a wagon, piled with luggage.

Ysa's Troops were still headed by old Lackel, now so ancient as to be well-nigh fabulous. Whatever the Duchess's failings, Einaar mused, disloyalty to those who served her faithfully was not among them. Lackel looked too stooped and frail even to carry the sword at his side, Einaar observed, let alone wield it. He wondered how the old fellow could manage to stay on his horse.

The Troopers themselves were gray-haired but the only battles they might be expected to fight would be those of Court gossip and innuendo. Against them, men's weapons were useless.

Down in the inner ward, Ysa was taking her time, unhurriedly descending from her carriage, helped by her ladies, settling her voluminous emerald green cloak about her shoulders, accepting her lapdog—a lapdog! Bringing something like that into a castle where warkats roamed freely? Einaar shook his head. Trust Ysa to create trouble in ways both small and large.

The hood slipped back, revealing Ysa's face. Her Grace, Einaar noted, had aged far more than a woman of her years would have been expected to do. Deep wrinkles bracketed her mouth—still bravely painted scarlet—and scored her forehead. The skin of her neck drooped, even though Ysa had tried to hide it with a fur boa. Also, her shoulders were beginning to stoop, making her look shorter than she really was. He thought a moment, counting years. He was now in his late thirties. His brother Gaurin was some ten years older. Ashen was about forty-five. But Ysa actually looked older than Madame Zazar, who had lived uncounted years, though she had to be only in her mid- to late sixties—still comparatively young for a well-maintained upper-class woman.

Ysa was rumored to have dabbled widely in magic, using it to maintain the freshness of her first youth. There was always a price to pay for such doings, Einaar thought, and he was now looking at it.

The Duchess paused, obviously making certain that her retinue had all arrived safely into the main ward of the inner keep, and Einaar knew that he must hurry down so he could be with the greeting party. Not to do so would have been an unforgivable breach of good manners, and even someone not so punctilious as Ysa would be sure to notice. He lingered only long enough to glimpse Princess Elin, also clad in green, emerging from the coach as well, and then headed for the stairs.

The NordornKing and NordornQueen were already waiting in the vestibule of the Great Hall with their own retinue around them. Einaar saw his wife Elibit just as she caught sight of him. She was with child again; the way her face lit up at his appearance always warmed him through and through. Young Yngvar stood at her side, decorous as always.

"My lord," Elibit exclaimed, hurrying to his side. "You are almost late!"

"But not quite, my lady Duchess," he said, and kissed her on the cheek. "And you, Yngvar. How goes my son and heir?"

"Very well, my lord father," Yngvar replied gravely.

"I am pleased," Einaar told him. The boy was very much like Einaar's foster father, for whom he had been named. A good old man, worthy of better than he had received at the hands of Bergtora, Einaar's mother. He hoped their new child would not be a girl; by custom, a girl would be named for her grandmother. He turned, a little belatedly, to his half-brother and Ashen.

"My lord King and brother." He bowed low.

Gaurin returned the gesture in the proper degree. "Your Grace." He smiled.

Einaar turned to Ashen. "My lady Queen and sister."

She held out her left hand to him and he took it gently, kissing her fingers through the glove she wore.

How frail they both looked, Einaar thought. Royance moved forward, his step youthful, his cheeks showing color.

"Greetings, my lord Earl," Einaar said.

"And to you as well," Royance returned. "How long must we play these Court games?"

At that, Einaar smiled broadly. Royance, despite the difference in their ages, had always been a kindred spirit both to him and to Gaurin. "No longer, sir!" Then he gathered the Lady Mjaurita in his arms and bussed her right heartily on the mouth.

"My lord husband!" Elibit exclaimed. "Whatever will Earl Royance be thinking!"

"That my lady finds favor in more eyes than mine," Royance

said, amused. He retrieved a laughing Mjaurita from Einaar's embrace.

"Fie, my lord Duke! Your wife got not nearly as warm a welcome as I," Mjaurita said teasingly, glancing at Elibit.

"Just wait until we are in private," Einaar told her.

Elibit blushed. She had never become fully accustomed to the teasing that went on among some of them in the inner circle of kindred and near-kinship. "We must compose ourselves, my lords and ladies," she said, "for our guests are arriving."

The Court, including Gaurin's gentlemen and Ashen's ladies, moved out from the vestibule onto the big landing at the top of the stone stairway leading from the ward to the Great Hall of the castle just as Ysa reached the foot of the stairs.

"Greeting, my lady Duchess!" Gaurin said. "We make you right welcome to the Castle of Fire and Ice."

"Thank you, Gaurin NordornKing. Have Royance and Mjaurita married yet?"

"We were waiting for you," Royance said genially, putting his arm around Mjaurita's waist.

"Elin, welcome home, my dear daughter. Come inside, all of you, please," Ashen said. "You must be wearied by your journey. We have food for all, and warmed wine with snowberry juice."

"Thank you, Ashen. It grows cold early this year. Mjaurita, greetings. As lovely as ever. Royance is a lucky man, even if he is more tardy than any other woman would tolerate. Where are my grandsons?" Ysa asked as she climbed the stairs to the landing.

"I am here, Granddam Ysa," Bjaudin NordornPrince said, stepping out of the crowd. He bowed low. "Alas, I think Mikkel is off hunting, unaware that you were to arrive today. My apologies for him."

"Oh, no apologies necessary—"

At that moment, Rohan emerged from the Hall. "I am here, Granddam Ysa!" he cried. "Sorry I was late."

With a flourish, he produced an emerald-green silk rose out of nowhere and presented it to her. The crimson stone on his new thumb ring glowed in the noontime light. It didn't escape Ysa's notice.

"You've come up in the world, with your fancy jewels," she commented. "I didn't think you the type for rubies."

"It's a fire-stone. My dear foster mother and father, Ashen NordornQueen and Gaurin NordornKing, were kind enough to provide me with a replacement for the badge of the Sea-Rover Chieftain. My grandfather's went with him to a watery grave."

"Oh," Ysa said, scarcely chastened. "Yes. Well, greetings, Rohan. I didn't expect to see you here."

"You wouldn't have, except that I delayed my departure for the purposes of seeing my Lord Royance wed, and greeting you again. One week hence, I return to New Vold on *Spume Maiden.*"

"So soon! But the gowns, the flowers—"

"All arranged for, Madame Mother," Ashen said. "You are to rest and enjoy the festivities without a care."

"Then why send for me? I have no duties."

"Ah, I meant only that the hard work was done. But believe me, there are many final details of protocol that will be perfect only with your expert touch!"

"Hmph," replied Ysa, scarcely mollified. "Where am I to stay?"

"Your old apartments have been cleaned and warmed. Everything is much as you left it," Ashen said.

"When I was asked to leave by you, if I remember well," Ysa retorted. "Well, no matter. I'm back now."

And so she was, Einaar thought wryly. Further, he had no doubt that she would stay as long as she pleased—or until she was asked again to leave.

"I wish to examine the completed castle," Royance told Gaurin the next morning at breakfast in the small room off the Great Hall, close to the fire. The room had served many purposes since the castle's construction; now it functioned as a private dining room, easy to warm. "The women are busy with whatever it is that occupies them, and I'm always interested in this kind of architecture. The inner barbican is a late addition. And that tower by the Water Gate—that's even newer, isn't it?"

"It is," Gaurin said, setting aside his bowl of bread scraps soaked in flat ale, the customary breakfast of Nordorners. "We could not build a guardian castle to that gate, such as exists in Rendel wherein the Lord High Marshal resides, but we constructed a residence for our own Lord High Marshal in the great barbican."

"Very wise," Royance commented.

"I will ask my brother to act as your guide. A would-be invader would have a hard time coming at us from Cyornas Fjord, and an even worse time trying a land assault. It would disturb and annoy our Lord High Marshal and I know I would hate to go against Svarteper when he is angry."

Royance laughed out loud. "As would I. It is an impressive fortification. Your engineer must know his business."

"Indeed he does," Einaar said. "Come, sir, and I will gladly show you whatever you desire to see."

Cyornas Castle—the Castle of Fire and Ice—was a formidable structure indeed, looming high and proud on the north cliff-face of the fjord. No danger of invasion from the southern face, for it was taken up with a great ice-river that frequently dropped massive floes of ice, making navigation dangerous. Out in Cyornas Fjord, no good anchorage had ever been found, so ships moored to permanent buoys positioned where the ice would be unlikely to be a hazard. A loading wharf was now under construction, attached to the land.

Almost rectangular in shape, the castle boasted great towers at each corner, with lesser towers punctuating the curtain walls and a new open gorge tower in the middle of the east wall. It was built of pale buff native stone whitewashed to rival snow so that the eyes of potential enemies might be dazzled. At certain times of the year, it loomed as cold, forbidding, and formidable as the ice-river across the fjord.

The Cyornasberg Barbican Gatehouse, a late addition, was almost as strong as the Water Gatehouse, boasting two portcullises and double walls with arrow slits affording a wide angle of fire. If an enemy could make it through the town—a difficult proposition, as the town walls were thick and also well provided with defensive towers—he would face a daunting challenge at the barbican. Then he would have to fight hard to gain the gate to the castle itself. The Lord High Marshal's banner, a silver devil-tree on a black ground, flew from a staff atop the highest tower. A second banner, a white snow-fox on a deep blue ground, proclaimed that Admiral-General Tordenskjold was in residence in his apartment in the barbican.

The castle had proven barely adequate to house all the permanent residents, outgrown even before it was finished, and so a veritable village of outbuildings had sprung up, like weeds, between the castle and the town wall, crowding even the fixed bridge between the barbican and the castle gate against which a sturdy drawbridge could be raised. Here were smithies and stables, reserve barracks and mews, fullers, tailors, bakers, shoemakers, all hoping for patronage from the castle itself as well as the town residents, and all seldom disappointed. The spinners' and weavers' guild was important enough to rate its own defense tower and a wall with its own gate, in a corner where town walls met castle curtain. Income from the spun and woven snow-thistle silk created a substantial part of Nordorn wealth.

Cyornasberg had grown to become a very respectable city, the primary defense against wild northern tribes—Fridians, untamed Aslaugors, stubbornly independent Nordorners, even the fabled, warlike Wykenig wanderers, said to be moving steadily southward.

"I have already delivered this message to Gaurin and Ashen, and will tell you in turn," Royance said. "King Peres and Queen Hegrin are very much in the debt of the Nordorners, standing as they do as a bulwark between Rendel and their enemies. Kinship is kinship, but such alliances have broken in the past."

"Not these. Let us hope that Rendel remains ever in peace, due to our efforts," Einaar replied. "Are Their Majesties well?"

"Thriving. Queen Hegrin just presented us with another prince—Arnaldr."

"That makes—how many?"

"Four. Boroth the Younger, the heir; Prince Nollan; Princess Gizela, and now the new one. I fear, among all those boys, Gizela may be a bit spoiled."

Einaar laughed. "And why not. Our own Princess Elin is a bit spoiled as well. There is no harm to it, when they are young."

"And yet the young have a way of growing older," Royance observed. "Was that the dinner bell?"

"It was. We should be returning to the Hall."

"This afternoon my lady wishes to take a drive with me out into the countryside while late autumn still holds and the snows have not yet begun. She would rather go to Åskar to inspect the new fortified manor house I have built for her," Royance said, "but that would take several days. I daresay she has become weary of the wedding preparations as much as I. If it were not for friends and relatives, we would steal into the Fane and let Esander the Good say the words over us in private and have done with it."

A sudden suspicion, coupled with the expression on Royance's face and the tone of his voice, dawned on Einaar. "If I didn't know better, I would think you had already visited the Fane, and Esander. But of course you haven't—have you?"

To his delight, Earl Royance blushed to the roots of his hair. "My lady Mjaurita is a good and virtuous woman. She would not— Well, she insisted that we, um, regularize our relationship some years back. Now, we are just making it all public for propriety's sake, and because she is weary of keeping up a long outgrown pretense."

Einaar laughed aloud. "That is wonderful, sir! And you kept your secret all this time."

"Ysa would never forgive us, if she knew," Royance said.

"Then if only for that, be easy, my lord Earl; I will not betray you."

"We need to move now if we're going to leave on *GorGull*," Tjórvi told Mikkel. "Fritji is even more tired of all the fuss about the wedding than the rest of us are. He plans to leave with the dawn tide. Wind in the sails and waves favoring." He indicated a bundle tucked under his arm. "Have you got your goods?"

"In my room. Come and see."

The boys went out into the corridor of the castle wing that had been assigned to the Sea-Rovers. As they passed by the door in the room just beside Tjórvi's, they could hear soft voices, male and female, and an occasional giggle coming from within. Mikkel raised his eyebrows, a question directed at Tjórvi.

"Oh, that's just Obern with one of the castle maids," Tjórvi said dismissively. "I told you he'd be easy to get around. He should have brought Hallfríðr Snolladóttir with him. She'd keep him attending to his business."

"Who's that?"

"His wife. Her great-grandmother was Great-Grandda Snolli's sister, or half-sister or something. From what I've heard about *him*, Hallfríðr inherited his disposition. Obern would be unwise to provoke her, even this far away."

Mikkel smothered a laugh. "It sounds like fun, to live in New Vold. A lot more fun than stuck off here in Cyornas Castle."

"You wouldn't think it so much fun if you actually were there."

"If I were far enough away from Yngvar, it would. He's a regular little prissy-pants. Here we are." Mikkel pushed open the door to his apartment and the boys entered. He closed it carefully behind them. "I've got my trunk in the bedroom."

"Trunk!" Tjórvi echoed disbelievingly. "What kind of pleasure cruise d'you think you're going on?"

"Just a few things," Mikkel protested.

Tjórvi brushed past him and opened the offending article—a very small trunk, Mikkel thought—and began tossing the contents onto the floor.

"You won't need these," he said, indicating snow-thistle silk hosen, "or this." An embroidered coat—Mikkel's second-best—followed the rejected hosen. "Haven't you got any rough clothes, like you'd work in? Or do you ever work?"

Stung, Mikkel retorted hotly, "Of course I work! There's real work clothes down in the bottom of the trunk. You just didn't look hard enough!"

"Well, these are still too fancy but more like it." Tjórvi held up a pair of trews made of coarse snow-thistle fabric. They were the sort of warm, long-lasting garments the common people favored, only somewhat nicer. "D'you have shirts, too?"

"Of course."

"Well, then, that's not so bad. But you'll have to leave these other fine things behind. And no trunk."

"But—"

"Look you. How d'you think you're going to manage to lug something like this onto the *GorGull* and not be seen? You'll have Yngvar on us in no time flat and he's just the sort to tattle. Tie everything up in a bundle like mine, and we'll manage to get us a sea chest later on."

"Very well. What about a blanket? Can I take a blanket?"

Tjórvi swore. Obviously, he had forgotten to pack a blanket.

"That's all right," Mikkel said. "There are lots of blankets made out of snow-thistle silk. Light as anything and they fold down really small. I'll get you some, too."

Under the other boy's guidance, Mikkel picked out two changes of clothing, a pair of stout shoes, and three pairs of stockings. He rolled all of these things up into one of the shirts. As if by accident, he allowed the amulet he had borrowed from Mother's jewel box, bearing her Ash emblem, to slip outside his shirt and noted Tjórvi's raised eyebrow with delight. No need to mention that he had not gotten permission to borrow it first.

When they were finished with his packing, his bundle looked much like Tjórvi's.

"There now. We'll make our appearance in the Hall for dinner, and then slip away separately and into our special place in *GorGull* for the night," Tjórvi said. "When we wake up we'll be well out to sea."

Mikkel smiled. At odd moments, particularly when the crew were busy with their duties, the boys had clambered aboard *GorGull*, one among many vessels now crowded in the fjord. The ships flew many banners—Yuland, Rendel, Aslaugor, Fridian, and more.

They raced from forecastle to aftercastle, ducked around the single mast, laughing and shouting. Ostensibly they were just youngsters playing, but they had systematically created a snug berth for themselves in a larder well belowdecks, on the starboard side near the bow. They had shifted barrels of flour and grain until they had created a wall of sorts behind which—they hoped—they would be well-nigh invisible.

"There will be lots of coming and going on the portside. The larder opposite ours holds barrels of salt pork and cheese and other spoilables," Tjórvi told Mikkel. "Or, it will, once Fritji arranges for them to be brought on board. No sense starting out with stale provisions. The kegs with the spirits are over on that side, too."

Mikkel secretly looked forward to tasting spirits for the first time, but Tjórvi wouldn't allow any tapping of the kegs, not now when they could easily be caught. Mikkel reasoned that his turn would come sooner or later. For a long time he had wondered what spirits tasted like.

That evening, once dinner was over and the dancing begun, first Tjórvi and then Mikkel would steal out through the Water Gate, down the stairs set against the cliff face, and thence into a small boat they had hidden under the wharf. To Mikkel's relief, Yngvar was nowhere to be seen. But, as he was making his way across the castle ward, Talkin appeared out of the shadows and moved to tag along at Mikkel's heels.

"No," Mikkel told the warkat. "You can't go with me this time. A Sea-Rover ship is no place for you."

Undeterred, Talkin padded along beside him, through the Water Gate and down the stairs. He had to be physically shoved away from the little boat as the boys climbed in.

"Go find Weyse and play with her," Mikkel ordered. "Please."

"You sound like that beast can understand you," Tjórvi said, a little scornfully.

"He can. Or he could if he wanted to," Mikkel said. "Look, Talkin, I'd take you if I could. But I can't. So go back to the castle now. We'll go hunting when I get back."

Talkin was almost pure white now with the coming winter. Mikkel put the furry head between his hands and kissed the warkat on his forehead. "Good-bye for a while."

The boys, under Tjórvi's direction, turned the little boat toward the *GorGull* and began rowing, very quietly, the oarlocks muffled with rags. Because this was their last night in safe port for some time to come, Captain Fritji had given the crew leave. If there was anybody left aboard, they were apt to be fast asleep. It was the perfect opportunity for Tjórvi and Mikkel to smuggle themselves aboard.

As they pulled farther and farther away from the wharf, Mikkel could see Talkin, not returning to the castle as instructed. The young warkat had sat down, ears pricked forward. He watched and watched until Mikkel had climbed the rope ladder and disappeared from view.

Three

*E*lin prepared with special care for the evening's banquet, of-
ficially welcoming Granddam Ysa's arrival. Lady Kandice
had to do her hair three times before she was satisfied. Lady
Hanna searched through every chest and brought out gown after
gown until Elin found one that suited her —a rose-pink snow-
thistle satin with matching coat, hosen, and slippers, the very picture of innocence. When the ladies had finished with her, she
presented herself for Ysa's inspection and approval. She was, as
Granddam said, growing up. And a grown-up Princess of the Nordorners was marriageable.

Not that she had any intention of putting herself in the position of being ruled by any man, regardless of who or what he was,
or how noble he thought himself to be. Granddam Ysa obviously
thought otherwise.

"How like me you are, Granddaughter," Ysa said. "Of high
mind, spirited. Marriage is in the air, and you must be wed, and
soon. Else, you will become a lodestone for every jumped-up little
princeling seeking alliance with the mighty NordornLand. I've no
doubt that the NordornKing is already in correspondence if not

actual negotiations with both Writham and Yuland, not to mention lands to the east."

"I do not wish to be married."

"That is beside the point. I did not seek marriage with Boroth, but it happened. He was almost impossible to manage and it wasn't until he fell ill that I could do it."

Ysa rubbed her thumbs and forefingers together, perhaps unconsciously. Her huge emerald ring, the Great Signet of the House of Yew, flashed green fire.

"You tended him while he was ill?" Elin asked cautiously.

"Of course. It was my duty. And, while he lay, apparently on the point of death, the four Rings of Power he wore on thumbs and forefingers transferred themselves to me."

Ah, thought Elin. That explained the rubbing of the fingers. How interesting.

"Come, sit, and I will set a few curls to right on your hair while I tell you the tale. Everyone thought them the Great Rings of legend," Ysa continued, "but they were only spirit-rings, given by them to the one most fit to wield the Power that was in them. That was me."

Obediently, Elin sat down as Ysa picked up a slender comb. "What happened to them, Granddam?"

"When their time was finished, they fell into dust."

"Surely then you are the person best suited in all the world to guide me."

"Of course I am, child."

"Who has the other rings? I've seen a sapphire on Mother's hand—"

"Yes. The Signet of Ash. Years ago, before you were born, the scholars delving in the lost city of Galinth found the ancient Signets. They gave the sapphire to Ashen, and gave this one, the emerald, to me. Your sister's husband, King Peres of Rendel, wears the ruby Signet of Oak, and the Lady Rannore, wife of the Lord High Marshal and Defender of Rendel, Lathrom, bears the topaz Signet of Rowan."

A wave of longing to have one—or preferably more—of these powerful jewels swept over Elin so sharply that her mouth began to water. To keep Granddam Ysa from perceiving this longing and mistaking it for greed, she shifted the subject.

"I have heard that you arranged my mother's marriage."

"Both of them, actually. You see, at the time, Ashen was no one of note—just a by-blow of my late husband's, though," she added hastily, "no less loved by me. Your second name is that of her mother, Alditha of Ash. Wait. I have some rose-colored jeweled hair clips that would look lovely with that dress."

Ysa set the ornaments in place and then, satisfied with her efforts, laid the comb aside.

"Thank you, Granddam," Elin said, consulting her image in a hand mirror. The clips sparkled with every move of her head.

Yes, she thought, I, Elin-Alditha, am surely entitled to the sapphire. And perhaps to other Great Rings as well. "Please, tell me more."

She arose from her seat and poured her grandmother a goblet of snowberry juice laced with wine that was being kept warm on the hearth. She wanted to keep Ysa talking. Weak as the mixture was, it would help.

"Ashen's first husband was Obern of the Sea-Rovers. He was nearly sick with love of her, and so I granted his petition to wed her. Unfortunately—"

"What, Granddam?"

"He died, and my son Florian with him."

Granddam Ysa shook her head and closed her lips firmly on the memory. Elin decided not to pursue it—at least not at this time but eventually.

"Again Ashen was free for any to claim. Though a royal ward, she had very little in the way of dowry besides the old Oakenkeep, which I had given her. However, Rendel—which I ruled, remember—needed an alliance with the Nordorners."

"But Father and Mother— That sounds as if they had to be dragged before the priest!"

"Not exactly," Ysa said, as she drank deeply from the goblet. "It is fortunate that they had at least met prior to the wedding. And it worked out well. Now, we need to find a way to make sure things work out well for you."

Quite a different story from the one that had entered Nordorn folklore—the Sunburst at Midnight between Count Gaurin and Lady Ashen, when first they met. Elin had heard that Granddam Ysa sometimes rewrote history to suit herself, but before now had not experienced this phenomenon directly. Most interesting. She filed the information away carefully for examination at another time. Now, there were other matters to consider.

"We have an hour," Ysa said. "Let us draw up a preliminary list of husbands for you. Eliminate the unsuitable now. It is always wise to have one's plans in place early."

The Duchess moved to a table where pen, ink, and paper lay, and seated herself. She drew a sheet of paper close and dipped the pen into the ink. At her gesture, Elin joined her.

Painstakingly, the two of them began listing sons of the Nordorn nobility. Yngvar, Einaar's son, was rejected at once on the grounds of too-close kinship. Hugin, Admiral-General Tordenskjold's son, was already married, as were Axel, Baldrian the Fair's son and Ludde and Lars, sons of Lord High Marshal Svarteper of Råttnos. Baron Arngrim of Rimfaxe was a widower but far too old and his origins far too humble—he had been born a farmer and attained his barony by feats of arms—to be considered as a royal bridegroom. Neither of his sons Thorgrim or Kolgrim found favor, either. And as for Baron Gangerolf's sons Nils and Edvard—well, the idea was simply laughable that she wed either one. They were oafs who took after their father too strongly.

"Isn't there anyone else?" Ysa demanded. "Surely there must be someone."

"Well, one," Elin admitted reluctantly. "But he's not much more than nine years old."

"His name, girl. His lineage."

"It's Count Mjødulf of Mithlond's son Mårten."

"Hmmm. Mjødulf, eh. The Snow-Fox of the Midlands. I remember him from years past. Very intelligent. Good head on his shoulders. Never spoke without thinking it through beforehand. At least you wouldn't be marrying a dunce."

"But Granddam! I told you, he's only a boy!"

"And I told *you* that if you're to avoid being a lodestone and having a match out of a nightmare, you have to act now. And furthermore, you would be wise to act at my direction. I have been in the world longer than you, and know how these things are done." Ysa took a deep swallow of her wine-and-berry juice. "Unless, of course, you relish the thought of being used nightly by a savage from one of the eastern lands or stuck away in some minor jumped-up kingdom like Writham or Yuland. Or perhaps sent away to the Wykenigs to buy peace."

"No, Granddam, I do not."

"Well, then. So Mårten is only nine years old. You are twelve? Thirteen? That isn't all that much older, and when it comes to royal matches, age is not the primary consideration. Further, consider that we are speaking of betrothal only. The actual wedding wouldn't take place for years, of course, and in the meantime any number of things might happen. Mårten could die. Children do, sometimes. You could fall in love with each other and decide that the match would be an agreeable one. You might grow to loathe each other but learn how to coexist without violence. A better match might be found elsewhere. But in all this, you have bought the most important, essential element you seek—time. Oh, you might not think much of it now, but I assure you, my dear, that with time working for you rather than against you, you have the opportunity to seek the best course of action to make all your ambitions into reality."

If only you knew, Granddam Ysa, Elin thought. *If only you knew.*

"I promise that I will be guided by you in all things," she said, "even to a betrothal with Mårten."

"Good. Tomorrow I will begin making the proper inquiries."

And then, as if innocently changing the subject, Elin asked,

"May I try on your beautiful emerald? Perhaps wear it just until we go down to your welcoming feast? I think I have never seen a bigger one, or a finer."

It was not until he awoke to the pitching and rolling of the ship that Mikkel realized he had fallen asleep and that they had raised anchor and set sail. He was very warm on one side and chilled on the other; he roused a little and discovered that, beyond all possibility, Talkin was stretched out beside him, so close he might as well have been attached with glue. He was also hogging the blanket.

"Where'd *you* come from?" he whispered. For answer, Talkin sighed heavily and flexed his paws, showing the heavy claws. He snuggled closer to Mikkel. "Well, you're here, and I'll find out how later."

Mikkel couldn't believe his good fortune, nor how glad he was that his feline friend had found a way to be with him after all. He extricated the blanket from under the young warkat and pulled it up over both of them, covering up his ears and hoping it would muffle the sound of his wildly beating heart. They were actually on their way!

He wondered if Tjórvi was as excited as he was but determined not to say anything lest he be shamed by his friend, to whom such adventure must seem commonplace.

"Mikkel?" Tjórvi whispered hoarsely. "You awake?"

Mikkel decided to pretend he had been asleep. "I am now," he said.

"I saw your warkat come in a while ago. How'd you manage to get him on board?"

"I didn't. I have no idea how he got here."

"Well, there's no turning back now for any of us. You have any regrets?"

"No. You?"

"Not a one. I think we should not go out on deck in the morning, but stay here until we're found. That way we're bound to be far enough out to sea that Fritji won't turn back."

"We should have brought some food with us."

"Don't you think I thought of that?" Tjórvi said, a trifle scornfully. There was a clink, as of glass, as he pushed a bundle over to where Mikkel could see it in the dim light coming through the open hatch to the storage locker where they lay. "Pinched it this morning. Two loaves of bread, and some of that fruit juice you people like so much."

"Good. We won't starve, then."

He could practically see Tjórvi grinning in the darkness. "Not until Fritji gets hold of us, that is. Go to sleep."

Mikkel settled back down into the warm spot he had created, pulled his blanket over his head once more, and let the motion of the old ship lull him back into slumber. He grasped his amulet. Surely it, like Tjórvi's, would bring him luck.

Both boys awoke at first light, filtered through faceted glass globes inset in the ceiling of the storage locker. The globes carried light from outside and provided surprisingly good illumination, quite enough to rouse them—that, plus Talkin nudging them as if asking for some breakfast. The boys each took a loaf of bread, broke off a chunk, and ate, washing it down with swallows of snowberry juice. Talkin got a share of the bread, but rejected the juice after one taste.

There really wasn't much to do but lie there, hiding. They didn't dare talk to one another, lest the sound of their voices be overheard. Nor did they move from their hiding place. Mikkel wished he had thought to bring a King's Soldiers game board with him. He played with Talkin's ears, then began counting the threads in the woven design of his blanket, out of sheer boredom. He even began to long for discovery, just to have something better with which to pass the time.

"Don't be so quick to ask for more," Tjórvi advised, when Mikkel whispered his feelings to his friend. "Fritji won't be pleased at being put on the hot seat by the Chieftain's son, not to mention a Nordorn prince, and who do you think he'll take it out on? Me more than you, but even your rank won't count for beans."

Tjórvi's prediction came true an hour or so later when the Sea-Rover Ferbus, *GorGull*'s cook, came down to the storage locker for more flour.

"Look what I found!" Ferbus announced as he dragged Tjórvi and Mikkel out onto the deck. "Two rats, I'll be bound, digging into our vittles! And the cat with 'em!"

Captain Fritji came swaggering up to where Tjórvi and Mikkel dangled by their collars, still in their captor's grasp. "Rats, d'ye say."

"Just little ones. Didn't eat much, I expect."

"Rats!" Fritji exclaimed again as he examined the two boys. "Rats indeed. Come, everyone! Take a look, my lads. We're privileged to have our Chieftain's boy Tjórvi with us. We all know him. But who's this?" He grasped Mikkel's shoulder in an iron grip. "The warkat's owner, I'll be bound."

"I—I'm just a Nordorner," Mikkel stammered.

"More than just that, I'll warrant. You're one of the royal family. Youngest, aren't you. Prince Mikkel."

Mikkel hung his head. "Yes, sir."

"Off to find adventure and make your fortunes, both of you, eh." Fritji glanced around at the Sea-Rovers who had gathered, amused, to enjoy the discomfiture of the two stowaways. "Well, lads, what should we do with them, eh?"

"Keep the cat for a mascot, throw the stowaways in a boat and let them row back to shore!"

"Never mind the boat, just throw them in the water and let them swim!" cried another, which provoked hearty laughs from his companions.

Even less kind suggestions were shouted from the crowd. Mikkel was now feeling very uneasy about the wisdom of his actions. Would they really lop off his ears and nail them—and him—to the mast? What would Talkin do in such a horrid event?

Finally Captain Fritji held up his hand for silence. "They're ours now, to do with as we will, and it isn't the way of the Sea-Rovers to abuse anyone unnecessarily, even stowaways. Don't fear, boys. Your lives are safe enough but I'll put you to work. That ought to cure your romantic notions about a life at sea."

He put them in the charge of his third mate, Dorsus, who set them to laboring with scrub brushes, pumice stone, and water, to make the ancient decking shine like new. Both boys developed blisters on their hands in short order and, when they began to bleed, Dorsus granted them a brief rest. The Spirit Drummer and Wave Reader, Jens, called them over to the spot where he was customarily stationed. He eyed them up and down.

"Well, you're getting the life you wanted," Jens commented, grinning. He tied a small bucket to a line and tossed it overboard, bringing it up again full of salt water. Then he dropped a powder into the water and stirred to dissolve it. "Soak your hands in this, to toughen them. While you're soaking, want me to see what the Spirit Drum might tell us?"

"Oh, yes, please, sir," Tjórvi said.

"Then be quiet, and keep soaking those hands. Don't bite at the loose skin." Jens took out a small drum from where it had been carefully wrapped and began to stroke it.

"Well, now," he said. "Well, now. You will both be in peril, but should live through it if you're lucky. Mikkel—well, your fate is a mystery even to me. I see snow, and ice, and hidden cities, and strange creatures, but nothing clearly. It looks like Tjórvi is going to do well by himself, though. I see him in surroundings much more luxurious than he is accustomed to. That is all, though, because you are both very young and as yet unformed. Now, get back to work. Wrap your hands in these rags and finish your scrubbing before dinner."

The boys did as Jens told them, and found that the treated salt water, though it stung horribly, had already begun to heal and toughen their hands. With the rag wrappings, they could manage what otherwise might have been impossible.

Nobody at the benches at the crew's table seemed inclined to move over and give them room, so they found places on the deck.

Mikkel noted that Captain Fritji wasn't quite as harsh as he made out to be; he heard him giving orders to Ferbus, and presently the cook set down two bowls for Talkin, one full of meat scraps and the other filled with fresh water.

Both boys would have fallen asleep with their heads in their empty bowls, except that members of the crew roused them roughly, but not unkindly, and sent them off to bed amid much laughter.

They were not given hammocks to sleep in—and would not be, Tjórvi told Mikkel, to his suppressed horror, until somebody died and made room for them—but their belongings had been moved to another locker, this one containing spare sails and coiled lines. There they could create passable beds atop the folded sails in much greater comfort than the grain larder had provided. They were also given an old arrow chest they could share, to put their clothing in. Another chest contained signal rockets, Tjórvi said, not to be touched save by the captain.

By the middle of the next day, the boys were trusted enough to help the cook serve in the crew's mess and to eat with them as well. Later, perhaps, they would earn the privilege of waiting on Captain Fritji and his officers.

Talkin wandered among the men, accepting petting and praise, and generally behaving as if he had been born on a Sea-Rover vessel. From listening, Mikkel learned that the young warkat had succeeded in getting into a boat while the seamen were loading the rest of their supplies, and refused to leave. Laughing, the men decided to let him go on board and return him on their last trip back but by then, Talkin had disappeared.

"Looked to me like yon beastie would have swam out if we'd not taken him," one of the men remarked. "I never knew they could, or would, swim."

"I know they can, and will," said another. "We chucked him over, one trip, trying to make him go back. He paddled right on after us, and climbed back into the boat."

"I was there. Fur's so thick he never even got properly wet," a third commented. "I think he might bring us luck."

"That's in the hands of the Ruler of Waves, but I think so, too."

There never seemed an end to the tasks that Third Mate Dorsus could find for the two boys to do. Dorsus's main responsibility, as the boys learned, was being the leader of the Marines, who were primarily archers. He was also out on his first adventure a-roving. If either of the boys thought this latter circumstance would create some measure of sympathetic kinship with them, they were very much mistaken.

Tjórvi hit on the idea of asking Dorsus to give them lessons in archery.

"Maybe that would sidetrack him, just a little, from finding every nail that needs polishing, or line that needs waxing," he said. "And we could do well to learn a new skill. Well," he added a bit boastfully, "hone the skill I already have, that is."

"Hah," Mikkel said. "And who was it who brought down a coney with his bow, when we went hunting?"

"You missed another," Tjórvi jeered companionably. "It wouldn't hurt you a bit to take a lesson from an expert. He learned from Chief Archer Dordon, his father, you know."

"I've heard Uncle Rohan speak of him. Well, it costs nothing to ask."

Mikkel settled into his bed, trying to find a comfortable spot, a problem that never concerned Talkin who seemed able to relax completely wherever he was. The spare sails made a mattress much harder than anything Mikkel had been used to, and they smelled stale and musty to boot. He was tired as he had never been before in his life, with half-healed blisters on his hands and muscles he never knew he had aching abominably, much too tired and sore to sleep. He smiled, utterly happy and content, and fell asleep the moment he closed his eyes.

The next morning, they were hard at work under Dorsus's watchful eye, when the lookout spotted sails from another ship on the horizon. At once, Captain Fritji ordered them below to their quarters, with instructions to stay out of sight.

"But—" Mikkel started to say, but Fritji stopped him before he could protest further.

"We don't know if these are honest merchants who'll pay us our tithe to let them sail on, or if they're brigands after our blood. You'd be a hindrance if there's a fight," he told them sternly, "and no help if there isn't. We can't afford to assign men to guard you. You will obey me. Take the warkat with you."

Already the Spirit Drum, in the hands of Jens, was whispering. It would make smooth the waves under the bow of *GorGull* and roughen the waters through which an enemy must go to reach them. Third Mate Dorsus was busy with his Marine archers, handing out quivers of arrows and making certain that every man had a sound bowstring on his weapon, and another safely in reserve. Second Mate Arund was seeing to the distribution of swords to those who had the skill to use them and cudgels to those who did not. Even the cook, Ferbus, laid aside his pothook for a wicked-looking blade.

"Go! Now!" Fritji was not to be defied.

Crestfallen, the boys, followed by Talkin, headed for the midships ladder leading down into the lower part of the ship, disappointed that their first brush with real excitement was going to go unexperienced, the sweetness of danger untasted.

Rohan Sea-Rover was furious, and not troubling to hide it. He called Obern into his apartment and closed the door ungently behind him.

"Tjórvi is missing and Mikkel with him," he said as soon as he was sure they were alone.

"They—they've probably gone out hunting."

"I think not. Their disappearance coincides with *GorGull*'s sailing. Frode consulted the Spirit Drum, and confirmed my fears. They're on board. How could you let this happen, and right under your nose?" he demanded of his eldest son.

"I can't be everywhere," Obern returned, more than a little defensively. "And Mikkel's whereabouts is not the concern of the Sea-Rovers."

"It is my concern. And should be yours." Rohan's voice dropped to a growl. "If you'd pay more attention to your duties and less to the castle maids you wouldn't be standing there looking stupid while your brother and a prince of the Nordorners sails off a-roving with an inexperienced captain."

Still Obern stood silent, glowering, showing no outward sign of chagrin or acknowledgment of error. Rohan's eyes narrowed.

"Shall I inform Hallfriðr Snolladóttir of your—your pleasant activities among the castle serving women?" he asked.

Obern started, stung at the mention of his wife. "No!" he shouted. And then, more calmly, "No. I will find him."

"How? Do you propose to take *Spume Maiden* out in some random direction and call it a search? Hope that the Ruler of Waves will bring them to you? No, I will tell you what you will do. You will return to New Vold on *Spume Maiden* while I take *Ice Princess* in pursuit of *GorGull*. We should be able to catch up with her within a day, two at the most, with Frode to guide us with his Spirit Drum."

"But Frode is with *Spume Maiden*," Obern objected.

Rohan stared with some distaste at his eldest son, disliking the slowness of his mind and wondering what he could do to make the boy think at least as well as the lowliest Sea-Rover at New Vold. "Frode is now with me. You do not have his services. Surely you are competent to follow the coastline back south."

"Yes, Father," Obern said meekly.

"Now you will accompany me and wait outside while I break the news to Gaurin NordornKing and Ashen NordornQueen. I would not blame either of them if they called you in and decided to have you flogged until your back is raw. For that matter, I haven't decided against such a thing myself. You can only hope that this turn of events does not disturb the festivities surrounding the marriage between Earl Royance and Countess Mjaurita."

Andre Norton & Sasha Miller

He started toward the door, then hesitated and turned toward his son again. "Most of all, you should hope that the Duchess Ysa does not get wind of this. If her plans are disturbed she'll devise a punishment that will have you longing for the sweet and gentle taste of the flog. Now, go!"

Four

ohan sent a steward urgently requesting a private meeting with the Nordorn rulers; his request was granted automatically, and the steward sent to escort him into the sitting room of the royal apartments. In happier times, he and Gaurin had exchanged pleasantries in this chamber while Ashen and Anamara puzzled over how to solve the riddle of the Dragon Box, wherein had lain a bracelet composed of small teeth—not all human—and an ancient parchment containing the history of the Mother Ice Dragon and the fabled Dragon Blade.

Today, Rohan was fairly blazing with anger. Ashen had never, to her recollection, seen him in such a state before.

"How now, good Chieftain, kinsman, and friend," Gaurin said. "What troubles you?"

"I am the bearer of ill news," Rohan replied. He began to stride back and forth in front of the NordornKing and NordornQueen, too agitated to take the chair they offered him. "My son Tjórvi has gone missing, and worse, so has Prince Mikkel. From all the evidence, the boys have stowed away on *GorGull* to go a-roving and it's all Obern's fault for not keeping a proper eye on them."

"Why, those scamps!" Gaurin exclaimed.

"No wonder they've been absent from table at the evening meals," Ashen said. "But isn't this something that every young Sea-Rover does, sooner or later? Going out to sea, I mean?"

"Yes," Rohan ground out from between gritted teeth, "but not on the first voyage of an untried captain. We always arrange these adventures carefully, to make sure the youngster comes back safely if at all possible. I knew that Tjórvi was planning to escape and go out a-roving; he might as well have had it written across his forehead. It was Obern's duty to keep him safe and on shore. To keep *them* safe. Heir Obern might be, but he hasn't any more sense than he needs, and I haven't yet made up my mind how to deal with him."

She remembered an incident, years earlier, when she had been sailing on *Spume Maiden* down the coast to New Vold. Obern had been a toddler in leading-strings then, reckless as only a young child could be, and had fallen into the water. She still recalled the rough jokes about how to deal with the obstreperous child, and how he had been more outraged than hurt by the incident. Apparently, listening to Rohan talk about his heir, the young man had learned little in the way of prudence or foresight as he grew.

"You are beginning to frighten me a little, Rohan," she said.

"As well you might be, if I allowed this little misadventure to go on much further. The Duchess Ysa may have some of her wedding planning spoiled, but my part in them was minor at best. I will ask Tordenskjold for permission to go after the boys on *Ice Princess*. I should be back within two days, no more than three. Frode will guide me to where the *GorGull* will be found. You can rest assured that Tjórvi will have a good hiding when I get my hands on him. Mikkel— Well, he's yours to discipline, not mine. But if I had my way, I would impress on him the utter stupidity of running off on some wild adventure without so much as a by-your-leave."

"Do as you deem best," Gaurin told the agitated Sea-Rover Chieftain. "You know your boy better than I do. I will deal with the Duchess, if need be."

"For not having my head for my carelessness, I thank you, Gaurin NordornKing. And thank you, Ashen NordornQueen," Rohan said formally. He bowed. "Now I take my leave. The soonest departed, the more quickly returned."

Then he was gone, leaving Ashen and Gaurin to stare at one another.

"I never thought Mikkel would do such a thing," Ashen said. "Tjórvi must have put him up to it."

"Undoubtedly," Gaurin replied, "but the notion fell on fertile ground. Do not fret, my Ashen. Rohan is a good Chieftain, a good father, and a good uncle to all our children. I have no doubt that he will bring the boys home, much chastened."

"Surely he will."

Privately, Ashen determined to seek Zazar's advice and counsel. As Rohan had his Spirit Drummer Frode, so did she have the old Wysen-wyf, Zazar. If anyone could reassure her about the outcome of this harebrained boyish misadventure, it would be Zazar.

In spite of herself, Zazar was startled when Ashen told her the news. "I thought I was past being surprised. They are idiots. Imbeciles. Just like all males. It's a wonder any of 'em ever grow up, the reckless way they act."

"I was hoping you could, could do something. Perform a ritual, perhaps. Look into the future."

The Wysen-wyf stared at Ashen, thinking. Should she admit that it was possible she could have warded off this incident by consulting the Web castings, if only she hadn't had that *brandewijn*? Better to wait.

"Too soon for that." Or too late, Zazar thought glumly. "Let Rohan do what he's skilled at—chasing around the open seas going after a prize."

"He has set sail already."

"Good. Don't borrow trouble until you know the true face of it, is my advice. He'll bring the boys back if anybody can, most likely none the worse for wear except for a good soaking. You've got enough to worry about here, what with the wedding and having to keep a rein on Ysa. There's no telling what she could or would make of this opportunity to cause trouble, not to mention what a tantrum she's apt to throw now that her beautiful plans may be disturbed."

"Ysa!" Ashen exclaimed. "I had forgotten about her. Is there any way to keep this from her?"

"I wouldn't count too heavily on it. The word has to be out, and widely, by now. I saw Elin hurrying in the direction of Ysa's apartments, and I have to think she was eager to let her granddam know what had happened. Elin, I think, likes to be the bearer of news, whether good or ill."

At that very moment, the Princess Elin was rapping on the door to Granddam Ysa's apartment. "May I come in?"

Lady Gertrude answered. "Is there a warkat with you?" she asked. "Or that creature Madame Zazar harbors? Poor little Alfonse gets so frightened—"

The tales of Ysa's lapdog and his encounters with any creature larger than he, which encompassed almost all the animals living in Cyornas Castle, were well known to Elin. The warkats especially seemed to think Alfonse was some sort of toy, created for their enjoyment. They never hurt him, but loved to terrify him. "No, Lady Gertrude, I made sure that I was alone."

"Then come in, child!" Ysa called from the inner chamber beyond the sitting room. "Your company is always welcome!"

"The more so when you hear what I have to tell you," Elin replied as she entered. "Mikkel has run away!"

"No!" Ysa exclaimed. "Grisella, bring the Princess Elin a cup of hot berry juice. She looks quite out of breath. And yes, a little hot wine in it. Not too much, mind you."

Elin accepted the beverage gratefully. "Thank you. And yes, I did hurry here, Granddam. I thought you should know in case you—you wanted to remake some of your plans. For the wedding, I mean."

"Then tell me, child."

Quickly, Elin relayed to Ysa the information about Tjórvi and Mikkel's running away to sea, and how Uncle Rohan had gone in pursuit of them. "He told Mother and Father that he'd leave Mikkel's punishment to them, but I think he'll give both of them a good beating."

Ysa thought a moment, eyes narrowed. "Ladies, please leave us," she said.

Obediently, the three—Grisella, Ingrid, and Gertrude—arose and, with a rustle of snow-thistle silk skirts, went into the outer room. Little Alfonse, who had been napping on a chair in that chamber, trotted back to his mistress quickly, before the door closed.

"There might be an opportunity for us in what might otherwise be thought of as a calamity," Ysa said as soon as they were alone. She reached for a plate of sugar cakes that had grown stale and began feeding bits to the dog.

"That's what I thought, Granddam. And so, I was all impatience to get to you."

"You acted wisely. Now. As to the wedding itself, the absence of the Sea-Rover Chieftain is unfortunate, but something we can cover. Your brother— Well, frankly, we won't miss him in the least, nor that boy he is such good friends with. What's his name? Turvus? Turvi? Something like that."

"Tjórvi," Elin said. "They would probably spoil things by pointing and whispering anyway, or not even show up. It would be worse than—" She closed her lips firmly. She had been on the verge of saying, worse than Alfonse being chased by one or more of the warkats.

Word of the young Prince's disappearance, and that of the Sea-Rover's son, spread quickly through the castle. Like any other small community, the doings of all of its inhabitants was a matter for great discussion, and this one was amusing as well as unusual. The castle servants eagerly took up the news, having served the great ones in the Hall and now free to have their own dinner.

"I always thought His Highness Mikkel was better suited to live in a crofter's cot than here," Rols remarked as he heaped his truncheon with roast fallowbeeste flesh from one of the big bowls.

"No!" exclaimed Grete, one of the maids. "The young master is missing? And what of Their Majesties? I expect Ashen Nordorn-Queen is right well beside herself with worry. She fair dotes on all her children."

"She is holding up well," Rols said, happy to be speaking with Grete. He was sweet on her, as the saying went, and she mostly ignored him. "The Sea-Rover Chieftain has gone out to find the young master and his own son and bring 'em back in some disgrace."

A ripple of laughter went around the table.

"And the little warkat with them, I expect," said Arne.

"Oh, yes, that's right," Rols said. "I also heard that one of the warkats is missing. The little 'un."

Rols had once been charged with caring for the warkats in Cyornas Castle. As he had advanced in rank among the servants, this task had fallen to Arne.

"His mama, Finola, wouldn't touch the plate of fallowbeeste I gave her earlier," Arne told the people around the table. "From the tenderest joint, too. Madame Zazar's familiar, Weyse, is down in spirit as well."

"It is sad, very sad," Beatha said. She had made herself useful as an assistant cook, and so ate with the other servants.

"Well, I daresay that all will be put to rights within a few days," Huldra said. Second in rank only to Ayfare, her word carried a great deal of weight among the servants. "I will not be pleased if word of your tattling and mumbling over Their Majesties' misfortune, minor though we all hope it may be, gets back to them."

A murmur of acquiescence went around the table, and so the subject was closed—at least for the time being.

Despite Huldra's warning, and orders from Ayfare and Nalren as well, castle gossip about the very unlikely missing trio continued unabated, if quietly, until the midmorning the warning bell announced that the new ship, *Ice Princess*, had returned to Cyornas Fjord and dropped anchor.

Only one boy, much chastened, trailed in Rohan Sea-Rover's wake as he made his way straight to the Great Hall of Cyornas Castle. If the Sea-Rover Chieftain had had a face like thunder when he departed, a veritable storm cloud sat on his brow now.

Word of his arrival preceded him. Immediately on sighting the ship, Gaurin gave orders for a full, formal Court, convened as hastily as possible. He and Ashen and a sizable number of the nobility were already waiting in the Hall when Rohan made his entrance. Those not yet in attendance were on their way.

"Welcome," Gaurin said to him. "What news?"

"I will tell it here and now," Rohan replied, glancing around at the servants and others who were crowding in to learn firsthand what had transpired, "as soon as all have arrived."

Bjaudin NordornPrince rushed into the room, hair mussed, clothing a bit untidy. "Greetings and apologies, Uncle," he said, running his fingers through his hair. He took his seat at the High Table, at Gaurin's right hand. "I was at practice with the sword. What news of my little brother?"

Princess Elin and the Duchess Ysa also hurried into the Hall before Rohan could reply. From another direction, Duke Einaar appeared, fastening his doublet. This was the hour at which he was usually hard at work in the chamber that served him as office, taking care of the brunt of NordornLand business.

Various barons and counts entered, seating themselves where they could find chairs or benches, otherwise standing like the others.

"Well, most of you seem to be here," Rohan observed, "even Earl Royance and Lady Mjaurita."

"I believe this concerns all of us," Royance said.

Rohan glanced around again; in the short time it had taken for the nobles to gather, more servants and even townspeople had filled every available out-of-the-way niche to learn the news.

Rohan bowed. "Sir, Madame, I regret to inform you that the *GorGull* is no more."

A murmur of disbelief ran through the room.

"The ship is gone, sunk, destroyed, and with it a sizable number of my men. We came upon the *GorGull* as it was under attack by Wykenigs and would have given battle but they turned and ran. We needed to save those who could be saved, and so the Wykenigs escaped."

"But what—" Gaurin cleared his throat. "What of Mikkel?"

Rohan turned to his son. "Answer the NordornKing," he said, and his voice was not gentle.

"I—I think he is with them," Tjórvi said, faltering. "It was very confusing, after the ship began to sink. We were within sight of land, barely. Captain Fritji put us into a small boat and told us to pull toward the shore and then hide ourselves. But then the Wykenigs caught up with us, and I went into the water—"

Five

Tjórvi **and Mikkel searched** for a way to see what was happening above-decks. But the locker that served as their quarters was tightly sealed and the door firmly closed. There seemed to be nothing for the boys to do but wait, every muscle at stretch, until they were let out again.

Under Tjórvi's direction, the boys put on as much of their clothing as they could and folded their blankets into flat, tight squares that they tucked next to their skins and held in place with their belts.

"I've heard about this," Tjórvi said. "Probably wasted effort, but it's something to do."

They could hear what was happening, though. Beside him, in the gloom, Mikkel heard Talkin growling deep in his throat and knew that the young warkat was no less eager to fling himself into the fray than he. A ridge of fur stood up along his back and he quivered like an arrow nocked to the string.

"Be patient, Talkin," he told the warkat. "Our turn will surely come."

Talkin settled down, but only a little, licking his lips and shaking his fur back into place. He moved close to Mikkel, who put his arm around his companion.

Topside, all seemed to be chaos, with shouts and orders being bellowed and sailors and Marines flying in all directions, forecastle and aftercastle according to their battle stations, as the two ships drew near one another.

"I'm hearing a different rhythm from the Spirit Drum," Tjórvi said, his head cocked. "I don't know that one—"

A gigantic shock ran through the ship and interrupted him, throwing boys and warkat across the weapons locker.

"We're rammed!" Tjórvi cried.

The door burst open, flinging them into the galleyway. They had barely regained their feet before the ship heeled over as the attacking ship pulled free, and they fell again. *GorGull* righted herself, reluctantly. A grinding sound echoed from below as a gush of icy water spewed up from someplace aft, near the keel.

"Maybe they'll board us and we'll be fighting for our lives." Tjórvi's voice had dropped to a near whisper. "Or maybe they'll just let us sink while they watch."

They heard no clash of steel, no outcries of men in combat. Apparently *GorGull* hadn't been boarded, at least yet. The shouting and running and preparations for combat above abruptly shifted, as men sought to save themselves. The whole vessel shuddered, not from the impact and release, but by what could only be the screaming of a ship mortally wounded.

"What do we do?" Mikkel asked. "We can't stay here. We'll drown. We can't go up there. We'd get killed instantly."

"Maybe not."

Both boys turned toward the man who had spoken. Captain Fritji had made his way down the ladder and was now wading toward them. He ducked inside the locker, opened the chest of rockets, and took one out.

"Come on, you two. And your warkat. The Ruler of Waves is not with us this day. I'm putting you in a boat. We're near enough to land that you could make it if you row hard. You've got a chance to get away unseen during the confusion. Hurry, now."

They followed him toward the aft ladder, floundering through shockingly cold water. The initial spout and gush of water had now been replaced by a relentlessly rising flood, mixed with splinters and other debris. Even to someone lacking in experience, it was plain that *GorGull* had only moments to remain afloat. Mikkel remembered the little skiff that was rigged at the rear of the ship snug against the hull, halfway between rudder and deck. It was the captain's personal property, as he had learned, and now, apparently, was to be passed on to the stowaways.

"Sir, sir," he said through chattering teeth. "We can't take your boat! What will you do?"

"Don't argue," Fritji ordered.

They gained the rear deck of the aftercastle. Fighting had begun amidships, where Wykenig warriors were now boarding the stricken vessel to engage Sea-Rovers who, presumably, had most of the fight taken out of them by now. Some Wykenigs were preparing to swing themselves over by ropes attached to lofty spars. For a short time, until it broke up, no portion of the ship would be free of combat. There was not a second to lose.

"We're already down at midships almost to the rails," Fritji said. "Slide down and get in. I'll cut the lines, and you two get clear and row for all you're worth."

"But sir—" Mikkel began again.

"I'll hold them off. Now get going."

Obediently, Tjórvi and Mikkel did as they were bid. Talkin jumped into the skiff after Mikkel and had to be shoved to the bow to get him out of the way. As soon as they had gotten seated, Fritji slashed through the lines holding the little boat to its davits. They were so low in the water, the skiff scarcely splashed as it dropped.

With their oars, the boys pushed off from the ship and then began rowing toward the rock-encrusted shore. Fritji waved, and turned back to the battle. Presently, the signal rocket roared aloft.

"Will we ever see him again?" Mikkel asked, fearfully.

"Who knows?"

Mikkel stared at his friend. He was scowling, and holding onto his oar much harder than was strictly necessary. Mikkel realized that Tjórvi was just as afraid, just as horrified, as he.

"Wait," Tjórvi said. "Look."

The *GorGull* was breaking up under the sheer weight of the water filling her hold. Only forecastle and aftercastle were above the waves, and they were sinking rapidly. With a groan that rivaled the one the ship had made when the Wykenig ship's ram had pierced her hull, the big mast leaned, and cracked, and broke. With another sickening wrench, the ship split in two. Forecastle and aftercastle, released from the midsection, bobbed up high but only for a moment, as both began to sink again. Already men were splashing in the frigid water, seeking bits of wreckage they could cling to, lest they drown.

A movement on the horizon prompted Mikkel to wrench his attention from the dying ship long enough to spot another ship bearing down at top speed. "It's *Ice Princess*! *Ice Princess*!" he cried. "They saw the rocket!"

"That's my da!" Tjórvi exclaimed proudly. "My da would not let us drown, and *GorGull* go to the bottom without a fight!"

"I hope he's come in time," Mikkel said. "Look."

Small boats from the Wykenig vessel were now moving rapidly among the Sea-Rovers now virtually filling the sea around the foundering ship. Both boys watched, open-mouthed, as Fritji was hauled on board one of the boats despite his strong resistance. Being captain, Mikkel thought numbly, he might bring a fair ransom. The Wykenigs looked to be cheated of any other prize because of the *GorGull*'s demise and the Sea-Rover ship now within arm's reach.

"We'd better get out of the way and not wait for Da," Tjórvi said. He took up his oar and the skiff thunked on something unyielding.

A Wykenig boat had cut across their bow unnoticed and the men seized the skiff to draw it alongside.

"Too late, I think," one of the Wykenigs said. "You're ours now."

"Small fish," another commented.

"Yes, but Rovers don't often have two boys on board. There's bound to be profit with them somewhere."

"You'll take us at great cost," Mikkel said fiercely. He balled his hands into fists. Talkin took up a position directly in front of Mikkel, baring his teeth and growling.

"*Krigpus!*" one of the men cried. "Be careful!"

"We don't have time to wrestle both of you and a *krigpus* into the boat," the first Wykenig told them. "Even if it would come. I thought those things were untamable."

"Maybe we should kill it," another said.

Yet another put his hand on the hilt of a long, wicked knife.

"No! You'll have to kill me first! Talkin is my friend!" Mikkel shouted. "Take all of us! If you can't, then take me, and leave Talkin and Tjórvi alone!"

"I'm more valuable to you than Mikkel," Tjórvi cried stoutly. "My da's the Sea-Rover Chieftain!"

"Likely story, that," said the Wykenig, apparently the leader of the boat crew. He gave a short laugh. "We don't have time to argue the point. Take the one with the *krigpus*. Anybody who can tame a *krigpus* has to have more to him than first glance shows. We'll keep him until we decide what to do with him. Throw the other into the water."

Suiting words to action, one of the Wykenigs upended the skiff and tossed Tjórvi overboard. Another seized Mikkel and dragged him into the larger boat. At once, Talkin launched himself at the man, only to be knocked aside in mid-leap, splashing into the water beside Tjórvi.

"Damn beast attacked me!" a Wykenig shouted.

"Tjórvi! Talkin!" Mikkel cried. "Don't drown them! Talkin only wants to be with me!"

"Well, there he'll stay, unless you can control him," Mikkel's captor growled into his ear. "Do it, and we'll let the *krigpus* stay with you and the boy can climb back into the skiff if he can manage it before he freezes."

"Talkin," Mikkel called through chattering teeth. "Talkin, I'm all right. I need you now. Come into the boat and stay with me. Please."

"You don't know what you're doing!" Tjórvi shouted. "I'm the one you want!"

"Tjórvi!"

"Don't worry about me." Tjórvi's teeth, too, were chattering, and his face had grown pale with the cold. He would not last long in the frigid water. "Save yourself!"

Mikkel's captor loosened his grip enough so the boy could help Talkin scramble into the boat. He shook himself, and then put both front paws on Mikkel's shoulders, looking back at their captors as if daring anybody to come close. Mikkel put his arms around the wiry, feline body and held him close.

"Take the oars and let the Sea-Rover boat drift," the leader said. "Is the *krigpus* being good and not attacking again?"

"I think so."

"Back to *Dragon Blood*," the leader ordered. "We have to get out of here now!"

Mikkel stared despairingly across the water at Tjórvi as the Wykenig boat widened the gap between them. "Tell Father— tell him!" he called. "And Mother. She will worry."

Tjórvi waved. He had grabbed hold of the skiff and gotten one leg over the gunwale, but the distance between them was now so great that it was likely he hadn't heard anything. Then the Wykenig boat reached the ship, and Mikkel and Talkin were drawn on board and into their new life.

"—and that was the last I saw of him, Sir." Tjórvi hung his head. "I am most heartily sorry. If it hadn't been for me, we would both still be here at Cyornas Castle, hunting conies."

"What other losses?" Gaurin asked grimly.

"Most of the men who went into the water were saved," Rohan said. "Captain Fritji was taken captive and I expect that we can ransom him and Mikkel both. A few others were captured as well.

There was ice in the water. Some men froze before we could get to them. Others fell in the fighting. They died well."

"I didn't entirely freeze because I wasn't in the water that long," Tjórvi explained. "Also, I had put on extra clothes and had my—I mean the ones Mikkel gave me—the snow-thistle silk blankets under my shirt. We both did. I got back into the skiff before I could drown."

Gaurin turned to Ashen, who was sitting very still, her face dead white. "The boys both showed resourcefulness. They were lucky, but they saved themselves."

"Ransom," Ashen murmured through stiff lips.

"Whatever the price, we will pay it gladly," Gaurin told Rohan. "What are your plans now?"

Rohan turned to the most experienced seaman he knew. "Admiral-General Tordenskjold, what is the advisability of taking more than one ship back north?"

"I think just the one," Tordenskjold commented. "I know that country well, and also I know a little of Wykenigs and their customs. One Nordorn ship is on a mission; more than that, and it becomes an invasion." He turned to Ashen. "Rest assured, Madame, the Chieftain and I will do everything in our power to bring your son, Rohan's nephew, back to you."

"So swear I," Rohan said. "We depart in a matter of hours. Let the wind be in our sails and the waves favoring. While we are absent, I will leave my own son Tjórvi as hostage until I fulfill my vow and bring Mikkel home once more."

"Not as hostage, but as our treasured guest. He is as a grandson to us," Gaurin told him. "We will rear him as our own, if need be."

The Duchess Ysa was seated nearby, as befitted her rank. "Grandson!" she said, not so loud as to be an interruption but loud enough to be heard.

"Yes, grandson," Einaar said. "And my kinsman as well. Pray do not make a bad matter worse."

Ysa sniffed. Plainly, she was not impressed with the arrangements being made to ransom Mikkel. Elin, nearby, reached out and took Ysa's hand.

"Resupply your ship, and go at once to retrieve your people and ours," Gaurin told Rohan. "The treasury is open to you."

"Sir."

Royance spoke up. "With regret, I must now say that your plans for my wedding to the handsome Mjaurita are for naught. We cannot have a gala celebration under such circumstances."

"I agree with my lord—my lord Earl," Mjaurita said.

"But the invitations have gone out already!" Ysa protested. "And the gowns, the flowers—"

Royance looked at Mjaurita, and she nodded. "Let us then turn the occasion into a celebration for those already wed," the Earl stated.

"Yes," Mjaurita said. She arose and swept a full curtsy to the Court. "My lord Earl is my lord husband, and has been for some time now. We had hoped to have kept our secret for the comfort and rejoicing of our friends, but the time for this pleasant game is past."

"The flowers," Ysa repeated. She seemed entirely stunned at the news.

From the chair behind Ashen Zazar muttered something under her breath. It could have been a curse, Ashen thought, but Zazar had spoken too softly for it to be clearly audible.

"I must retire," Ashen said, "and perhaps take to my bed for a time. This has been more than a shock. Zazar? Please come with me."

Once they had reached the royal apartments, Ashen dismissed her ladies. "Zazar has tended me for many years," she told them. "I want only her with me now."

"You aren't as faint as you were earlier. You have something in mind," Zazar said when they were alone.

"I do. I want you to perform that ritual you have spoken of before, and look into the future. It is not a frivolous request, nor an order. It is a plea. Now is the time to do it."

Zazar stared at her for a long moment. "Well, come on then," she said. "I'll need you with me, and that means you have to climb some stairs, will or nill."

Under Zazar's instructions, Ashen put on a dark cloak to disguise herself as best she could. Then the two of them started off toward the tower where the old Wysen-wyf's apartment was located.

"Don't let Ysa see what we're up to, or sure as the Powers she'll recover from her shock over having her plans spoiled and want to put in her bit as well, the way she did back when we three fought the Great Foulness. We needed her then, true enough, but there's no book-magic she could find that would help us now. Not in time, that is." Puffing, Zazar led the way up.

The Castle of Fire and Ice had been built for defense. Its tower staircases were constructed around a central column and wound upward from left to right. An enemy, fighting up, would be hampered in his attack as the center column would get in the way of his sword arm whereas a defender, fighting down, had a strong advantage. A single swordsman could defend successfully against a dozen or more invaders, if need be.

"Careful here, Ashen," Zazar cautioned. "False step."

This was an additional defense in every tower staircase, the step that was two or three finger-spans higher than the rest. An invader could easily trip on it, and so would have Ashen if Zazar had not warned her. There was no such false step on the staircase leading to the Great Hall. That was in the living quarters of the castle, and defenders, in case of attack, would be marshaled elsewhere. Ashen navigated the false step carefully. Then, a few more feet, and they were on a small landing where a door led to Zazar's private quarters.

"You have never seen this before, and you wouldn't be seeing it now except that your youngest is involved," the Wysen-wyf told Ashen when they were inside and the door safely shut behind them. "The last time I worked the Ritual of Asking, we had returned from battling the Mother Ice Dragon and your fate and Gaurin's hung by a thread. The time before, I was waiting to be summoned to the battle with the Great Foulness. This time, the Web castings called to me, but— Never mind. Weyse? Get out of that chair and let the NordornQueen sit down."

The odd little creature roused, blinked, and climbed down out of the chair close to the fire that she customarily occupied. Then she waddled over to Zazar's worktable, and with an agility belying her plumpness, leaped up onto it. There she sat hunkered on her hindquarters, and crossed her clever little paws over her belly as if to say, "Yes, you need me."

Zazar set one of her kettles on the worktable and poured a little water into it. "Some of this, and a little of that," Zazar told Weyse as she began adding ingredients. "Do you think we need henbane?"

With the Wysen-wyf consulting Weyse at every addition, eventually they achieved a mixture that suited both of them. Then Zazar set the kettle on the pothook over the fire and took up a paddle. As she stirred the heating mixture, she droned a tuneless song. Weyse squeaked and trilled, as if in counterpoint. Ashen watched and listened, fascinated. Indeed, she had never encountered even a hint of this ritual except in Zazar's recent, cryptic references.

The concoction in the kettle began to steam. "Now you can look into it," Zazar said. She drew her chair close. Then, using a rag to shield her hands from the heat of the fire, she lifted the kettle off the hook and set it on the hearth between them. "Here. Give it a stir yourself."

Obediently, Ashen took the paddle with both hands and moved it through the steaming concoction.

"What do you see?"

"Streaks of colors. A trace of red. Silver and gold. Strong lines of green, red, purple. But mostly sea-blue green. Two shades, one light and one dark. Both entwined with white."

"Good. Now watch closely."

With that, Zazar added a few bits of thread from the ball she had taken from a box on one of her high shelves. The mixture in the kettle foamed and a cloud of smoke billowed upward. Startled, Ashen sat back in her chair.

"What was that?" she cried in alarm.

"That, my girl," Zazar replied calmly, "was what happens when you employ castings from the Web of the Weavers. This was what I did when you were carrying Elin."

"Yes, but I thought it was—"

"You seemed to think it was fortune-telling. Well, it is not. Now be still. I still have the last part of the ritual to perform."

The Wysen-wyf took the paddle from Ashen. As she stirred, she sang again, a different song, one with words.

> *Youngest child, Nordorn-born, restless in this world.*
> *Too young yet to seek his fate, yet his fate has sought him out.*
> *When will he return?*
> *Where will he find his home?"*

Zazar stared into the kettle. "I should have done this earlier," she muttered as if to herself. "Perhaps I could have avoided— Well, no matter now. It is interesting. Very interesting."

"What? Please tell me."

"Look at the pattern. Try to alter it." She handed the paddle back to Ashen.

She moved the paddle through the thick mixture. "It won't change, no matter how I stir it," Ashen said. "What does it mean?"

"It means that Mikkel's fate, once in question, has become almost certain. I do not know what it is; the kettle cannot tell me that."

"No!" Ashen cried.

"There is more. Oh, and you'd better move back."

Suiting actions to words, Zazar shifted her chair back to its place beside, but not facing, the hearth. Ashen did likewise just as a muffled explosion erupted from the kettle. An orange glow lit up the entire room and was as quickly extinguished.

Instinctively, Ashen checked herself for burns, and found nothing. She peered into the kettle. "Everything is gone!" she exclaimed. "And you hadn't told me all that the Web casting had to say!"

"Well, don't you think I have any memory left these days?" Zazar said testily. "Watch your tongue, or I'll keep the rest to myself."

"I apologize. But this is about Mikkel—"

"Yes, Mikkel and Ysa and Elin and Bjaudin and you and Gaurin and a lot of others, including Royance, Mjaurita, and Einaar, and even young Yngvar and Tjórvi."

"So many," Ashen murmured.

"Do you know nothing of the Web of the Weavers, girl? All our lives are intertwined—even mine—with others'. Oh, you may think the Weavers are just folktale characters, made up by the superstitious to try to explain what happens in their lives, but this"—Zazar brandished the small ball of threads—"proves otherwise. The dark-handed Weavers rule all, even the Almighty One of whom we do not speak.

"Each life is a thread in the Web Everlasting. We think we are free to make decisions, free to act as we think fit, but our threads go through the fingers of a Weaver nonetheless. Some live, some die, kingdoms rise and fall and are forgotten. And all, all is recorded in the Web. Therein lies all history from the first glimmers of time."

"Then all is foretold?" Ashen asked.

"Not exactly. Today's weaving is not yet complete. There is always the possibility of change. You yourself, in case you didn't know it, were a Changer, and the Change you wrought was great indeed. You brought the entire land of Rendel back from the Darkness. I had thought that ended it, but you had one more Change in you, it would appear, for it was through you that the Nordorn-Land was saved when you slew the Mother Ice Dragon."

"Is Mikkel's fate tied up with that adventure?"

"No, that has been accomplished and his fate is still forming. Others' are more settled, true, but nothing is entirely certain until the Weavers are finished and move on to another section of the Web. When I use the castings, I can see the way things are probably going to go. That is all, and often it is enough. The pattern tells me that Mikkel will not die or even be seriously harmed, but it also says that he will not return quickly to the NordornLand. There is much change in store for him."

"Ill tidings."

"I told you this is no mere fortune-telling. If it were, I would say he would return on the next tide."

"How come you by these threads?"

"Various mysterious ways," Zazar responded with a trace of a smile. "Do you remember how, when you were little, visitors would come occasionally to my house? It was always in the black of night, and they welcomed my hearth fire."

"Yes. They were all heavily cloaked and seemed to walk ever in shadow."

"It was from such as these, when I was still living in the Bog, I would buy Web threads with trade-pearls when I could find them, and hoard them carefully until they should be needed. Sometimes others who know earth-magic as I do would share, as Nayla does nowadays. But where do they actually come from? Who knows, maybe the Weavers drop these castings where they can be found and then amuse themselves by watching us try to make sense with our rituals and attempts to peer into the future. But I will say that I am right more often than I am not."

"I just wish you could be more specific. I want Mikkel back."

"I think that in the coming days you are going to have more than enough here at home to keep you occupied." Zazar pondered a moment, staring at the now-empty kettle. "I did not see him dead. That was very plain. And I will confess to you, I think I could have avoided this whole sorry adventure if only I had paid heed that night when you welcomed Ysa back to Cyornasberg."

"The night Gaurin made you dance with him," Ashen said, smiling a little in spite of herself.

"Yes, that one. Well, I came back here, and had a little *bran-dewijn*. The castings were, well, calling to me in a way they have, and I paid no attention. I regret that now. I could have seen to it that he and that other boy, Tjórvi, didn't smuggle themselves onto the *GorGull* on a lark and go out to sea."

Ashen digested this in silence. Finally she spoke. "I could be angry, wish things had turned out differently, but it wouldn't change the past," she said. "Mikkel is alive. You have said it, and the kettle has shown it to you. Rohan and Tordenskjold are sailing out from Cyornas Fjord within hours, carrying ransom enough to buy back an emperor. If anyone can bring the boy back, he can."

Zazar muttered under her breath again. Ashen could not be certain, but it seemed she said, "Perhaps."

"What a disaster!" Ysa cried. "All the beautiful wedding plans for naught, and all because a couple of naughty boys ran off for a life of adventure at sea!"

Elin, not ordinarily given to overfondness for her younger brother, nevertheless rose to his defense. "I'm sure he didn't deliberately ruin your plans, Granddam. And he is being held captive by barbarians, you know."

"Oh, yes, yes, I know. I don't want to seem insensitive. It is a sad situation all the way around, but I'm sure the Admiral-General and Rohan will set it all to rights once more. In the meantime, we should try to make the best of things. Do you agree?"

"Oh, yes, of course. But Mother is very upset. And I daresay Father is, too."

"That is only natural. They need diversion now, as they never have before. I suggest that you go and entertain them. Sing to them. Or play games with them. They are fond of King's Soldiers. You might even bring that priest, Esander, to comfort them. Anything to keep their minds off their troubles."

"Yes, Granddam."

"I worry about the NordornLand. For some time now, neither Gaurin nor Ashen has been truly able to govern, and so the brunt of this work falls on the shoulders of Bjaudin and Einaar. It would be reasonable for Gaurin and Ashen both to step down, but Bjaudin is still too young for such responsibilities to fall on his shoulders."

Bjaudin, Elin thought, *is anything but too young for this. What is Granddam Ysa getting at this time?*

"Whereas Einaar, while mature enough, is hardheaded and willful. I do not think he would accept much guidance."

"At the moment, I don't think there is much to worry about," Elin pointed out. "The Aslaugors are peaceful among themselves, or at least not in open warfare, and the Fridians haven't caused any trouble for, well, for years now. We have good reason to be cautious of the Wykenigs, now that they hold my brother as a hostage, but I'm sure the Aslaugors will be more than ready to turn from fighting each other to battling with them instead. Therefore, where lie the problems that would plague either Bjaudin or Einaar if they should shoulder the responsibility for ruling the Nordorn-Land? This is not to say," Elin continued carefully, "that the northern tribes are at permanent peace. They are always touchy at best."

"How quickly you grasp the political situation, my dear!" Ysa exclaimed. "You really are quite precocious!"

"Father and Mother deserve peace. They have striven long and hard for the NordornLand. Perhaps, as you say, it would be wise if they relinquished their burden to another, now that they have grown old in their labor."

"Ah, yes, but to whom? Duke Einaar is the logical choice, but—"

"My uncle of Åsåfin has a reputation of being fiercely loyal to my father. He would resist such a suggestion."

"Well, my dear, I will tell you something you do not know. Many years ago, before you were born, the Duke approached me with just such a scheme, while your father and mother were off on the adventure that cost them so dearly, the destruction of the Mother Ice Dragon. Should they have not returned—or should they have returned unable to continue ruling—he would have assumed the throne. We talked about it at some length."

"No, truly?" Elin was delighted to have this fresh piece of information. So Bjaudin had nearly been supplanted!

"Then Royance had to come and butt in, and turned Einaar against me. I daresay that he, with me to guide him, would have become the kind of ruler the NordornLand requires. But his notion of 'honor' held him back."

"I daresay," Elin murmured. "Lucky would be he—or she—who has you for a mentor."

Ysa turned and stared at Elin as if seeing her for the first time. Elin did not quail under the Duchess's appraisal, but met her gaze unflinchingly.

"When this celebration is finished and some degree of normalcy regained—well, as normal as it can be with a Prince of the NordornLand missing—you must return with me to Iselin."

"Thank you, Granddam," Elin replied demurely. "I would like that very much. I think we have a lot to talk about."

Dragon Blood had moved about a league from the site of the battle lest she be fouled by the wreckage and was now riding at sea anchor. The sails were neatly furled and a blood-red banner now floated free. It bore a device in gold of a fishtailed man armed with a three-pronged spear—Draig the Sea-terror. The Wykenigs were prepared to wait. All but a few of the captives had been thrown into lockers below decks, and the doors secured behind them. Mikkel and Talkin remained on deck under guard.

Fritji alone of the adults was taken directly to the captain's cabin, where a meal had been laid out. Large horn cups with silver bases were already full of some unknown liquid. The captain, a big man with wild yellow hair scarcely tamed by forcing some of it into braids, offered him one of the cups. "You look like you could use a good draft of Wykenig *björr*," he said. "Better than that unfermented berry juice you Southerners are so fond of drinking."

"Who are you?" Fritji demanded. "The least you can do is give me my captor's name. Why did you ram my ship without so much as a parley?"

"Holger den Forferdelig," the Wykenig captain replied genially. He sat back in his chair. "That means 'Holger the Terrible.' You'd do well to remember that I come by the name as a tribute to my own deeds. *Dragon Blood* is my ship; I have two more. I also have the largest steading in our settlement. I am the Knight King, Ridder of Ridders in the Upplands."

"Where is that?"

"You'll find out soon enough. As to why we rammed your ship, it was because there was no need to fight or parley. You rode too high in the water; there was no plunder in your hold. Better to remove you from our way, send as many as possible down to the Sea-terror Draig's lair, and take what captives we could for ransom. Such as the boy. He is interesting. How came you by him?"

"He stowed away. Other than that, I know nothing."

"I don't believe that, but no matter. We have eight of your men, by the way, in addition to the boy. Would you like to see them, reassure them that Wykenigs don't eat their captives alive?" Holger laughed hugely. "We are quite a hospitable people, in the right circumstances."

"I will stay with my men. I do not wish to have special treatment."

Holger laughed again. "Then you should not have been the captain of your ship!" He took a large swallow of *björr* and glanced out a porthole. "Ah, I see that the *Marmel* is in sight. Good. Keep your seat, I must go supervise something."

With that, Holger left his unwilling guest behind and strode out on deck where some of his men were already preparing to launch one of the ship's boats, scarcely dry since being put back into its davits.

"Take the boy and the *krigpus* to the *Marmel* and bid Shraig sail with all speed back to Forferdelig Sound. They are not to be harmed, either one of them. I have a premonition that might as well have come out of Old Askepott's kettle. Move. We can't be more than a day and a half from Cyornas Fjord, and if ever a man had his war face on, it was the captain of that three-masted wave cutter. He'll be back as soon as he can dump off the people he fished out of the Icy Sea, mark my words, and then we'll haggle over the rest." He surveyed his crew with a hard eye. "Why are you still standing around looking stupid?"

The men immediately leaped to do their captain's bidding. Talkin might have given them a fight, but Mikkel soothed him enough so that they could both be put into the boat, and thence into the water to be rowed across the short distance separating the two ships. This one also flaunted a red Draig banner, and on the ground it bore what looked like a crescent moon—a difference, for those learned enough to recognize it.

Holger returned to his cabin in the aftercastle, where he found Fritji hungrily gnawing on a hunk of bread he had dipped into his bowl of stew. Lacking a little in meat, nevertheless it was hot and thick with turnips and tubers.

"If it makes you feel better, your men are eating the same as us. We don't bother to starve our captives because they aren't with us long enough. One more bowl of stew more or less won't make any difference."

So saying, he resumed his chair and pulled the dish closer so he could ladle out a helping for himself.

"Now, while we wait for your brave rescuers to arrive, would you like to have a game of *Hnefa-Tafl*? That would be—let's see . . . King's Table in your language."

"The Nordorners call it 'King's Soldiers.' But Sea-Rovers do not play games," Fritji said stiffly. He pushed aside his bowl of stew and half-eaten crust of bread.

It was a futile, defiant lie; Holger knew that Sea-Rovers were very fond of games of all sorts. "Then I'll teach you."

Unperturbed, the Wykenig took an exquisitely carved board from a cupboard and began setting out the men. To Holger's amusement, Fritji watched, trying to appear not to be watching.

The pieces were pegged so they would not be dislodged if the ship happened to be in heavy seas. First, Holger placed the King in the center square, the Throne. He was guarded front, back and sides, by twelve warrior women in files of three, Walkyrye, clad in white, the King's elite Guard. The Guard faced the Dark Attackers, in ranks of six on each of the four sides. The corner squares were marked, but not filled. These were for the King's use only.

" '*Who are the maids that fight weaponless around their lord, the fair ever sheltering and the dark ever attacking him?*'" he murmured. Then, aloud, "Here are the rules. Since you are a beginner, we will cast dice. That shows us who can move, or if we can move. Odd numbers move, evens lose a turn. You move either up, down, or sideways. No diagonal moves, no jumping over pieces. I will give you White. This gives you a slight advantage, despite being outnumbered. You are trying to save the King by getting him to a corner square, one of his Strongholds. If you can manage to get a single clear path to any of these Strongholds, you must say '*Raichi.*' That's 'Check' in your language. If you manage to get a double clear path, you say '*Tuichi*' or 'Checkmate.' Then you move the King to a corner square and you win. But that won't happen."

"What happens if one of your pieces gets between one of mine and a corner square?"

Holger smiled. Fritji was interested in spite of himself. No doubt he had played a similar game, though he denied it.

"In that unlikely event, you can capture my Dark Attacker and remove him from the board. More likely, I will outflank your King instead. I will tell you 'Watch your King,' and then I will capture him. Shall we begin?"

Mikkel had understood only part of what the Wykenig captain was telling his men, but enough that he grasped what was happening.

He and Talkin were being sent from the big Wykenig ship—not as big nor as sleek as *Ice Princess* but big enough—to be rowed across a short stretch of sea and put on board the smaller ship, the *Marmel*. They would then be taken—where? The *Marmel* was even smaller than the old *GorGull* and could be easily outrun by the *Ice Princess* or even the ship they were on. Then the strategy became clear to him. The Wykenig captain would deliberately allow himself to be caught, and while negotiations for Fritji and the Sea-Rovers were going on, the *Marmel* would slip away undetected.

Vaguely he remembered having read something about marmels. Tiny merpeople, as he recalled.

Then the boat was bumping against the hull and a rope ladder let down for the captives to climb. Mikkel was apprehensive about Talkin's being able to manage, but he need not have worried. He took one of Talkin's paws, and then the other, and placed them on the rungs, mimicking climbing. Understanding at once, the warkat raced up the ladder and onto the deck far ahead of Mikkel.

"Don't be afraid of the *krigpus*, Ridder Shraig," one of the Wykenigs told the *Marmel* captain. "It's tame. Or at least, tame enough. You're to go to Forferdelig Sound through the hidden way and wait for Ridder Holger to return. The boy and the *krigpus* are not to be harmed."

"Very well," said Shraig. "We'll put them in a locker down in the hold. But if the *krigpus* becomes a danger to me or my men, it dies. Make sail!"

A light but steady breeze began filling the striped canvas and the ship moved away from *Dragon Blood* at a good clip. Mikkel watched it grow small in the distance, knowing that people he knew were on that ship, and knowing that he had no idea of their fate, or his, until Wykenigs took him belowdecks and put him and Talkin into a small locker, not unlike the one he had lately shared with Tjórvi. Spare sails and coils of rope were stored in this one as well. With a pang, Mikkel realized he was on his own, with only his own wits to sustain him.

The door opened again, briefly, and a Wykenig tossed a rough blanket in to him. "I'm Blixt. I've been put in charge of you. We'll bring food as soon as there is any. Might as well get some sleep," the man said. "You may not be going anywhere, but we are." Then, laughing at his own joke, Blixt closed the door again and, by the sound, locked it.

Mikkel stared at Talkin, who was staring at the door as if judging its strength. "I'm sorry you got yourself into this," Mikkel said. "But you insisted on coming along."

He shook out the blanket. It was rough-woven, and if he didn't know better he would think it inferior snow-thistle silk. That was impossible, of course; snow-thistle silk came from the NordornLand. He placed it over a stack of sails, hoping to make a passable bed and wondering how he could do that and stay warm at the same time in the chilly hold. Inured as he was to snowy weather, the farther north they had come, the more he was beginning to feel the grip of a different, more intense cold.

Then, belatedly, he remembered Tjórvi's prescient advice about putting on extra clothing and, even more important, folding his snow-thistle silk blankets and putting them under his shirt.

He pulled them out now—two wonderfully light, warm, compact blankets, finely made—and laid one over the rough one. He settled down, and covered both himself and Talkin with the other. They quickly warmed under the silk. Despite the cold, the boy began to doze.

Late in the afternoon, Blixt brought food, a rather thin soup and a hunk of coarse bread.

"If you promise to keep that beast under control, I'll let you come out on deck for a while. There's something ahead that's worth seeing," he told the boy.

"Talkin won't make any trouble," Mikkel promised, adding *I hope* under his breath. "We'll be glad to get out of this locker for a while. We have scarcely seen the sky in so long I don't remember."

"Come up topside then. We've made the turn, and are lowering the boats now."

Puzzled, Mikkel quickly swallowed a mouthful of soup, leaving the rest for the warkat, and, taking the crust of bread to gnaw on, followed the seaman up the ladder and onto the deck of the Wykenig vessel.

The sun was past midafternoon, but as far north as they were,

Andre Norton & Sasha Miller

it was likely to linger in place long after full dark had fallen in more southern climes. The light cast mysterious shadows on the line of cliffs the ship faced, creating the appearance of being guarded by ranks of trolls—big ones, little ones, some standing on others' shoulders. All seemed to be watching as the *Marmel*'s boats maneuvered into place and, lines attached to the vessel, the men began rowing toward a dark area in the cliff that Mikkel now could recognize as a narrow inlet.

He moved toward the rail. Quickly, he understood why the ship was being towed in. There was room, perhaps, for a vessel such as the two-masted ship he had been aboard so briefly, but a larger craft would be apt to scrape on one side or perhaps both. No ship, whatever size, could maneuver through unscathed if it were under sail.

The rocky walls of the inlet rose almost vertically. Bits of hardy vegetation clung to cracks in the walls, and, ahead, Mikkel could see the jagged tops of mountains that formed the sides of a bowl-like rock structure.

He gazed in wonder, taking it all in. The water they moved through was so clear he could see that the underwater walls were as vertical as those above. He fancied he could have made out the bottom if shadow had not shielded the waters from further view. There was only a hint of the murkiness of decaying vegetation.

Ahead, the mountains held ice-rivers in their laps. They were full of music, and everywhere the splash and tinkle of pure running water created a counterpoint to the rhythmic dip and plash of the oars.

Fascinated, Mikkel held out one hand toward the stone wall that seemed close enough to touch.

"Better not," a Wykenig said.

Mikkel turned; he recognized Shraig, the captain. Ridder Shraig, one had called him.

"Why?"

"You may be caught by a Rock-Maiden and carried off, never to be seen again." The man was smiling a little.

In an enchanted spot like this, Mikkel was ready to believe that anything, even being taken by a Rock-Maiden—whatever that might be—could happen. And so, prudently, he kept his hands on the railing and did not risk being captured anew. Talkin emerged onto the deck and moved close to Mikkel. The warkat paid little or no attention to the unworldliness of their surroundings, but calmly sat down to wash his face and paws.

Presently—too soon—they were through the dark, beautiful inlet to the more open water beyond. It was a fjord, Mikkel realized, but one much narrower and even more dangerous than Cyornas Fjord. It also was fed by the ice-rivers above.

Like the entry, the fjord was filled with bright music. Waterfalls, sparkling in the weak sun on one side and glittering softly in reflected light on the other, cascaded down from all directions. Mikkel thought he had never seen a spot so beautiful. He wondered if they were going to stay here for the night, hidden from view.

He turned to ask Shraig only to find that the captain had gone to the aft castle, to supervise as other seamen took up long poles and made ready to use them. He recognized Blixt, his caretaker, among them. Pulled by the small boats, the ship was heading straight for the far wall of the fjord.

Now the helmsman of the *Marmel* spun the wheel, turning it, deftly maneuvering the little ship so that its course paralleled the far cliff face. As it drifted close, the men wielding the poles kept it from colliding with the wall of rock as the rowers redoubled their efforts to coax the vessel in the direction it should go.

The ship swung around and steadied under the helmsman's skillful work with the rudder. A brief pause as the ship adjusted to its new course and now Mikkel could see that they were heading down a deep and narrow channel hidden from anyone who entered the fjord and wasn't aware of its existence. It was so small and the rocky walls so close that trees overhead formed a roof. In the resulting twilight, the men in the small boats towed the Wykenig ship a good league until they were in clear, open water

Andre Norton & Sasha Miller

once again. Trees clung precariously here and there, stubbornly trying to survive in spite of the stony ground. The tops of the masts occasionally touched the lowest branches of some of the trees, sending showers of thin green pine needles down upon the ship.

There was no chance of any ship anchoring here, if the steepness of the mountains on either side was any indication. Perhaps they could have tied up, if such had been their intention. Clearly, however, it was not. The peaks soared skyward like lance points threatening to stab the sky, so sharp that snow could not cling except in cracks in the rocky slopes.

Blixt returned. "You've seen the show. I hope you enjoyed it. Now, it's on to Forferdelig Sound and the Upplands," the man said, "where they'll decide what to do with you."

Six

Under the circumstances it no longer seemed fitting to hold a great celebration for Earl Royance and Countess Mjaurita. Nevertheless, guests had been invited, festive clothing made, food and drink prepared, and though the festivities might have a shadow over them, the honor due such a revered and honorable ally as Royance would take place.

The Great Hall of the Castle of Fire and Ice was ablaze with light, every holder of the great chandeliers filled with gleaming candles. Everywhere crystal drops and snowflakes had been hung until the very air twinkled.

Granddam Ysa, as Mistress of Protocol, and Elin as her assistant, took on themselves the ordering of the guests as they arrived. Every spare room in Cyornas Castle that could be turned into sleeping quarters was commandeered, cleaned, and made ready. Those guests whose status did not entitle them to lodgings in the castle had to find places to stay in the town. The counts and barons who had residences in Cyornasberg opened their doors, more or less hospitably, to ease the crowding.

Elin consulted one of the many lists she was making. Uncle

Rohan and Aunt Anamara were to stay in the castle as were her brother-in-law Peres and her sister Hegrin, King and Queen of Rendel; the Rendelian Lord High Marshal and Lady Rannore, Ashen NordornQueen's dearest friend, would stay in Svarteper's quarters in the barbican.

"But what shall we do with people like Mayor Doffen of Pettervil?" Ysa said fretfully. "Or that grotesque Chaggi, leader of the Fridians? His face is covered with tattoos!"

"We will find places, most likely in Cyornasberg. All who are coming are friends to Royance, or to Mjaurita, or to Father and Mother," Elin said. "I have heard that the Great Chieftain of the Aslaugors is close to arriving as well."

Ysa searched her memory. "Öydis."

"I understand that Öydis is getting on in years and her Marshal, Patin, has taken on most of her duties. She still holds the title, though. They will both be here."

"Could Patin possibly be a bit weary of living in Öydis's shadow?" Ysa inquired delicately.

Elin smiled at Granddam Ysa, knowing perfectly well what she was getting at. "Not likely," she said. "Öydis is his mother."

"That is no obstacle. Speak to him at one of the banquets. Find out if he harbors any resentment for the delay in his coming to his just position."

"Yes, Granddam," Elin replied demurely.

"The standards on the towers will be crowded with pennons. It already is with your father's, your mother's, the Nordorn-Prince's, yours, mine—"

"Uncle Einaar's, Aunt Elibet's, Peres's, Hegrin's, on and on. And that doesn't even take into consideration other countries or their protectorates. We must find a staff for everyone or deliver a deep insult."

Ysa stared thoughtfully at nothing in particular, and Elin knew the hint she had dropped had fallen on fallow ground.

"I think we should also inquire as to how relations are progressing twixt Writham and Yuland; they will have representatives here," Ysa commented.

"More banners."

"Yes. And the people from the Bog—that was well before your time, my dear, and nowadays they call it the Lowlands—are sending a delegation, headed by Tusser. I remember when he was no more than a savage. Less. But he's coming with a number of scholars who have been excavating the ruined city of Galinth. It seems that our Earl Royance has contributed generously to funding this project."

"The Aslaugors and the Fridians are still tribal, aren't they? I mean, the Aslaugors have united under their Great Chieftain—"

"Not all. There are those, I understand, who still object to being led by a woman. Or her son who leads in her name."

"You have stayed well informed, even while you were away from Court," Elin said tactfully. Ysa obviously had a good spy system.

"I have always found it useful to know what is going on around me," Ysa said. "Iselin is not all that isolated, you know. Let me see your list."

Obediently, Elin handed it to the Duchess.

"Yes, yes. Very good. Thorough. I see you have assigned Prince Karl of Writham and Duke Bernhard of Yuland rooms in the castle. You need to pay attention to these young men. I am certain they have been sent as potential suitors. Flirt with them. Make them each feel as if they have a chance to join Nordorn nobility."

Elin made a face. "I am not the least bit interested in either of them."

"Of course you aren't—not seriously. But you can certainly amuse yourself. Call it practice. You must get out of yourself, my dear, if you don't mind my saying so. Look outward. You'll never accomplish anything if you are thinking only of yourself."

With difficulty, Elin restrained herself from making a harsh—and unwise—retort. "Do you truly believe I think of no one but myself?"

"It is perfectly normal at your age, dear granddaughter. I was very like you when I was young. All I am saying is that it is now time for you to look outward, start exerting your power and influence as a princess, and as a budding woman. I can think of no better subjects for this practice than the envoys from Yuland and Writham. Nor can I think of anyone better to guide you than me. Would that I had had such a tutor when I was young and still beautiful." The Duchess laid Elin's list on her worktable, smoothing it with her hands. They had grown thin, the veins standing out sharply against the bones, and her rings hung loose. "Let me see what I can add to this, and where I can have people share quarters. We are seriously crowded, but surely room can be made for the most important. Now, run along. Surely there are matters you need to attend to elsewhere. And remember what I have told you."

"Yes, Granddam." Elin got to her feet, curtsied, and left Ysa's apartment. *No fear of any visitor being lodged in there,* she thought, *any more than in mine or Bjaudin's, or Father's and Mother's rooms.*

She had already devised a solution of sorts for the plethora of banners. Those of the nobility would, of course, fly in ranks on the staffs atop the castle towers. Those of lesser folk—in this case, barons, counts, ambassadors—would be displayed along the ramparts of the castle walls where they would make a brave show. But better she should order this at the last minute, to keep Granddam Ysa from claiming it as her idea. Elin was already very aware of Ysa's penchant not only for scheming, but also for taking credit where it was not due her.

She smiled; her first thought had been to reject Granddam Ysa's advice about dallying with the would-be suitors. But on second thought, she decided to obey. It would be good practice. Also, she realized, there was a good chance that the Court, especially her father and mother, would be so taken up with this new facet of their daughter's personality that Granddam Ysa would be able to do very much as she pleased.

Yes. By the end of the four days' feasting they should have Fridians warring with Lowlanders, the new name the former Bogmen had chosen for themselves; Aslaugors warring with Aslaugors and with Fridians; and possibly even Writham declaring war on

Yuland. Never mind that Writham was located well west of Rendel and Yuland was an island kingdom to the south and east, if provocation were great enough a way would be found.

She had already met the Writham prince, Karl, and knew that he found her attractive. If the delegate from the Island Kingdom of Yuland were also young enough and vulnerable enough, she could possibly stir up a rivalry that might bear fruit when she chose.

Each to her own strengths. The Duchess was beyond the age for flirtation; it would be an absurdity and laughed at. Therefore, let her stir up trouble with the Aslaugors and the Fridians and the former Bog-Men. They were rough people, often ill-mannered and even dirty and smelly. Elin had a more pleasant task by far. She would encounter Duke Bernhard this very evening. Then she would see.

Her new peach-colored snow-thistle silk dress lay on her bed, ready, with its matching coat, hosen, and slippers. Fortunately, the fashion was to dress children very much like adults, so she would not look like she had just come from the nursery.

She sat down at her dressing table and let Lady Hanna touch up the rouge that reddened her cheeks and lips. It made her look very grown-up, she thought. It would have been nice if Granddam Ysa would permit her to wear her beautiful emerald ring, but she had allowed it only that one time. Instead, she would wear pearls at neck and ears. They would look beautiful against her clear skin. Nevertheless, she longed for the time when she, too, would possess really important jewels such as a Great Signet.

As people gathered in the Great Hall before dinner, Princess Elin discovered to her surprise that Granddam Ysa had been right— again. It was a new pleasure—watching people, actually listening to what they were saying, rather than ignoring what was going on around her while she stayed in her own private half-dream world.

As if for the first time she observed her brother Bjaudin as he paid court to one of the newcomers. The girl was pretty enough, Elin supposed, with her soft brown eyes and hair.

She stopped a passing maidservant. "Who is that lady?" she asked.

"That is Lady Laherne, ma'am, daughter of the Lord High Marshal of Rendel and the Lady Rannore."

With a gesture, Elin sent the girl about her duties as she studied this Laherne without openly staring.

Interesting. Lady Rannore was Mother's closest friend and had been for years. Bjaudin needed to find a marital alliance outside of the NordornLand. Rendel and the NordornLand were fast allies already, of course, but the prospect of civil war should Bjaudin choose someone from Nordorn nobility was too great; this she had learned from Granddam Ysa.

She turned from scrutinizing Laherne and saw Duke Bernhard of Yuland not too far distant in the crowd. He was well dressed and very good-looking, and quite aware of it. She could tell by the carefully trimmed beard and the slightly self-consciously graceful way he carried himself. When she danced with him later, at least she could be reasonably certain he would not tread on her new peach-colored slippers.

Just as Bernhard, who seemed to feel the weight of her gaze on him, turned to meet her eyes, the crowd shifted and she found herself observing Count Mjødulf of Mithlond with his wife, the Countess Ekla. They were accompanied by their daughters Fidelina and Emelina, and their son, Mårten. To her surprise, Mårten did not look nearly as much a child as she previously described him to be. Indeed, he had a gravity of manner suitable to one three times his age. If Mikkel and Tjórvi had been present they would have shunned Mårten as a baby. That, Elin realized, was another fundamental difference between boys and girls; boys matured much later.

She decided to dance with Mårten as well, at least once. After all, Granddam Ysa would be negotiating for a betrothal between them in a matter of days. In the meantime, of course, she felt free to enjoy herself as she would.

Prince Karl of Writham appeared at her elbow. "Will you sit with me at the feast?" he asked.

"Alas," she answered, eyes downcast, "I must sit with my father and mother. I dare not do otherwise. But I will dance with you later, I do promise."

"With that, then, I will be content." He kissed her hand.

The Seneschal sent stewards through the crowd ringing bells—the signal for dinner. With not entirely feigned regret, Elin disengaged her hand from Karl's and made her way to the dais where the royal family were already finding their chairs. Mother and Father, dressed in spring green, took their places at the center table; the chairs on either side of the King and Queen were empty.

Presently, the Chief Musician, Lady Pernille, ascended the shallow steps to the musicians' gallery. She was joined by players on the tambour, the horn, and the pipe. They struck up a tune used for a progression, and the chatter by eager and famished guests ceased. Earl Royance and his Countess, the handsome Mjaurita, entered the Hall to much applause. They were followed by Cyornas Castle's priest, Esander the Good, and Royance's gentlemen escorting Mjaurita's ladies. Smiling, the Earl and the Countess progressed straight down the center of the room until they stood before the royal dais where three tables had been set up for the family. As one, they bowed low to the sovereigns.

Both Gaurin and Ashen arose from their places and bowed in turn. "Most hearty welcome, our friends," Gaurin said. "Let our guests welcome and rejoice with you in your good fortune!"

Esander moved to the side of the Hall while Royance led his lady past all the tables until they had made a complete circle of the room. More applause preceded them and accompanied them; in spite of the fact that there had been no actual wedding, it was plain that this was a popular match.

"Now take your seats in the most honored places on either

side of Ashen NordornQueen and me," said Gaurin, "and let the feasting begin!"

At once the guests began to fall to heartily and the sounds of eating, drinking, lively conversations, laughter, filled the air.

Elin found herself wanting this part of the evening over with so that her real purpose could begin. She had to force herself to calmness and not bolt her food. That would not make the banquet go faster, only upset her stomach. She dallied with her trencher, so daintily that the stewards who were bringing around new platters of delicacies for those who were not tempted by roast fallow-beeste or crisp baked fowl or broiled fish, paid her close attention.

Her mother leaned forward. "Your appetite seems off, Elin," she said. "Are you feeling well?"

"Oh, very well, my lady Mother. I ate a few bites of bread before coming down to the Hall, so that I wouldn't make a greedy spectacle of myself, that's all."

"Like me?" Hegrin asked tartly. Her platter was full and she was applying herself to it with a right good will.

For answer, Elin put her tongue out at her sister. She was turning into a fat cow, with all her many pregnancies and her immoderate appetite.

Ashen laughed softly. "Indeed, my Elin, you are growing up, at least in some ways. It was not so long ago that you would eat heartily in public and not care who saw you. And for whom are you showing yourself the lady?"

"Oh, no one in particular," she said, truthfully.

She caught Granddam Ysa's eye where she sat at a table scarcely lower than the one set aside for the immediate family. Ysa nodded with a smile; apparently she had noticed Elin's demeanor and approved as well.

Eventually, the sweet was brought in, signaling the feasting was nearing its end. The musicians struck up a different tune. This time, the melody came from the curious stringed instrument Pernille held on her lap, strumming rather than plucking the strings. The plangent notes of "The Song" began to fill the air and

Pernille and her musicians sang to their own accompaniment. At once couples arose from their seats and began to dance.

Out of the corner of her eye, Elin saw Granddam Zazar making for the door, apparently feeling that the festivities were over for her. The good Esander also left the Hall, but it had ever been his custom to do so after the meal was finished.

Almost too quickly for propriety, Prince Karl approached the dais. "Sir, Madame," he said to Gaurin and Ashen. "With your permission, may I dance with your lovely daughter?"

"You may," Gaurin said.

The three tables on the dais allowed enough room between them for stewards to come and go—or for young princesses to take the dance floor. At once Elin stepped down and laid her fingertips on Karl's outstretched hand.

Behind her, she heard Countess Mjaurita speaking to Mother. "The Princess's loss of appetite might be due to the pangs of first love," she observed. "There may be another wedding very soon, one that you can plan."

But most likely not with this swain, Elin thought, smiling at Karl.

As she had planned, she seldom sat down for the balance of the evening. She danced first with Karl, then with Bernhard and others, occasionally, with young Mårten who made a surprisingly agile partner. She did not enjoy her courtesy dance with her brother-in-law King Peres nearly as much, which surprised her even more.

The royal members of the Court and their guests kept a strict protocol for the first few verses of "The Song" and then chose their partners as they pleased. She could not help observing that Bjaudin danced most often with Laherne, after his duty dances with his mother, Lady Rannore, Countess Mjaurita, and Granddam Ysa. If the ladies at the head dais were looking for a love match to gossip over, let them look no further than the heir to the Nordorn crown.

Most amusing, however, was the ease with which she discovered she could foster a polite, controlled, but definite jealousy between

Prince Karl and Duke Bernhard—just enough to have them glaring at each other out of carefully neutral faces, and not so much that they were apt to challenge one another to a duel.

Yes, interesting. Very interesting. None of this would have occurred to her before she and her grandmother had begun to talk. She was learning a great deal from Granddam Ysa. She looked forward to learning even more.

Seven

*R*ohan and Tordenskjold, in *Ice Princess*, fairly flew through the Icy Sea toward where they hoped the Wykenig vessel might be located.

"They're wanting to be found," the Admiral-General said, "so they won't have gone far. I daresay they'll be hove to in sight of our northern shoreline, not far from where the *GorGull* went down."

"I hope you're right, sir," Rohan replied. "Winter is beginning to close in. There are streaks of light in the night sky, and ice floating in the water."

"But no more bodies, and no one in a small boat crying out to be rescued. That means that the Wykenig has taken those he thinks will bring him the best ransom. Surely we will find Prince Mikkel among them."

"Surely." Rohan took out his far-see glass, a legacy from his grandfather, and with it scanned the horizon. "There," he said. "Just where you said it would be."

Tordenskjold took a look as well and then began issuing orders to the seamen. Quickly, mainsail, foresail, and lateen stern sail all came down, and were furled away neatly. *Ice Princess* slowed, now carrying only a small square sail on the bowsprit. Gradually they came alongside the Wykenig vessel.

A large man dressed in rough clothing with a cloak slung over his shoulders stood atop the rail, holding onto some rope rigging with one hand for balance. His hair was yellow, and he wore it in two untidy braids. A long sword in a decorated scabbard hung from a baldric and his other hand rested lightly on the hilt. He wore an incongrously delicate and ornate silver necklace—possibly a badge of office or authority—set with an enormous green gem. "Welcome to *Dragon Blood*," he called. "Will you come aboard, or shall we shout at one another across the water?"

"There are quite enough Sea-Rovers on your ship now," Rohan returned. "Do not think it unmannerly if we choose not to add to those numbers."

The man laughed. "Point taken. But who is the man standing at your side? He doesn't have the look of a Rover about him."

"I am Admiral-General Tordenskjold of the NordornLand," he said, scowling. "And I am not nearly as genial as my companion, Rohan, High Chieftain of the Sea-Rovers, whose son you nearly drowned."

"Ah. One of the boys told me as much, but I didn't believe him. Perhaps I should have. I am Ridder Holger den Forferdelig."

"Holger the Terrible," Tordenskjold said. "Knight-King of the Upplands. I have heard of you."

"Which is more than I can say of you," Holger said. "Or the Sea-Rover with you. He must pursue milder pleasures these days than going a-roving."

"That is no concern of yours," Tordenskjold said. His scowl grew deeper. "We have no time for small talk. You have captives we want returned."

"Well, so I do, but there is no reason to be unpleasant about it," Holger said. "I could hoist sail in a minute and leave you here."

"Not for long," Rohan told him. "You would have a problem, trying to outsail my ship."

"Not if you were stopping frequently, to fish one of these captives—I prefer to call them guests—out of the water."

Rohan turned away so the Wykenig could not see or hear him speak. "Impasse," he muttered to Tordenskjold. "He has all the advantages and we have nothing."

"Don't forget the ransom," Tordenskjold reminded him. "He is bluffing. Amusing himself, playing with us. It is a very good bluff, but we have a better hand to play in this game than he thinks."

Rohan nodded, then turned around again. "Point taken in turn, Captain Holger."

The Wykenig laughed. "Then we are even. Look you. We have something you want. You have something we want—payment. We must trust one another at least a little, or neither of us will come out even, let alone winners."

"Show us your—your goods," Rohan said.

Holger stepped down from the rail and issued an order. A freshening wind blew his words away before those on the *Ice Princess* could hear what he said. But presently, nine men emerged from the aftercastle of the Wykenig ship.

"Sir!" one of them said.

"Fritji," Rohan replied. "Are you whole? Have you been mistreated?"

"I—all of us have been treated well," Fritji said. "Apart from what we suffered in the fight, in the water, and the humiliation of being taken captive."

"How much do you want for them, Captain Holger?" Rohan demanded.

"Ten gold pennies each. Twenty for the captain."

"Done. Are these all?" Tordenskjold asked.

"There was another," Holger answered warily. "But he is not here. I may have let him drown."

"He is our main demand," Rohan told him. "We will pay you well for his return—better than the trifling sum you asked for my men."

"He must have been very special."

"He is the youngest son of the NordornKing."

"He made no claim to be a prince of the Nordorners. He should have, I think. He interested me only because he had a tame *krigpus* with him. But I grow bored easily. How well will you pay, supposing he can be found? What if I asked for the ship you're on? It looks like a fair fast one."

"Even the ship," Rohan got out through gritted teeth.

"With a hole in her bottom so you drown before you can get her to your pirate's lair," Tordenskjold added under his breath. He scowled.

"I must consider this turn of events. It's a generous offer but one that I cannot accept at the moment. In the meantime, prepare to receive your men—a little the worse for wear, I am afraid—on board."

"He has Mikkel," Tordenskjold muttered. "But not here. He has sent the boy to his stronghold, or I'm land-bound."

"We will send two of our boats," Rohan replied. "One to carry the men, the other with the gold and full of archers to guard against any tricks you may decide to play on us."

"I would do no less." He turned to one of the Wykenigs standing nearby. "Let down the ladders."

The boat from the Wykenig ship and the boats from the *Ice Princess* met halfway between the larger vessels. When the nine men from the Wykenig ship had been transferred to the *Ice Princess*'s boat and the payment made, Rohan waited impatiently for Holger den Forferdelig to take up the bargaining over Mikkel's return. But, with the Nordorn gold safely in his possession, the Wykenig captain gave every appearance of having forgotten about the matter. Finally, Rohan was forced to speak up, knowing he was forfeiting any advantage he might have had.

"Ridder Holger!" he called. "What of the boy?"

"Boy? Ah, yes, the boy," Holger replied. "And the *krigpus* with him. Well, as it turns out, both survived, though it was a near thing. As I said, I was interested in a lad who could tame one of those creatures and even make it do his bidding."

"And?" Rohan prompted.

Holger shrugged. "I have no idea where he is at the moment. But if I do happen to come across him, I might send a message. You say he really is kindred to the NordornKing? The one who slew the Mother Ice Dragon? I had heard he died and his Queen with him."

"Both live. Mikkel is their son, as I told you," Rohan said grimly. "Their Maimed Majesties will be grateful in many ways for his return."

"And as I told *you*, I might send a message if I find him. And if I remember. I will have to think on it."

"Think not too long," Tordenskjold told him, even more grimly. "Lest you find a war on your hands."

Holger's amiability vanished in a twinkling. "In which case, the boy—supposing he even exists and I come into possession of him—would perish instantly."

Rohan forced himself into a calmer, more reasonable frame of mind. "The boy is, you might say, a nephew of mine. His mother, Ashen NordornQueen, is in fragile health herself, from the encounter with the Mother Ice Dragon. To hear of Mikkel's death would kill her as well. Would you have that on your conscience?"

"There are those who think I have none. I will tell you again: I do not know where he is. But I will keep your words in mind supposing he shows up. Now, return with those you have ransomed. If we meet again, let us hope it is under happier circumstances."

The two ships raised sail and the Wykenig vessel turned northward, tacking awkwardly against the wind. The *Ice Princess*, whose radical new design would have made such a maneuver trivial, turned back south, making for Cyornas Fjord.

After clearing the enchanted fjord and the narrow passage leading from it, the *Marmel* finally reached the unobstructed light of late afternoon, twi-night as it was called in the northernmost climes. For only a few hours a day would there be real darkness until winter had passed. Winter lights already streaked the sky.

Up came the sails as the ship entered out into clear water. Looking back whence they had come, Mikkel found it hard to locate the notch where they had emerged from the tunnel-like exit of that fjord. Islands and headlands massed to their stern and high, sharp-edged mountains ranged to the south; to the north, a solid wall of white marked a region of snow and ice that never melts. Mikkel understood how difficult it would be to reach Forferdelig Sound by that or the secret route. The inhabitants of the Uppland villages could rest easy, secure from all but the most determined attack.

What passed for night was behind them and midmorning upon them before they arrived at their destination and turned into the wide, deep sound. Down came the sails again, and the ship's boats once more were pressed into service to tow the *Marmel* to its mooring. Atop the headland, a lookout sounded a signal on a huge horn—three short blasts.

The village, or steading, as the Wykenigs called their townships, was actually a fortress. A double stockade fence made of tree trunks with towers on the four corners guarded a group of huts surrounding a larger edifice. Mikkel realized they were made of daub and wattle like the poor folks back home used to build their homes. These materials were cheap, sturdy, and snug—ideal for cold climes.

The stockade fence was almost hidden by stacks of firewood. There might have been other buildings beyond the fortress, close to the line of trees and, indeed, other steadings might be scattered along the irregular shores of the sound, but they were invisible to Mikkel from his place on the deck of the ship. All the buildings in the establishment they were approaching, save the central one, appeared to be made of daub and wattle or of wood; the big one was constructed at least partially of stone. It was hard to tell, as the walls were high; however, Mikkel could see by the thatched roofs that many other buildings were attached, seemingly at random. Tiles surrounded the sheltered vents from which wisps of smoke rose, indicating that most of the huts were occupied.

A child's shrill voice echoed the horn blasts heralding their arrival. Within moments it seemed that the entire population had emerged from the gatehouse and gathered at the dock.

"You're back soon enough!" a woman called. By her demeanor, she was someone of consequence. Her hair shone gold; it was plaited neatly with strings of beads woven into the braids. She wore a dress somewhat finer than those worn by the other women in the crowd, and her jewelry glittered in the twi-night sun. "What did you bring?"

"Naught but a boy," Shraig answered. "And a *krigpus.*"

"A *krigpus*? Go back out to sea and drown yourself. You've gone mad."

"If I have gone mad, then Holger den Forferdelig is even crazier, for it was your husband who bade me bring them here to his steading."

The woman stood, fists planted on hips, frowning. "I'll put the boy in Old Askepott's charge. As for the *krigpus*, well, I don't know."

"Let the boy see to him. If either of them gets killed, nobody's the worse for it."

"Come ahead, then." She turned to a woman standing nearby. "Go and notify Askepott that she's got another orphan to look after." She addressed a man in the crowd, a metalworker judging by the apron he wore. "You make ready an iron collar. Just the boy. No need to risk yourself collaring the *krigpus.*"

"Yes, Mistress Gunnora," the man said.

"Now, everyone, back to work. There are no treasures to be doled out, and we have new mouths to feed."

Mikkel had stood still, thunderstruck by this woman and the aura of Power she radiated. The hairs on his head lifted, and might have stood straight up if not for his braids.

He had lived with the Power of magic, to one degree or another, all his life. Mother had it, inborn, although she almost never used it, as if she were afraid of it. Granddam Zazar had it, old as the earth, and not to be taken lightly. Granddam Ysa had it, true it

Andre Norton & Sasha Miller

was out of books, but Power nonetheless. His brother Bjaudin and sister Elin had it; perhaps that was why they fought so much. Even Uncle Rohan had a tiny bit of Power with the silk roses he could take out of the air.

He had none, and neither did Father, as far as he knew. But Mikkel could sense Power when he saw it or touched it, or it touched him. This Wykenig woman, Gunnora, possessed Power so strongly the air around her presence well nigh shimmered. He wondered that nobody else seemed to be aware of it. And further-more, while it did not seem to be exactly malignant, neither was it entirely benign.

The iron collar was not, as Mikkel expected, welded onto his neck. Rather, it was a torque, such as the silver or gold necklets some highborn people wore, locked in place with a little peg to keep the hinge from opening. The collar bore the mark of Holger den Forferdelig, and notified any who encountered one of his slaves or vassals that they were under Holger's protection. This was not jewelry, but a sign of ownership and the wise bearer did not remove it.

Old Askepott regarded him with some distaste when the smith brought him to her door and left him and Talkin there.

"Another younker gets himself caught up in matters too big for him and he gets dumped here, for me to take care of. I'll say this for you, though, you're different with your *krigpus* guarding you. No need, I don't bite and the kitte would have a rare fight on his paws if he decided to attack me. Are you hungry? I expect so, with naught but ship grub for—how long?"

"I—I lost count of the days."

"Well, come on, come on. And your kitte, too."

Askepott bustled inside. The room was larger than it looked from the outside; like the main building, its size was obscured by the number of outbuildings attached to it like barnacles. Mikkel discovered that he had entered a big kitchen. Women moved here and there through the room, setting out stacks of wooden platters, pulling feathers off a couple of fowl, sweeping the floor. Three women kneaded batches of dough at one flour-covered table. All surveyed the warkat with a wary eye, and took care to stay between him and a table or other substantial piece of furniture.

Good smells were coming from a large kettle set close to the fire, and the old woman was already ladling out two generous bowls of stew that looked, smelled, and tasted much more appetizing than anything he had had since he and Tjörvi had smuggled themselves aboard the *GorGull*.

"Needs more tubers, and more salt," Askepott muttered.

Mikkel sat at an unused table, applying himself to his meal; Talkin crouched at his feet, lapping up his portion. Askepott pulled up another chair and sat down with her new charges.

"Where'd you come from, then?" she demanded.

"I'm—I'm from the NordornLand," Mikkel muttered around a mouthful of tender meat that tasted similar to fallowbeeste, but was subtly different.

"Ran away to sea, did you?"

"Yes, ma'am."

Askepott laughed aloud. "No need to 'ma'am' me, younker. I'm Askepott. That's what they call me, anyway, at least to my face. What's your name?"

Mikkel was beginning to like this brusque old woman; she reminded him in many ways of Granddam Zazar. She had Power, no doubt; she might even possess much the same sort of Power his Granddam did. "I'm Mikkel. And my warkat is Talkin. What's to become of us?"

"Well, you've been given into my care, so I can assure you you aren't going to get eaten by some wild Upplander. You look too bulky for your size. Wearing everything you own, are you? Are those the only clothes you've got?"

A little startled by the abrupt change of subject, Mikkel brushed at his sleeve self-consciously. "Yes, ma—I mean, yes, Askepott."

"Too fine for the work you'll be doing, Mikkel. When you've finished, I'll get you some breeks and a shirt and smock more suitable. Things you can get dirty if you need to. Save your good clothes for feast days. I'll find you a box to keep your belongings in and tell the others to leave them alone or they'll answer to me."

"But these—" Mikkel stifled his protest. He had thought his garments rough indeed, but considering his surroundings, he was willing to save them, as Askepott said, for special occasions. He would be especially grateful if he could hide the two snow-thistle silk blankets he had refolded and returned to their hiding place against his skin and, perhaps, retain possession of them.

When he had finished eating, Askepott showed him to the room down a short hallway adjoining the kitchen where he was expected to sleep. There were six piles of straw arranged around three walls; five were covered with the kind of rough blankets he had seen in the ship that he'd thought made of inferior snow-thistle silk. Each sleeping place with bedding had a box at its head containing, Mikkel supposed, that person's belongings. It seemed to be a custom among these people. A table stood in the center of the room, with a pitcher and basin on it, and a few rags. Mikkel wondered if they were supposed to be towels to dry one's face and hands.

"That," Askepott said, indicating the unoccupied straw pile, "is where Hultz used to sleep. He's left to go on his own, built a house outside the village, the fool. Now it is your place."

"Who else lives here?" Mikkel asked.

Askepott pointed to three piles in turn. "Lucas, Willin, Tark. Over here, against the other wall, is Haldon's place. She was taken out of her village and left to die because the people thought her mother had had aught to do with a troll. The mother did die, stoned to death."

"How did Haldon survive?"

"Oh, some of the men from our steading found the infant and brought her here. This is the only home she's ever known."

Mikkel digested this in silence.

"The other girl is Petra. She claims she's a Rock-Maiden—a princess, no less. Always singing something about sea-green glass." She tapped her forehead. "Touched. Now, you'd better get out of those clothes while I go and find a box for you to keep them in."

"I—I'd rather not."

"Don't be a noddle-noodle," Askepott said sharply. "You think you have something I have never seen before? I'll bring you proper clothes. And I need to look at everything you own, so I'll know if someone tries to take anything. Now, do as I say!"

Reluctantly, Mikkel began removing clothing, shivering a little in the dank air. Presently, Askepott returned carrying not only a box for his belongings, but trailed by Talkin. The box was already full of clothing, with blankets on top. She dumped everything out on the pile of straw.

Mikkel had laid out his two changes of clothing, his three pairs of stockings, and his shoes beside the straw pile, leaving him barefoot and shivering in his underbreeks. The blankets were hidden beneath his clothing. He took the trews, shirt, and smock Askepott gave him and put them on gratefully.

"Keep your stockings, at least for now," Askepott told him. "And your shoes, at least until you outgrow them." She began placing the old garments into the box, and uncovered the two snow-thistle blankets he had thought to hide. "What's this?"

"Oh, just something from home."

"Well, now." The old woman moved to the bed belonging to Petra and turned back a corner of the blanket. "Our little Princess has something similar. She lined her good, honest bedding with them. I expect you'll want to do the same."

"Yes, thank you." Mikkel found himself relieved not to have to hide the silk coverings in his belongings box. If he dared use them, he would have had to take them off in the mornings, retrieve them at night, and hope not to be discovered. Also, someone else possessed snow-thistle silk. . . . He resolved to befriend this Petra, if possible.

Askepott had begun stowing Mikkel's belongings in the box

and now was staring at him, an unfathomable expression on her wrinkled old face. "Very dainty. Are you a prince, then?"

"Ma'am? I mean—"

"Well, Petra claims to be a princess, and you possess these silken covers that only Gunnora the Golden has here in Holger's house. The rest of us make do with not nearly so fine stuff. Also, you are accompanied by a *krigpus* that nobody yet has tamed." She reached out and Talkin craned his neck so she could scratch him under the chin. "Must have found him as a kitten. So again I ask: Are you a prince, then?"

Mikkel knew it was only a matter of time before his identity was discovered; Uncle Rohan would be virtually in Holger's wake, taking the wind from his sails in his determination to ransom his men and his nephew.

"Yes, I am," he said. "I am the youngest son of Gaurin NordornKing and Ashen NordornQueen."

"Their Maimed Majesties. That is why you wear the Ash badge?"

Mikkel touched the amulet he had almost forgotten he wore. "I took it out of Mother's jewel chest and put it on before I left, for luck. Not that it brought me much."

Askepott gave a sharp bark of laughter. "You don't recognize luck when it slaps you in the face, boy!"

She got up and shook out the blankets over the straw with practiced speed, smoothing the snow-thistle silk between the rougher layers. Then she straightened the belongings box at the head of the bed, and brushed straws off her skirt. Talkin stepped onto the new bed, kneaded it a few times, and curled up for a nap.

"Come back to the kitchen with me now. I'll brew us some tea and we will talk more. You might as well know your princely status means less than nothing here. You'll be expected to work for your keep. You'll follow me around for a day, learning where things are, while I decide what you'd be best doing, and then you'll be no better, no worse, than any of the other children."

"You told me about Haldon and how she came to be here. What about the others?"

"Orphans, cast-outs, bits of flotsam fished out of the sea. We can always use more hands to do the work. Holger can be kind under his gruffness, but never take him for granted. He can also be as cruel and as harsh as anybody in the Upplands. I have seen it."

The activities in the kitchen had picked up as more women worked, preparing the evening meal. Apparently, it was to be more stew with, possibly, the addition of the fowl. This stew seemed to be a staple among the Wykenigs, the big kettle never being allowed to empty entirely. The women kneading the bread had disappeared, but the smells of baking wafted through the room. Apparently the oven was nearby; perhaps it was reached through one of the several doors leading from the room.

Askepott guided him into the inglenook, where they could converse in relative privacy. "This is my spot. No one else comes here. They wouldn't dare."

There was one chair and a small table beside it. A little cabinet stood in the corner, containing jars of unknown substances. A small tea kettle with a lid and a spout sat on a raised iron grate away from the fire. She gestured to one of the women who brought her a jug of fresh water. She poured a little water into the kettle and set it and the grate on the fire to heat while she measured some dried leaves from a jar and cast them into the water.

"That reminds me of— Oh, never mind," Mikkel said.

"Might as well tell me. I'll have it out of you anyway."

"Well, it reminds me of Granddam Zazar."

"Zazar. I think I have heard the name."

"She once was the Wysen-wyf of the Bog. My mother, Ashen NordornQueen, was her ward, before she was NordornQueen, I mean, and now she lives in The Castle of Fire and Ice. There is a new Wysen-wyf now."

"Nayla," Askepott muttered, almost inaudibly.

She placed the steaming mugs on the table and sat down. Seeing no second chair and unwilling to leave the warmth of the inglenook to find one, Mikkel lowered himself to the floor.

"You have seen fit to trust me with your secret," Askepott

continued. "Now you may hear one of mine. Steinvor is my true name though I never use it and I, too, am a Wysen-wyf."

"You!" Mikkel exclaimed, startled. "No wonder I—"

"What?"

"Well, you reminded me of Granddam Zazar. That's all."

"It's quite a bit." The old woman sipped at her tea thoughtfully. "Did any of the people you were with survive when Holger attacked?"

Mikkel nodded. He had scalded his tongue on the tea, and was unwilling to trust it to speak at the moment.

"Holger must have stayed to collect ransom. That is why the *Marmel* came back before him, with you on board. That means that Holger either is unaware of the kind of important fish he has caught, or has just recently learned. Otherwise he would have kept you with him and made your people buy you back at a dear cost."

Mikkel risked speech; the scalding tea seemed to heal even as it burned. "How long will I be here?"

"If you aren't returned at once to your homeland—in exchange for a handsome payment—then Holger will have decided to amuse himself at the Nordorners' expense. If that is the case, there is no way to tell how long you will remain. It could be years."

"Mother is not strong," he said. "She is not at all strong. She may die, not knowing what has become of me."

"Now, listen to me, boy. Holger does not find amusement in making ladies die of grief. I have watched his dealings with hostages before. My guess is that he will send reports from time to time about you—your health, how you've grown. How much he has come to like you, so that he does not wish to be parted from you."

"What do you think he will do with me?"

"I have no idea. But if you're a smart lad, you'll work hard, stay out of sight, do as you're told. If Holger decides to pay attention to you, then you'll be at his elbow as long as he wants you to be." Askepott set her tea aside and arose.

"The Nordorn army and navy both will come looking for me."

"I do not think so. Holger will find a way to deny them, keep them bottled up at home, gnawing on their shields. There will be no brave, rash rescue for you, lad."

Mikkel swallowed hard, remembering his manners. "Then I thank you for your kindness. How can I repay you?"

Askepott emitted another bark of laughter. "Oh, never fear about *that*, boy! I'll keep you hopping. Can you milk a snow-cow? Gather honey without being stung? Thatch a roof? Brew *björr*? No? You'll learn. Just do your work so Holger has no opportunity to change his mind and decide you're more bother than you're worth. At the moment, I'll warrant, he will be inclined to make a pet of you. I think he will find it amusing. Be pleasant with him, but do not fawn over him or he'll know something isn't right. Show him your amulet."

"What good will that do?" Mikkel said, touching the gold disk.

"It is the Ash badge. The Wykenigs revere the Great Ash Tree, from which all life derives. As a son of the Ash, you are special, under its protection."

The old woman reached out and patted Mikkel on the shoulder. "All is not as dark as you fear, younker. There is still hope. Now, go to the larder—that's through yonder door—and fetch tubers for the dinner tonight."

Eight

The Duchess Ysa watched contentedly as Elin NordornPrincess enjoyed herself during four of the five days the celebration was due to last. She might as well have been born a coquette. But then, considering the grandmother she had been named for—her husband Boroth's unlawful mistress—perhaps this was not surprising. On alternate days, Elin favored Prince Karl and Duke Bernhard, with the most satisfactory result that the two young men glared daggers at each other on every occasion when they met.

This did not go unremarked by the ladies of the Court, even the visitors. Ysa bided her time and, when she judged the situation was becoming critical, invited Ashen, Hegrin, Mjaurita, Elibit, and Rannore to tea in her apartment. Skillfully, she guided the conversation in the direction she wanted it to go.

"Princess Elin is growing up fast," Ysa remarked. "She is turning into a very lovely young woman." To hide any telltale expression she might have had, she bent over to place a plate of spice cake crumbs on the floor for Alfonse. The little dog began gobbling the treat greedily.

"And too aware of it, if you don't mind my saying so," Mjaurita stated. "I am taking full advantage of my greater years and experience, Ashen NordornQueen, so please forgive me if I give offense. Your daughter is behaving, well, rashly. One would think that she was deliberately playing with those two young men."

"Oh, surely not," Rannore protested.

"Oh, surely so," Hegrin said as she helped herself to another sugary spice cake. "She's just as bad in her way as I was when I was her age, only I was more interested in fighting with the boys and beating them than I was in flirting with them."

"Alas, I fear Queen Hegrin knows her sister very well," Mjaurita said. "You have a gentle heart, Rannore my dear, but none here save the Duchess and I have lived long enough to see clearly what is happening. Or the remedy."

"And what would that be?" Elibit asked.

"Well," Ysa said judiciously, "it seems to me that if Elin were betrothed—"

"No!" Ashen exclaimed.

"Betrothed," Ysa repeated. "If Elin were betrothed, that would possibly settle both Prince Karl and Duke Bernhard enough that they don't start a war between their two countries. Such a war would be sure to involve both Rendel and the NordornLand as well! And we all know that betrothals aren't the same as marriages. Elin, for all her precociousness, is far too young for that."

"But who would make a good match for her?" Rannore asked.

The ladies, to Ysa's immense satisfaction, then virtually repeated the conversation she and Elin had had on the subject earlier, and to her even greater satisfaction, after they considered every possible suitor of noble or near-noble blood, came to the same conclusion. If Princess Elin was not to be bestowed upon a commoner or sent to another kingdom, the only real candidate was Mårten.

"My great-nephew is a very intelligent young man," Mjaurita said. "That is not just a doting aunt's claim. He shows every sign of growing up to be as long-headed as his father. Mårten may be young, but I am certain his father and the Countess Ekla will welcome the opportunity to ally themselves even more closely to the royal house of the NordornLand."

Before someone could point out that the House of Mithlond stood to become even more powerful than it currently was, what with Mjaurita's marriage to Earl Royance, Ysa voiced her approval. "Yes, I agree, my dear. Mjødulf has always been one of Gaurin's most loyal supporters. Now, given Princess Elin's disposition at times, especially when she does not have her way in all matters, this match between them might not be a totally unmixed blessing—" She laughed at her own jest, and the other ladies, save Ashen, joined in a little uncertainly. "No, not totally unmixed, but not a match that would be seen as grotesque, such as a liaison with, say one of Arngrim's sons." She shuddered delicately. "Their manners at table—well, those young men are most unsuitable in every particular, as I sure all here will agree."

"I am still not in favor of a betrothal at such an early age," Ashen said.

"How old is she? Twelve? And how old were you, Hegrin my dear, when you married Peres?"

"Thirteen," the Rendelian queen said, a trifle defiantly. "Closer to fourteen."

"I think not. Closer to twelve, I think. Nor were you betrothed. Peres announced that you were to wed, and so you did at once. And you gave birth to Boroth the Younger at fifteen?"

"Yes." Hegrin's face flamed.

"Even though you were discouraged from beginning the intimate part of your marriage until you were sixteen at least."

"Yes." Hegrin flushed even deeper.

"Well, then," Ysa said, turning to Ashen, "it would seem that Elin could be betrothed to Mårten now, and no one—save you—would find reason to object. I daresay that after a little thought, you will see the wisdom in this course of action."

"I suppose that I am being a little overprotective, as I was with Hegrin," Ashen said reluctantly.

"Then it's settled!" Ysa turned to the other ladies. "Shall we all agree, to preserve peace between Writham and Yuland enough that the two countries don't declare war on one another here in the Castle of Fire and Ice, and also to rein in the Nordorn-Princess a bit for her own good and the NordornLand's, that Elin and Mårten's betrothal shall be announced tomorrow evening. Yes?"

"Well, it might be considered polite if we notified Mjødulf of our plans for his son," Mjaurita said a bit tartly. "Not that he'll have any objection, of course. Still."

"Of course, my dear. We are just arranging matters among ourselves, as women do. I would never overlook that courtesy. With Ashen's permission I will give that assignment into your capable hands. And, since Elin and I have grown close these last weeks, I will inform her of the plans for her future."

"It seems to me that this is all proceeding too hastily," Elibit said. "Do these two even like one another?"

"Of course!" Ysa said. "Or, if not, they will grow to do so. Mårten might be a little young yet to appreciate the necessity and significance of such a liaison, but Elin surely will. I will send for her this afternoon."

"Then we should absent ourselves, and leave you to your interview," said Elibit, rising from her chair.

Ysa did not miss the glance that passed between Ashen and Hegrin. Those two would have some things to discuss in private. Rannore looked faintly troubled, as if events were proceeding far too swiftly for her comfort. She and Elibit would be having a similar discussion, Ysa would wager anything on it.

"Does it have to be now?" Elin asked petulantly. "I had plans to go out riding today with Prince Karl. And if Bernhard happened to be out riding as well, it would have been most amusing when the two of them met."

"Undoubtedly. And I suppose that you would see to it that he knew when and where to find you. But the game is played out."

"Oh, I suppose. How did you get Mother to agree?"

"I have my ways, Granddaughter. Now, sit you down at my desk and we will begin composing notes to both Bernhard and Karl, telling them that you regret that you shall not see them again. Don't give them a reason; we'll announce the betrothal tomorrow night. And consider that you will have the pleasure of watching both Prince Karl and Duke Bernhard nearly strangle themselves, trying to hide their anger and disappointment."

Elin brightened. "Yes, that will be nice to see. You are very wise, Granddam." As she was bid, she took the chair offered. Alfonse stood up, his paws on her knee, and whined to be picked up. She settled the little dog on her lap.

"Never doubt it, girl. There is no other like me. Now, write."

"I am still heartbroken," Elin said sadly, as she dipped the quill into the inkwell. "Could you let me wear your emerald ring again tonight?"

"You seem entirely too fond of the Great Signet of Yew."

"It is the emerald I am fond of. It is so beautiful I can scarcely take my eyes off it. I wish I had one half as lovely."

"I have heard that the fire mountains in the Upplands, where your brother is at present, create green gems, just as the fire mountains in the NordornLand produce red fire-stones. When we finally hear from him, shall we ask him to bring back a green stone for you?"

"Oh, yes, Granddam!" Elin exclaimed. "A big one."

"A bag full," Ysa promised. "Enough to make rings and bracelets and necklaces—"

"And even a tiara?"

"Yes, even a tiara."

Satisfied, at least for the moment, Elin applied herself to the task Granddam Ysa had set for her. And truthfully, the game she had been playing with Bernhard and Karl had begun to take on the tinge of too much danger. She was glad to have it done with.

"So Ysa is plotting again," Duke Einaar said when Elibit had told him of the proposed betrothal.

"She was most insistent. It was almost as if she had reached this conclusion well beforehand, and was all but pushing us in the direction she wanted us to go."

"That was ever Ysa's way." Einaar thought back to the days when he had first come to Cyornas Castle, and Ysa had come within a hair of persuading him to seize the throne in the absence of both the NordornKing and NordornQueen, even usurping the rightful accession of Bjaudin NordornPrince. Yes, Ysa could be very persuasive and very forceful as well.

"Furthermore," he continued, "this proposed betrothal is eminently sensible in a dynastic sense. Even as it would make sense for Bjaudin to marry Laherne, Lathrom and Rannore's daughter."

"Is that being proposed? Ysa said nothing about it."

"I suppose that is because she hadn't arranged it," Einaar told her. "Or, alternatively, that she had no objection. The Duchess never does anything, or refrains from doing something, without having a reason. I am not sure, yet, of what Ysa's reasons are concerning the marriages and betrothals of our niece and nephew, but we can be certain that there are plenty of them. I must go and consult with Earl Royance."

"The Countess Mjaurita seemed to accept the proposed betrothal between Elin and Mårten without objection—yea, with great approval."

"As I said, it makes perfect dynastic sense. And also, Mjaurita hasn't the depth of experience with Ysa that I, or even you, have. Well, we shall see how things play out. Now that we have an inkling of what Ysa's plans are, if not the reasons behind them, we can better be on guard."

"I am glad that I brought this to you, my dear lord and husband.

You have ever been wise and careful in all matters concerning the well-being of the NordornLand."

For answer, Einaar folded his wife in his arms. As he held her close, he felt, even through their voluminous clothing, the new child kicking. It would be a vigorous one, and, again, he hoped it would be a boy. No child of Elibit's deserved to be forced to bear the name of his faithless mother.

Later, he called a meeting with Mjødulf, Royance, Peres, and Gaurin in the Council chamber.

"My good lords," he said, when all were assembled, "what think you of this newest scheme of the Duchess Ysa?"

"Oh, yes. Aunt Mjaurita has so informed me." Mjødulf bowed in Gaurin's direction and, as was his habit, folded his long, slender hands in front of him on the polished tabletop. "I am both humbled and flattered that a liaison between my son and the royal family of the NordornLand is even contemplated."

"Such a connection would not be unwelcome," Gaurin said. "You have always been unswervingly loyal. The children are close enough in age that such a betrothal would not occasion whispers and knowing laughs behind hands. I would like to hear the opinion of my brother and of Earl Royance as well."

"The Duchess Ysa is very astute when it comes to politics and political scheming," the Earl said. "I have observed her at it for years. Also, it is almost unknown for her to act without having at least one hidden motive. However, in this instance, I cannot fathom what that might be."

"Nor can I," Einaar said. "Our thoughts run in the same vein. I said as much to Elibit."

"In this case," Gaurin said, "I am inclined to think that her motives are straightforward."

"Yuland occupies the southeastern boundary of Rendel," Peres noted. "And Writham provides a not inconsiderable shield for both our lands from the peoples of the far west. It would not be wise to alienate either country."

"Agreed," Gaurin said. "My lady Ashen has informed me of what

I, a mere man, had overlooked, namely that the Princess Elin was, we must think inadvertently, stirring up a rivalry between Prince Karl of Writham and Duke Bernhard of Yuland. I had thought it just young people's high spirits. But she assures me that such high spirits could result in unforgivable insult." He took a swallow of the snowberry juice and hot wine that had been provided for the participants in the meeting. "I well remember my own feelings when I first met Ashen only to learn that she was freshly wed to another."

The other men nodded. This tale was well known throughout the land, about how the Sunburst at Midnight had engulfed them both, and how they had nobly resisted yielding to almost unbearable temptation. It was the stuff of legend.

"If I may suggest," Earl Royance said.

"Of course, my good friend," Gaurin replied.

"The Lady Anamara is kindred to Ashen NordornQueen, and her husband, Chieftain Rohan Sea-Rover, is a man whose station is not to be despised. Could we propose a match between his daughter— What is her name? Oh yes, Amilia. A match between her and the Duke Bernhard would, I think, be adequate consolation for his rejection as Elin's suitor."

"That is well thought on," Gaurin said. "Rohan should be returning at any hour now. When he arrives, I will ask him."

"And I will offer the hand of my daughter Gizela to Prince Karl," Peres said. "That should strengthen our presently shaky alliance with Writham and thus avoid the potential for warfare between that country and Yuland, with Rendel caught in between."

"How fortunate, then, that the Duchess decided to step in to avert what could have been a very dangerous situation!" Mjødulf observed. "There will be good outcome in all cases, I think."

Indeed there would, Einaar thought, a trifle cynically. Even though such ideas might never have crossed the scheming Duchess's mind.

At that moment, the ringing of deep-toned bells in the lookout station atop the Water Tower announced the arrival of Rohan and Tordenskjold.

"Now we can inform Rohan of our plans and get his approval. Go and inform Esander, Einaar, and have him make ready to perform the betrothal ceremonies," Gaurin said. "We will ask Court ladies to stand proxy for Gizela and Amilia. Let us hope that Rohan brings us good news in turn."

Nine

$\mathcal{M}$ikkel met the other "younkers" that afternoon. Lucas was about his age; Tark somewhat older; Willin, a frail boy, much younger. The two girls, Petra and Haldon, looked about his age as well. Neither girl seemed inclined to friendliness. Per haps they had seen too many of Holger's younkers come and go.

Oddly, Petra's pale skin bore silver-colored marks apparently tattooed to emphasize the planes of her face and make it seem that her features were chiseled of stone. He recalled that Askepott had said the girl claimed to be a Rock-Maiden. *Perhaps*, Mikkel thought, *it is some kind of tribal marking.*

He was glad when Lucas suggested they go outside and fetch water and more wood for the fire. "It will get us out from under foot and maybe save us a scolding from Askepott," he said. "Always a good idea to stay on Askepott's good side—if you can find it."

Mikkel laughed, and followed the other boy out of the kitchen and into the open. The long twi-night made all seem bathed in wet green light. Here and there veils of mysterious colored light ebbed and flickered in the sky. But the boys dared not stay and watch the show. They both grabbed pails and Mikkel followed Lucas up the

Andre Norton & Sasha Miller

hill to where the steading's primary well was located. They passed a cattle pen on their way, with several—Mikkel couldn't count them in the uncertain light—beasts in it. He supposed these were the snow-cows Askepott had mentioned. They bore a slight resemblance to fallowbeeste. Some of them had impressive racks of antlers on their heads. He wondered if the bits of meat he had devoured so hungrily were snow cow flesh.

Atop the rise, Mikkel got his first good look, despite the twinight, of the steading and its surroundings. Many huts crowded the stockade wall, as if for protection. Higher up the slope, a line of black trees stood at the edge of what passed for civilization below. Low hills created natural boundaries, and lines of smoke from domestic fires marked the steadings of other Wykenigs.

"Do all the villages here have their own docks? Their own ships?" Mikkel asked.

"I think so. Each steading keeps to itself, except when there's a war. But Holger's is the best and biggest. His only real rival is Thialfi Hamarwieldar, two steadings over. Some day they will go to war with each other, I think."

"Do you like it here?"

Lucas shrugged. "It's better than starving, or freezing to death. Either one would have been my fate if one of Holger's jarls hadn't carried me back with him after a raid."

"Then you're not from the Upplands."

"No more than you are. But I'm not a prince, like I heard you are."

"Whether I am or not, it makes no difference."

"Why is your hair so red?"

Mikkel self-consciously touched his braids, now sorely in need of attention. "I don't know where I got it from. My—my mam is very fair, and my da not much darker."

"Upplanders think red hair is special. I expect that is why Holger decided to send you here when he attacked the ship you were on. That, and your pet *krigpus*."

This place is worse for gossip even than the Castle of Fire and Ice.

Is there anything, Mikkel wondered, *that Lucas doesn't already know?*

"Any scrap of news travels fast," Lucas said. "If you don't want everyone to know everything, then don't say it, not to anyone, not even Askepott. You never know who's going to be listening in." He paused, considering. "Well, maybe you could say it to me, if we're out away from the main buildings like this. But not many others."

"Thank you for the advice," Mikkel said.

Then the boys busied themselves with hauling the bucket up from the well and filling their pails. They would have to make a second foray for the firewood and that, Mikkel thought, would be agreeable. He liked the fresh air, cold though it was, after the stifling closeness of the busy kitchen.

"Where is your kitte?" Lucas asked as they made their way back down the hill.

"I left him asleep on my bed."

"Will he hurt anyone? I heard you got him as a kitten and tamed him to your liking."

"Well, I have known Talkin ever since he was a kitten," Mikkel admitted truthfully, "but I have never seen him hurt anything or anyone except when I've taken him out hunting. Then conies had better run fast and hide. Mostly, he likes people, if he can see that I like them, too."

Lucas laughed. "Well, show him that you like me and maybe he'll come help keep me warm tonight. From the looks of that sky, we're due for snow and there isn't any firepot in our cubby. Too dangerous to leave unattended while we sleep."

"Maybe, if there isn't too much work to do some day, we can take him out hunting."

"Likely chance," the other boy said scornfully. "Old Askepott keeps us jumping morning till night."

They reached the door to the kitchen and left the water pails inside, then brought in as much firewood as they could carry. Askepott acknowledged their efforts with a curt nod of her head.

"Go and wash your filthy hands and get ready to serve at supper," she told them. "Look lively!"

And so the two boys made their way toward the sleeping area. The other four children were standing outside the door.

"There's a—a *krigpus* inside!" one of the girls said fearfully. "We told Askepott and she just laughed at us. I don't think she believed us."

"Well, unless he's moved there *is* a warkat inside—that's what we call them—but he won't hurt anybody. He's my friend." Mikkel opened the door.

Talkin looked up from where he had been asleep, blinked sleepily, shook his ears, and gave one paw a lick with his long red tongue.

"Here are new friends," Mikkel said. He turned toward the others. "Come in, come in, it's perfectly safe."

One by one he encouraged the other children to approach Talkin and, if they were brave enough, to stroke his head.

"Will he—will he come to the Long House tonight?" Haldon, one of the girls, asked, still fearful.

"He will if he wants to," Mikkel told her.

"Better not," Tark said. "There are dogs. Many dogs."

"I think I like him," said the other girl, Petra. The silvery markings on her face showed even in the dim light. She sat down on Mikkel's bed, stroked Talkin, and started to sing. As she sang, Talkin began to purr.

> *Bring to me my sea-green glass*
> *Sea-green glass so fine, so fine.*
> *Bring to me my sea-green glass*
> *Glass so fine.*
> *Bring to me my sea-green glass*
> *I must have it ere you pass,*
> *It is mine.*

The melody was plaintive, haunting, and one Mikkel had never heard before.

"What is sea-green glass?" he asked the girl.

"Something my people crave and collect. That, and snow gems."

"Where does it come from?"

But Petra only looked away and refused to say more.

"Holger wears a necklace with a green gem in it."

Still silence.

"Leave her, her head is cracked," Tark said. "If she doesn't get washed up and back into the kitchen quickly, though, Askepott will see to it that it's cracked even more and ours with it."

Mikkel took his turn with the others at the basin of water, drying his face and hands on one of the rags provided. Reluctantly, Petra also washed, though by now the water didn't look clean enough to do any good. Then the children all returned to the kitchen to begin serving food to those gathered in the Long House. Prudently, considering that dogs roamed the room where the men of the steading customarily ate, Mikkel closed the door, keeping Talkin inside. He would return with a bowl of water and whatever meat scraps he could beg from Askepott.

The Long House, the main building of the steading, was fully as large as the Great Hall back at Cyornas Castle. Torches in iron holders lit rows of weapons hung from the walls, along with many racks of antlers. This reminded Mikkel with a pang of home. But there the resemblance ended.

Missing was the big stone fireplace on the far wall topped with the mantel on or over which were displayed various trophies and awards—standing cups won by Father in tourneys, the hilt of the famous Dragon Blade, now cemented into its mother-of-pearl scabbard to hide the blade's absence, the gem-encrusted box that had held a very odd bracelet and a document relating the history of the Ice Dragons, and other items of more sentimental than actual value. There, at the High Table, was where Father and Mother had their chairs.

Instead, the Long House had a huge central hearth rimmed almost knee-high with stone, in which blazed a truly impressive fire, too hot to sit near, designed to warm the large room almost to the walls. Most of the smoke rose to the ceiling where it could escape through a roofed vent, but enough remained in the room to make the air heavy. Four thick wood columns, carved with images of beasts out of legend, supported the roof around the hearth; more columns, also carved, were spaced along the length of the room.

The walls, which had doors leading from the room in all directions, were lined with trestle tables, with more stacked against the far back wall to be put to use when needed. Men were already gathering at the tables, finding their accustomed places, some arguing over who had the best vantage point for seeing all that might be happening in the room. Before each man a wooden platter had been placed on the table. The platter contained a flat rusk of stale bread to soak up the stew juices, and cups of various designs were now appearing as the men placed their own drinking vessels on the table.

Women entered from the kitchen in pairs, one woman holding a pot of stew and the other a large ladle. They passed along the tables, serving each man in turn, and returning to the kitchen to replenish as necessary. Other women carried pitchers and filled the men's cups that were eagerly held up to them.

Mikkel and the other children were expected to carry trays of fresh flatbread and serve everyone. When all the men had been served, the women and the children would eat at tables at the back of the room. The good smells of food and bread were almost too much to bear and maintain any semblance of decorum. Mikkel hoped he could refrain from grabbing a round of bread and stuffing it into his mouth. The aroma wafting up from the tray was almost irresistible. No wonder the dogs seemed so intent on tripping him and the other servers. Now and then, one of the women snatched a piece of bread, tore it into pieces, and threw them at the dogs to gain a moment's respite.

He noticed that one of the other tables, positioned in the center of the wall opposite the kitchen, was also set on a slightly raised dais and on it were chairs rather than benches. Behind the dais only one door had been cut into the wall. Nobody occupied the ornately carved center chair. The golden-haired woman, Gunnora, from the *Marmel*'s landing was seated in the chair to the right, only slightly less ornate than the central one. Tonight she wore a deep crimson dress, and her necklace and rings were set with blue and red stones.

That would be the Wykenig version of the High Table. The central chair, he realized, was Holger's customary place and the woman, the only one in the main part of the room, must be his wife. The chair to her right was also empty, but the one to what would have been Holger's left was occupied by Captain Shraig of the *Marmel*, the one who called himself "Ridder." He recognized Blixt as well, and a few others from that vessel whose names he did not know. Off to one side, he saw another dais with chairs and musical instruments on it.

Behind Holger's chair, several game boards hung on the wall; apparently the Wykenig chieftain was fond of some form of King's Soldiers. Mikkel gazed in awe at the most ornate board, nineteen-by-nineteen squares. It had apparently seen less play than another that was thirteen-by-thirteen from which the gilt was missing in spots. He had never played on any other than an eleven-by-eleven, though he had heard that even smaller boards existed.

The back of his neck began to tingle.

"Get moving," Petra whispered in his ear. "Gunnora is frowning at you."

With a start, Mikkel took up his task, hoping to have avoided possible punishment for his lapse. His neck tingled more and he knew he was still the object of the woman's scrutiny.

As he made his way through the room, doling out bread to the hungry inhabitants of the steading, the ill-mannered dogs crowded even harder against him, occasionally even leaping up, apparently hoping to make him drop the bread to them.

He was glad he had confined Talkin to the sleeping room. Warkats were, by and large, indifferent to dogs, except possibly as prey, but with some dogs, particularly of the hunting variety as these were, their aggressive canine natures could bring them to grief. If a dog started an altercation, a warkat would be sure to end it. Back home, many a torn ear or raked flank attested to a rash young dog's lessons in the wisdom of keeping a good distance between itself and the castle's resident warkats. An adult warkat stood taller than all but the largest dog; Talkin had yet to reach his full growth, however, and he might have been the one to come to some grief against such long odds.

At last, the diners seemed content with what they had been given and Mikkel and the others were left in peace to eat their suppers as well. They got up only when someone called for more bread, or another ladle of stew, or a cup of *björr* before the others had finished eating and the serious drinking had begun.

"Is it always like this?" Mikkel asked Petra, who happened to be sitting beside him.

Now she seemed inclined to talk. "Not always. This is a celebration, welcoming Ridder Shraig back safely, and with him a hostage that will bring more wealth to the steading. You."

Mikkel thought about that in silence, as he chewed on the crust of the very tasty bread. "I think Holger—"

"You must always refer to him as Ridder. Or, sometimes, as King. Perhaps Knight-King."

"What's that mean, 'Ridder'?"

"It's a title of nobility. I think a Ridder might also be called a knight. Someone who is not as important as a Ridder is called an Adelig. Men of the steading are called jarls."

"It is similar to my homeland. Very well, then, I think that Ridder Holger could have had as much wealth as he wanted, had he left me on his ship and bargained with my uncle who surely came after me."

"How do you know your uncle did this?"

"Because if he had not, Ridder Holger would have been back here by now."

It was Petra's turn to consider Mikkel's words. "That is very good, Mikkel," she said finally. "You can think matters through."

He didn't tell her that Askepott had figured it out long before he had. "Who is missing at the High Table, besides Holger?"

"Ridder Gudbrand Grå. He is the commander of the Chieftain's second-best ship. It is the *Ice Rider.*"

At that moment, four musicians mounted the platform, took up their instruments, and began to play. To Mikkel's astonishment, the tune was very like "The Song," only in a different rhythm and at a much livelier pace. Three musicians played long-necked stringed instruments and a fourth held a drum and coaxed a strong rhythm from it with a double-ended padded hammer. The entire company began to sing:

> En bedre . . . byrde ingen mannbjørn
> på måten enn hans morvidd;
> og ingen verre foranstaltningsboks . . . han bærer med ham
> enn en dyp dyp dypgung av björr.

"What does that mean?" Mikkel asked.

Lucas translated: " 'A better burden . . . no man can bear on the way than his mother wit; and no worse provision . . . can he carry with him than a deep deep draught of *björr.*' "

"That means they'll be drinking late into the night," Haldon observed. "They don't always do that."

"It also means that we'll be sent off to bed early," Willin said. He looked tired, and there were dark circles under his eyes.

"Gunnora is already leaving the hall," Petra said.

Mikkel glanced toward the High Table, dreading the resumption of the tingling on his neck. But the Wykenig woman seemed to have forgotten him. She had, indeed, arisen from her chair and had opened the door on that side of the room.

"Can any of you play King's Soldiers?" he asked.

"What's that? A game?" Willin asked. "Not for me. I am tired."

And indeed the boy looked as if he could fall asleep with his head in his empty platter.

"Yes, a game. You play it on a board like one of the ones behind Holger's chair."

"Then it's not for you, either," Tark told him. "Valuable hostage or no, if you touch one of the Ridder's precious game boards you'll be missing one or both hands when he hears of it."

Mikkel made no reply. In days to come, he decided, he would try to make a board of his own and teach one or more of the others to play. It would ease the monotony of their lives.

Two days later, the horn atop the lookout mountain at the entrance to the sound gave voice again—one long note, followed by two shorter blasts.

"That's Ridder Holger, returning, and Ridder Gudbrand Grå with him!" Lucas told Mikkel. "There'll be a proper feast tonight, you can be sure!"

And indeed, Askepott already had the women in the kitchen running here and there, instructing one of the house jarls to bring out a side of snow-cow from the cold locker, already prepared and held back for this occasion. All other work was suspended, at least for the moment. Women left their looms and their mending, their brewing and their other regular tasks to help in preparing the feast.

Quickly, the men spitted the meat and put it on the rack to roast over the great kitchen fireplace. At first, Mikkel was assigned the task of turning the spit, but Talkin made such a nuisance of himself, as if this were a game that he would win by snagging bits of meat, that Askepott put Willin to the task instead.

"You go bring in more firewood," she instructed Mikkel. "And take that kitte with you. Let him run off some of his excess energy."

Everywhere the inhabitants of the steading seemed to have but one thought in mind—the great feast that would welcome

Ridder Holger back from his last foray of the season. Snow had fallen the past two nights, and even now drifted lightly through the chilly air as Mikkel and Talkin went about obeying Askepott's instructions.

Mikkel had laid aside his heavy shoes in favor of Wykenig soft leather footwear covered with heavy cloth or fur that was gaitored around the wearer's legs to the knee and kept him warm and dry no matter how deep the snow. He was, of course, not allowed to wear a dagger from his belt, nor a purse. He didn't have any coins or other treasures to put into a purse anyway. All he had that was truly his was his Ash amulet, and that he kept hidden around his neck under his shirt.

None of this mattered to Talkin. Like all warkats, his coat was dense, three layers thick, and he didn't feel the cold even through his paws that were likewise heavily furred. He raced up the hill and back down again at full gallop, leaping high, twisting and turning, scrambling up fence posts and alarming the snow-cows in their pen. As content as he had been in Mikkel's company and enjoying the attentions of the other younkers, he seemed enormously relieved and happy to be outside for a while.

Mikkel kicked at a weed in the cabbage patch. Soon the cabbages would all be gathered and put into a cold locker with onions and barrels of tubers, turnips, and peas to help get the steading through the coming winter. In another locker, cheese was stored along with casks of butter, salted meats, and dried fish. Yet another held seemingly endless casks and barrels of the *björr* that the Wykenigs drank in such huge quantities. This, Mikkel had discovered, was fermented from the fruit of what looked very much like the snowberries of his homeland, only wild and uncultivated.

It was becoming ever more clear to Mikkel that the Wykenigs, hard as it was to believe, were, in fact, much the same peoples and kindred to the Nordorners, the Rendelians, and perhaps even the Aslaugors and Fridians and Lowlanders. At what time ages ago had tribes or clans or families gone their own way and then become, if not enemies, then not friends?

Mikkel tucked this insight away to ponder later and, perhaps, even to talk about with Willin. Now he had to persuade Talkin to come back inside. Left to his own devices, the warkat was fully capable of bringing down a snow-cow, hiding the carcass, and devouring it at his leisure.

"Come, Talkin," he said. "I'll find you meat broth to drink. Nice and warm. Mixed with milk, perhaps."

Interested, Talkin trailed Mikkel back to the kitchen that had become his home. The boy took the load of firewood to the great hearth and put it in the niche let into the thick wall where it would be added, as necessary, to the roasting fire.

"Here, you, Mikkel, if you're at loose ends, go into the common room and help lay the tables for the feast tonight," Askepott said when she spotted him.

"I was hoping for a bowl of warm broth and milk for Talkin," he said. "I promised him." He didn't add that it was a bribe to keep him from decreasing the steading's herd by at least one.

"You do as you're told. I'll feed your kitte."

The haunch of snow-cow on the spit was beginning to smell wonderful, as Haldon mopped it with a mixture of honey and *björr* mingled with spices. Mikkel lingered a moment and was relieved to see Talkin merely sniff and turn to his bowl of meat broth and milk, clearly disappointed that the humans were spoiling perfectly good meat by burning it in such a fashion.

Relieved that the warkat wasn't going to cause any disruption, at least for the moment, Mikkel went to do as he was bidden.

More tables than for Ridder Shraig's homecoming feast had been set up, and women were placing platters on them, along with carved wooden spoons. At intervals women set dishes of salt and deep bowls to be filled with more of the savory basting sauce and shared by all the diners, and pots of honey for the bread. Each diner would provide his own personal knife for cutting the meat, and, as before, his own drinking horn or cup.

The wall torches lifted only a part of the darkness in the windowless room. The main light for the diners was provided by many thick candles set in low dishes obviously made for that task on every table. The wax smelled sweet, like honey.

At the head table, special care was being taken for laying out the platters and ornamented silver cups. Beside each platter, a woman had placed a napkin, and in the center of the table there was also a dish of salt, a sauce bowl, and a pot of honey for these diners' exclusive use.

Gunnora moved through the room, supervising the preparations with a sharp eye, now and then moving a platter or a bowl to suit her. Most of all, though, she paid attention to the head table.

"You there, Berna," she said sharply. "Those napkins look like they've been used. Go and fetch fresh ones."

"Yes, Lady," the woman said. She went through the door Mikkel now knew led to the private quarters of Ridder Holger and Lady Gunnora. He was curious as to what it looked like.

"What're you staring at, boy?" Gunnora demanded. "You're the one who thinks he's a prince, aren't you? I think you must be mad."

"No, Lady," Mikkel said. His neck tingled sharply and he knew he must be careful around this formidable woman. "I do not think I am mad. Though I am the son of a king, I will not ask for special favors nor require being addressed by a lofty title. I have been knighted, though, so I might be called Ridder if this finds favor in your or Ridder Holger's eyes."

Gunnora regarded him at some length. Then she began to laugh. "Now, that is amusing! A boy your age, a Ridder! We must be sure to tell my husband that. He'll either laugh himself sick or knock you across the room. Now, get busy."

Gratefully, Mikkel turned away to try and look busy and escape Gunnora's attention.

While the feast was being prepared under Gunnora's watchful eye, Holger and a few of his Ridders and Adeligs went out into a small hut outside the protective walls for a sweat bath. As an unexpected reprieve, Mikkel was called away from work in the banquet hall to fetch water for pouring over rocks heated nearly to the melting point to create the necessary steam and then to fetch buckets of snow for the after-bath cleansing.

The Knight-King himself seemed to have nothing on his mind more important than this refreshing ritual. Perhaps, Mikkel thought, he had forgotten about his prisoner entirely.

But no. When Ridder Holger, having profusely sweated out impurities through his skin, was ready for the snow in the bucket Mikkel carried, he addressed the boy directly for the first time since arriving at Forferdelig Sound and the Upplands.

"They say you're a prince. Son of the NordornKing. Is that right?"

"Yes, sir," Mikkel said. He dared to look Holger in the eye. "His youngest, if it please you."

Holger laughed. "And even if it doesn't," he said genially. He seemed to be in a good mood after his bath, scrubbing his skin with the snow and turning it red.

"Did—did my father offer ransom for me?" Mikkel asked, more than a little hesitant lest he ruin Holger's pleasant frame of mind.

"Ransom in plenty!" Holger exclaimed. "The fellow we talked to, the one captaining the sharp-bowed new ship, offered it to me in exchange for you. They must think highly of you."

The *Ice Princess*! Father and Mother must want him back very much indeed if they were willing to give up the prize of the Nordorn navy. Mikkel tried to keep his expression from giving away his thoughts.

"That was my Uncle Rohan, Chieftain of the Sea-Rovers, you spoke to. Was there another man with him?"

"Yes. Gruff, older, looked like he'd been at sea most of his life."

"That would be Count Tordenskjold, Admiral-General of the Nordorn fleet."

"Well, he looked to be capable of being very unpleasant if the mood took him." Holger toweled himself off and began donning the festive garments laid out ready for him. "Wouldn't fancy meeting him in battle. I wager he knows what he's about. Not like that fool whose ship you were on. He was barely worth the twenty gold pennies I got for him."

Mikkel decided to risk one more question. "And will you trade? Me for the ship?"

"Haven't made up my mind yet. Now, run along. I'm sure Gunnora has plenty of work for you to do and if she doesn't, then Askepott will."

Mikkel went to do as he was bid. Despite the Ridder's careless attitude, he felt more hopeful than at any time since being taken aboard the Wykenig ship that he would, eventually, be returned to his home.

When the hall—the room Askepott called the Long House—was full of men, many with their ladies at separate tables, Mikkel almost forgot how strongly Gunnora's aura of Power told him she was, in her own way, far more dangerous than Ridder Holger could ever dream of being. Her attention was turned elsewhere.

No stew for the diners tonight. This was a real feast. In addition to the roasted meat, there were platters of honey glazed vegetables—turnips, carrots, cabbages, leeks—and mounds of fresh flatbread. These, Gunnora served with her own two hands to her husband and to the Ridders at the High Table, an honor that she would cede to no other. Another smell of honey, not from the candles, began filling the air in the hall as the women poured the first draft into the diners' cups. This was *mjöð*, the honey brew, reserved for grand and great occasions; *björr* was for all other times.

The skalds, the musicians, struck up a tune and began to sing:

> *Comes now forth Gunnora the Golden,*
> *queen of Holger, heart of the Upplands;*
> *heedful of courtesy is she,*
> *gold-decked, greeting the guests in hall;*
> *and the high-born lady hands the treasured cup*
> *first to the Wykenigs' heir and warden,*

bids him be blithe at the welcoming mjöð-carouse,
the land's beloved one.
Lustily takes he
banquet and beaker, battle-famed king.
To those at the High Table then goes Holger's Lady,
to younger and older waiting there, till comes the moment
when the ring-graced queen, the royal-hearted,
gives thanks in wisdom's words, that
she has wed a hero on whom her hope could lean
for comfort in terrors. The cup he takes,
hardy-in-war, from Gunnora's hand, and drinks.
Bright with gold the stately dame by her spouse sits down.

When Holger and those in the hall had drunk the cup of *mjöð*, the women began refilling all beakers with *björr*. This, too, Gunnora served him with her own hand in his own ornamented silver cup from a pitcher she had personally prepared. Lesser men had to make do with carved wood or horn served by women of the house.

Later, when the women had cleared away the platters and thrown the scraps to the dogs, the men would fall to the serious drinking. If there were dancing in the Wykenig Long House, it would be in the form of an entertainment—not participated in by the onlookers—but this would not be the night for that kind of frivolity.

While Gunnora ate, sharing her platter with Holger, she was constantly surveying the room with her sharp eyes. Mikkel could almost see her committing small transgressions and breaches of manners to memory to be used later against the malefactors.

His nape hairs rose again as her gaze fell on him. She leaned toward Holger and whispered something in his ear, causing him to turn and stare at her. Then he laughed uproariously.

"I think she's told Ridder Holger something about me," Mikkel muttered to Petra, who was sitting beside him. "Nothing good, I'd wager."

"You'll find out soon enough," Petra said. "Look."

Holger was beckoning to Mikkel. Resignedly, he arose from the table and made his way through the revelers until he had reached the High Table.

"Sir?"

"My lady wife tells me that in addition to being a prince, you fancy yourself a Ridder!"

"My father, the NordornKing, knighted me on my tenth birthday," Mikkel answered, trying to sound humble. "It is a custom among the Nordorners."

"Now I am glad I decided to keep you for a while, young Ridder." He turned a shade more serious. "Look you. I have had a good season. The treasury is full. The larders have enough in them to feed us through the winter that is hard upon us, if we are lucky with hunting and fishing. The winter lights fill the sky, there is ice in Forferdelig Sound, and no Nordorn ship, no matter how well captained, will risk sailing northward at this time of year. You are my guest whether you wish it or not. It is an added benefit that I find you amusing. Some of my guests are not so lucky."

Unconsciously, Mikkel put his hand on his amulet.

"What's that?" Gunnora demanded.

"Nothing, Lady. Just—just something from home."

"Let me see it."

There was no denying her, Mikkel knew. So he pulled the chain over his head and handed it to her. She held it to the light, examining the device. Then she passed it to Holger who scrutinized it in turn.

"The Ash Tree," he said. "Well now, young Ridder. There is definitely more to you than first appears. Tell me. Do you know how to play *Hnefa-Tafl*?"

"If it is like King's Soldiers, I do."

"Close enough, I'll warrant. Very well, young Ridder— What is your name, anyway?"

"Mikkel."

"Mikkel. That means 'Red Fox' in our language. So, young

Ridder Red Fox, after dinner we will have our first game. And then, if I'm in a good mood, I'll send word to the NordornKing that his son still lives. For now."

He handed Mikkel his amulet, then threw his head back and laughed loudly at his own wit.

"You told me you were the son of a king, but not a son of the NordornKing," Gunnora said accusingly. "Your parents, they are the ones who slew the great Ice Dragon? The Mother?"

"Yes, Lady."

"And they received certain items in a gem-heavy box, to help them on their mission?"

"Yes, Lady. The Dragon Box has a place of honor in my father's Hall."

"I see. Get back to your table now."

Mikkel escaped gratefully to his table where his companions nearly swamped him with questions.

"Not now," he told them. "Later, when we have all gone to bed. Then we will talk."

He wanted to think about the implications of what Holger had said and the questions Gunnora had all but skewered him with. Also, he wanted to remember, as nearly as possible, what Askepott had told him about the Great Ash Tree. Perhaps this amulet he had borrowed from Mother's jewel box was going to bring him luck after all.

Ten

Again the Great Hall of Cyornas Castle blazed with light, the crystal drops—more like icicles—and twinkling snowflakes reminding knowing onlookers that this was, indeed, the Castle of Fire and Ice.

Dinner was over, the tables cleared, but the music and other entertainment not yet begun. Three young men stood before the dais occupied by Gaurin NordornKing, Ashen NordornQueen, and the heir, Bjaudin NordornPrince. One could be counted little more than a boy, but the other two, though young, were grown men. Of the three, the boy looked the most at ease; the other two, though they tried to hide it, seemed a little stunned at this turn of events.

Three women stood nearby, waiting, as did the crowd of courtiers who had come to witness the ceremonies before the last feast of the celebration of Earl Royance and Countess Mjaurita's wedding. Esander the Good, priest of the Fane of the Castle of Fire and Ice, entered the Hall and took his place before the three young men.

"Come you now to be betrothed," Esander said. "So say you all?"

"So say I, Prince Karl of Writham."

"So say I, Duke Bernhard of Yuland."

"So say I, Mårten of Mithlond."

"And where are the beloveds? Who comes to be betrothed to Prince Karl of Writham?"

One of Ashen's ladies, Kaisa, who had replaced Lady Elibit when Duke Einaar claimed her in marriage, moved forward. "I stand proxy for Princess Gizela of Rendel," she said.

"And who will be betrothed to Duke Bernhard of Yuland?"

Another of Ashen's ladies, Frida, came forward. "I stand proxy for Amilia of the Sea-Rovers."

"And who will be betrothed to Mårten of Mithlond?"

Elin stepped forward, barely hiding a scowl, and took her place beside Mårten. "I, Elin-Alditha NordornPrincess."

Esander smiled on the six standing before him. "Then, I—"

"Wait, good Esander!"

All heads turned as Bjaudin NordornPrince left the dais and strode down the length of the Great Hall, to return hand-clasped with Lady Laherne. "We come also to be betrothed," he said as he reached the place where the others were standing.

"And you, my dear?" asked Esander of Laherne. "Is this your wish also?"

"It is." She looked at Bjaudin, her face glowing, her eyes full of love. "I, Laherne of Rendel, do wish with all my heart to be betrothed this day to Bjaudin NordornPrince."

"Our great friends' marriage, Earl Royance and Countess Mjaurita of Grattenbor and of Åskar, has prompted an outpouring of affection unlooked for but happily found," Esander said placidly. "I charge you—all of you—to seek patiently for deeper affection between you, so that when you wed you will find true happiness and contentment." He held out his hands, blessing all eight young people lined up before him.

"Did you know anything of this?" Gaurin whispered to Ashen.

"No, nothing." She glanced at Rannore, who seemed as taken aback as any. "Though I cannot think of a better match for our son."

He smiled at her with the trace of mischief in his eyes that always made her heart skip. "Then I will say nothing in opposition."

Lady Pernille, Chief Musician at Cyornas Castle since old Master Oskar's permanent retirement, signaled the players who struck up "The Song." At once, four of Gaurin's gentlemen claimed their counterparts of Ashen's ladies as partners; Frida and Kaisa, of course, would dance with Prince Karl and Duke Bernhard. Elin's ladies Hanna and Kandice took Frida's and Kaisa's places with Gaurin's other two gentlemen so none were awkwardly left without partners. With an aplomb far beyond his years, Mårten took Elin's hand and led her to her place in the ring of dancers.

"Come, my Ashen," Gaurin said, as he arose from his chair. "It is a good day in many ways. I have laid aside my staff, at least for this evening."

With a heart made light and glad Ashen took his proffered hand. Let the morrow bring snow and aching cold; this day was a happy one with but a single dark cloud on the horizon. If only Mikkel were here. . . .

To make up for her gloomy thought, she smiled at Tjórvi, now her foster son, who had been bidden—all but ordered—and had reluctantly come to the Hall for the celebration. Uncertainly, Tjórvi returned the smile. But he did not join the dancing.

When the tedious evening was nearing completion, Elin found a moment to speak with Granddam Ysa at a small table at the far end of the room where they could be reasonably sure of not being overheard.

"I thought you said that we would be creating . . . unrest in the NordornLand," she said a trifle petulantly, "not celebrations."

Ysa stared at her granddaughter. "And do you expect duels to break out in the Great Hall? Do you think Aslaugors are going to draw weapons against Lowlanders? Or Fridians? Shall the scholars of Galinth turn their quill pens into daggers?"

"I—I don't know what I expected."

"These things take time. While you have been enjoying your-self and flirting shamelessly with those two young men, poor be-fuddled souls, I have been working quietly, behind the scenes. And not so incidentally, you've done a fairly good job of creating unrest yourself. Look at Duke Bernhard and Prince Karl."

Truthfully, the two barely exchanged glances and when they did those looks were loaded with icy daggers. "But they aren't do-ing anything about it."

Ysa sighed. "Child, child, you must learn patience and the art of diplomacy."

"This is diplomacy?"

"It can work both ways—creating peace or destroying it." Ysa straightened in her chair, her silk skirts rustling. "You must come back with me to Iselin. I see that I still have much to teach you. Also, we can work more openly there, without the great need for secrecy."

Elin brightened. "And I can bring that bracelet of Mother's I told you about!"

"What bracelet?"

"Oh—I must have forgotten. There's a bracelet with nine little teeth strung on a thin chain. I got the oddest feelings when I touched them. Maybe you can help unlock the riddle. You and I together," she amended.

"That sounds interesting." Ysa smiled. "Yes, definitely, you must bring the bracelet when you come. Now," she continued, "here is what you should do. Tell your mother and father that it is most un-seemly for you and your betrothed to live in such close proximity; therefore, you should live apart for a while. Royance will be too busy with his new bride to pay much attention to you, and there is not another place suitable unless you went to live with your sister in Rendel."

"Oh, please, not that," Elin said, making a face. "Fortunately, Mother won't want me to go that far distant, with Mikkel still missing."

"Just so. Therefore, if you're to stay in the NordornLand, it must be Iselin. It's the only place fit to house Nordorn royalty, short of Cyornas Castle. I'll speak to Ashen and Gaurin in the morning."

"Thank you, Granddam," Elin said demurely. "Now I feel able to stay the evening without pleading a headache and taking to my room."

"Haven't I told you that everything will work out all right?" Ysa said. "There, there, you're young, my darling, and you lack experience, that's all. Never you fear. We have time on our side. And with time, all the *problems*"—she put a special emphasis on the word, which Elin understood immediately—"will work themselves out and you will achieve the station in life that was destined for you in the Loom of Time."

Indeed, Ysa thought, *I have been busy. There is unrest brewing on the eastern borders and also with isolated tribes of Fridians and Aslaugors to the north.*

She had promised wealth, dropping broad hints that Their Maimed Majesties had hoarded the vast trove of fire-stones from the Mother Ice Dragon's lair, and were keeping them for themselves. She had dared even spread tendrils of doubt into the border area where Grattenbor merged into Åskar, Earl Royance's domain, and to Yuland, along the southwestern border of Rendel, and the wealthy island Kingdom of Writham to the west.

Even if these last two seeds failed to bear fruit, the others looked ripe to break into a civil war sooner or later unless stronger, cooler heads prevailed.

The day following the feast, *Ice Princess* sailed back into Cyornas Fjord. The NordornKing and NordornQueen immediately called a meeting of the Council, so that Rohan and Tordenskjold could report to all the results of their ransom voyage. Each noble had his own chair now, carved and painted with his device and crest. The order of precedence had been altered; Ashen was now seated beside

Gaurin instead of at the other end of the table. That position was occupied by Duke Einaar, with Bjaudin NordornPrince beside him. One chair was empty—Gangerolf, late as usual—so Rohan took that one. The Council meeting would surely have ended before Baron Gangerolf the Tardy showed up.

"We retrieved nine of Rohan's men," Tordenskjold told the nobles seated around the table. "Eight Rovers, and their captain, Fritji. A hundred gold pennies in all; Fritji cost us double. I'll wager he won't be going out to sea alone again for a while, not until he gets more experience under his belt."

Gaurin glanced at Ashen. She was pale, her hands tightly gripping the arms of her chair. "And what of our son?"

"The captain of the Wykenig ship, Holger den Forferdelig, played a little game with us," Rohan said. "First he claimed not to know of whom I spoke. Then he said he thought he remembered him, but he might have let the boy drown."

Ashen gasped.

"No, Ashen NordornQueen, remember, he was enjoying playing with us. Finally he did pretend to remember Mikkel. I think he will send a message asking for ransom."

"Ransom!" Tordenskjold snorted aloud. "We offered him the *Ice Princess* for the boy! What more ransom could he want?"

"Oh, I expect he would be able to think of something."

"Whatever it is, we will pay it," Gaurin said. He reached out and took Ashen's hand. "And I believe also that he will send a message to us concerning our son's welfare."

"He seemed taken with the notion," Tordenskjold said. "Incidentally, the little warkat is with him. I think Holger thought the warkat's presence and loyalty to Mikkel was special enough to save his life, whereas he left Tjórvi to live or die as best he may."

"How does my son?" Rohan asked.

"He fares well. He has been keeping much to himself, and not appearing in the Hall but eating his meals with the servants unless ordered otherwise."

"Well, I'll instruct him otherwise, as it seems he will be staying here an indefinite period of time," Rohan said.

"You are relieved of your vow, if vow it was, to leave Tjórvi as surety for the return of Prince Mikkel," Gaurin said.

"I thank you, but will abide by my promise."

"What say my nobles?" Gaurin looked from man to man seated around the table. "What say you to this news?"

Svarteper, NordornLand's Lord High Marshal, spoke first as was his right. "We should assemble an army and take Prince Mikkel back by force of arms."

"I concur," Baron Arngrim said.

Most of the other nobles—Baldrian, Håkon, even Einaar and Bjaudin nodded their agreement. Their eyes were alight with the thought of battle and forceful retrieval of their young Prince.

"Holger den Forferdelig is known as 'the Terrible' for good reason. He can laugh one minute and burn a village or sink a ship the next. He said that any such move would result in Mikkel's death at once, and I believe him," Tordenskjold informed them.

The war spirit evaporated like spring mist. No one else seemed to have a suggestion. Then Count Mjødulf spoke. As was his habit, he put his hands on the table and laced his long, slender fingers in front of him so that they were reflected in the high polish of the table top. "I believe, from what Chieftain Rohan and Admiral-General Tordenskjold have reported to us, that this Holger the Terrible might be, in his own way, a man of honor. I have heard it said that such exist among the Wykenigs. Let us then go on the assumption that this is the case. Let us await a message from him concerning Mikkel and after a reasonable time—say, a month—if we have not heard from him, then let us meet again and make other plans."

"Alas, I fear that is our only recourse," Gaurin said somberly. He turned to Ashen and kissed the hand he still held. "Our midwinter celebrations will be dimmed, I fear, even with the presence of young Tjórvi to brighten our days."

At that moment, Gangerolf made one of his typical noisy entrances into the Council Chamber, sending the door crashing into the wall. "I see you started without me, as usual," he said. "Well, then, what's happened?"

Snow had begun falling and the many visitors to the Castle of Fire and Ice knew that they must be on their way or risk a much longer stay than they had anticipated. Royance and Mjaurita would be leaving to travel to their elegant manor in Åskar, leaving the *Silver Burhawk* at winter anchor in the pens of Cyornas Fjord until they could take a pleasure cruise. Those with longer journeys to make dared not linger.

"This winter looks to be an early one, and a hard one as well," Gaurin commented to Ashen. "Prince Karl is making ready his vessel even now; he will have difficult sailing if a storm catches him on the way. Our Rendelian kindred probably have the easiest return of any. Bernhard of Yuland will be traveling with them as far as Rendelsham, but then he has an overland journey south and east. He may find his coach mired in snowy mud even in those milder climes."

"Elin wants to go to Iselin with Ysa," Ashen said. "Those two have taken quite a liking to one another."

"And Ysa? Is she agreeable?"

"Yes. In fact, she claims it would be highly improper for Elin to continue to live so closely to her betrothed."

Gaurin raised one eyebrow. "Well, she does still fancy herself the Mistress of Court Protocol. And you, are you agreeable?"

"Gaurin, would you think it horrible of me to say that having Elin in the care of another for a while would suit me well? She is entering into a very difficult time of her life. I know how I felt, just becoming a woman. I don't think she would be willing to accept instruction from either Zazar or me. If she will do so from Ysa, then I say let her have her visit." She smiled, a trifle shakily. "She can always come home again when she and Ysa quarrel."

Gaurin laughed out loud, the first time in a long time; then he sobered. "Whatever will bring you ease, my Ashen. I know you grieve daily for Mikkel. But look you, with the onset of winter, it has become impossible for us to parley with his captors and ransom him. It would be unsafe. He is as secure as we can reasonably expect him to be."

Only partially reassured, Ashen determined to consult with Zazar again. The Wysen-wyf had peered into matters unknown before; she would repeat the ritual even if Ashen had to order it done. Zazar, unfortunately, was lying abed with a cold and so any such petition would have to wait.

The NordornQueen forced herself to remain calm on the surface. Her nerves were stretched to their breaking point, however, and she felt that the slightest touch would shatter her entirely. If that happened, she would begin weeping and never stop.

Before Zazar had recovered, she and Gaurin received the looked-for message, delivered by the least prepossessing of messengers. An Aslaugor from the far north arrived in Cyornasberg, obviously having traveled through deep snow. He bore a packet wrapped in the oiled skin of some cold-weather animal, and asked for directions to the Castle of Fire and Ice. A townsman pointed him toward the barbican gatehouse.

"Here," the man said, thrusting the packet into the hands of one of the guards. "Got it from a Fridian passing through my village. Said this here is for the great ones. You take it and save me the trouble."

Then he tightened the wolvine-rimmed hood of his tunic over his head, turned, and disappeared back the way he had come, not stopping long enough to receive a reward.

At the news, Zazar pulled herself out of bed and, heavily wrapped and muffled and accompanied by Weyse, joined Ashen, Gaurin, Einaar, and Bjaudin in the sitting room of the private quarters Ashen and Gaurin shared. She brought with her a small bottle of her own special cough remedy and when she opened it to

Andre Norton & Sasha Miller

take a sip, a strong smell of *brandewijn* mixed with some of her medicines filled the room.

The five people drew up chairs around a table and watched while Gaurin opened the packet.

Inside the many layers of protective wrapping was a folded letter addressed simply to "King," sealed with a drop of wax bearing the likeness of a creature out of legend.

"That's Draig the Sea-terror," Zazar commented. She coughed and took another sip of her elixir. "Wouldn't be surprised if this Holger took it for his device. What's that?"

"That" was another letter, wrapped in rough snow-thistle fabric that had been treated with wax to make it waterproof. The covering bore a single word in characters Ashen recognized as having seen before: ᛗᛁᛂᛁᛊ·

"That's mine," Zazar said, taking the letter. "It's got my name on it."

Gaurin handed it to her and opened his letter. The writing was childlike, as if the writer were not used to using a pen. The message was brief:

> He's alive, winter is here, will send another update when I feel like it. H.

"Well, that's short and to the point," Einaar commented. "This Holger is not a man of many written words."

"I am glad to know that my brother lives," Bjaudin said. "I, too, feel that this Holger is merely playing with us. We are currently at his mercy. Yet I do not think Mikkel is in any great danger presently—not nearly as much as when he was on the *GorGull* when it was being attacked."

"I don't know whether to laugh or cry," Ashen said.

"And what is in your letter, Madame Zazar?" Gaurin asked.

For answer, she opened the parcel and spread it out on the table so all could look at, if not read, it. Another package, much smaller and smelling of herbs, tumbled out and Zazar put it aside.

The Knight of the Red Beard

ᚠ ᛘᛘ'ᛏᛘᛘᛈ ᛈᚱᛏᛁᛏ' ᛈ ᛘᛘ''ᛏᛘᛘᛈ ᛁᚦᛏ ᛈᛈᛘ ᛁ' ᚾᛁᛏᛏᚱ ᛉᛘ ᛈᛁᛈᚱ
ᛁ ᛘᛏᛈᛈ ᛘᛏᚱᛈ ᚦᛁᛉ ᚦᛈ ᚱᛏ ᛈᚾᛁ ᛏᚦᛁᛁ ' ᛈᛈᛈᛏ ᛈᛈᚱ ᚦᛁᛉ ᚦᛈᛈᛏ ᛈᛈ ᛈᛏᚱᛏ
ᛈᛈᚱ ᚦᛁ' 'ᛈᛈᛏᛁᛘ ᛘᚦᛏᛈ ᚦᛏᚷ ᛈᛈᛈᛏᚱ 'ᛏᛈᛏ' ᛘᛁᚱᛏ ᛏᛈ ᛘᛈᚾ ᛁ ᛘᛁᛁᚾ ᛒᚾᛁ
ᛏᛈᛈᛏᚦᛏᚱ ᛈᛈᛏᛏ ᛁᛈ ᛁᛏ ᛁ ᛈᛁᛈᛏ ᛘᛈᚾ ᛈ ᛈᛁᛈᛏ ᛘᛈᚾ ᛈᛉᛈᛘ ᛘᚦᛏᛏ ᛏᛈ ᛏᛈ
ᛘᛁᛏᚦ ᛁᛏ 'ᛏᛏᛈᛈ ᛈᚱ ᛈ'ᚦᛒᛈᛏᛏ

"Can you read it?" Ashen asked.

"With a little time, yes. I'm out of practice, you know." Zazar gathered up the letter, the packet—much like the bundles and packets of herbs she had prepared for so many years—and left the room with Weyse to return to her lofty apartment, trailing the aroma of medicine-laced *brandewijn*.

Ashen wanted to go with her, but knew that she would only get the rough side of Zazar's tongue for her presumption. When the old Wysen-wyf had deciphered her letter—then and only then would she send for the NordornQueen. If at all.

Eleven

Life in the Upplands village settled into a routine for Mikkel. He worked hard through the day, served meals, fell into his bed of straw gratefully and slept soundly until morning. There was always wood to be brought in or water to be drawn from the well, providing he could crack the film of ice that covered it. There were bowstrings and fishing lines to be waxed and made ready for the hunters and fishers, and their bounty cleaned and made ready for table or for the special cooking house, the *soðhús* where women boiled the meat in a large kettle and salted it down for winter storage.

He had never given any thought to the incredible amount of work involved in keeping a large household running. Undoubtedly, this much or even more went on at Cyornas Castle, but he had been oblivious. When he wanted fresh clothing, it was available. When he was hungry, food was provided.

Talkin had become a favorite among most of the men. They laughed hugely when Talkin showed up to help dispose of any spare bits when they were dressing the meat after a hunt. As for the warkat's presence among the dogs in Holger's Long House, Talkin seemed to pick his time and his opponent before establishing his authority. One or two skirmishes and the house dogs tried hard to ignore him. The house cats, on the other hand, adored him and loved to cuddle up with him in a heap wherever he decided to take one of his frequent naps.

Though the people customarily had two meals a day—the *dagmál* or "day-meal" about two hours after sun-up, and the *náttmál* in the evenings—the younkers who helped in the kitchen could almost always count on being able to filch a handful of cold meat or raw vegetables to ease a growing child's appetite. Mikkel quickly learned that volunteering to chop vegetables was a good way to get an extra serving of food under the guise of offering to help. Askepott generally turned a tolerant eye on such goings-on unless the younker exhibited too much greed, whereupon he or she was summarily turned out of the kitchen to be put to such household tasks as Gunnora the Golden might deem necessary. There was always spinning and weaving to be done, to manufacture the cloth necessary for such a sizable village. From time to time, people went out into the forest area to search for a special plant that lay half-hidden under the snow, with only the spiked, deep rose-colored flower visible.

This plant had a very thick stalk that, when opened, yielded a spray of light, strong fibers that could be dried, spun, and mixed with wool. With a slight shock of recognition, Mikkel realized he was seeing snow-thistles for the first time.

The women and the girls also worked at milking the snow-cows and turning the results into butter, buttermilk, whey, the fresh soft cheese known as *skyr*, curds, and regular firm cheese. Here the boys helped by preparing seawater in shallow vessels so it could evaporate, leaving the salt necessary to help preserve the new cheeses. Only a lucky few were allowed to sample any of this food, and for that reason the girls preferred to work in the kitchen. Often they were set to grinding grain, a task that Petra liked. The hand mill in

Askepott's kitchen was heavy and the work hard; Petra, however, had a knack of making the large grindstone almost float against the base stone and as she worked, she would sing her song about the sea-green glass. She could grind enough grain for the day's bread well before noon, an astonishing feat for such a slight girl.

During the warm months there was the struggle to grow enough grain for the mill and during the cold months there was the problem of how to portion it out so that it would last and yet not let the steading go hungry. Some of the grain was used to make ale, but most was used for bread and other dishes. Grain porridge was a staple at the day-meal, usually cooked in water and eaten plain, but prepared with milk and butter when there was a surplus. Special buildings housed the grain, and there the house cats earned their keep, ruthlessly tracking rodents and other vermin and destroying them.

In Holger's village, one farmer, nicknamed *Smjör-Hringr* or "Butter-Ring" because of his great fondness for bread and butter, was experimenting with sheltered fields, constructing awninglike coverings over the all-important plants. This technique looked to be able to lengthen the growing time, but when full winter was upon them, the protected fields lay fallow like any other.

The Wykenigs, Mikkel Red Fox learned, were very clean people. In addition to the sweat bath there were bathhouses for men and for women, also constructed well outside the stockade walls. These, he learned, had hot water piped in from natural hot springs in the area. No matter that it smelled of brimstone; these baths were very popular with everyone in the steading.

Some of this water was also piped into a wash house where clothing could be scrubbed. Fur or leather garments were cleaned elsewhere by other means.

Mikkel had formed an impression while on shipboard that the Wykenigs were filthy by nature. Now, he realized, they were as cleanly in their habits as Nordorners. Furthermore, he developed a healthy respect for those servants back home, who had been charged with the task of cleaning the clothing he so carelessly soiled. There were no natural hot springs in Cyornasberg or Cyornas Castle.

In the evenings, when most of the work had been done, the men of the steading relaxed in the Long House. Sometimes one would amuse the others with song or storytelling; often the men engaged in wrestling matches or sparring with wooden weapons. With luck, these matches would serve to ward off or at least delay a full-out *hólmgang* or "duel of honor," fought to the death on a small islet out in the sound. Once, at Holger's urging, Gunnora danced, but the performance was not repeated.

The most favored pastimes were games of *Hnefa-Tafl*. Many men brought their own boards to the Long House but, perhaps deliberately, they were of inferior quality to the ones hanging behind Holger's chair.

The first evening Holger invited Mikkel to play, to his pleasure the boy caught on quickly enough that the Ridder actually had to work for his victory. Thereafter, a game an evening became almost a ritual with them.

"You are better than any boy your age has a right to be, Ridder Red Fox," Holger said, grinning. "By the time I get through teaching you, you'll win money from fools who think they can get the better of you."

"Perhaps," Mikkel said before he thought, "I could win enough to pay my ransom."

He was immediately frightened that he had insulted or annoyed the Ridder Chieftain. Instead, Holger threw his head back and bellowed with laughter.

"And you're brave and daring, too! Not many would have had the stones to address me as you did! More and more I am glad I decided to save your life and bring you here, young Red Fox. Here," he said, taking down an eleven-by-eleven board from his wall. It had seen much play. "Take this as a gift from me to a young but worthy opponent."

From a corner of the room, Mikkel observed Askepott watching them. She might have nodded; in the dim light, he could not be sure.

Mikkel had been in the Wykenig village a moon's turning before Holger informed him that he had decided to write to the Nor-dornLand monarchs and inform them that their son yet lived.

"I am very considerate that way," he said. "Later, I may write to them again."

"Thank you, Ridder Holger," Mikkel said.

"Thank me indeed. It was against Gunnora's wishes. If she had her way, you'd be bones on the bottom of the sound, or I miss my guess. She has taken a dislike to you."

"I am sorry for that," Mikkel said. "I will be careful as much as possible not to annoy her."

"She doesn't like your red hair or your ice-blue eyes. None of which you can help."

"No, sir. But I will try to stay out of her way anyhow."

"Oh, she is just a woman. Do not pay a lot of attention to her or any woman—except for Askepott. She rules the house, even rules Gunnora." Holger laughed, pleased at his own wit. "Askepott will send the letter. She knows of such things."

Mikkel determined to ask Askepott, as soon as he could find a moment to do so without being overheard, how she was going to do this thing. Maybe he could even add a line to Holger's letter. It would make him feel better, and would certainly lighten Mother's and Father's hearts.

But he was doomed to be disappointed. Askepott refused any such addition.

"Do you not think Holger would know if I allowed you to write directly to your parents? Do you not think that if he wanted you to write to them he would have suggested it himself? No, Ridder Red Fox, not this time. Nor the next, I warrant."

"Yes, Askepott," Mikkel said, chastened. "But at least you can tell me how you propose to send the letter. By ship?"

"Where are your eyes, boy? Don't you realize that all three of Holger's ships are at winter rest and propped up on blocks? Men have been at work for days, scraping the hulls and getting them ready for new pitch to be applied."

Mikkel had, indeed, seen the work going on down at the shore. Somehow, he hoped that a vessel could be taken out of its framework and put out to sea once more.

"You are still thinking like a Nordorner prince, Mikkel," Askepott continued. "You are important, yes, but not important enough for Holger to risk a ship this time of year. But I will send off his note with a man on an ice-sleigh and let you watch him leave. You'll like that."

It seemed to Mikkel that the packet was a bit bulkier than it needed to be if all it contained was Holger's letter. But this thought was quickly lost in his fascination with the ice-sleigh.

Indulgently, Rødiger, the man chosen for the errand, put the ice-sleigh through some maneuverings for Mikkel.

"See here, young Red Fox?" he said. "You have to kick it to make it go. Would you like to try it?"

"Oh, yes, please!" He hopped on and Rødiger positioned the boy between his knees.

"Kick it *here* and then hold on."

Mikkel did as Rødiger directed and the vehicle fairly leaped into motion. Rødiger took the steering rod and skillfully guided it through and around the village, returning much too soon to the starting place.

"Oh, please, may we do that again?"

"Perhaps when I return, Red Fox. But now you must get down so I can be on my way."

Reluctantly, Mikkel dismounted from the sleigh. Rødiger tucked the precious packet containing Holger's letter well wrapped in waterproof trappings into his tunic. Then, with a spurt of speed that sent snow flying in his wake, he was off.

At last Zazar sent word to Ashen. The Wysen-wyf's cold had improved greatly, though the smell of the *brandewijn* medicine still lingered. The air in Zazar's apartment was warm enough, possibly because the fire in the hearth blazed more brightly than usual, but the floor was still cold. There were cracks in the plank flooring that allowed chill air to seep through.

"I will send you some wolf hides to use as rugs," Ashen told Zazar. "You need to keep your feet warm. While you are recovering from your cold," she added hastily.

"I don't need your coddling," Zazar retorted, her tone surly, but she did not refuse the offer. "Come on, come on, sit down. Put your delicate feet up on a stool and take a look at what I received from Holger den Forferdelig's house."

She spread out the original letter, and placed beside it another piece of paper, smudged with many erasures and words crossed out and rewritten. "As you can see—well, maybe you can't—some of the letters are upside-down and the spelling is atrocious. She is as unused to the act of writing as Holger the Terrible is. But here it is."

Ashen pulled a candle close and began to read.

> a wysenwyf gretes a wysenwyf the boy is under my kare i well werk him hard but that s good for him have no fere for his safety when nex holger sends wird to you i will put another note in it i give you a gift you know what to do with it stenvor ashpott

"Who is this person?" Ashen asked. "Do you know her?"

"I know of her, and she knows of me. Wysen-wyves are a diminishing breed. There aren't many of us."

Ashen's mind seemed to be working very slowly. "Then this Stenvor is a Wysen-wyf."

"It's Steinvor, and she's known as Askepott, not Ashpott. Mikkel could not have been more fortunate, to have wound up where he is after such a brainless escapade. I doubt Holger would dare touch the boy, even if he decided to do him harm."

"What did this Askepott mean, that she sent you a gift?"

Zazar smiled, just a little. "Wysen-wyf business. If anything comes of it, I will let you know. You look terrible. Much too pale. You might as well have been brushed by a spirit from the next world."

"In a way, I have. Some part of me was convinced that Mikkel was dead. To learn that he is alive, and as safe as he is—well, it is as if I had just seen a ghost."

"Here." Zazar took down a flask from a shelf, unstoppered it, and poured a generous amount into a smaller flask. "Take this to your apartment, drink it, and lie down. It's neat *brandewijn*. I made it myself. No cough remedy in it. It's pure and wholesome, and it'll be good for you. You'll sleep for the rest of the day and through the night. You need it. Now, go."

Late that evening, Zazar made her preparations. She thought there might be enough herbs in the packet Steinvor Askepott had smuggled to her for more than one "meeting" if she were frugal with their use.

She had not performed such a rite in years—not, she thought, searching her memory, since she had barged in on some of Ysa's spell-making—meddling was more like it—and introduced her to Ashen. Also, if truth were told, she did it to show Ysa that she was not the only one who could call upon Power.

That had been years earlier when she had taken Ashen to the ruins of the scholars' city, Galinth, and left her there to be found and eventually taken to Rendelsham and her rightful inheritance. No harm in showing Ysa that Ashen was more than a mere Bog-waif, abandoned by a woman ashamed to death of what she bore. That Ashen had sought to contact Zazar by ingesting one of Zazar's potions only confirmed the Power the then-girl possessed; Zazar merely seized the opportunity offered. It had been a gratifying exercise.

Back then Zazar had sought a cave, primarily for the secrecy it offered. None to be had around here, but the tower room might do. Also, there had been a pillar of fire. Now there would have to be another, but not of her devising.

"Well, Weyse, what do you think?" she asked the fat little unearthly creature who had become her constant companion. No longer could she call on Bog-creatures to bring her information; even if the Bog had still existed, another had that Power now. Only Weyse remained. "Are you willing to risk the fire to help Ashen and Mikkel?"

For answer, Weyse jumped down from the chair where she had been sleeping, waddled over to where Zazar stood on the bare wooden floor, and climbed her dress until she could wrap her paws around Zazar's neck.

"Good," the Wysen-wyf said.

If ever she was going to meet Steinvor Askepott, now was the moment. She took about half of the mixture the other Wysen-wyf had sent her and sprinkled it in a circle around the two of them. Taking a deep breath, she summoned up an old Power and pointed at the magical circle, invoking the Ritual of Travel. Nothing happened. Reluctantly, she poured out the remainder of the mixture, tried again, and this time it burst into flames. In less than a heartbeat the fire became a pillar surrounding them. It began to spiral—a very nice touch, Zazar thought—and then, unexpectedly, the motion came to a halt.

The outlines of the tower room faded until there was only cold, blank emptiness outside the frozen spiral of flame. Weyse, whimpering a little, clung even harder to her neck, gazing about in fear.

Have I erred? Zazar thought. *Is this a trap, to some purpose unknown to me? Am I now never to guide Ashen through the rest of her stay on this earth, and give her what help I can to ease her hurts?*

She could not get out. She could only stand, frozen as the motionless twisted flames, awaiting her fate.

Twelve

*O*h, *I am so glad* to be going to live with you for a while, Granddam," Princess Elin exclaimed.

Outside the Duchess Ysa's coach, snow was falling, thick and white and deceptively gentle, muffling most sounds and making the country through which they traveled a wondrous place. Inside, the Duchess and Princess Elin were warmly wrapped in cloaks and fur lap-robes. Little Alfonse had his own bed on the floor between the two ladies, though he preferred to be on Ysa's lap, as well wrapped as she.

Everywhere, the evergreens bore their snowy mantles lightly, and only seldom did one see the tracks of conies or snow-foxes or fallowbeeste. It seemed that all who lived out in the open had now gone to ground, where they could keep warm and await the coming of spring.

"We are lucky that we don't have a howling gale to contend with," Ysa replied. She pulled the fur lap-robe higher, as if she would disappear under it entirely.

"That would be exciting," Elin said.

"You only think so because you have never seen one except

from the safety of Cyornas Castle. If you are out in it, it is not exciting at all."

"Will they be expecting us at Iselin?"

"Indeed. I had Lackel send Ruffen, one of his Troopers, ahead so we will receive a warm welcome and something to take the chill off. My ladies especially will welcome this."

If Ysa's ladies had hoped to return to Iselin in the relative comfort of the carriage, they were disappointed. They had to ride between the carriage and the Troopers, because of Elin's presence, as they had traveled on the journey to Cyornasberg. Again, Elin's ladies rode with them. Bringing up the rear were two wagons carrying an additional load of luggage—all in all, an unwieldy caravan.

Elin had barely given any of the ladies a thought.

"Why do you care, Granddam?" she asked Ysa. "They are just servants, after all. They should be glad of their station in life to minister to royalty and not be assigned to kitchen scullery duty, or perhaps worse."

"Child!" Ysa exclaimed. "Have you no heart at all? No compassion? Have you never wondered why, for example, I have but three ladies and your mother has six?"

"Yes, and I have only two. It isn't fair—"

"Listen and learn, young lady. Your mother is a queen. When I was a queen, I had even more ladies than she, though Ingrid, Gertrude, and Grisella were always my favorites. They stayed with me when I left Rendelsham Castle for the Yewkeep, a vastly less comfortable residence. They go with me wherever else I may journey. They are loyal to me, for they know I am loyal to them. You have but two ladies for that is all your present station entitles you to. Look to their comfort and safety, or you won't have them for long."

Chastened and taken aback by her grandmother's stern tone, Elin bowed her head. "Yes, Granddam. I heed your words."

"See to it that you do," Ysa said, slightly mollified. "Oh, look, we're nearly home!"

And the ladies can thaw out, Elin thought. *What a fuss over mere servants*. And yet, Granddam Ysa's three ladies had grown old in her service, so perhaps it would be wise to model her behavior on Ysa's. In that respect, at least. As for other matters— Well, that remained to be seen.

The entourage turned onto the great wooded road to Iselin Manor. The beautiful circular drive had been made even more so by the thick, soft snow. The blanket of white was scarcely marred by footprints; most of the inhabitants of the houses and other buildings that flanked the manor house would be at the main building, waiting to welcome their Duchess home again.

Elin watched carefully what Granddam Ysa said and did, once they were all dismounted and had entered into Iselin Manor. Lackel took the House Troops off in another direction to the barracks where they lived.

Servants and courtiers waited inside in two rows. The Duchess greeted them all in turn. Three men—Elin vaguely remembered them as the barons who formed Ysa's ridiculously small Council— bowed low to her and to Elin. They wore the deep blue Court color Ysa prescribed, even at the Castle of Fire and Ice, and in Elin's eyes looked as if they would be more at ease in the garb of a farmer. She allowed one of them to kiss her hand.

"Let my granddaughter and me recover from our journey and we will all be together at meat tonight, my good lord Baron Gustav," she told him. "We are tired. I am not as young as I used to be. But be assured that I treasure your love and loyalty to me."

"Your Grace," said Gustav. They bowed themselves out of the entry hall.

"Go and warm yourselves," Ysa said to her three ladies. "Then you may unpack my belongings and set all to rights in my apartment. My granddaughter will occupy the rooms she had when she visited me before; I think I will make them hers permanently."

"Thank you, Granddam," Elin said. Her tone was soft and even kindly. "And you, Hanna and Kandice, go with the other ladies and warm yourselves likewise before you make my rooms neat and tidy. I'm sure my granddam's ladies will show you the way if you have forgotten. This journey back to Iselin must have been hard on you all." She turned to Ysa with a sweet and innocent smile that summoned up a fleeting dimple. "If we are to continue traveling back and forth from here to Cyornas Castle, I might have to petition my father for another coach so that all may ride in comfort!"

The ladies laughed, a bit uncertainly but gratefully. It was interesting, watching their reactions.

They were not used to this side of the NordornPrincess, Elin thought. Perhaps I should cultivate it more.

"That is a good suggestion, Elin," Ysa said. "But surely by the time we return, the weather will have moderated. For now, we will settle in and enjoy each other's company. Now, join me by the fire in my Great Room while our ladies make all ready for us."

The Duchess's Hall was nowhere near the size of the Great Room at the Castle of Fire and Ice. This made it easier to heat, though, and it was quite comfortable with the fire roaring in the fireplace. As was the custom in all residences of this type, chairs and a table had been set up close enough to the fire for comfort, but not so close as to risk danger from flying sparks. A screen closed in the area to make all cozy; it would be removed in the event of a formal dinner or other celebration and trestle tables set up. Now, Harald, Ysa's Seneschal, bowed Ysa and Elin into this warm area where they would wait until their rooms had been prepared. Alfonse trotted at Ysa's heels.

"I have hot snowberry juice to be mixed with wine, Madame," Harald told the Duchess, "and Ania has instructed the cook to make hot meat pies as well, to be ready for you when you should arrive."

"Excellent," Ysa replied. "I am glad I took your advice and named her Iselin's Chatelaine."

Maids hovered, ready to take their velvet cloaks away and hang them up so the snow could be brushed from them. There was a surprising amount of it, considering that Elin and Ysa had merely walked from the carriage to the door.

"Our poor ladies would likely drown if the snow they gathered happened to melt too quickly," Ysa said, and Elin nodded agreement.

She took a seat and motioned Elin to the chair opposite. "This is almost the best part of returning home. The staff is always glad to see me."

"I feel very much at home here, Granddam," Elin said.

They applied themselves to the savory meat pies. Alfonse got an entire pie to himself. He snuffled over it greedily and then curled up in his little basket with a happy sigh. The ladies ate with much more decorum but with every bit as much appreciation. Ysa kept an excellent chef. There was very little to return to the kitchen.

"Now," the Duchess said as she settled herself where she could put her feet up on a cushion and warm them at the fire, "while we wait, let us take a look at that bracelet you told me about. I assume you had the wit to put it into your reticule and not trust it to the luggage."

"Yes, Granddam," Elin replied with another of her dimpled smiles. "Here it is." She opened the little handbag that matched her velvet traveling cloak and took out a small parcel wrapped in a kerchief. She handed it to Ysa, being careful not to touch the contents.

"Well," Ysa said as she unwrapped the kerchief. "Interesting. Very interesting." Tentatively she put a fingertip to one of the teeth strung on the thin chain. "You said you have touched this. Am I correct?"

"Yes, Granddam, and got a very funny feeling."

Ysa was gingerly handling each tooth in turn. "The same 'funny' feeling for all of them? Or different?"

"Different, I think. My fingers tingled. With some of the little teeth, the tingling reached up to my elbow. With others, it was just my fingertips."

"This is a mystery indeed," Ysa commented. "I will have to consult my books to see if I can learn anything about this artifact. Do you see the little gems?"

"I didn't look closely enough to see gems," Elin said.

"Well, each tooth is strung on silver wire, and there is a tiny gem between it and the place where it is fastened onto the chain." She picked up the bracelet by its ends and held it where the light from the fire shone on it. "You have to hold it just right to glimpse them."

"Now I do see!" Elin exclaimed. "Red, yellow, blue, green, orange. Another red, deeper in hue. And clear gems, with no color to them."

"Those mark the three teeth that are from a human—or something close to a human. I suspect they once belonged to a wizard's offspring, or perhaps the children of three wizards. I will know more once I have looked through my books, and perhaps found someone to help me perform a Ritual of Asking."

"Oh, how exciting!" Elin exclaimed. "May I be there when you do it?"

The Duchess Ysa gazed at her granddaughter. "Yes," she said finally. "Yes, if it is possible I think you should be. After all, you were the one to find the bracelet, and you had the wit to bring it to me, the only person who could fathom what it is and why it was made." She folded the bracelet in the kerchief again and tucked it into her own reticule. "But you must be patient. Ancient knowledge—and I suspect this is very ancient indeed—is sometimes difficult to ferret out. I will be long hours with my books. You must find other ways to entertain yourself."

"Needlework," Elin said with a small grimace of distaste. "Mother insisted that I bring it with me. At least she didn't make me bring Karina, the lady who was teaching me."

"Karina. She is new, isn't she?"

"Yes," Elin said, happy to be relating gossip. "She replaced Lady Dinna, who was, well, lavish with her favors. Rumor has it that she occupied Uncle Einaar's bed for a while."

"No! Really? That must have outraged Ashen when she found out."

"Oh, I think Mother never did—or if so, she kept it to herself. She knew about Dinna's liaison with Braute, one of her House Troops, but it was when Dinna was found out in the stable with one of the house jarls that she was summarily dismissed from service."

"Well, I did know a little of Dinna's escapades back when I lived in Cyornas Castle. In fact, I found them amusing. But Ashen was right to dismiss her. A little flirtation is just to be expected, but Dinna carried matters entirely too far."

"It's said she went to live with Blåmann, the jarl she had been discovered with—they didn't have on any clothes—and now lives at Baron Håkon's country estate at Erlend as a part of his household. She took a child, rumored to have been fathered by Blåmann, with her. She is not permitted to come to Cyornasberg and the Baron's town house. Mother's orders."

"Well, well, what does go on when one does not adequately supervise one's people—not that I am criticizing Ashen. She never had to exert her power and control when she was growing up, the way you are learning to do, my dear, and so one cannot expect her to have done any better. And some ladies are very good at subterfuge."

Elin took the message Granddam Ysa was sending her. "I will always keep an eye on Hanna and Kandice, though I believe Mother would have been very careful to select ladies of good character for me."

"Of course," Ysa said. "Of course."

If Elin had expected life to be more exciting in Iselin than it had been at the Cyornas Castle, she was doomed to disappointment. There was a difference between the short stay she had had earlier, when she had come to coax Granddam Ysa back to Cyornasberg for Earl Royance's and Countess Mjaurita's wedding and this extended sojourn—possibly permanent—in Iselin.

If there was a difference between *here* and *there* it was that *here* was much more sedate. Cyornas Castle was always astir with activity, paid performers coming and going, keeping all amused. Except for Ysa's female fool, Tinka-Lillfot, such entertainments were rare as both the duchy and its manor were very much off the main routes. And, of course, it was winter when sensible folk stayed indoors. People amused themselves as best they could.

Perhaps this was another of Granddam Ysa's lessons. Surely she had had to endure worse during her lifetime, but she still put a good face on it. So Elin prepared herself to find the best in the situation that, after all, she had chosen.

Ysa forbade her to go out hunting as the men did, though once or twice she went hawking with Baron Gustav, the Council head, and Barons Caspar and Isak and their followers.

The hawking was interesting, or would have been if the hawk Gustav allowed her to fly liked her. It was always bateing, as if impatient to get away from her, and would not stay in place until game was flushed.

"Delion was trained to catch prey on the ground," Gustav told her. "Show her some conies and then watch her in action."

"Conies?" Elin said. "That's boring. I like it when your hawk takes a bird in midair."

"It took a long time to train Albia properly. Forgive me, Your Highness, but she requires a practiced handler. Delion does not. Just let her go her ways." Despite his burly appearance, Gustav demonstrated a gentle touch with the bird.

Elin soon decided that she did not care for hawking. She preferred to stay inside. There was always embroidery and other needlework in the daytime and it was a way to pass the time, if tediously. At least her cheeks stayed warm and her fingers did not develop chilblains. As at Cyornas Castle, at Iselin even the high-born ladies contributed to clothing the members of the household and did not scorn to stitch a shirt or mend an elbow. In the evening, after an entertainment there were the usual games.

The men played King's Soldiers, of course, but Elin preferred the game of Tables. The opponents rolled dice to determine the movement of counters over the game board. She also liked Merrils, because that took more thought. Sometimes, with Ysa's permission, she gambled small coins on the outcome of games and frequently won.

Granddam Ysa seldom participated in such activities. She kept much to her rooms, studying.

To Elin's surprise, there was no real Fane at Iselin, as there was at Cyornas. There was but a single, high-vaulted chamber set aside for spiritual matters, presided over by an elderly priest named Mattis. It was small, compared to what she had heard about Fanes elsewhere, such as the magnificent structure at Rendelsham Castle, but every detail was perfect. Once a week she had gone to the Fane at Cyornas Castle and confided her activities to Esander the Good. Not all, of course, for though he had a reputation for keeping secrets, there were some she did not care to mention.

Out of habit, she visited the beautiful room at Iselin weekly but was even less inclined to confide in Mattis than she had been with Esander. She never saw Granddam Ysa there, and occasionally wondered if she ever entered.

The primary bright point to ease Elin's boredom was the novelty that the Duchess had installed at her little Court, Tinka-Lillfot, who provided the bulk of the entertainment in the evenings.

She stood perhaps waist high and the twinkling grace and agility of her movements almost disguised how her body and limbs were half the size of a full-grown woman's. It pleased Ysa to dress Tinka-Lillfot—nobody ever used less than her full name when speaking of or to her—in miniature versions of her own gowns, and Lady Gertrude was tasked with the duty of informing the fool of Ysa's choice of gown for that day.

Elin never tired of Tinka-Lillfot's antics. She had a remarkable gift for mimicry and telling funny stories. Alfonse was fond of her, and Tinka-Lillfot had trained him to do any number of amusing tricks.

There was no such Court fool at Cyornas Castle, for there was no real need for it. Throughout the year the castle was frequently visited by all sorts of entertainers— troupes of mimes and players, acrobats and tumblers. The troupes would visit, stay for a week or so, and then move on.

By far the best of the acrobats were the troupes of little people like Tinka-Lillfot, only most of them not perfectly formed as she was. They seemed to have no bones in their small bodies, rolling themselves up into balls at will and dancing upon ropes strung between posts.

Elin didn't know where they originated. There were no such deformed children among the Nordorners. Perhaps, she thought without much interest, they gave them to the troupe masters as they traveled through the countryside.

Tinka-Lillfot was, therefore, the first of such Elin had ever encountered on a sustained basis. She found herself looking forward to seeing what new japery the little woman had created for an evening's entertainment.

All this changed, however, the night Tinka-Lillfot, accompanied by Alfonse, minced into the Hall wearing a duplicate of Elin's gown. Alfonse wore his own costume—a ruffled collar, a set of vaguely feline ears, and a long tail that dragged behind him.

"Come, my brave warkat!" Tinka-Lillfot cried. "You must protect me. You must save me. I think I saw a fierce coney lurking in a bush and I've lost my hawk. Oh! Oh!"

She drew her skirts around herself, peering here and there, and put the back of one hand to her forehead as she pretended to feel faint. "Whatever have I done, to find myself abandoned here in the outlands instead of the center of all eyes in my grand home! And beset on all sides by conies! However shall I endure!"

The men and women seated at dinner in Ysa's Hall laughed heartily. Elin was forced to laugh along with them though she seethed inside. Oh, to have the power to blast the little creature into cinders! At the least, she most urgently wanted to throw Tinka-Lillfot into the nearest dungeon and destroy the key.

Then, at the fool's signal, the musicians struck up a tune and Tinka-Lillfot began to sing and dance—a song that mercifully did not refer to Elin at all—while Alfonse twirled in time to the music. The crisis had passed.

Though Elin thought she had successfully hidden her surge of anger from those seated in the Hall, she found Granddam Ysa regarding her through narrowed eyes.

"When the meal is finished, you will come with me so that we may speak in private," she said.

It was not a request.

"Yes, Granddam," Elin said meekly. She managed to smile.

When at last the wretched supper had ended and the two were alone in the inner chamber of the Duchess's apartment, Ysa poured warmed wine into a goblet and handed it to her granddaughter.

"Here," she said. "Its stronger than you're used to, but I think you need this. I intend to speak plainly with you and it may be the first of several shocks. This was the first time you've been openly laughed at, isn't it?"

"I—I've never been laughed at," Elin replied, a little defensively. She took a generous swallow from the goblet and tried not to cough. She had never before tasted neat wine. "Well, my brother Bjaudin would laugh at me but that doesn't count. Not ordinary people."

"Be that as it may. You've had your first brush with it and you might as well begin getting used to it. You showed that you were angered and upset. You must never do that. Laugh along, and the people will love you."

"Yes, Granddam."

"However, that was not why I called you in here—not the entire reason, that is." Ysa opened a small box on the table between the two chairs they occupied and took out the bracelet made of teeth. "I find that this is an even stranger—and yes, even more powerful—article than I first thought. To fathom its real purpose, I must return to Cyornas Castle and there consult with Zazar."

"Return to Cyornas Castle!" Elin echoed, dismayed. "Why, I only just got here!"

"I did not say that *we* would be returning. I will go alone. You may stay here in warmth and comfort." Ysa put the bracelet into her reticule.

"But you said—you promised—I should be present when you performed— What was it? A Ritual of Asking."

"I promised nothing. I said 'if possible.' It is not. I need Zazar. She knows the ritual. Further, she has contact with certain Powers. Well, I do, too, a little, and so do you—or did you know that?"

"Is that why the bracelet made my fingers tingle?"

"Yes. But your abilities are far from developed. Not yet."

"Wh-when do you leave?" Elin was having a bit of trouble grasping this unexpected news. She finished the wine unsteadily.

Ysa refilled the goblet with the usual weak wine and berry mixture that was so popular among Nordorners. "As soon as my ladies can pack. My priest, Mattis, says all the signs point to a few days' respite from the snow, and I plan to use them for travel."

"And when will you return?"

"That I do not know."

"But—but Granddam, what of our plans? I mean, what of the Fridians, and the Aslaugors, and—"

"We are in the dead of winter. The seeds I have sown will not begin to sprout until the season has passed. And, if need be, there is still time to turn any . . . difficulties aside."

Elin opened her mouth to protest, and Ysa silenced her with a look.

"Yes, turned aside for another time if the situation requires it. I thought I had been teaching you, but you seem determined not to learn." Abruptly, she seemed to change the subject. "Did you speak with the Aslaugor Marshal, Patin, as I told you to do?"

Elin started guiltily. An excuse rose to her lips but she instinctively knew this was not the time for it. "No, Granddam, I did not. I forgot."

"Of course you forgot. You were too busy enjoying all the attention being danced upon you by two handsome young men. Well, I did not forget. As a result, I know the situation between Patin and his mother Öydis. I know also of how matters lie between the Aslaugors and the Fridians and with the Lowlanders. You do not."

"I am sorry, Granddam. I will try to do better."

"Very well, then, listen for once and pay heed, for you are to have your first opportunity at governance."

Elin's heart was beating rapidly while Ysa outlined what was expected of her.

As Gertrude, Ingrid, and Grisella would be accompanying the Duchess, she was assigning two noblewomen to Elin—Lady Brithania, wife of Baron Gustav and Lady Rebecka, wife of Baron Caspar. They would, of course, keep a record of any improprieties Elin might commit, and then report to the Duchess upon her return.

Elin was to leave the management of the manor house to Harald and Ania; they were in charge of the household staff and quite competent to carry on in Ysa's absence. Further, they would resent it if a child such as Elin tried to meddle. She might ride out when the men went hunting, if she were inclined to do so and they inclined to allow it, but otherwise she would remain safe, indoors.

Elin was to continue visiting the Fane room and must be certain to be seen doing so. She would do well to begin taking the priest, Mattis, into her confidence.

If disputes arose, she was not to try to settle them by herself, but was to bring them before the Council. Baron Gustav was entirely competent to give advice that Elin would be wise to heed. He and the other barons, Caspar and Isak, had lived in Iselin all their lives; there were few doings that they did not know of.

"But Granddam," Elin said, when these and other instructions had been laid before her, "what shall I actually *do*?"

"Watch and learn, Granddaughter. And practice for the time when you receive Iselin as an inheritance upon my death—which, I assure you, is yet very distant."

Elin almost dropped her goblet. "But—but—"

"How did I know? The same way I know how you have long thought of me as just an old woman, well past her prime, and someone to be used when it suited you." The Duchess arose from her chair and pulled herself up to her full height, the stoop to her shoulders vanquished for the moment. "Never, ever underestimate me, child. It amused me to watch you try to maneuver me—for a while. I am amused no longer. Now, you will become my pupil in truth or, be assured, I will cast you away without a second thought. I am still powerful enough both personally and politically to do great things, never doubt that. Together we can accomplish even greater deeds, even to creating civil unrest that will topple a kingdom and set father against son until the only one left with a claim to rule the country is a daughter. But"—Ysa swooped unexpectedly and grasped Elin's face in one hand, forcing her to look the older woman in the eye—"only if that one is loyal to me and only me."

Elin felt as if she had been stripped bare; her heart sank within her. All her secret thoughts and ambitions—what she had thought were her secrets—were plain to Ysa, and apparently, had always been. She had seriously underestimated the woman she had thought to use to her own advantage. And, gazing into Ysa's eyes, she realized how close she had come not only to being cast aside but perhaps even finding Ysa her enemy.

A cold shudder went through her. She had thoughtlessly come much too close to the ruination of all her ambitions. Bad enough that Ysa was displeased with her; much worse would be to have her enmity replace what love or affection she currently had for the Princess.

"I swear, Granddam," Elin said. "I most heartily swear to be your most loyal pupil in word, thought, and deed, from this moment hence."

"Good." Ysa released Elin from her grasp. "Now you may call the Court ladies in so they may learn of your new status."

Thirteen

The twisted strands of the frozen flame surrounding Zazar gradually began to thaw and move again. A hand reached through the flame and Zazar grasped it. A couple of steps, and she had emerged into a small mud-walled room lined with wooden shelves crammed with blankets and other goods, carefully placed to be safely out of the flames. She found herself staring face to face with a person who could only be Steinvor Askepott.

"Apologies, Zazar," the Wysen-wyf said. "You are Zazar, aren't you? Someone else didn't get hold of the bundle of herbs of Transport, did they?"

"No, you got Zazar, for good or for ill. I thought for a moment I had fallen prey to a trap from which I couldn't escape."

"Apologies again. Sorry to leave you waiting like that. I didn't know when you would use the herbs, so I was a little unprepared to, um, receive visitors. Had to excuse myself and clean this storeroom so I could fix a landing place in here. Next time things will go easier." Askepott grinned. "I didn't think you'd want the column of fire to appear in the middle of Gunnora's bath, would you?"

"Even not knowing who Gunnora is, no, I wouldn't."

Weyse loosened her grip on Zazar's neck and clambered down from her perch. She waddled over to Askepott, sniffed her thoroughly, and stood up, begging to be held.

"Well, now," Askepott said. "A benevolent summat. It's been many a year since I've seen one of your ilk. Too cold up here for you. The other sort, however—" She shuddered. "They don't leave anything when they catch you—even footprints in the snow."

"Tell me of Mikkel."

"That is why you've come, of course." Askepott set Weyse down.

Unexpectedly, the odd creature's little round ears pricked up. She uttered a trilling chirp that was answered by a *chuff!* from someplace beyond the confines of the room. She scampered toward the half-closed door only to be nearly hit on the nose as the warkat Talkin pushed through it. In moments the two were rolling around ecstatically on the wooden floor.

"Well, he's grown and flourished anyway," Zazar commented, indicating the warkat.

"I'll take you to the boy—Ridder Red Fox, as he's known around here. You can make up your own mind."

Leaving Weyse and Talkin behind, the two women made their way down a darkened corridor. At the far end, the flickering light of a banked fire and smells of cooking told Zazar that this was a kitchen complex. Askepott gently opened a door down the corridor. For light, she gathered sparks that glinted off the walls and ceiling and held them in the palm of her hand.

"His place is over here," she said softly.

Six sleeping forms occupied six piles of straw serving as beds. Zazar made her way to where Mikkel lay, deep in slumber. She reached out and almost touched his hair, now unkempt and needing a comb, and stopped herself.

Then she held her hand, palm down, over him and a different light appeared. Mikkel's face, hair, and body, as much as could be seen under the blankets, glowed in an aura of pale green, the color of health and growth. To her relief, no sign of illness touched him. "Yes, he is well," Zazar murmured.

One of the other children tossed and cried out in her sleep.

"We must leave," Askepott whispered. "I don't have the materials at hand to make anybody think they'd had a dream."

"This is enough, at least for now," Zazar told her once the door had closed behind them. "At least for me. His mother—well, she is a different matter."

"Mothers always are. But I must say this is the first time any of the household younkers' mothers have come into consideration. Of course, it is also the first time we've had a prince of the Nordorners in our midst."

"How long will your traveling herb mixture let me stay?"

"Long enough for a little chat and a cup of tea. Follow me."

Askepott led Zazar down the corridor toward the warmth and comfort of the kitchen. A pot of tea was already brewed and being kept warm on the grate in the inglenook.

Askepott handed Zazar another bundle like the one that had been included in Holger's letter. "This is all I have until I prepare some more. There's enough for another brief visit. Say, three days from now? At the full moon? That'll give me time to prepare the closet properly." She grinned. "Also, I needed to make sure of who or what I was dealing with before I arranged a longer stay."

"I can't blame you for that. But I am Zazar and that's all I will ever be."

"I'll have a fresh supply ready when next you hear from Holger," Askepott said as she poured tea into a mug and handed it to the other Wysen-wyf. "Come at the first full moon. I'll see to it that he sends regular messages. Then we won't have this hurry-hurry scraping together of a landing spot for you. And perhaps you can bring a packet of Transport herbs for me as well. I have a hankering to know what sort of place young Ridder Red Fox hails from."

"Gladly. I must say, Steinvor Askepott, that though you frightened the wits out of me at first, I feel much better in my heart about Prince Mikkel. Now I have to figure out a way to transmit this to his mother without her demanding that I bring her along with me next time."

"That would be awkward. She'd be sure to cry and carry on and I'm not sure I can create an adequate veil of Silence to keep the entire steading from being roused."

"Leave that to me. I've known Ashen all her life. Caught her as she dropped, being born. Knew then that she was a Changer, and destined for great things. I thought she had done with all that when she killed the Mother Ice Dragon, but perhaps there's still something the Weavers have planned for her to do."

"I've heard somewhat about that adventure. Tell me about it."

The two Wysen-wyves conversed for the better part of an hourglass's turning. Weyse and Talkin eventually made their way into the kitchen and curled up together nearby. By the time the Transport herbs had burnt low and Zazar was forced to return, her heart was at peace, for she knew she had truly met another of her kind, one whose gruff exterior hid their kind's fierce compulsion to see all disorder put to rights.

She thanked the Weavers and every other Power, both known and unknown for this blessing. Mikkel was safe. It was well.

When the promised wolf skins arrived, a gift from the Nordorn-Queen, Zazar almost refused them. What a mess they would make, if the fire of the Transport herbs touched them! But then she realized that the floor really was much warmer with the skins in place and anyway, they could always be pushed aside when need be.

A more pressing problem was the replenishing of her stocks of herbs and other materials from which to formulate her own Transport blend. That, and reassuring Ashen that her son was alive, well, in good hands, and actually thriving.

On pretext of thanking Ashen for the wolf skins, Zazar invited her to the tower rooms to share a cup of tea and see for herself how much warmer the floors were. When Ashen was properly seated and taking a cautious sip of the hot liquid, Zazar told her what she had learned about Mikkel.

Ashen nearly dropped her cup. "Are you sure? But how? And when? Was it really Mikkel?"

"Hush now, or I'll have to put a soothing remedy in your tea and put you down for a nap. Yes, it really was Mikkel. She really is a Wysen-wyf, too. Knew what sort of creature Weyse is, though I have never told another soul."

"What might that be?" Ashen held onto her cup as if this mundane article was all that was keeping her connected to this world.

"She's a summat. A benevolent one. In the land beyond the Isle of Writhram, the dangerous ones are known as the Shapeless Shadow, the Devil Tiger, the mist that pursues. You always wondered how she could pop out of sight and re-appear without anyone knowing where she'd been or how she'd gotten there? Well, now you know."

"And you've seen Mikkel?"

"Do you remember the packet that Askepott sent me in Holger den Forferdelig's all-too-short note? Well, that contained a mixture that allowed me to travel to where she lived and see Mikkel with my own two eyes. A night or so ago I used the mixture. I saw Mikkel as he slept. Stayed nearly an hour, and Askepott and I visited and got to know one another." Zazar refilled Ashen's cup. "You've had a brief experience with herbs of Transport yourself."

Ashen thought, brow furrowed. Then her face cleared. "I was in Galinth, tending to Obern when he was injured. I sought to contact you—and wound up in a cave, being introduced to Ysa!"

"Just so. Askepott will send me another packet of Transport when next Holger communicates with us." Zazar found herself saying words she had definitely not intended to utter. "If it turns out that I can take you with me on one of these excursions, I will."

She bit her tongue, wishing she could take back her rash words. The NordornQueen's eyes filled with tears that threatened to spill onto her cheeks. She set her cup down.

"Oh, yes, how I would love to see with my own eyes. I couldn't really believe that he was dead, but neither could I believe he was alive. Now I know."

"I always did. Now, I am planning to return and even to bring Askepott here, later. To find another Wysen-wyf—another *older* Wysen-wyf, that is. Nayla is still young as our ilk goes. Let's just say that Askepott and I have a lot to discuss other than Mikkel's well-being."

"I am so grateful." Ashen stopped trying to hold back her tears. She put her head in both her gloved, maimed hands, and sobbed openly.

On the night of the full moon, Zazar again visited the Wykenig stronghold. Askepott reported that Holger den Forferdelig had no immediate plans to send another message. He was not a good correspondent; that, or Askepott was unable to cajole him into more frequent contact. In the meantime, the two Wysen-wyves could manage with their herbs of Transport, though they both knew that keeping their activities a secret would be accomplished more by accident than by design.

"Gunnora is watching me closely," Askepott said. "And she keeps an eye on Ridder Red Fox, too. It's as if she knew or suspected some secret about him."

A week later, Askepott, using Zazar's traveling mixture, appeared in the high tower room. She seemed very interested in observing where Mikkel had come from originally, and Zazar was not loath to show her as much of the town and countryside as could be seen from her tower window. Then the two Wysen-wyves descended the stairs so the woman from the Wykenig steading could get a good impression of her surroundings.

She whistled softly as they glided through the Great Hall. Earlier that evening there had been a feast such as Gaurin was in the habit of giving his nobles from time to time, to thank them for their unswerving loyalty. Half-burned candles still stood in the great chandeliers, and though the dishes had been cleared away, tracings of the meal remained. Here and there, a house dog gnawed on a meaty bone.

"Ashen won't be pleased with this," Zazar said, frowning, "nor will Ayfare. She's the Chatelaine here and both like things kept clean. No dirt on the floor, and no scraps of food tossed into the corners."

Three of the four resident warkats, sensing something new and different, arose from their places near the banked embers of the fireplace and came to look them over.

"That one's the mam of Ridder Red Fox's kitte?" Askepott asked, indicating one of the females.

"No, it's the one holding Weyse in her paws and giving her a bath."

Askepott shook her head. "What a household."

"Yes. A happy one, mainly."

"Let us hope it becomes even more so."

"Have you heard something?"

"Nothing to put your finger on. Just some thoughts I'd like to share with you."

"Come along, then, lest we wake someone we don't intend to."

They ascended the stairs to Zazar's apartment again and Askepott continued with what she had been mulling in her mind.

"Something is definitely brewing with Gunnora the Golden. She spends too much time in the little room she made Holger build for her, just off her private quarters. I think she is up to some mischief and is searching for the right ingredients with which to do it."

"Do you know what those ingredients might be?"

"No. I don't think it has anything to do with our lore. Nevertheless, I won't let her into my stock of supplies, you can be sure."

"The fire has nearly died away," Zazar observed, indicating the smoldering herb circle.

"I think we've pressed our luck on these excursions as far as we can. It's just as well that we have used our store of Transport and you'll have to wait until next you hear from Holger before you visit again."

"My very thoughts. I would not like either of us to get caught. Ashen wants to come with me and see Mikkel for herself."

"I appreciate a mother's concern, but that is not a good idea."

"I know. I will have to deal with her carefully."

"Well, until the next time."

The Wysen-wyves clasped hands. Then Askepott stepped into the smoldering circle. The flames arose, spun, and she was gone.

While Zazar waited for the next note from Holger, the Duchess Ysa returned to the Castle of Fire and Ice unbidden and unexpected. With the heavy snowfall and dropping temperatures, the Great Hall was used now only for feasting, as it was too difficult to heat. The NordornKing and NordornQueen received their kinswoman in the outer room of their private apartment where they had been amusing themselves with a game of King's Soldiers.

"Oh, yes, Elin is well," Ysa told Ashen and Gaurin. "I just thought I'd leave her alone for a while to play at being a duchess in her own right. It should deliver a few valuable lessons—not that I think you are not rearing her correctly."

"There's nothing like firsthand experience," Gaurin agreed politely. "Would that I had had similar opportunity, when my cousin died and I became his heir."

"Oh, you've done reasonably well," Ysa said airily. "Now, what news do you have since last we spoke? Have you heard from Royance and his handsome Mjaurita? Did the Prince and the Duke return safely to their lands? Are they now pleased with their betrothals? And what of Einaar and his lady? The new babe must be almost due by now."

"The Earl and his Countess are in their residence in Åskar," Gaurin told her. "We have heard from Yuland; their Duke has returned safely. Nothing from Prince Karl, however. I expect the Icy Sea is much too hazardous for a ship to risk delivering a message."

"My sister-in-law is very near her time," Ashen said. "Zazar is with her."

"In the Duke's suite?"

"In a small chamber adjacent."

"Why, then, I must go and pay my respects! Don't worry, I won't tire the Duchess. I remember how dreadfully hard it was with me, as I waited for Florian's birth. I labored for several days."

"Your kind concern does you credit, Madame Mother. Your usual living quarters will be ready for you and your ladies when you want them."

"Thank you, Daughter Ashen." Ysa swept a brief but correct curtsy and left the room. The NordornLand rulers looked at one another.

"Whatever does she have brewing now?" Ashen said, not expecting an answer.

"It must be something she deems important, or it could be nothing more than a whim on her part. Perhaps she really is concerned about Elibit."

"She barely acknowledged Elibit's presence when she was here before. Now, she invokes the supposed difficulty when Florian the Forgotten was born."

"Well, I daresay we'll find out, sooner or later. Now, let us return to the game. As I recall, I was beating you soundly."

"I must speak with you in private," Ysa told Zazar at the first opportunity.

"I am busy."

The Duchess spared a glance at the frail figure lying in the bed. She was sleeping, and drenched with sweat that Hermine, one of her ladies, was gently sponging off her. "She'll be all right for a while. Come. This is important."

"So is the birth of Duke Einaar's second child," Zazar retorted, but she followed Ysa out the door of the labor room. "Now, what is it?"

"We really should be in private."

"Perhaps, but this is as far as I am willing to go when the Duchess may need me at any moment."

"Very well. Do you know aught of this?" Ysa took a bundle wrapped in a kerchief from her reticule and opened it enough so that Zazar could glimpse the strange silver bracelet.

"Yes." Zazar frowned, thinking. "It was in the Dragon Box, where we found the map that led us to the Mother Ice Dragon's lair. I thought it had been lost. How do you happen to have it?"

"That doesn't matter. What does matter is that it is in my possession, and it is an item of Power. I need your help to discover just what sort of Power it is. When do you think you'll be available?"

"Not until the Duchess has given birth and is out of danger." Zazar shook her head. "You never cease to amaze me with your selfish insistence that you and only you are the center of the entire world."

"Not so! By all means, go back and minister to the woman. I hope she lives and her child prospers. I will be waiting, though, for the moment when you graciously decide to honor me with your presence and your knowledge."

"Oh, go feed your fat dog a spice cake," Zazar retorted, and returned to the room she had so recently left. With an effort she refrained from slamming the door.

One mystery in this tangle was no mystery at all. The only way the Duchess could have come into possession of the bracelet was that Elin had taken it from its resting place in Ashen's jewel box and given it to her.

Out of sight, out of mind. She hadn't thought of the bracelet in years; now Ysa had given her something to think about. She wondered if her skills, grown rusty over the years, would be equal to fathoming the Power residing in the thing. If she could not, then surely two Wysen-wyves working together could unravel it.

She would have to find some way to get the bracelet away from Ysa and, if not returned to where Elin had found it, then put away in a secure place, preferably under lock and key. Whatever its use and meaning, it was not something that should be left for any snoop to find.

She seated herself beside the Duchess Elibit and glanced at Hermine.

"She rests," Hermine told her. "I think it is in preparation for the next step. My lady will be lighter of a fair son before the next hour's turning."

"You're sure it's to be a boy?" Zazar had come to that conclusion some time previously, but was curious to know how Elibit's lady had decided the gender of the new child.

"Oh, yes. My lady wants a boy and her lord likewise. In the NordornLand, the first daughter is always named for the husband's mother."

Zazar understood at once. Everyone knew of the day when Baron Einaar of Asbjørg, a small, insignificant island to the northern part of the NordornLand—came to Court. And all knew of the illicit liaison between Gaurin's father and Bergtora, Einaar's mother. Duke Einaar had no reason to love or revere that mother or to perpetuate her name.

"If the child turns out to be a girl, we'll break custom. We might even call her Zazar."

At that, Lady Hermine laughed, but softly lest she disturb the sleeping Duchess.

A day later, Elibit having been delivered of a son and considered out of danger, Zazar sent word to Ysa.

"The young Duchess is well, then?" Ysa said, puffing as she came through the door to Zazar's tower rooms. "And the boy is healthy?"

"Hale enough to be given his name, Cirion, and put in Beatha's care. She's glad enough to be out of the kitchen and back to doing what she loves best."

"But that isn't what brings me here," Ysa said. "Do you have any snowberry juice and wine? That is quite a climb."

"Almost as difficult as the one back in Rendelsham Castle to the tower where you did your magic-making," Zazar retorted a little more sharply than absolutely necessary. "But that was years ago."

Nevertheless, she set the already prepared pitcher closer to the fire so it could warm more quickly. Then she drew up the two chairs facing and indicated that the Duchess should take one.

"Give me the bracelet," she told Ysa.

The Duchess took the kerchief out of her reticule and handed it to Zazar. "I haven't touched it since—well, for a long time."

"Makes your fingers tingle, doesn't it? I can feel a buzz even through the kerchief." She set it aside.

Weyse, who had been napping nearby, roused a little and sniffed at the bundle. Then she drew back, fur standing up in a ridge down her back. As fast as she could go, she trundled off toward Zazar's sleeping room and, if one went by her actions, would gladly have slammed the door behind her if she had been able and there had been a door.

"Well!" Ysa exclaimed. "That was odd."

"Not so, when you consider that she is a creature of Power herself. Whatever is hidden in the teeth on that bracelet, it is something not to be trifled with. You were wise to bring it to me."

"It is just a loan, until you learn what is the true nature of the Power it holds."

"Oh, yes, of course," Zazar replied, not meaning a word of it. In Zazar's opinion, Ysa led the list of all the people in the world who should not have this item in their possession.

"How soon do you think you'll have any information?" Ysa asked.

"I don't know. It might be a day, it might be a year."

"Well, if it looks to be that long perhaps I should take it back with me to Iselin."

"No. It isn't yours to take. If it belongs to anyone, it belongs to Ashen. You are curious, that is all, so don't get yourself all upset for nothing. Give me some time to work on the problem before you give up on me."

"Well," the Duchess admitted, a little reluctantly it seemed to Zazar, "I suppose that, in a way, Ashen could claim it. But it is mine now. And I did come all this way to seek your guidance."

"Then learn patience, Madame. Learn patience."

When Ysa finally departed Zazar's tower rooms, the Wysen-wyf unwrapped the kerchief and laid it out flat on her worktable. "Weyse," she said, "come here, please."

The little creature poked her nose around the opening in the curtain, but didn't venture farther into the main room.

"Oh, come on. I won't let anything happen to you and you don't have to touch any of the teeth on the bracelet. I just need to borrow some of your Power."

Very reluctantly, Weyse waddled slowly into the room but did not, as was her wont, jump up in Zazar's lap. She had to reach down and lift Weyse up, where she turned her back firmly on the table and clung to Zazar's shoulder and began to whimper a little.

"Yes, I know it is evil. I just don't know what kind of evil it is, or what its purpose is, or why it was among the things hidden in the Dragon Box." She thought for a moment, and then made a decision. "We need to return to the Wykenigs' steading and ask Askepott. After all, she knew what you are, when I had only a suspicion. I supposed you could say she has been stuck away from everything and everybody, up there in the wild north, but then I have quite a store of knowledge—of a different type—and I was stuck away for countless years in the Bog."

She reached around Weyse and folded the kerchief up into a square and tucked it away into the waterproof pouch that had contained Askepott's letter and bundle of herbs of Transport.

Weyse immediately relaxed. Zazar got up and transferred her to the other chair while she began rummaging around in her store of herbs and other items on the shelves lining the chamber.

"I've had other matters occupying me, but I do need to make some Transport mixture as well and have it ready the next time Holger den Forferdelig sends word and I know when to return to his steading. It is becoming more and more important that Askepott be able to visit me here, and also that I can travel there when I please."

She peered out the window. From her vantage point, she had a good view of the countryside to the north and east. It had been several weeks since the first letter; surely by now Askepott had been able to persuade Holger to write again.

Nothing for it but to wait, however. And while she waited, Zazar would continue to try every avenue open to her to discover what lay behind the strange bracelet strung with even stranger little teeth.

Ten days later, the eagerly awaited messenger arrived, this time a Fridian who did not scorn a reward for his troubles. Zazar made certain she was among the people in the outer room of the monarchs' private quarters when the parcel was opened.

Again, another bundle addressed to Zazar dropped out. And again, Holger's message was brief:

The boy is eating me out of house and home. H.

"Well, that is curt to the point of impoliteness," Ysa noted with a scornful sniff.

"It is what we crave to hear," Ashen told her. "And it is what we have come to expect from the Wykenig who holds Mikkel captive."

"If he had grown weary of his game, the message would have been otherwise," Gaurin observed. "But he tells us that Mikkel is well, and thriving, and it still amuses him to make certain that he is well cared for."

"It is good news, then," Einaar said. "As good as possible under the circumstances."

"Yes, dear brother," Ashen said.

Ysa reached for the bundle addressed to Zazar but she retrieved it neatly, almost from under the Duchess's fingers. "This is mine," she told her.

"Well, of course," Ysa responded a bit huffily. "I wasn't going to steal it. Just smell it. There's an odd odor about your parcel. Your correspondent uses a strange perfume."

Zazar permitted herself to smile. Ysa was so transparent. "Yes," she said, and refused to elaborate further. Instead, she turned to Ashen and Gaurin. "I may be at meat tonight, and I may not. I have work to do."

"Can anyone be of help to you?" Elibit asked.

"Only to the extent of keeping the curious away from my door," Zazar told her, but her tone was softer than her usual wont. Einaar's Duchess was a sweet little thing and Zazar feared that she would not live long, particularly if she continued bearing children. Her slight body was not made for it. She made a note to provide Elibit with medicine that would help prevent another pregnancy—at least too soon.

"There, there," she said, patting Elibit on the hand. "I'm just a cranky old woman and I want to be alone for a while. That's all."

"Then you shall have your wish, Madame Zazar," Elibit responded, "and more besides. I owe you much."

"You owe me nothing." Zazar looked around the small room, nodded, and left, closing the door behind her.

It was yet two days before the full moon and Zazar had a great deal to accomplish, starting with deciphering the note that was bound to be wrapped around the herbs of Transport.

This time it was a little easier to translate:

> a wysenwyf gretes a wysenwyf the boy is doing well
> he wants to go home he is growing up and his kitte too
> when you come this time you can stay longer we will talk
> stenvor ashpott

The invitation to "stay longer" suited Zazar immensely. The two Wysen-wyves now had even more to say to one another. Between them . . .

The possibilities seemed endless.

In the meantime, she continued to study the strange bracelet, ignoring the sometimes painful tingling in her fingers as she turned each tooth over, seeking the answer to the riddle.

It seemed impossible for time to drag any more slowly, but the full moon finally arrived. Zazar made her final preparations.

First, she carefully pushed the wolf-skin floor coverings aside and weighted them down so they would not unfold and reach the burning circle. She didn't want to have to explain to Ashen how they got burnt. The magical fire did have an effect on its surroundings; her wooden floor bore the marks of the several expeditions. She poured out the mixture along those marks, leaving a space open in the circle.

She returned the bracelet of teeth to the waterproof covering of Holger's earlier letter and put the bundle into her carry-sack along with a few other items she thought might be useful, including a sack filled with the mixture of dried berries and grain that Weyse loved so much. To coax the little creature to come along, she offered a handful tucked into a fold of her shawl if Weyse would climb to Zazar's shoulder. Weyse reluctantly climbed up and clung to her with one paw while she transferred the delicacies to her mouth with the other, greed winning out over her fear of what else lay in the carry-sack. Zazar filled in the gap in the circle, said the word, and ignited the herbs of Transport.

Again the column of flame arose and began swirling around the two. Zazar was almost tempted to reach out and touch the spiral, to see if it was really hot. She resisted the impulse, however. As before, the flames took her directly to the little closet in Askepott's kitchen house. Askepott was waiting for her.

"Come, come," the other Wysen-wyf said. "It's a raw, cold night and I have tea to warm you. You'll want to look in on Ridder Red Fox first, I expect."

"It is definitely cold," Zazar said. She blew on her fingers, wishing she had thought to wear gloves. "How do the children keep from freezing with no firepot?"

"Heh. The secret is in the straw they sleep upon. I put a little of a certain mixture into it. Not only do they sleep warm but there's no vermin to trouble 'em either." She laughed. "And, I expect, it builds character as well to think they're enduring such hardships."

She led the way, with Weyse scampering ahead of both women. Talkin came bounding out of the children's sleeping room to greet his unearthly little friend and the two immediately headed off together on some errand known only to them.

Zazar checked on Mikkel; as before, he slumbered in fine health. And he had definitely grown. Were those crimson hairs on his chin? "He'll be a man in no time," she murmured.

"And that worries me," Askepott said. "It isn't natural. Something is making him grow much faster than he should. That's one of the things I wanted to talk to you about."

They hurried on down the corridor toward the light and warmth of the kitchen. There, Askepott poured tea for them and they sat down at one of her tables where, in addition to the hot liquid, a platter of meat pasties awaited them. A candle, smelling of honey, burned in a dish on the table.

"I can't keep young Red Fox in clothes," Askepott said. "I'm used to a boy making rags of his clothing, but Red Fox outgrows everything almost before he puts it on."

"Has anybody else noticed this?" Zazar asked around a mouthful of the savory meat pie. She made a note to remember to save some for Weyse.

"Holger has. He thinks it's funny to tell the boy that he'll be going out on raids when winter is past. And Gunnora. She looks at Mikkel and I can see in her eyes that she's measuring him for something. If you want my opinion, I think Gunnora is the one behind this unnatural growth. Perhaps she wants him gone, and Holger wouldn't send a boy away. He would, a man."

"Tell me of her."

"I don't know very much about her. Holger's father, Ivar Groznoy—Ivar the Cruel—found her living in a kind of palace,

Ivar claimed, made of ice. How she survived, nobody knows except that she was tended by the remnants of a force of warriors that had once fought against the NordornLand."

A chill not born of the cold swept over Zazar. "Did—did she ever mention a name, perhaps?"

"Once. She said her mother was someone named Flavielle. Who her father was, nobody knows. The leader of the ones who took care of her was called Farod. He had been sore wounded in some great war, run through with a sword and left for dead, but he survived. Crawled off to die and didn't. He returned to the ice palace and there he stayed."

Zazar's head was spinning. Farod had been the lieutenant of the Great Foulness, an Ice Dragon Rider, and she had watched, in company with Ysa and Ashen, as he and Gaurin had fought on the plain below the rock on which the women stood. His body had never been accounted for, and everyone had assumed it had been buried under the tons of snow the Great Foulness had brought down on them.

"Ivar finished the job on the man. Ran him through again and cut his head off so he'd stay dead. Then he brought the girl back and gave her to his wife, Jindra, to give her a proper Wykenig upbringing."

Zazar forced her lips to move. "And did you have any influence over this Gunnora?"

"Only enough to know that she has Power, and a lot of it. She married Holger when they were old enough, and has ruled this steading with an iron hand ever since."

"Your story is one that brought back many memories. I watched while Gaurin, later NordornKing, and Farod, second to the Great Foulness, battled at the foot of a spur of rock. It was Gaurin who dealt what we thought was a deathblow to Farod."

"You do get around," Askepott observed. "In high company, too."

"High enough. Ashen, later NordornQueen, Ysa, Dowager Queen of Rendel, now Duchess of Iselin, and I worked our magics together to defeat the entity that had begun that great war, where the Four Armies fought Ice Dragons and their Riders."

"Dragons!" Askepott snorted. Then she picked up the teapot and poured fresh cups of the steaming beverage for both. "Dragons fascinate Gunnora no end."

"How," Zazar asked carefully, "does she satisfy her curiosity about dragons?"

"Well, I've seen the books she reads and I've read some in them as well. Also she has sent out searchers to the ruined ice palace, seeking a certain artifact. It's said to have so much Power in it the one who wields it cannot be brought down."

Zazar reached into her carry-sack and brought out the bundle containing the silver bracelet. She laid it on the table and unfolded the wrapping. "Could it be something like this?"

Askepott drew in her breath sharply. The teeth had a glow in the dim light of the kitchen, and the almost-hidden gems shone with a malevolent gleam. Zazar watched the other Wysen-wyf's face grow pale.

"A picture of this is in one of Gunnora's books!" Askepott reached out and hastily scrambled the bracelet into its wrappings. "Put it away! Put it away! Gunnora is apt to sense it and come searching!"

With a calm that she did not entirely feel, Zazar rewrapped the bracelet and sprinkled a few drops from a vial onto the bundle. A scent of spices filled the air.

"I came searching also, seeking just a little knowledge, and now I find more than I hoped for."

"You do know what six of those—those objects are, don't you?"

"Yes. Shell-teeth. The—the creatures used them to break their way out of their shells. Then the teeth were discarded."

"And carefully saved. I think we both know why."

"Yes. But what of the three others? Those I cannot decipher."

"Each is the cast-off tooth of one who became a mighty sorcerer, or sorceress, and can likewise be invoked if the summoner is strong enough in his—or her—purpose."

"Flavielle was known as the Sorceress," Zazar said, almost under her breath.

"How," Askepott asked, "did you come by that—that artifact?"

Then Zazar told her the story of the Dragon Box and its contents, and how the NordornKing and NordornQueen had come to slay the Mother Ice Dragon and the remnants of her last brood.

"And maimed themselves in the doing," said Askepott.

"Yes. Everything that was in the Dragon Box save that"—she indicated the parcel, still smelling innocently of spice—"was put to good use. Ashen kept it in her jewel box, until a mischievous child filched it. The Power residing in this thing is gradually entangling those who know of it in the NordornLand and, it would appear, here, too. It was Duchess Ysa who last came into possession of it and gave it to me to unravel the mystery."

A faint sound, as if of a door opening, followed by footsteps, came from a room beyond the kitchen.

"Quick," Askepott whispered, "go and hide in yonder cupboard. That is Gunnora or I miss my guess."

Zazar did as she was bid, taking her cup and the carry-sack with her. She could only hope that Talkin and Weyse, wherever they might be, would have the good sense to stay out of sight.

She had no sooner closed the door behind her than a woman entered the kitchen. She put her eye to a crack in the door, where she could see but not be seen.

Even if she couldn't sense the Power emanating from her, the bright yellow of the woman's hair and her air of command told Zazar plainly that this was Gunnora the Golden. She had a silken robe clutched around her, and held a hollow silvery rod of a type that Zazar remembered, with another cold chill, seeing before.

"What are you doing up?" Gunnora demanded.

"Are you the only one who can't sleep every now and then?" Askepott said. "I woke up and came in here, where it's warm. Would you like some tea? It might help you get back to sleep."

"I felt something. Well, not felt exactly so much as *smelled* something. It seemed to come from here."

Askepott laughed shortly. "You were dreaming. Here, this is what you smelled. Have a pasty. It'll make your dreams sweeter."

With a start, Zazar realized she had left her half-eaten pasty behind on the wooden platter. Perhaps Askepott's quick wit would cover the lapse.

"It wasn't a meat pasty I smelled. But never mind." Gunnora turned, as if to return from where she had come, and paused. "If you're lying, I'll have it out of you sooner or later."

"You see old Steinvor Askepott having a cup of tea and a little something to eat in the middle of the night," Askepott said flatly. "Where's the lie in that?"

Gunnora made no answer, but left the kitchen. Askepott arose from the table and tiptoed softly to the door from where she had entered, listening. When she was satisfied, she released Zazar from the cupboard and they returned to the table. Then she poured out Zazar's cup of tea, dropped a few crushed leaves into the pot, and filled it with hot water. When the leaves had steeped a few minutes, she refilled both cups with the brew. She and Zazar took a swallow.

"Should have thought of this in the first place." Askepott's voice seemed to come from a distance. "Gunnora sleeps, if she sleeps, with one eye open. But even she can't hear us now."

"What was that thing she was holding?"

"An artifact she brought back with her from the ice palace. It was, she said, a souvenir of her childhood, a silvery rod that looks hollow. It's supposed to be a weapon, I think, though nobody knows how to use it. Gunnora keeps it in her jewel box." Askepott laughed a little. "It seems to be a favorite place for ladies to keep things they do not fully understand."

"I cannot stay as long as I would have liked," Zazar said.

"No. And I am sorry for that."

"Well, no matter. We have filled in some pieces of an old puzzle, however, and between us we'll fill in more. Here is a fresh package of herbs of Transport that will take you to my tower room at Cyornas Castle. I've said the words over them. There's enough, I think, for two more good visits. All we need to do is set a time."

"At the full moon," Askepott said. "That will give me time to put Gunnora's suspicions to rest."

"The full moon, then." Zazar pursed her lips and whistled a low note. Weyse came scampering into the room and climbed up into Zazar's lap. Without hesitation she reached for the discarded pasty. "Oh, you're more trouble than you're worth," Zazar told the little creature. "If you must, bring it along with you."

"Until next time," Askepott said.

"Yes. Until next time."

Zazar hurried back to the closet and stepped into the fire ring that still blazed there, ankle-high. Askepott made a sign with her fingers and the fire shot up into the familiar swirl. Zazar closed her eyes and when she opened them again she was in her tower room once more.

Zazar shivered, seized with a chill that no fire or blanket could warm. She had no proof, of course, but her strong feeling was that Gunnora, daughter of Flavielle, was, if not the physical then definitely the spiritual daughter of the Great Foulness of too recent memory.

Fourteen

*I*n Iselin, **Princess Elin** was finding the thought of ruling to be more agreeable than actually having to do it. Every night, the same boring faces at the dinner table, and every night the fool, Tinka-Lillfot, with her entertainment. At least, she did not ridicule Elin again; perhaps someone had informed her that her efforts had caused anger, not amusement.

Of course, old Lackel and the Seneschal Harald helped in the day-to-day matters inside the manor. Gustav actually ran things in the duchy, with Caspar and Isak, so there was little left for her to do save put her name on a paper now and then.

She let her embroidery cool in her lap while she gazed out the window at the falling snow. *Don't worry your young head; you just enjoy yourself.* She had heard that so often that she now wanted, very much, to throw something at the next person who said it. Yes, she wanted to enjoy herself—and would, if these stodgy old men would get out of her way—but she wanted also to savor real power. She wanted to get a taste of what she would be doing once she received Iselin permanently, and nobody was the least bit willing for her to do it, or so it seemed.

In a way, she almost envied Mikkel. The details of his misadventure were widely known, even here in Iselin. Through no fault of his own, other than sheer stupidity, he had been whisked off to a Wykenig stronghold where he had to be an honored guest. He was probably living a life of ease, feasting every night. Waited on hand and foot. Perhaps, she thought, he would even decide to take the Wykenig stronghold for his own, with Father's help, of course. That would surely be a sound political move. Better to turn your opponent into an ally than let him become your open enemy, according to Granddam Ysa. Who, she wondered, would be the Nordorn emissary to the Wykenigs?

One of the ladies, Cataya, cleared her throat meaningfully. She had not been specifically assigned to her, but had joined the others at their stitching. Elin took up her hated embroidery once more. It was to be a panel of a wall hanging, with a flower garden worked in wool thread. She had started it willingly enough, but now was incredibly bored with it. There were too many stupid snow roses to count, let alone stitch. Maybe she could lay it aside and work on something easier.

She arose from her chair, and her ladies all leaped to their feet as well. "Do not alarm yourselves," Elin said. "I just feel a need to walk awhile, and perhaps even visit Mattis. I've not been there in almost a week. Too much sitting makes one logy."

"Yes, Madame," they said, almost in unison.

"Would you be wanting someone to accompany you to the Fane room?" Lady Brithania inquired.

"I know the way. Be patient, and I will return anon."

With scarcely disguised relief, Elin let herself out of the cozy, overheated room and into a chilly corridor, remembering too late that she had left her shawl behind. The cold had the effect of revitalizing her instantly, if uncomfortably. She hurried in the direction of the Fane room where there would be some heat, at least.

She found the priest sitting by a window, reading. He laid his book aside.

"Come in, Your Highness!" he said. "Will you sit? Shall I ring for some warm wine or cakes perhaps?"

"A little warm wine would be nice," Elin said. She summoned her dimpled smile. "My ladies are too careful of me to let me get warm inside as well as out."

"Well, not too much, then."

Mattis bustled about, found another chair, and poked up the coals in the firepot, adding more wood. "Have you a—a spiritual matter you wished to discuss with me?" he asked delicately.

"Oh, no, not really. It's just that I was very bored and tired of my ladies' company. Actually," she added, as a thought struck her, "I was looking for something to read. I understand that my grand-dam, the Duchess, has many interesting books."

"So she does. Iselin has the finest library between Cyornasberg and Rendelsham."

"Then could I borrow a book? Or two?"

"The library is Your Highness's to read as she will," Mattis said, bowing. "Is there a particular subject you would like to read on?"

"Oh, no," Elin replied as guilelessly as possible. "Let me look through the volumes and see what catches my fancy."

"This way, then," Mattis said.

He opened a door leading to another, bigger chamber off the Fane room, and stood back to allow Elin to enter ahead of him.

She breathed in the smells of old paper, glue, ink, gilt, and something else—she could not recognize it. The library was as cold as the corridors and she shivered a little.

"Shall I bring the firepot in here?" Mattis asked. "We do not keep this room warm because of the danger to the books."

"Oh, I'm quite all right," she assured him. "I'll be quick about it. Thank you."

He hesitated, but took the hint. "If you need me, I'll be just outside."

"Thank you again."

The door closed behind him, though he did not latch it. That was all right; Elin would make this errand a short one. She immediately began to search through the shelves lining the room. The ones set up in the middle of the room she glanced at, but did not pause to examine closely. What she sought would be found in an inconspicuous place, or she missed her guess.

And there they were. Almost an entire shelf, devoted to magic and the making of magic. Quickly, she read through the titles and selected three more or less at random. She didn't really know what she was looking for, other than that she would recognize it when she came across it.

She placed another book, filled with poems, on top of the other volumes and tapped on the door. Mattis opened it immediately.

"Did Your Highness find what you sought?" he inquired.

"Perhaps. I think I'll spend the rest of the afternoon in my room, reading. I'll be sure to bring these back when I've finished."

She left him still bowing, and hurried off to her apartment where she dismissed her ladies with their infernal needlework.

"Tomorrow, I will stitch twice as much," she said. "Today, I want solitude until dinnertime."

"Yes, Your Highness," Lady Brithania said. She swept a deep curtsy, closely followed by the other ladies. "If you want anything, you have but to touch the bell."

When they had left, Elin settled down in a chair and put her feet up. She opened one of the books on magic at random, and began to read where the pages fell open of their own accord. It was a ritual designed to create a little flying creature that would act as eyes and ears for the one who created it. Useful, but not practical, she decided. She turned the page and read on.

Askepott took Mikkel aside. "You must know that your kitte is maturing," she told him. "The time is very close, if it hasn't arrived already, when you must let him go."

"No!" Mikkel protested.

"Yes. It's nothing you have done; it's just the way of the *krigpus*. They mate for life. He must seek a female of his own kind."

Mikkel stared at her, trying to find a way to refute her words. But he could not. The warkats at Cyornas Castle—Keltin and Bitta, Rajesh and Finola—were, as she said, mated for life. But to give up his friend? It was too much to ask.

"I can't do it."

"You can, and you must." She handed Mikkel a mug of tea, her sovereign cure for what ailed anyone. "He will not desert you. When it is time, he will return, with his mate, and then you will have two *krigpus.* Not many can boast of even one."

"When must I do this?"

"When the weather eases a bit. Look you. You will not be turning a helpless creature out to fend for himself. He is perfectly capable of taking care of himself and his mate, too. Have faith in your friend."

Mikkel regarded the old Wysen-wyf through a haze of tears. Impatiently, he dashed them away. He was far too old for such things. His voice had changed, and the hairs on his chin were growing more numerous, it seemed, with every passing day.

"Do you promise that it is a needful thing?"

"I do so promise. Your kitte has stayed with you longer than he would have with his mam out in the wild. He loves you just as you love him. This will not change, that I vow."

Mikkel swallowed hard. "How soon must I do this?"

"As I said, when the weather has let up a little. Maybe a week, maybe longer. But no more than that. You have a few days. I'll let some of your chores go, so you can spend more time with him."

Mikkel nodded, unable to speak.

The word spread quickly among the other younkers.

"I'm sorry, Mikkel," Haldon said. She put her hand on his shoulder. "He's so nice. I'll miss him."

"I think we all will," Lucas said.

The other younkers nodded, except for Petra. Her face, with its silvery tattoos, was expressionless. She reached for Mikkel's other hand.

"When you go to set him free, let me go with you," she said quietly.

"That would be very kind of you," Mikkel told her.

That evening, all the children made much over Talkin, giving him extra treats and tidbits saved back from their dinners. The warkat, either not knowing or not caring that he would shortly be granted his freedom, greedily ate everything he was given and searched for more.

"That's it, that's all I have," Willin protested, laughing, as Talkin nudged him so hard he fell over. The warkat then shoved him halfway across the room with his nose, butting and rolling him, apparently enjoying this new game. When he began taking Willin's tunic in his teeth and pulling so hard the fabric threatened to tear, Mikkel stepped in and stopped it.

"You have been my true friend for a long, long time," he told the warkat, cupping his face between his hands. "And, I hope that you'll be my true friend again." He looked up at Petra. "Yes, thank you, I would appreciate it if you went with me. Maybe it won't be so hard, if somebody else is there."

"When will we go?"

"Askepott said the first clear day."

"I'll be ready."

"Askepott will have your hide for shirking your tasks," Haldon observed. "And if not her, then Gunnora."

"No, they won't," Petra said. "This is much more important."

That night, all the younkers vied in coaxing Talkin to sleep cuddled up with them. Obligingly, he moved from bed to bed, ending up, as usual, with Mikkel. He hugged the warkat as tightly as he dared, dreading what was sure to come.

For three days, the skies were heavy with clouds, and the air full of light snow. But on the fourth, the day dawned bright and fair, and at breakfast, Askepott glanced meaningfully at Mikkel.

"Yes," she told him, and he could not pretend to misunderstand her meaning.

Andre Norton & Sasha Miller

"Yes," he replied.

All the younkers looked at him sadly. Petra slipped away from the table and vanished, meeting Mikkel outside as he tightened the wolvine-furred hood of his tunic.

"Where did you go?" he asked.

"I had something to take care of," she replied. "We might as well get started."

The two left the compound, with Talkin bounding ahead of them and then doubling back as if to show how much he loved being outdoors even if it were in the company of clumsy children, and headed toward the line of dark trees topping the hill behind the walled village.

"Do you have any idea where you're going?" Mikkel asked.

"Yes. Over that way." She pointed to a spot higher up and to the right.

"What's there?"

"You'll see."

And that was all he could get out of her until they were deep into the forest and had reached a glade where the tops of the trees nearly met overhead.

Talkin stopped, ears pricked forward, listening. From a distance came a low cry, like and unlike a cat. Talkin took a step forward, then looked back at Mikkel.

"It's a female *krigpus* seeking a mate, just like Talkin," Petra told him.

Mikkel went down on his knees, his arms around Talkin. "Yes, you must go now and be a real warkat. But remember, you'll always be my friend, and if you ever want to come back, I'll be so glad to see you." Tears were running down his cheeks, and he wiped them on Talkin's soft, thick fur. "Now, go."

He got up. Talkin took a step forward, stopped, turned back to look at Mikkel one last time. Then he turned again, and began to trot in the direction of the cry. The trot became a gallop and, in a twinkling, the warkat had disappeared from sight.

"He'll be all right," Petra said. "There isn't anything in these woods that is a danger to a *krigpus*. He'll be a king wherever he goes."

"Thank you."

"Now," Petra continued, "you must do something for me."

"What?"

"You must help me get back to my home."

"What? How can I do that?"

"Well, first, take this thing off me." Petra loosened her hood and pulled her hair off her neck.

For the first time, Mikkel saw that the iron torque she wore was wrapped in cloth.

"I don't understand."

"I don't expect you to. Just take it off. Don't let the iron touch my skin."

Gingerly, he freed enough of the hinge so he could pull out the pin that held it in place. Then he slipped it off her neck. Despite the wrappings, the skin under the torque was chaffed and red, as if scorched.

"Now you," Petra said. "The presence of iron hurts me, and you won't be taking it with you anyway."

"Why not?"

"Because you're going with me to my home."

Mikkel just stared at her. "What makes you think I'm going to run away from Holger's village? That is my home!"

Petra lifted her arms, seeming to grow taller now that the torque had been removed. "What about the NordornLand?"

He shook his head. "I know nothing about any NordornLand." He gestured in the direction from which they had come. "That is where I live. It is home."

"Then how did you come to be there?"

"Oh," Mikkel said, a little vaguely, "I was taken off a ship and brought back here. Holger adopted me."

"And put you in with the other younkers? The castoffs? The strays?"

"He thought it would be good for me."

"Your story makes no sense."

"Well, then, neither does yours. NordornLand, indeed. There is no such place."

"You do not remember? Then you really are a ninny! Do you have to have everything explained to you?"

"I suppose so," he said, more than a little angry.

"Even if Holger's village is 'home' to you now, you'll never be able to go back, not if Gunnora has anything to do with it."

"Why is that?"

"She's the one who's been making you grow so fast."

"That's silly. Everybody grows. There's nothing odd or unusual about that."

"Except that you're growing with unnatural swiftness. Mark my words, she has some black fate in mind for you."

"You must be mistaken. I know Gunnora doesn't like me, but why would she do something like this? You may go your ways, but I'm not."

"Mikkel, believe me, you don't have a choice. Quickly, rid yourself of any other iron you might have on you as well. Your golden necklace is all right. You may keep that." Petra reached into her tunic and pulled out an ornate silver chain with a pendant bearing a large green gem.

"That's Holger's!" Mikkel exclaimed. "You stole it!"

"He stole it from me first when he took me from my people."

"He's my father."

"If you say so. But father or no, believe me when I say he will kill you as readily as he will me. So you see, you really don't have a choice."

Mikkel could only stare. Her song, about the sea-green glass. And her claims about her origins.

"Are you really a Rock-Maiden?"

"Yes, I am. Now will you take off that horrible iron thing from around your neck? There's an entrance to the City 'Neath the Waves nearby."

Fumbling a little, Mikkel managed to unclasp his torque. At Petra's direction, he buried both under a rock.

"That's better." Petra straightened up more. Somehow, she had become nearly as tall as Mikkel, though reed-thin, and her skin had taken on a distinctly different tone, as if she were carved of alabaster.

"My city is well hidden," she told him as she led him away from the glade. "Be on the lookout. Somewhere around here there is a passageway, a stone tube. It will look like just another little hole where small animals make their lair."

Eventually, they found it, a depression in a larger boulder.

"This is too small for anyone to go through," Mikkel objected.

"It is now. But watch." With nimble white fingers, she pulled the hole open and widened it until it formed a doorway big enough that they both could walk through without touching. "Rock-Maidens can manipulate stone. We can push it into any shape we like. It grows heavy or light at our bidding and sometimes even floats if we want it to. Didn't you ever wonder how I could manage that big grindstone back in Askepott's kitchen? It was easy for me."

Mikkel could only blink. The wonders were coming too rapidly for him. He felt as if he had tumbled into a story such as minstrels spun, full of unbelievable creatures and heroic deeds. He followed Petra through the doorway and watched it shrink behind them. The air was warm. Petra took off her heavy tunic and after a moment Mikkel did the same.

"Here," Petra said.

"Here" was a stone tube. A door slid aside to reveal a platform seemingly poised on air. It bounced just a little when the girl stepped onto it, and a little more when Mikkel followed her. Then it began to descend.

"I do not like this," he said.

"It is nothing but a lift," she said. "How else do you think we go in and out of the city? We come up onto the land at times." She fingered her necklace.

The platform continued to descend until Mikkel thought he had surely reached the center of the earth. Eventually, however, it stopped. Another door in the tube slid aside and the two stepped out into wonders that Mikkel could never have dreamed existed.

"Welcome to the City 'Neath the Waves," Petra said.

Holger den Forferdelig's wrath was nothing short of earthshaking when he learned that Petra and his valuable hostage were gone, taking the *krigpus* with them. The loss of his prized green glass amulet only added fuel to his rage.

"You dared do this!" he bellowed at Askepott. He raised his fist threateningly. "*You're* to blame!"

"Dare, is it? Put your hand down," Askepott said, scowling. "You don't dare strike me and you know it."

For answer, Holger turned and smashed a table in half with a single blow. Then, for good measure, he shattered a stack of wooden platters, broke two bowls, and kicked Askepott's tea kettle across the room.

"Well, do you feel better now?" Askepott asked sarcastically. "Maybe you'd like to tear my kitchen apart entirely. Of course, then you'd go hungry. . . ."

"Silence, witch," Holger growled. "Maybe I'll let you live, if you tell me where they've gone."

"So you can send men out looking for them? You'll do that in any case. As it happens, I have no idea where they've gotten off to. Young Ridder Red Fox took his kitte out to let him go. He was ready to find a mate, and that wasn't likely, cooped up here in your stronghold. I gave him leave to go, and that's all I did. I didn't know that Petra had gone with them until she turned up missing. And that's all."

"Don't believe her, husband."

Gunnora the Golden had come into the kitchen unnoticed until she spoke up. The woman fixed Askepott with a malevolent eye. "She is up to something. Getting up in the middle of the night, having tea, serving meat pasties on a platter, more than one person could reasonably eat. She's been entertaining—somebody. Or maybe something. And I know it can't be good."

Askepott returned Gunnora's glare, adding a measure of dislike of her own. "Jealousy does not become you."

"Jealousy, is it!" Gunnora laughed, a cold and brittle sound. "You think you own so much Power! You are nothing compared to me."

Holger was staring uncomprehendingly first at one, then the other of the quarreling women. "Keep your differences to yourselves," he ordered. "If you are going to be no help in bringing back what is mine or in acquiring what you covet, then keep quiet."

Gunnora merely shrugged and turned away. Askepott took a broom and began sweeping up shards of shattered pottery. Holger stormed out and began calling his men, organizing a search party. A few of the women started to sidle into the kitchen, now that the violence seemed to have passed, at least for the moment.

"Well?" Askepott demanded of Gunnora. "Are you going to help? If not, then please leave so that I may put to rights what your husband has smashed."

With a sniff and another hate-filled glare, Gunnora turned on her heel and stalked out of the kitchen and into the common room. *Probably she is headed for her private chamber and her books,* Askepott thought, *to see what kind of mischief she can do to me.*

"Here," she said to Lotte, handing her the broom. She was probably the best of the lot. "You take charge. I must go and compose myself for a while."

"Yes, Askepott," the woman said. "All will be cleared away by the time you return."

And maybe not, Askepott thought as she hurried down the corridor past the younkers' room to her own quarters. There she kept her special kettle, the one she consulted when situations required it. If ever there was such an occasion, this was it.

She wished for a companion like Weyse. Doubtless Zazar invoked the little creature's help when she stirred the divining mixture. However, since she had none, she would just have to do the best she could.

She locked the door behind her and set a chair against it in case somebody tried to open it anyway. Then she began taking jars from the shelf and measuring ingredients into the kettle, stirring and singing a tuneless, wordless song. As she stirred, the contents liquefied, and became a mixture of colors never blending, but swirling in the wake of her paddle. When she judged the time to be right, she took another jar from the shelf and extracted a few bits of thread from those stored therein. She dropped the threads into the kettle and stepped back as the mixture foamed and belched forth a cloud of smoke.

A few more experimental strokes with the paddle, and she was satisfied that the pattern had solidified. A bright red streak dominated the design—not unexpected. Young Ridder Red Fox. Another thread, green, must be Petra with her cracked-brain song about the sea-green glass. They had doubtless run away together, but why those two? Why not Mikkel alone, or Petra with the other girl? Or, for that matter, Petra alone? She peered closer, to read all that the kettle had to tell her.

The streak of red bore a black edge. Nearby, a gold streak. That could only be Gunnora. Askepott knew she had done something to Mikkel, but until now she thought Gunnora had merely accelerated Mikkel's growth as an idle exercise in magic. Now she knew better; Gunnora had a purpose in mind.

She gave the kettle another stir. It was plain as daylight for anyone who knew how to see. Gunnora had brought harm to Mikkel.

But why?

She looked again. The gold streak that was Gunnora had sent tendrils out as if attempting to ensnare the others. She recognized the gray streak that represented herself, and knew that with Mikkel's absence she had now become the prime target of Gunnora's enmity. Colored specks dotted the space just out of the reach of the tendrils—two dots of different reds, dots of yellow, blue, green, orange.

The realization hit her with the cold force of an avalanche.

Gunnora. And the bracelet. She is closer to it than she has ever been. What you covet, Holger had said.

Of course she has gotten him to promise to include the bracelet as part of the trade, Askepott thought. *He all but said it aloud, there in the kitchen.*

All the pieces were there, and had always been but only now did everything become clear. Either Gunnora believed Askepott had the bracelet and was hiding it from her, or she thought she could force Holger to hurry the trade of the boy for the ship if she put him under a spell that made him grow too suddenly, and made it seem as if his life were about to be cut short.

Zazar and I were careless, she thought, dazed. *It is only luck that kept Gunnora from seeing the bracelet with her own eyes. She did say she* smelled *it. Now, with Mikkel vanished, she has nothing. Holger has nothing.*

In which case, though Holger might not dare harm her, Gunnora would have no such compunctions.

Why hadn't she consulted the kettle before now? Because, she told herself with a trace of self-contempt, she had thought she knew it all and had everything under control. Not so.

Askepott knew one thing with great certainty now; she had to flee for her life.

The contents of the kettle abruptly arose from the sides and folded in on itself, destroying the pattern. Askepott stepped back just as the muffled explosion sent up another cloud of smoke and an orange glow.

No time to lose. But how to get away? As she began to gather her few belongings, Askepott also began to formulate the beginnings of a plan. She knew where she must go—but how to get there?

Fifteen

*A*shen NordornQueen, **with the** good priest Esander at her side, gazed at the young Sea-Rover standing before her, wondering how to get him to talk to her.

Tjórvi resolutely refused to meet her eyes.

She tried again. "Are you happy here? Are you content?"

"Yes, Madame."

"You don't look either happy or contented."

"I am, Madame."

"Then why do you never smile? Your tutors tell me that you do your work listlessly, forever staring out the window as if wishing you were many miles away."

"I am sorry, Madame. I will try to do better."

"Tjórvi, you make me sad. I have tried everything I know to make your life comfortable and pleasant. But you will have none of it. Do you miss your home in New Vold so much? Would you rather return there?"

"My father has bidden me stay here, Madame."

"He will change that order if I ask him to. So I ask again, would you rather return to your home?"

"I will do as I am bid, Madame."

Esander spoke up. "You called me to this interview because I may have a slightly better understanding of a boy than you do, Your Majesty. May I break in?"

"Yes, of course. Please do."

Esander turned to the boy. "Now, Tjórvi, you miss Prince Mikkel, don't you?"

"Yes, sir, I do."

For the first time Tjórvi's unnatural composure slipped and Ashen thought his voice wavered a bit.

"Do you think you should have been the one the Wykenigs took as hostage?"

"I—I offered myself, sir. They wouldn't take me. Instead, they left me to drown. Or freeze."

"And yet you live."

"Yes, sir." Tjórvi looked down at his shoes.

"And you feel it is somehow unfair, even disloyal, that you are here, safe and sound and warm in the Castle of Fire and Ice, eating your meals at Mikkel's place, living in his quarters, wearing his clothes, while Mikkel is—"

"It *isn't* fair!" Tjórvi burst out. "If it hadn't been for me, Mikkel wouldn't have stowed away on the *GorGull* and none of this would have happened!"

"I see. And you think that you are solely to blame."

Tjórvi brushed away a tear. "For what happened to Mikkel, yes, sir, I do."

Esander appeared to change the subject. "Tjórvi, have you ever heard of the Web of the Weavers?"

Tjórvi blinked, a little taken aback. "Something, sir."

"It's said that the Weavers work the strands of our lives into their Web, and try as we might, we can neither foresee what direction our lives will take, nor change what the Weavers have foretold for us. Oh, they don't occupy themselves with trivialities such as whether you'll have porridge or toasted bread for breakfast, but the great events of your life—they are, for the most part, given to you as choices."

"Then," Tjórvi said slowly, "the Weavers decided that Mikkel would be taken, and I would not?"

"You boys could have stayed behind and attended Earl Royance's wedding, and still the Wykenigs would have attacked and sunk the *GorGull*. I think that the moment the Wykenig ship appeared on the horizon, the general shape of your futures were sealed. And once they captured the skiff, it was inevitable that you would stay behind while they captured Prince Mikkel. The variables? At that point, several. You could have drowned, or frozen to death. The little warkat could have attacked the Wykenigs and both he and Prince Mikkel would have perished at once. Tell me. Do you think you could have changed any of this?"

Tjórvi was frowning, trying to work out what the priest was telling him. "I—I don't think so."

"Of course you couldn't." Esander's voice was very kind. "It was as it was. All the protesting in the world, all the avoiding attending meals in the Hall, all the trying to make yourself invisible—they are for naught. Nothing will ever change what has already happened. Had you ever considered that you are valuable to Ashen NordornQueen and Gaurin NordornKing and that they want you to let them love you?"

"I—I don't see how they could."

"Ah, but we do," Ashen exclaimed. "You were Mikkel's friend! In many ways, you knew him better even than I, or his father. You were the last person from our world to see him. And you are my foster son Rohan's boy. Please, please, let us in."

Tjórvi bowed to her, awkwardly, but still a bow. "I must think on what the priest has told me. Forgive me, Madame."

"With all my heart."

"And be assured, young Tjórvi, that my door is ever open to you if you want to come and talk with me some more."

Tjórvi then took his leave and Ashen and Esander exchanged glances.

"Do you think you have gotten through this shell of defense he's wrapped around himself?" she asked.

"Perhaps I've made a crack in it, Your Majesty. But that is more than we had before this interview. I think, in time, he will be reconciled to the fate that landed him here, while it placed Mikkel out of anyone's knowledge."

"Then I shall be content. Thank you."

The Duchess Ysa was growing impatient. Surely Zazar had had sufficient time to solve the riddle of the strange bracelet. She had not descended from her tower in several days and finally Ysa decided to make the arduous climb again. She took with her a basket of delicacies.

How Zazar managed the climb on almost a daily basis, Ysa could not fathom. She had to pause frequently and catch her breath, a stitch in her side threatening to stop her entirely. Alfonse hovered beside her, occasionally pawing at the basket until she resumed the climb. At last she reached the door and rapped on it.

"Go away."

"Zazar, it's me. Open the door at once."

"Or what? You'll huff and puff and blow it to Iselin?"

"Of course not. I want to talk with you, that's all."

"And you came all this way to do it. Oh, very well."

The door opened and Zazar grudgingly let the Duchess into the chamber she used as a workroom and in which she also received infrequent guests. "It wasn't locked."

"I am not accustomed to entering someone's rooms uninvited."

"When did that change?"

"Please. Let us not be enemies. See? I've brought you something."

"Give it to your dog."

"I'm sorry you are in such a short temper, but I really did want to talk with you."

"Very well, then." Zazar settled herself in her chair beside the fire, and indicated that Ysa should occupy the one facing. "Talk."

Andre Norton & Sasha Miller

The Duchess brought out a flask of wine and set it on the hearth to warm. "This is a special vintage," she told Zazar. "It comes from my own vineyards." She arranged some spice cakes on a small platter along with several jars of preserved fruit.

"Then I'm honored."

"Yes. Well, once we've gotten comfortable, you can tell me what you've learned about the bracelet of teeth."

"I could, but I won't—other than to tell you that it is an artifact of Power that you have no business having in your possession. It is extremely dangerous, both to the possessor, and to those against whom it can be used."

Ysa sat back in her chair, astonished. "Zazar, I should be used to your bluntness by now, but still—"

"It is all that you understand," Zazar told her. "You do not realize that I am actually trying to do you a good service. There is no way of telling what could happen to you if you tried to invoke the Power in the bracelet."

Ysa stared at her keenly. "You don't know what it actually does, do you?"

"No, not exactly. But what I do know is that Flavielle— remember her?—had a daughter, and the daughter wants the bracelet. That is enough to tell me that it is extremely dangerous and when I can figure out a way to do it, I will destroy it."

"No, you mustn't!" Ysa raised her hands to her mouth as if she would call back the words.

"And why not? Would you loose again the mischief of the Sorceress we fought so many years ago?"

"How do you know all this?"

"Let me just say I have my ways. Just as you have yours. And there's an end to it."

"Oh, I think not."

"You're not going to get your greedy hands on that evil thing again."

"As you said once before," the Duchess responded haughtily, "it isn't yours to bestow. Or withhold."

"Wait for it to be bestowed on you with one hand and whistle with the other. See which comes true first."

Weyse had trundled in to the workroom and was investigating the spice cakes. Alfonse barked, trying to scare her away, and Zazar picked him up unceremoniously and dumped him on the floor, well away from the cakes.

"There's no cause to abuse my little dog!" Ysa cried. She picked him up and cradled him in her lap. "Poor Alfonse. He's never been happy here in Cyornas Castle."

"Then take him—and yourself—back to Iselin at once before I set the warkats on him."

"I do not know what's gotten into you of late," Ysa said. She gathered her rumpled dignity about her, arose, and settled an equally rumpled Alfonse in her arms. "I'll return to Iselin, since there is no courtesy to be had in this place, and you can rest assured you'll hear from me."

"Oh, I've no doubt," Zazar told her. "Trust you to meddle and make trouble when the storm clouds are on the horizon. Now quit talking about it, and go!"

When the door had closed behind the Duchess, Zazar almost regretted her harsh words. But she had no time to soothe the spoiled Duchess when the critical concern was the bracelet and how to dispose of it—or at least take it well out of reach—before Gunnora could pry its whereabouts out of Askepott.

The bracelet had to be hidden permanently, or, better, destroyed. But how? Not for the world would she try to smash the dragon teeth; instinctively, she knew this would invoke terrors unimaginable. But where to hide it? If only she could have finished the conversation with Askepott. Now she worried that Gunnora would try to harm her, or Mikkel, or both. She had given Askepott a good supply of herbs of Transport to the tower room; Zazar hoped she would not wait until the next full moon to use them.

The bracelet, still wrapped as she had carried it to and from the Wykenig stronghold, lay on one of her shelves, behind a large pot she used for stirring various mixtures. It would not be easy to find there, unless someone could "smell" the dragon teeth as Gunnora claimed to be able to do. And it was far from being a satisfactory permanent hiding place.

"Well," she told Weyse, who was busily stuffing fruit-covered spice cakes into her mouth, "Gunnora is not apt to pay us a visit any time soon. Now that I've offended Ysa sufficiently that she might go home, we may have a breathing space before the next crisis hits."

Askepott found an excuse to go out beyond the fence surrounding the village, where she found Rødiger, whose ice-sleigh had seen good service in carrying letters to the NordornLand. The vehicle was stowed in a shed nearby.

"I am curious about your sleigh," Askepott told him. "And equally curious about how you find your way south in it."

"Simple enough, Askepott," the man responded. "There's a trail of sorts, y'see, and once I get to the first Fridian village I can deliver my package, and then turn around and come home again."

"Yes, that does sound easier than it appears." Askepott took a deep breath. "What kind of trail is it?"

"The trail itself is easy enough—you go with the land—and just check to find red rags tied to trees now and then."

"And what would happen if you tried to ride it farther than the Fridian village?"

"Oh, nothing much. It would still work. It charges itself overnight, y'see. Has something to do with the lights in the sky. I don't understand it; I just use it." He laughed hugely at his own joke.

"I need to visit the Fridians," she told him. "They have some things I want to trade for."

"Does Holger know about this?"

"Am I supposed to tell him everything, every time I take a breath?"

"Well, no . . ."

"It isn't any of his business." She lowered her voice to a confidential tone. "Woman business, if you must know. Gunnora is looking a little peaked lately, and I thought I'd mix something that will perk her up. I mean, if she's carrying—and I don't say she is, and I don't say she isn't—she needs it." She winked broadly at the man.

"Well then, why didn't you say so? Trouble is, I can't get away just now to take you."

"If there's a trail, I can take myself."

"Do you know how to drive an ice-sleigh?"

"What is there to it? I've watched you enough to know that you kick it and then hang on and steer. It goes best on ice, but I have enough sense not to turn it over if I hit some snow."

"Let me think about it."

Good, Askepott thought. *You think about it while I load my belongings on the sleigh and get me gone before Gunnora can stop me.*

She had left her bundle of goods outside the kitchen door. Picking her time carefully, she retrieved the bundle and shoved it into the sleigh. Then she settled her carry-sack near her feet and, as warmly dressed as she could manage against the cold, kicked the sleigh into action and roared off, sending a spray of snow in her wake.

Before anyone at the village could react, she was halfway out of sight and well beyond pursuit. She didn't spare a thought as to how the household would continue without her; Lotte had been one of her best assistants, and she could manage.

Rødiger had been correct about the trail. Askepott fancied she could make out the tracks of the last few passings, though that was clearly impossible. It followed a clear path, winding through the trees, and when the way was uncertain, a bit of red rag indicated the correct direction.

Late in the day, she came to the Fridian village. She had had no instruction in how to stop the sleigh, but managed by taking her foot off the kick pedal and dragging the other to slow the vehicle.

Fridians, laughing at her awkwardness, came swarming out of their huts to help. All bore facial tattoos.

"You not know how for sleigh!" one of them cried jovially.

"No, I not know how, but I'm here anyway," Askepott said. Stiffly, she climbed out of the conveyance, hoping that it would not take it into its head to run off without her. But the sleigh seemed to have stopped for the time being. Fridians pulled it into their village and parked it beside one of their conical houses.

"You stay here," said the man who had first spoken to her. "You from Wykenigs?"

"Yes, you might say so. Can I get a hot meal here?"

"Sure, sure, woman bring. You rest."

The house looked snug enough, constructed of thatch and hides. The curved tusks of a snow mammoth flanked the doorway. She brushed past the inevitable dogs and children standing around to gawk, and entered the house. A woman was busy kindling a fire in the center. She grinned and nodded, and placed a pot of water near the hearth.

"Thank you," Askepott said.

The woman obviously did not speak the common tongue, but understood her meaning. She bobbed her head, grinned some more, and scurried out only to return a moment later with Askepott's belongings from the sleigh, which she dropped just inside the door and ducked out again without waiting for thanks.

Quickly, she checked to see that a certain bundle was safe in her carry-sack, and stifled a yawn. She was more tired than she wanted to admit. Part of it, she knew, was from the tension caused by managing the unfamiliar vehicle. Tomorrow, she would do better. But now, all she wanted was some hot food, a bed, and sleep.

What she would do, once she was past the Fridian village, she did not know. But she would manage somehow.

The next morning, with the memory of a hot supper, a good night's sleep to refresh her, a dish of hot porridge inside her, she took a look at the surrounding countryside through which she proposed to go.

Ahead lay a range of fire mountains, some leaking smoke. In places, rivers of molten rock had hardened in the snow. There were bound to be hot springs nearby, but she had no time or inclination to tarry long enough to locate them, much as she longed for a good soak in scalding water.

She wrapped herself as warmly as possible and climbed back into the sleigh to settle herself beside her belongings. She accepted with gratitude a fur lap robe from her Fridian hosts.

"You go back now?" asked her host, indicating the direction from which she had come.

"No. That way." She pointed south.

The man looked troubled, and sucked his teeth. "Oh, oh. Very hard. Not many villages. You find *seter* maybe now and then or you freeze. Where you go?"

"I am headed for the Castle of Fire and Ice, in Cyornasberg."

The man's face cleared. "I take letter there two, three moons ago! I know way!"

"Can you show me?"

"Sure, sure, I show. You drive, I show." He rattled off something in his own tongue, pointing at the sleigh and then at himself, striking a boastful pose.

The villagers sent up a cheer. Laughing, they helped him into the sleigh behind Askepott and pressed bundles of food and cooking utensils into every available space. Then, with certain misgivings, Askepott kicked the sleigh into action and they were off again.

She could not have fallen into a better bit of luck. The Fridian, whose name she learned was Eir, apparently knew the countryside well. He guided her past another ridge of high mountains where more steam escaped through rifts in the uneasy surface and occasional hot springs, smelling strongly of brimstone, bubbled to the surface. Now and again the ground trembled as one of the mountains belched forth a particularly large spout of steam.

That night, Eir found a *seter*, a stone building erected for the use of anyone traveling through the land. Askepott, who had driven the sleigh with much more skill than the previous day, brought it to a halt and parked it beside the building.

Once inside, Eir kindled a fire and set a clay pot full of fresh snow on the stone central hearth to heat. Then he took some dried meat and crumbled it into the pot. Soon the scent of nourishing meat broth began to fill the air.

"We rest now, eat, sleep. Tomorrow, maybe reach Pettervil."

"Where's that?"

"Two days from city. Maybe more, if storm and snow."

"You will be well rewarded when we get there."

Eir grinned. "I know." He glanced toward the door, now covered with a wool mantle to block the cold wind. "Maybe sleigh?"

"Maybe. We have to get there first."

"We get. Now go to sleep."

Even under the improved conditions of travel, Askepott was almost as tired as she had been the first night. Despite the unforgiving stone floor and the inadequate mattress her spare clothing made, she promptly went to sleep and did not awaken until morning.

Eir petitioned to take over some of the driving task, and, reluctantly, Askepott exchanged seats with him. He proved to be a much better driver than she expected, and she suspected that Rødiger had allowed him to drive the sleigh around the village. No wonder he had volunteered to come with her.

On his urging, they bypassed Pettervil, just glimpsing the town walls at a distance.

"Too much stay, and want coin also," Eir explained. "But know where we are now."

Askepott thought about a purse in her carry-sack, containing an assortment of red and rare green stones. "I have no coins. I'd have liked— Never mind. Let's go on."

The farther south they progressed, the easier the journey became. Only one storm delayed them. For the last legs, they kept the Icy Sea within sight and traveled down the coastline. There were no *seters* here, so Eir built double lean-tos out of fragrant tree branches. These branches, covering the ground, made a bed so comfortable that Askepott overslept two mornings in a row.

"I am feeling my age," she grumbled, not thinking Eir was within earshot.

"Mighty much age, too," he said, grinning. "That good. Age brings wise."

"If you say so. How much farther now?"

"One day."

"Then let's get started."

True to Eir's prediction, next day the walls of Cyornasberg came into view, and a more welcome sight Askepott could not imagine. Normally she would not have sought out a city this size, but the present circumstances dictated that she now make it her home—if the NordornKing and NordornQueen would have her.

When they reached the city gates, she unloaded her bundle of belongings, leaving behind the pots and jars and packages of food the Fridians had provided.

"You need ice-sleigh now?"

Askepott hid a smile. Eir was completely transparent, anything but cunning in his desire for the magical conveyance. Holger had undoubtedly come into ownership by theft; it was only justice that he lose it by theft as well. Her conscience did not pinch her in the slightest.

"No. It is yours," she told him. "I don't have anything else to pay you with."

"No need more pay. I take. Make me big man in village!"

"Do you have enough food for your journey back?"

"We not eat all. Enough left over."

"Then travel safely."

"And fast, too!"

With that, grinning hugely, Eir hopped into the sleigh, kicked it into action, and was off in a cloud of snow particles.

Askepott lingered only long enough to see him out of sight.

She hoped he would not come to grief if ever Holger learned of his part in the ice-sleigh's disappearance.

Then, laden with her bundle of belongings and uncertain of how she would be received, she entered the city gate and made her way toward the imposing Castle of Fire and Ice.

Sixteen

Trying to remember not to gape like a yokel, Mikkel followed Petra through the streets of the City 'Neath the Waves. Everywhere, other Maidens greeted Petra gladly, and even followed her, touching her and chattering among themselves as they made their way toward the center of the city. All wore flowing white robes, some belted with gem-set silver chains, others with colored sashes. All went barefoot, their little feet pattering softly on the warm stone.

Overhead, Mikkel could see a transparent crystal dome, supported by towers that looked to be made out of stone lacework. Outside the dome, fish swam and an occasional ice-shark came into view knifing through the water, seeking food. Because of the twi-night above, the water was dark. The interior of the dome was lit with what looked to Mikkel like smooth polished pieces of bone firmly anchored in holders attached to the lacy towers. These bones emitted a strange glowing light, waxing and waning as people passed by.

From time to time Mikkel observed a rock-lace circular wall, behind which thick mud bubbled and gave off steam that smelled of brimstone when one approached close enough. Rising from the mud were stone tubes, much smaller than the one they had used to get here. Each of these tubes was capped and stone pipes had been attached to gather most of the heat emitted, very likely to be transferred elsewhere. Mikkel realized that this City 'Neath the Waves must be built in the cauldron of a sleeping underwater fire mountain. These stone fumaroles, rising from the unstable subsurface, had to be the city's method of heating.

"Where are we going?" he asked.

"To the Rock-Palace. It's where I live. I told you I was a princess."

The palace was small by Nordorn standards. It looked to have been created from the same kind of clear crystal as the city's dome, and great mirrored panels flanked the doorway. Inside, graceful curtains provided privacy when needed. The walls were set with white gems that gave off a glowing iridescence in the light of the bones.

More Rock-Maidens, evidently having received the news of Petra's return, came rushing out of the palace to greet her. They enveloped her in loving arms, cooing and laughing and petting her hair, her hands, her face, speaking in a language Mikkel did not know. Some of them looked at Mikkel curiously, but then ignored him. He wondered what he was supposed to do now, besides stand by and be silent.

One Rock-Maiden stood a little apart. When the crush of greeting had ebbed, she bowed to Petra, and then the two clasped each other in their arms. Apparently, they were close friends. Perhaps this one had ruled in Petra's absence.

Petra extricated herself from the other's embrace and spoke to the Maidens in their language. As one, they turned to stare at Mikkel and he knew she was telling them of his part in her rescue. Shyly, they approached him and began touching his hair, hands, and face as well. Then, with muffled giggles, they fled back to their Princess and regarded him with questioning eyes.

"You will live in the palace, in a guest suite," Petra told him. "You will be fed and washed, and given suitable clothing. Then we will see what is to become of you."

"I had been wondering."

The deep tones of his voice sent the Maidens into more fits of giggles, barely stifled behind their hands.

"Be patient, Mikkel. They have never seen an Outsider Man before."

It was on the tip of Mikkel's tongue to say that he was still considered a boy, but when he saw himself revealed head to foot in the mirrored walls of the Rock-Palace, he could not claim that status and be believed. He was tall, perhaps even taller than Holger, and wide of shoulder. His muscles lay smooth on his frame, speaking of strength. His hair was unkempt and a red beard covered his chin.

Tentatively, he touched it, then tugged on it. It was real, all right. When they had left the village, it had been but a few hairs. They must have been longer on their way than he thought.

He allowed the Maidens to lead him into the palace and a bathing room where hot water in plenty awaited him. By signs and gestures, he indicated that he wanted to bathe himself, alone. Giggling, the Maidens trailed out and left him, though by the expressions on their faces and the tone of their chattering to each other, they clearly thought his preference very silly.

He investigated what the room had to offer. There were thick towels in plenty, and a dish made from a big shell filled with pieces of some soft substance that worked up into foamy suds that cleansed his skin. Over the tub was a shelf of crystal flasks filled with what he discovered to be perfumed oils of varying scents. He left those alone. Experimentally, he tried another liquid that also foamed, and washed his hair with it. It smelled good but not like perfume, faintly reminiscent of fruit and fresh grass. He ducked under the water again and again, enjoying the feeling of being thoroughly clean. Younkers in Holger den Forferdelig's village seldom had the time to bathe adequately. A quick dip and splash, and it was back to work for them.

Reluctantly he emerged from the bath and dried off, using several of the thick towels that seemed to be made of coarsely woven silk. Looking into a hand mirror, he applied a carved ivory comb to his hair. He attempted to put it into braids, but made a botch of it; he had never had to do this for himself until he had been taken captive.

Still wrapped in a towel, he followed the Rock-Maidens who showed him to what must be his sleeping room. There he found fresh clothing made of white snow-thistle silk waiting for him. His old clothing had been taken away, perhaps to be cleaned or, perhaps, copied. Rock-Maidens were, he surmised, unfamiliar with the clothing of Outsiders; the garments they gave him consisted of flowing robes, rather than tunics and trews, with a silk sash for a belt.

As soon as he got his robe over his head, Maidens entered the room. Despite his protests, they combed and braided his hair, working pearls and iridescent white stones into the braids. Mikkel tried to remember where he had seen the like of these gems before. Somewhere, there had been a bracelet. It swam before his eyes. A slim blonde woman wore it. He could almost remember who she was. . . . Another Maiden trimmed his beard neatly.

Before they finished, he discovered that he was ravenous. More Rock-Maidens waited outside his chamber and he made a gesture—fingers toward mouth, rubbing his stomach—that they immediately interpreted correctly. They led him at once to another part of the palace where a table of covered dishes awaited. Petra entered the room almost at the same time. She, too, was dressed in long white silk robes. She still wore the green-glass jewel, along with bracelets and necklaces of iridescent white stones like those of his adornments, translucent and shot with rainbows. Her belt and tiara were made of the same kind of stone.

"You do look like a princess," Mikkel told Petra.

"You are no proper Rock-Man," she responded, "because no Rock-Man is so slender and handsome. You are now Ridder Rødskjegg—the Knight of the Red Beard. It is very becoming."

Taken aback, Mikkel could only stammer a denial.

"Rock-Men," Petra continued as she took the covers off various dishes and began filling her plate, "are big, ugly brutes. They're much more, well, rocklike than the women. They are objectionable enough that we prefer to live well apart from them."

Mikkel was filling his own plate from platters of broiled fish and small whole lobsters. A bowl of shrimp, still in the shells, came in for its share of attention as well. He held one by the tail and squeezed the meat into his mouth.

"You're leaving the best part," Petra said. "We eat clams and crab, lobster and shrimp, shells and all." Suiting action to words, she picked up a shrimp and crunched it between her teeth. Then she smiled at his reaction. "You're lucky we didn't serve you chunks of stone and see you try to eat it!"

"Oh, now you're just joking with me," Mikkel said.

She laughed, a silvery sound. "It is easy to do."

The two moved to a small stone table, in a little alcove. Mikkel applied himself to his food with a good appetite. It was a welcome change from the usual diet of stew and porridge that, though undoubtedly nutritious and as tasty as Askepott could devise, nevertheless had become very monotonous.

As if she had read his thought, Petra said, "Sometimes we make stews of fish and eels und certain seaweed. I have missed this, very much."

"How did you come to be in Holger den Forferdelig's power?"

"I was out searching for the plants that make the silk—"

"Snow-thistles, is what we call them."

"Yes. Well, I got separated from my Maidens, and Holger and his men chanced on me. I tried to run but they were too fast and too strong for me. The iron they carried hurt me and made me weak. They captured me and Holger took my royal jewel." She touched her pendant. "I told him it was only sea-green glass—you remember the song—but it is a rare gem. We find it occasionally where it has been belched up by a fire mountain."

"Farther south, we find the same, only the gems are red."

"Mostly the ones here are red as well. Green gems are more highly prized."

"What are those white stones?"

"We call them snow-gems."

"I once saw a bracelet carved out of a big piece of it."

"The one who wore it is very fortunate. Snow-gems are very valuable."

"I think that bracelet had some magical powers."

"Such jewels often do."

"Who was the Maiden who greeted you so affectionately?"

"Hild. You would call her my sister."

As they ate and chatted about trivialities, Mikkel wondered about Petra's remark earlier about finding what to do with him. The Rock-Maidens had been all cordiality and helpfulness and full of charming giggles up until now, but he had a feeling that could change in the blink of an eye.

Rock-Maidens cleared away their dishes and removed the un-eaten food, and gave them a hot beverage that Petra said was brewed of certain sea plants.

"Tomorrow," Petra said, "there will be a great celebration throughout the city. You will be a part of it as well."

"Then have you decided what is to be done with me?" he asked.

"Yes, if you agree."

"I have to know what you have in mind first."

Close by the ocean wall of the City 'Neath the Waves, lay a sunken ship. Preserved in the icy northernmost waters, it had suffered little decay. Only the hole in the hull, beneath the waterline where some horned sea creature had attacked, showed the cause for the vessel's demise. Otherwise the ship was intact. Masts, spars, rigging, sails were all still in place, if tattered from the motion of the tides. If the vessel could be raised and its hull repaired, even as obsolete as the design was, it could once more ride the waves as proudly as when it was first launched.

Until now, the Rock-Maidens had only gazed at the vessel, enjoying its presence as a decoration outside their walls. But then their Princess was abducted, and by a man who sailed in such a ship. On land, they could never be his equal, let alone defeat him. At sea, however, it might be a different story.

The Rock-Maidens hated Holger den Forferdelig with a passion such as they had never previously known. He had stolen their Princess from them, had tortured her with the cold iron torque, the marks from which she still bore on her beautiful neck. Now, with Mikkel's presence among them, they might challenge Holger on the open sea.

"But I know nothing of sailing," Mikkel objected.

"You will come to it," Petra reassured him.

"Why not ask Rock-Men for their help?"

Petra laughed scornfully. "Do you know aught of Nisse? Some call them gnomes?"

"I have heard of them. They are tiny creatures who live in gardens."

"Not so. In the land of the Wykenigs, the Nisse are large and strong and their main pastime is seeking out trolls to fight. They look like they have been chiseled, very roughly, out of rock. They have strength many times that of a man, can run faster than a snow elk, and have eyesight better than a hawk. Their manners are no better than trolls', though, and no Rock-Maiden will have anything to do with them, willingly. They are, however, the best gem-cutters and jewelers in existence, so we trade with them from time to time. We have to be on our guard then, for sometimes one of us disappears, a victim of what passes for love to one of them. At any rate, they can be no help to us. Our problem is not your skill or theirs, but the ship itself."

"How so?"

"There are iron nails and fittings. And neither Maidens nor Nisse can bear the touch or even the presence of iron."

"What has that got to do with me?"

"You can remove the iron. We can then replace it with wooden pegs, or stone fittings where there are now iron ones."

"Yes," Mikkel said slowly, "that might work. But we would still need new lines, new sails—"

"We will have them, all made of snow-thistle silk and stronger than any canvas. We Rock-Maidens discovered the secret of snow-thistle silk long ago, and some parts of the world are just now catching up with us."

"And what about the crew?"

"Rock-Maidens will crew the ship. And we will fight Holger den Forferdelig when we find him, and we will best him, too. There are few things that can seriously harm us. Here. Try to stab my hand." She held out a silver knife.

"No!"

"I promise you, I will not be harmed."

Reluctantly, he did as he was told. The knife just slid off her thick, smooth skin.

"We can be hurt by an iron arrowhead, but it cannot penetrate deeply. Our movements are slow in cold climes and in the presence of iron; we tolerate great heat but can melt in a fire mountain if we stay too long."

Mikkel had a sudden visual picture of a *Hnefa-Tafl* board, populated with living beings. He was the King, and occupied the center square. Rock-Maidens, dressed in white snow-thistle silk and armed with bows and alabaster-tipped arrows, guarded him in ranks and files from Wykenig Dark Attackers. Something that Holger had been in the habit of saying came to mind:

Who are the maids that fight weaponless around their lord, the fair ever sheltering and the dark ever attacking him?

It was madness, but a madness that just might work.

"Well," Mikkel said, "I suppose there is no harm in trying."

From the street, Askepott surveyed the Barbican Gate leading to the castle. She was uncertain of what she would do if the soldiers manning it kept her out. Therefore, she decided, she would approach with the air of someone who belonged in Cyornas Castle, and who was now returning. She got as far as the gatehouse before being challenged.

"State your business, woman," a guard said.

"Nothing that concerns you," Askepott returned sharply, with an assurance she did not really feel.

"Then you will not enter. Not until you give me a reason."

"It is my business and not yours. But I will say that Zazar and I are friends and it is she I have traveled many leagues to see."

"Madame Zazar, is it?" the guard said, visibly impressed. "Stay here and we will send word."

He showed her into what had to be a guardhouse, where other soldiers sat around a firepot, eating and drinking. They offered to share, and nothing loath, she accepted. And that is where Zazar found her, nearly an hour later, enjoying a hot drink laced with spirits and butter.

"I thought I was past being surprised!" she exclaimed. "How did you get here? And why? Not that you aren't welcome, for you are. But I don't understand."

"Nor could you be expected to," Askepott said. "I will explain all in good time."

"Then come with me. There are introductions to be made, and, if I am not mistaken, good-byes to be said to the Duchess Ysa, whom I have cordially invited to return to her little duchy where she can lord it over everyone and there's none to object to her regal ways."

Heavy snow had begun falling and the two hurried to get inside the castle walls.

"Maybe she won't return just yet," Askepott said, puffing a little, "and it just might be that we need her."

Zazar paused and stared at the other Wysen-wyf. "I can't think of a single reason why."

"I can, and that's one more thing we must discuss."

"Well, we're here, so come inside."

They climbed the castle's stone steps to the doors leading to the vestibule just off the Great Hall, and entered.

"Here, you, Rols," Zazar said, and the man immediately paused in his errand.

"Madame?"

"This is Steinvor Askepott. She's—she's a kind of sister. Take her belongings up to my tower and put them outside the door. We'll dispose of them later."

Askepott looked a question at Zazar.

"Oh, you needn't be concerned. Nobody in the NordornLand would dare meddle in my things, and that means yours are safe as well."

Rols took up Askepott's bundle and would have added her carry-sack only she didn't allow it. "Be lost without it," she muttered.

"I will take you first to Gaurin and Ashen, and then upstairs we'll go."

"Always good to have the host and hostess aware of your presence. Lead on."

Zazar kept the introductions to a minimum. Askepott was uncertain of how to behave—should she bow? Should she attempt a curtsy? She took her cue from Zazar and nodded her head, a gesture that was returned gravely.

"We are happy to have one of Madame Zazar's kindred come to visit," the NordornKing told her.

"May we hope that the visit will be a lengthy one?" said Ashen NordornQueen.

Zazar laughed. "From the looks of the weather outside, yes. None of us, save the huntsmen, will be apt to go anywhere any time soon."

"And shall I ask Ayfare to prepare quarters for you, Madame Steinvor?" the Queen inquired solicitously.

"Oh, Askepott will do, Your Majesty. And I'll snark down anywhere."

"She'll share my tower, if she's willing," Zazar said. "My bedroom is big, room enough for half a dozen soldiers. We'll hang a curtain down the middle, for privacy. We'll make do quite well."

"I will have another bed brought up there for you."

"Thank you, Your Majesty."

"Then shall we expect to see you at meat tonight?" the King asked. "We would like to get to know one of Zazar's friends."

"What he means is, I have never confessed to having a friend," Zazar said with more than a trace of sarcasm. "Yes, we'll be at meat. All the world's treasures couldn't pay me to miss the look on Ysa's face when she learns that there's another Wysen-wyf in the Castle of Fire and Ice!"

"Well, this is it," Zazar said, when they had reached the top of the stairs.

Askepott's bundle of belongings lay by the door, just as she had instructed. She picked it up, opened the door, and the two of them entered just as a couple of the castle servants arrived with the new bed, bedclothes, the dividing curtain, and a rod to hang it from. Quickly and efficiently they attached the rod to another corbel and supported the other end on the main rod. Then they hung the curtain, set up the bed in the sleeping area, put the coverings on it, and departed as if eager to get out of the tower chambers.

"Oh, this is like home!" Askepott exclaimed. She looked around at the shelves, the pots and jars, even the stack of reed mats. "What a wonderful, comfortable place you have."

"It's half yours, as long as you want to stay. What possessed you to leave Holger's village, anyway?"

"Brew me some tea, and I'll tell you."

Presently, over steaming mugs of Zazar's personal mixture, Askepott related the whole story—her theory of why Mikkel had experienced such an unnatural growth surge, his disappearance with the *krigpus* and the crazy girl who was always singing about green glass, Holger's rage, Askepott's certain knowledge that Gunnora would harm her, even kill her, if she stayed.

"What a story!" Zazar exclaimed, when the other had finished. "And what do you think has happened to Mikkel?"

"I can only hope that he found some safe refuge, perhaps with an enemy of Holger's," Askepott said. "Beyond that, I cannot say. Perhaps, with the two of us trying, we can find some indication of where he might be."

"I do not think he is dead. I would have felt it."

"You have a kettle. Do you perform the Ritual of Asking?"

"Of course. But I use certain, um, ingredients and my supply is currently low."

Askepott dug into her carry-sack and brought out a jar sealed with wax. She pulled the wax away and spilled a few threads onto the table between them. The jar was full nearly to the brim. "Ingredients like this?"

"I should have known you'd be familiar with them. How did you come by such a good supply?"

"Let's just say I have sources and perhaps can call on them even this far south. The Ritual of Asking is what told me the extent of my danger, and the reason. It's that dragon-tooth bracelet."

"The one that the Duchess Ysa is all a-twitter to learn the secret of." Zazar sighed.

"She's the one with the book-magic, isn't she."

"Yes."

"Unappealing as the prospect is, we might need her."

"I'd rather not. You don't know the woman; I do."

"I'd use Gunnora herself, if I could, and if it would save Mikkel and put that horrid bracelet out of harm's reach. Where is it, by the way?"

For answer, Zazar arose and went to the shelf, moved a couple of jars aside, and retrieved the bundle that held the item under discussion. "This is a very insecure hiding place, but the best I could think of until something better cropped up."

Askepott glanced around the room. The implements of a

Wysen-wyf's trade were everywhere. Zazar couldn't have chosen a better spot, even on this temporary basis. "I wouldn't worry about it too much. At least not yet. Put it back and let me stow my goods before we go back down those stairs again to dinner."

True to his word, Gaurin ordered that the two Wysen-wyves be seated directly across from their chairs at the High Table where he and Ashen could talk with them. One by one, the members of the Court came to be presented to the newcomer before taking their seats as well. Askepott found herself more than impressed by the deference showed to Zazar and, by extension, to her.

The NordornPrince, Bjaudin, occupied the position of honor, to the King's immediate right. A dark-haired man, dressed in the Court color, dark blue, sat at the Queen's left. This, Zazar informed Askepott, was Duke Einaar, and he and the Prince did most of the work involved in managing the kingdom. Next to the Duke sat his Duchess, a frail young woman who seemed very shy. A woman well along in years was placed next to the Nordorn-Prince. Zazar identified her as the Duchess of Iselin, Ysa, the one they would most likely need to unlock the secret of the bracelet. Then came the powerful counts, Svarteper and Tordenskjold, whose positions as Lord High Marshal and Admiral-General dictated that they live in the city, if not permanently in the castle. A parade of other nobles followed in close order.

Names without faces, faces without names. "I am not used to this," she muttered to Zazar, "all this deference. At Holger's village, I was just Old Askepott, a little soft in the head, good for nothing but running his household."

Zazar laughed shortly. "Just wait until someone asks you to dance."

Askepott pulled back a little and stared at Zazar. "What?"

"You heard me. They're great for dancing to 'The Song' around here."

"Well, I don't know how and I don't propose to learn, either."

Zazar laughed again. "That's what I said. But one does not say 'no' to Gaurin NordornKing."

"Then I'll plead fatigue when the music begins."

"Good plan. Too bad we're here at the High Table. We'll have to nod and bob our way out through the crowds. But everybody knows what a testy old crone I am anyway so we won't be hindered. Royance isn't here and Gaurin's leg is bothering him."

"Royance?"

"An old, old friend. He married recently after being a widower for many years. . . ."

The two Wysen-wyves continued to chat quietly through the meal—real meat, Askepott noted, and bread almost as good as what she made back in what used to be her home. No *björr* but a choice between ale—which seemed to be a paler, lighter *björr*— and hot wine mixed with snowberry juice.

"You've got us beat with this, at least," Askepott said as she drained her goblet. "We have never thought to cultivate snowberries to make them taste better."

"Both our cultures have much to share with each other, if only the day will come when they do not consider themselves enemies." Zazar wiped her platter with a piece of bread and stuffed it into her mouth. "Here come the musicians. Better pretend you can't keep your eyes open another minute. We'll get up to the tower and I'll give you a tot of *brandewijn*. I brew it myself. It'll help you sleep and tomorrow we'll start fresh to unravel the mystery of that *item* and how to find Mikkel and bring him home safely."

With the *brandewijn* warm in her belly and the fire in the main portion of the tower room banked for the night, Askepott was ready for sleep. The sound of snoring was already coming from the other side of the curtain—Zazar and Weyse, curled up together.

Despite the wall hangings, the shutters over the windows let enough cold air into the portion of the tower set aside as a sleeping chamber that she could see her breath. A chest sat against the wall, lid open, and inside was her bundle of goods, untouched. That was good. Tomorrow she would unpack it and arrange things to suit herself.

To her astonishment, she discovered that these people actually wore special clothing to bed, and also little hats that tied under the chin. Well, silly or not, she would go along with their custom. The night garment was thin but generously cut; it seemed to be made of a variety of snow-thistle silk.

More wonders awaited. Instead of a bed of honest straw covered with a blanket, she saw she was expected to sleep on a kind of cushion atop the straw. It seemed to be made of blankets such as she was used to, though of a finer weave, and stuffed with something soft. Feathers? Perhaps. Another cushioned cover awaited, turned down neatly. This one was stitched in a lozenge design. With a certain disdain for these soft people living in what they called the NordornLand and the way they pampered themselves, Askepott crawled into the bed and covered herself up.

To her surprise, she discovered how chilled she had been when her own warmth was returned to her almost instantly, even to her feet. Her feet were always cold but now even they were getting warm. The silly cushion turned out to be amazingly comfortable, holding her as if cradled, and the cover acted to hold in the warmth so that she would not shiver no matter how cold the chamber became.

Perhaps, she thought, *this isn't as ridiculous as I first thought.* And then she pulled the cover up to her chin and slept without dreaming until the morning awakened her.

Fascinated, Mikkel watched as Rock-Maidens built a crystal bubble surrounding the sunken ship. As far as Mikkel could tell, they simply pulled the city dome out and stretched it until the edges met, encompassing the wrecked vessel. Then they removed the water from the bubble, leaving the ship to dry out enough so that the necessary repairs and modifications could be made.

When Mikkel entered the bubble through the door that sealed behind him, he discovered that the air inside was considerably cooler than that inside the city. This, one of the Rock-Maidens who had a smattering of the common tongue told him, was to keep the ship happy and healthy.

"Ship has been cold very long," she told him. "It must like cold. Too warm, make ship sick."

It made sense, as much as anything in this underwater existence made sense. Though he had no knowledge or experience in how such things worked, he was nonetheless impressed with the way the Rock-Maidens—or, perhaps, Rock-Men in some long-ago period of amity—had harnessed the fire cauldron that their city was located in and made it yield up its warmth without destroying everything in its vicinity.

When he tried to find out how it all worked, all he got were blank looks as if he were slightly mad to ask.

"This is how it always has been," they would tell him. "We have always had the heat pipes and the lights from magical bones. Why do you question this? Is it not enough for you that these things exist?"

And so, though his curiosity was not satisfied, he stopped asking. More important matters now occupied him, for actual work had begun on the ship.

Mikkel reasoned that, since ships were built from the keel up, he should start with the keel and work up as well with the replacements and modifications.

He was pleased to discover that most of the ship's hull had been put together with wooden pegs instead of nails. This meant that the ship was even older than he thought, and that his chore wasn't going to be as difficult as he had feared.

In what had once been a weapons locker, besides iron-tipped arrows and spears, he found a copper tube and missiles carefully stored in a watertight box—signal rockets, undisturbed for possibly centuries. They might come in handy, so he set the tube aside to be cleaned and returned the box to the locker. The iron weapons he removed personally, to be replaced with those the Rock-Maidens favored.

As he explored, he found some sad remnants—bones of sailors who had gone down with their ship. The Maidens carefully removed the bones for burial in the sand outside the crystal walls.

One of these sets of bones had, apparently, belonged to the ship's carpenter, for Mikkel discovered them in a small locker where various tools of the carpentry trade had been stored. Some of these—hammers, axes—could be reclaimed and put to use, but the best find was the long-dead carpenter's chest. Watertight, as was prudent for the preservation of these tools, the chest yielded plumbs and levels, cord and chalk, spare nails and a roll of putty, and, best of all, an iron pry-bar.

Rock-Maidens, politely but carefully avoiding the iron, worked with him to locate places where, here and there, repairs to the ship had involved using ancient iron nails. He pried them up with the iron bar and the Maidens replaced them with either more wooden pegs or stone nails they precisely shaped to fit.

Within a week, he had reached the deck of the ship, where the work of replacing iron increased sharply. Every block, every stanchion, every place where iron lurked had to be searched out and stone or hardened wood substituted. At the same time, Maidens replaced the broken planks of the hull. These were overlapped in such a way that caulk was almost unnecessary. When the Maidens had finished, the repairs scarcely showed, and would be completely invisible once the hull had been painted.

From somewhere in the dim places of his memory where he realized he could not go, Mikkel recognized that this ship was of a type earlier than those he had seen—someplace. The hull was squat, offering more cargo space and better living quarters for the crew on long voyages. The rigging was not as complicated as he had first feared, being a lateen rig—triangular fore-and-aft sails set on a long, sloping yardarm—on two masts. This, he thought, would allow the ship to take advantage of a wind from the side of the vessel.

As he and his iron-locating Rock-Maidens cleared a portion of the ship, others came with pumice and seawater to cleanse away what residue remained from the vessel's underwater sojourn. Eventually the day came when the Rock-Maidens applied a coat of paint made with ground white nacre from certain shells, and prepared a place for the ship's name to go on her stern. After that, it was only a day's work to put up the sails and lash them in place with lines spun of thick snow-thistle fiber.

Mikkel called Petra to come and admire what the Rock-Maidens and he had accomplished. She strode to the work area, her long cloak swirling around her.

"It is truly beautiful," she said. "What is her name?"

"I thought you should have the honor of naming her."

"Well, then." She thought a moment, her brows drawn together a little. "*Snow Gem*. That's what she will be called. *Snow Gem*. And we will take her out as soon as possible."

"But a crew—"

She smiled. "You have been busy here and do not know what I have been doing in the meantime." She gestured to one of the Rock-Maidens and said something in their own language.

Within seconds, a group of Maidens, all clad in iridescent shell breastplates over brief tunics and carrying bows and spears, ranged themselves behind Petra. One of them, Hild, loosed the cape from around the Princess's shoulders and she, too, stood revealed in fighter's garb.

"Your crew, and your warriors," she told him, smiling. "Walkyrye."

Mikkel examined the arrowheads and the spearheads, all formed from hard white alabaster. "This is truly a marvel," he said. "Yes, as soon as *Snow Gem* has her name properly applied, we will take her out for a sea trial."

Seventeen

*J*n Cyornas Castle, Zazar and Askepott were trying to find a way to gain Ysa's cooperation in unlocking the secret of the dragon-tooth bracelet.

"I must have my books," the Duchess repeated stubbornly.

"Aren't there books enough in the Fane?"

"Esander won't let me have access to them."

"Well, I can remedy that," Zazar said decisively. "I'll be back in a little while. You two can get acquainted while I'm gone."

She left Askepott and Ysa staring at one another uncertainly while she descended from the tower and made her way across the inner ward to the Fane, where Esander the Good could be found.

"Yes, I do have some books the Duchess borrowed when we were trying to find the best way of dealing with the Arikarin when it should arrive at Cyornas Castle. She forgot to give them back, and I had to go to her and petition that they be returned to the Fane."

"Where are they now?" Zazar asked.

A smile crossed Esander's features. "When my lady Duchess came back here the first time, after vowing never to return to the castle, I put them under lock and key. There they remain."

"I need them now."

"For what purpose?"

Zazar was reluctant to tell the priest that she wished for Ysa to put her hands on the disputed volumes again, but saw no way to avoid it.

"No!" Esander exclaimed. "This is much too dangerous. My lady Duchess may do as she pleases in Iselin, but here she must not be allowed to work her spells!"

"Please believe me," Zazar told him, "there is more danger than you know here in Cyornas. And Ysa may be the key to disarming it. It has been this way before; she worked with me to defeat the Great Foulness. She can be capable of doing as much again."

"The Great Foulness has not returned?"

"No, but his spawn—or as close as he could come to siring something to live after him—is abroad and we must find a way to thwart the evil."

"And you need the books of magic."

"We do." Zazar stared at the priest, willing him to give over, just this once. "We must do it to save Mikkel."

The mention of Mikkel's name tipped the balance.

"Then you shall have the books. But you must also promise to return them once—once Mikkel is safe again."

"They will be returned as soon as possible, by me."

The priest opened the locked cabinet and began taking the volumes out one by one. Zazar wrapped them in her shawl for transport back up the stairs. They made a sizable bundle.

"Will you need help, Madame Zazar?"

"I can manage. And I'd rather that nobody else knew anything of what's going on."

"I understand."

Despite her protestations, he carried the package of books across the ward, into the castle, and as far as the door that led to the tower staircase. There he handed the package to her and she began the long, arduous climb.

She was puffing and completely out of breath by the time she reached her door. She paused a moment, listening. No voices raised. Maybe that was a good sign.

She managed to open the door wide enough to get an elbow in and pull it open so she could enter. Askepott immediately jumped up to help her. Ysa, Zazar noted, stayed where she was, in the chair closest to the fire.

"All right," she said as she dumped the books onto her worktable, "here they are. Now show us what you can do."

"I can't say that I like your tone," Ysa replied. Nevertheless, she arose from the chair and moved to the table where she began sorting the volumes by type and subject matter. Two books she set aside at once as being of no use in the present project. Three more she stacked in front of her. "These have to do with summoning, and if I remember correctly, there is a passage in one of them that has a spell for bringing dragons out of the mist and into our world. Perhaps it can be modified—"

The Duchess, Zazar noted, had become more animated than she had seen her in quite some time with the prospect of working some inventive mischief. Almost, she regretted the necessity of bringing out the bracelet for Ysa to examine and, perhaps, to say a spell over. Nevertheless, making sure that Ysa was too engrossed in her reading to notice what she was doing, she retrieved the little bundle from its hiding place and put it on another shelf.

Presently, Ysa looked up from her book and closed it, holding her place with her finger. "I need the bracelet now," she said. "But there's more. You and I have different magics; we learned that long ago. I must assume that Askepott has your kind of magic. I also need the kind of magic Ashen possesses."

"Ashen is not well."

"I know that, Zazar. Nevertheless, I—*we* need the magic that is inborn. I suspect that Elin has it as well. The weather has abated, for the moment. We could all journey to Iselin and enlist Elin's help in solving the problem. Or, better, bring Elin here."

"Iselin?" Askepott asked. "Where is it?"

"A few leagues distant. It is my duchy."

The kettle and the castings from the Weavers' Web had revealed to Zazar that the child Ashen had been carrying at the time she and Gaurin had faced the Mother Ice Dragon would also be affected by the magic that had enveloped her in a blazing fire. "Without fire there can be no Ash," the canting pun of her family motto declared, made manifest in that desperate moment. And then Zazar had told Ashen how unclear it had been as to whether this was for good or for ill. She had not been exactly candid with Ashen; her health and well-being had been far too fragile to encompass the indications that Elin would be ever drawn to the darker side of Power.

"I'm not sure of the wisdom of letting Elin substitute for her mother," Zazar said.

Ysa airily waved Zazar's objection away. "Oh, don't be such a stick. She'll be glad to help. After all, it was she who brought the bracelet to my attention in the first place."

"My point exactly." Zazar stared intently at Ysa, as if willing her to acknowledge an evident truth. "The Princess filched it from her mother's jewel chest. She is far too interested in this article of Power."

"But—" Whatever her rebuttal, it was never spoken. Ysa sat quietly, obviously thinking hard. Then she straightened up, removed her finger from the place she had marked in her book, and folded both hands over the volume. "Elin very likely does have the magical ability that we will need for this undertaking. But she is young, untried and—" She marshaled her thoughts, choosing her words carefully. "Elin does not have the experience necessary to ensure that she does not unknowingly use her abilities for less-than-noble purposes. Therefore, we will neither journey to Iselin nor send for the Princess but will call upon Ashen instead. In spite of her frail health, I think she will be able to muster enough strength to do what must be done."

"And that is . . . ?" Askepott inquired.

Ysa regarded both Wysen-wyves very seriously. "The references are clear. The bracelet is what you may have already surmised—the avatars of six dragons of varying attributes, abilities, and wickedness, plus those of three extremely powerful users of magic from the dimness of the past. If the proper spells are said over these avatars, they can be summoned from wherever they have been during the long years since the bracelet was made by the same smiths who created the Dragon Blade, and put for safekeeping into the Dragon Box. Surely, their reasoning went, the brave man who could wield the Dragon Blade, would be able to keep the secret of the Six Dragons safe."

Zazar moved a little, and found that her bones creaked. To hear what she had only suspected, said so calmly and with such assurance, was unsettling. She glanced at Askepott and knew that she was having much the same reaction.

"Unfortunately," Ysa continued, "the man who wielded the Dragon Blade cannot defend the bracelet against those who would unlock its secret to the detriment of our entire world. Nor can the woman who wielded the same blade. But her abilities, joined with ours, may prove enough to harness it or, failing that, to destroy it. So that is what we must do, when we can."

Just a few moments ago, Ysa seemed to have been set on freeing this Power and using it herself. Zazar knew she was still smarting, somewhere in the depths of her being, from her failure to wrest control of the NordornLand and rule it herself, if from behind a proxy. From where, Zazar wondered, had this burst of selfless nobility arisen? The same place, she told herself, where Ysa had found the strength and wisdom to rule Rendel so long and so well for the most part. Yes, a few lapses along the way, but without these lapses Ysa would not have been Ysa.

"Is the bracelet truly as powerful as you say?" Askepott asked.

"Perhaps even more so," Ysa said.

"Then no wonder Gunnora the Golden coveted it above all other artifacts."

"This Gunnora. She is the one of whom you spoke? The remnant of the Great Foulness?"

"One and the same."

"Then whatever befalls, the bracelet must not go into her hands."

"As long as there is breath in my body," Zazar declared. "I just wish—"

"Wish what?"

"That I could actually see Mikkel. Know whether it goes well or ill for him."

"Once I had a little flying servant," Ysa said. "Visp. But the means for creating another are now vanished."

"Visp, eh?" Askepott said, interested. "How did it work?"

"It appeared at my command, flew where I sent it, saw what there was to see. Then it returned to me; I looked into its eyes and it showed me what it had discovered."

"Handy," Askepott commented, "but clumsy compared to—"

"To what?"

"To what one of Holger's captives, a long time ago, claimed she could do."

"Tell us," Zazar urged. She arose, ignoring the creaking in her bones, and moved toward the fire where she poured a little *brandewijn* into a pitcher and mixed it with plain snowberry juice and hot water. She filled three goblets and, on consideration, added more *brandewijn* to the one intended for Ysa.

"Well," Askepott said, sipping the hot mixture, "this was a woman who didn't stay with Holger long. She was well connected with a wealthy family who paid Holger his ransom and then some. Before she left, though, we became acquainted. She said she could recognize a Wysen-wyf when she met one, though she had only book-magic, like the Duchess here."

Zazar glanced at Ysa, wondering how she would take the implied slight, but she was staring at Askepott, rapt.

"Anyway," Askepott continued, "when Holger let her go, he made her leave behind everything but the clothes she wore—all her jewels, all her finery, all her writings. Gunnora got the jewels and other fripperies, but I saved her documents before they could go into the fire—or into Gunnora's hands."

"And?" Zazar prompted, hardly daring to hope.

"I brought them with me." Askepott drained her goblet. "There's nothing to say that they contain the spell to create the Ritual of Seeing, but there's nothing to say they don't, either. I'll go get them."

As Askepott disappeared behind the curtain marking the sleeping area, Zazar and Ysa stared at each other. With a trembling hand, Ysa raised her goblet to her lips.

"I could wish for something a little stronger," she murmured.

"I think you'll find that is quite strong enough," Zazar replied. "In fact, I'd advise you to be cautious."

For answer, Ysa took a generous mouthful. Her eyes immediately teared and, by sheer bravado, she managed to keep herself from coughing. "Yes," she said when she could speak again, "I see what you mean. It is quite—effective."

Askepott returned with a bundle in her hand. They were obviously several documents of varying sizes, all rolled up together and tied with a ribbon. "Here," she said, handing the roll to Ysa. "You know this sort of thing. Open the packet."

The Duchess set her goblet aside and untied the ribbon. She unrolled the papers and spread them out on the table. The bundle had been tied so long it opened reluctantly and Ysa had to weigh down the corners so she could examine the contents. One by one she peeled away the layers.

"A spell to render spoiled food edible. Very handy. Here's one to let the user see through the backs of cards. Your lady," she said, glancing at Askepott, "was none too honest, it would seem." She returned to her task.

"Well, now. Here's one to render one's eyesight exceptionally sharp. Could this be the one she spoke to you about?"

"No. She was very specific. Said something about needing a bowl of clear water."

Ysa looked further, turning over a number of pages containing spells useful for everyday living or to enhance a woman's beauty. Then she paused, staring at the page. With a trembling hand, she reached for her goblet and took a deep swallow without coughing or blinking an eye.

"This is it. And it's something that we can do here, ourselves, with materials we have on hand. Quick, Zazar, bring me a bowl full of the freshest water you can find."

"I melt snow for my daily use. I will gather some fresh from the battlements."

"Good. While you are gone, with your permission I will find a suitable vessel for the water."

"Askepott will help you."

With that, Zazar, bucket in hand, left the warmth of her tower apartment, went down the stairs to the first landing, and thence onto the walkway between that tower and the next. New snow had fallen during the night and even now a few flakes drifted in the air. Nothing could be fresher or purer than this. As a precaution, she scrubbed out the already clean bucket and then filled it to the brim with the lightest and whitest snow she could find.

Askepott and Ysa had laid out a freshly washed earthenware bowl on a clean white cloth.

"Now we will melt the water and pour it into the bowl," Ysa said. "I will sit here. You two will stand on either side of me with your hands on my shoulders to lend me your strength while I say the words that will make Mikkel's image appear to us."

In Holger's stronghold, Lotte moved into Askepott's old quarters when it became apparent that she had left and was, in all probability, never returning.

Curious, the woman looked around the room. It bore all the marks of someone having made a hasty exit. A kettle lay abandoned, lying on its side in one corner. Elsewhere, Lotte found a pair of worn-out shoes, and a shawl with the fabric picked and rent. It was lying at the foot of the bed and Lotte thought it might have seen its final service keeping Askepott's feet warm. The bed itself, a simple wooden frame with rope supports and a straw mattress that seemed to bear a permanent imprint of Askepott's form, looked as if the old woman had just arisen from it. Lotte made a note to herself to have a fresh mattress brought in.

Otherwise, the room was quite serviceable or would be with a thorough cleaning. Bits of debris littered the floor, detritus of a hasty retreat. The one window was blocked with shutters, a sheet of oiled lambskin stretched over the opening, and curtains covering all so that most drafts were stopped before they could enter.

Yes, Lotte thought, *I can take Askepott's place despite her reputation for having magic. Life at the steading will go on, and soon Gunnora will be over her spell of temper and Holger likewise. It will be better for everyone once the ice breaks in Forferdelig Sound and he can be out in his ship again.*

Eighteen

Princess Elin regarded Tinka-Lillfot as she stood before her. The little woman seemed perfectly composed, her hands clasped lightly. On this day, at least, she had not attired herself in some grotesque mockery of Elin's or Ysa's gown but had, instead, chosen a plain green dress with matching coat that was actually quite becoming to her.

"Do you have anything to say to me?" Elin asked.

"No, Your Highness. You sent for me, and I am here."

"Very well. What I want to know is why, when I first came to Iselin, you held me up to ridicule."

"It is not my intention to ridicule, Your Highness, but to entertain. When, for example, I found that you did not enjoy it when I wore similar clothing to yours, I stopped doing it."

"Then you noticed my frowning."

"Of course, Your Highness. The ruler of Iselin, the Duchess Ysa, enjoyed my efforts; as you look to be the next ruler of Iselin and especially in the Duchess's absence, I altered my efforts to please you instead. Have I failed in this? Are you displeased?"

"Well," Elin replied reluctantly, "not displeased exactly. But I do not find you as entertaining as the rest of the Court does."

"Then I will strive to find other avenues of amusement that will please you."

"That will be acceptable."

"To that end, Your Highness, might I request that you give me a little dog?"

The question set Elin back. "A—a dog?"

"Yes, Your Highness. My Duchess took her little dog Alfonse with her when she journeyed to Cyornasberg. Without Alfonse, I feel I am not entertaining enough for anyone."

"You underrate yourself, Tinka-Lillfot. You sing and dance and tell stories. But you shall have a dog for your very own."

The little woman smiled for the first time since the interview began. "Thank you, Your Highness! I will train him to dance and jump through hoops and do other amusing tricks! You'll see."

With a wave of her hand, Elin dismissed the female fool. Who, she asked herself, would be most likely to have dogs or know of where a young dog could be found? Probably the Seneschal, Harald, or perhaps Baron Gustav. If neither of these could be of help she would ask Lord Lackel. He was unswervingly loyal to Duchess Ysa, but this was a small enough favor to ask of him.

She arose from Ysa's Chair of State, stepped down off the dais, and moved to one of the tall windows of the Presence Chamber where the interview with Tinka-Lillfot had taken place.

Outside the circle of warmth created by the fireplace and braziers near the Duchess's chair, the room was cold. The air was chilly enough that she could see her breath and the floor was frigid. Outside, it was snowing again. No chance of Granddam Ysa returning to Iselin until this harsh weather moderated. She pulled her fur-trimmed silk coat more closely around her.

The conversation with Tinka-Lillfot had left Elin curiously unsatisfied, though she had achieved what she sought—the female fool's pledge not to embarrass her. Then she realized what was wrong. She, Elin, had not given an order or even hinted at what had been troubling her; Tinka-Lillfot had been in charge of the entire interview right from the start and had even extracted the promise of being given a dog.

Should I be annoyed? Elin thought. Finally, she decided not to be, for she had gotten what she wanted.

I will call my ladies to go and embroider, she decided. *At least that is a small room, easy to keep warm.* The flower garden panel worked in wool thread was still only half done. Perhaps doing the snow roses wouldn't be so tedious this time.

In Zazar's tower room, the three women gathered around the bowl of melted snow. At the Duchess's signal, Zazar and Askepott placed their hands on Ysa's shoulders. Zazar could actually feel the Power flowing from her into Ysa as she invoked the Ritual of Seeing. She glanced at Askepott and knew she was experiencing the same thing.

Ysa murmured words under her breath, tentatively at first, and then with growing confidence. "Mikkel," she said clearly.

As the women watched, a vapor began forming over the bowl. Then it coalesced into an image as clear as if someone had carved a likeness. *But,* Zazar thought, *that cannot be the young Prince.* This person was fully grown, sporting a full red beard with pearls braided into it, and he seemed to be standing on the deck of a sailing vessel painted white. He was wearing a white cloak, possibly of wool, and it was lined with white fur. His hair blew in the wind.

"Your spell has gone awry," she told Ysa.

"I don't think so," Askepott said. "Remember I told you that Mikkel was experiencing unnatural growth, thanks to a spell put on him."

"Do not mention another name just yet," Ysa commanded. She reached out with both hands, appearing to caress the air around the image.

The miniature person turned. His lips moved, as if he spoke to someone as yet unseen. Another person, barely within the field created by the misty vapor from the bowl of water, moved in and then out of view. It was possibly a woman, clad in white. She turned her head as if something had briefly caught her attention.

"Well, I do not believe you have commanded the image of Prince Mikkel," Zazar declared. "This must be someone else."

The Duchess made a few more gestures. "Then name someone else you could recognize."

"Ashen."

The bearded man faded from view along with the mist from which his image had been formed. A new mist arose, and settled into an unmistakable likeness of the Nordorn Queen. She was sitting at a table with young Tjórvi, apparently helping him with one of his lessons. The boy's forehead was knotted with concentration and Ashen gently said something to him as she pointed to a page in the book he was laboring over. Tjórvi's face cleared immediately and he smiled as he began writing something down.

"Well?" Ysa said. "Are you satisfied?"

"Let me try," Askepott said.

Ysa nodded.

"Lotte," Askepott said clearly.

Again the image faded and vanished, as a new mist began to form. This time, a stout Wykenig woman emerged—two women, actually, as the Wykenig was apparently being lectured by another, a more slender woman with yellow hair who was dressed in blue snow-thistle silk.

"Is that—" Zazar hesitated, unwilling to name the powerful woman who craved the dragon-teeth bracelet. Ysa's spell might have unknown properties; perhaps Gunnora would be able to see through it and view them, even as they watched her, and then who knew how the security of the bracelet's hiding place would be compromised.

"It is."

"Well," Ysa said, looking back over her shoulder. "Are you satisfied now that the mist shows the true images?"

"Yes," Zazar admitted.

"I have someone I would see," Ysa said as she turned back toward the bowl. "Elin."

The Princess was sitting on an ornate chair that was much too big for her.

"That is my Chair of State," Ysa said. "What has the child been up to?"

Another person was in the range of vision, a very small woman dressed in green, with her back turned to the onlooker.

"That is Tinka-Lillfot, my female fool," Ysa told the others. "Whatever there is that prompted this meeting, I doubt that even the clever little Princess Elin will get the better of her."

Tinka-Lillfot turned, a smile apparent on her face before she vanished outside the scope of the viewing mist. Elin watched her go, a perplexed expression on her face.

"Show me the red-bearded man once more," Zazar said.

In the moment between the dissolving of one mist and the forming of another, Zazar had observed that the water level was very low; this final image would be the last until more pristine snow could be collected and melted.

Again, the mist showed the man on the deck of a ship. The woman who had been but barely glimpsed earlier now stood in the circle of his left arm; in his right hand he held a stone-tipped mace. Now Zazar could see clearly the Ash amulet on a golden chain, the one that had disappeared from Ashen's jewel box, around his neck. Another mystery solved.

The woman with Mikkel wore a short white tunic girded high. Her hair looked like it had been spun of translucent crystal filaments, and in her hand she held a bow. A quiver of white stone-tipped arrows was slung on her back. She wore a silver necklace set with a huge green stone. The stone and the man's hair and beard were the sole spots of color in the icy scene they were watching.

The woman looked up at the man and smiled. The planes of her face, Zazar saw, were sharply cut. They reflected light as if—With a peculiar thrill, Zazar realized she really was formed of a clear white stone, like alabaster.

She must be one of the fabled Rock-Maidens that were said to inhabit portions of the far north. But how had Mikkel come to be embroiled with them? And why were they on a ship? She wished that she could talk with this man, what Mikkel had become, for she had many, many questions to ask.

The images vanished; the bowl was now empty and dry.

"I saw Ashen's missing amulet. Now I know we have found Mikkel and observed what he has become—the captain of a peculiar white ship. We must show the people here what we have seen concerning him," Zazar said. "But first we will let Ashen know what we have discovered."

"My very thoughts," Ysa agreed. "Askepott, you will carry the earthenware bowl. Our efforts will be better if we can find a silver basin. Zazar, gather as much pure snow as you can."

For once, Zazar didn't resent the high-handed way Ysa issued orders. She left Askepott putting jars of herbs and bits of other items into a small carry-sack while she went back into the cold of the walkway atop the wall to gather as much fresh snow as her bucket would hold.

When the three women arrived at the NordornQueen's door, they were admitted immediately. Despite the blazing fire, the room was cool enough that the fashionable coats were a necessity. Outside, regardless of the hint of returning springtime, the snow-fall had intensified so that objects a few feet away could scarcely be discerned. It seemed a good day to stay inside, as warm as possible. Zazar brushed snow off her cloak.

"What brings you here?" Ashen inquired.

"We have that which we must show to you," Ysa said. "In private."

Ashen turned to Tjórvi. "Go back to your quarters, please, and continue your lessons. Mark the places where you do not understand and we will work on them later."

"Yes, Madame," the boy said. Obediently, he gathered his books and closed the door behind him.

Two of Ashen's ladies, Ragna and Karina, were sitting near the fire, embroidering. "You must leave us as well," Ashen said.

"Madame," Karina said.

Both ladies curtsied and left the room, though they did not take their embroidery with them.

"What is this mystery that is so important?" Ashen asked.

"We must show you, rather than tell you," Ysa replied.

Then, at the table where so many important private meetings had taken place, Askepott set the bowl at the place recently used by Ashen and Tjórvi. At the Duchess Ysa's direction, the Nordorn-Queen and the other two pulled chairs up around it.

"Do you have a silver bowl we may use?"

"Of course." Ashen called Lady Ragna and requested that the item be brought from the storeroom where such things were kept.

Zazar had made sure the pail was filled to its utmost from the freshest of the fresh fall. Ysa carefully packed it into the silver bowl Lady Ragna handed her. Then Ragna left the room again.

"We might get better results if we start with snow, rather than water." Ysa murmured a few words, gesturing with both hands. The snow immediately melted, but the water covered only the bottom of the bowl. "More," she said. "Let us bring the level up past halfway."

It took two more fillings and meltings before the Duchess was satisfied with the results. She spoke the words of the ritual, and the tableau unfolded before them. Ashen gasped and grew pale as she realized what she was seeing.

Zazar noted that the red-bearded man was no longer on the deck of the white ship. He now occupied a chair pulled up to a table whereon lay several charts and maps. A white candle in a stone holder atop the captain's desk, from which the chair had most likely come. Mikkel—Ridder Rødskjegg—moved the candle to the table and lit it for better illumination as he studied the materials before him. The silver bowl definitely made a great difference.

Ysa spoke again, unintelligible syllables to the uninitiated.

Outside the captain's cabin, to Zazar's surprise she heard a female voice. Mikkel looked up. "Are we there already?" he asked.

A woman entered, a blur at the edge of the window into Ridder Rødskjegg's world that the Duchess Ysa had opened. "We are," she replied, her voice thin and distant to those in the private chamber at Cyornas Castle. "*Snow Gem* is very easy to handle. She flies through the water."

"Can—can you widen the area we can see?" Ashen asked. Her voice was unsteady.

"I will try."

Ysa murmured a few more unintelligible words, made more gestures with her hands, and the scene before the watchers opened out. "We may have to add yet more snow water," the Duchess said. "Perhaps we can do it without losing our connection."

Zazar noted that the water level in the bowl was down to half of what it had been before the viewing began, most likely because they were now hearing as well as seeing. She exchanged glances with Askepott who nodded, understanding without having to be told. "We'll keep it coming as long as necessary," the other Wysenwyf said.

The new scene revealed the white vessel, *Snow Gem*, slipping into a berth in a kind of pier projecting from a nearly vertical mountain. It looked to be made all of ice. Slender, white-clad girls leaped out onto the pier and quickly secured the vessel while others lashed the snowy sails neatly until they should be needed again. The girl they had seen earlier was, Zazar realized, the leader of a troop of young warriors, all in white, all armed with throwing-spears or bows and alabaster-tipped arrows. Only she wore a necklace with a green gem in it.

Mikkel watched the work for a few minutes; then, apparently satisfied that all was being taken care of properly, turned to the young woman by his side.

"We need more snow," Ysa said.

Zazar cursed under her breath.

"Never mind, I'll go," Askepott offered. "You have more at stake with young Ridder Rødskjegg than I do. Tell me what happens when I get back." Taking the bucket, she slipped out the door.

The other women returned their attention to the tableau playing itself out on the table. Ashen NordornQueen watched raptly, absorbing every detail.

Ridder Rødskjegg and his companion walked past the icy crags toward what seemed to be the solid stone of the mountainside. The girl touched the stone, and it opened onto a small room, which the two entered. Zazar felt a little dizzy and realized that this "room" was conveying the inhabitants downward. In a moment, another door opened and the man and girl emerged into a world the watching women could never have dreamed of in all their imaginings.

It was a city, deep underwater, walled in crystal through which could be seen lazily swimming ocean creatures. Light was provided by glowing bones attached to the numerous columns. The inhabitants, all women similar in appearance to Mikkel's companion, bowed and smiled at the two as they made their way along a white-paved street toward what looked to be a small palace, not much larger than a Nordorn count's city home. The walls were clear crystal over white curtains, the doorway flanked with mirrored panels.

"I have seen magical light sources like those before," Ashen murmured. "The glowing bones. They were in Galinth. But never such a city nor such a palace."

The women interested Zazar. Though Mikkel's companion's garb was obviously designed for freedom of movement in battle, here in the city, the women dressed in long white robes that fluttered with every movement, girt with silver chains or pale sashes. All of the women were barefoot, some with pearl adornments. *The streets must be warm,* Zazar thought, *else they would have white shoes.*

"Is that where Ridder Rødskjegg is living now?" Askepott had entered unnoticed, and now stood staring, as rapt as the others, her bucket of snow forgotten in her hands.

"Yes." Ysa reached for the bucket. "The water is nearly all gone. Let me try—"

She scooped a handful of the snow in her hands and attempted to slide it under the vision. To no effect; it sputtered and vanished at the touch, leaving only a little water in the bowl.

"Shall I try again, Ashen?" Ysa asked with unwonted gentleness.

"Thank you, no, Madame Mother," Ashen said. Tears were now running down her cheeks. "Beyond all belief, I know now where Mikkel is, and have an idea of what he is doing. But how he came to be so grown up, I still do not know."

"Well, maybe I can help there." Askepott set the unwanted bucket of snow on the floor. "I've been thinking, and I believe I know when his unnatural growth began." She glanced at Zazar. "It was around the time of your second visit to Holger den Forferdelig's steading."

"*Second* visit!" Ysa exclaimed, but Ashen hushed her with a gesture.

"It seemed to me he then began a growth spurt the like of which I had never encountered before. Judging by the way he outgrew his clothing, he was acquiring a year's growth in a week."

"And do you think this is still continuing?" Ashen asked. Her face was deathly white but Zazar could detect no sign that she was going to faint.

"Brave Ashen," she murmured.

"I don't know," Askepott replied, "but I would doubt it since he is out of Gunnora's immediate presence. Nor," she added as if to forestall the NordornQueen's next question, "do I know if the process can be reversed."

"There is something else I would venture," Ashen said. "The Rock-Maiden. You recognized her."

"Yes. Her name is Petra. I think we earlier heard Red Fox address her as such. She, too, has changed, but not so much as Mikkel."

"It seemed to me that perhaps she sensed the spell as a human woman would detect a glowing spark, be it ever so small, in a darkened room."

Ysa raised her eyebrows. "Now that you mention it, it did so seem. I shall have to think on this and how we might turn it to our advantage."

"All will wait until Admiral-General Tordenskjold sails northward to unravel the mysteries we have but touched upon," Ashen said somberly. "Let us go down to the Council Chamber at once. I will call the family and what other nobles are currently in the city to meet us there as soon as possible. Then we will show them what has become of the child who so rashly ran away to seek his fortune."

It was Zazar's turn to gather more snow. By the time she reached the Council Chamber, a goodly number of people stood outside it, with a few stragglers hurrying down the corridor. Apparently rumors ran swiftly in Cyornas Castle and many of the inhabitants were avid for news of their missing prince. Inside, Zazar saw that Gaurin and Ashen occupied their chairs. With them were Bjaudin NordornPrince, Duke Einaar, Counts Tordenskjold and Svarteper, and, a little to her surprise, young Tjórvi as well. Ashen must have brought him.

Despite protests, only those invited were admitted. The last to enter the chamber was one who made Zazar's conscience bite her a little—Esander, the priest whom she had all but coerced into lending the books on magic. She hoped the results of his going against his instincts would mollify a well-deserved anger that the Duchess had once again meddled in matters Esander considered to be highly dangerous.

He fixed Zazar with a steady, disapproving eye, his usually cheerful expression now one of suspicious gloom. She would have some work to do, to rebuild a trust she knew was seriously damaged if not entirely destroyed.

"My lady Duchess," said Gaurin, when Esander had pulled the door closed behind him, "you have important information for us?"

"Yes, I do," Ysa replied. She did not take a chair at the table, but stood calmly, her hands clasped in front of her. "I have broken an agreement made long ago concerning my use of magic—"

A murmur arose from the two powerful counts, hushed when Gaurin raised his hand.

"Yes, I have broken the agreement. I and only I am to blame, but I am sure you will agree that I did so in a good cause. Further, it was not for my personal aggrandizement, but rather in an effort to ease your mind concerning the fate of your youngest child."

She glanced at Zazar, and then at Askepott, and nodded. Askepott immediately started clearing a space at the Council table. Zazar hefted her bucket of snow. It wasn't melting as fast as she wanted to make the pure water Ysa would need. Apparently Ysa noticed this as well, for she gestured and spoke a word, whereupon the snow immediately collapsed and turned into liquid.

"Ashen NordornQueen and these two ladies with me have seen what I am about to show to you," Ysa continued. "Please have no concern. Just observe."

Zazar poured some water from the bucket into the bowl. With a certain flourish, Ysa murmured a few more unintelligible words—and then, clearly, said, "Mikkel."

The mist rose from the bowl and the red-bearded man appeared, on his ship once more. Zazar noticed details she had missed before—the careful combing of his hair despite the teasing breeze, the neat braids, the tunic and trews of white silk, the way he stood so easily on the moving deck of the ship.

"That cannot be Mikkel," Gaurin objected.

"We thought the same, at first," Ysa answered. She turned to Askepott and nodded.

"He looks so—so old," Bjaudin said.

"Not much past twenty," Ysa responded. "How old was he when he was taken? Eleven? Then he would seem old to anyone who knew him then."

"I am searching for a trace of that eleven-year-old boy in the person you are showing me," Gaurin said. "He is gone, and I think he will never return. Nevertheless, it is Mikkel, grown."

There was no mistaking the red hair or the ice-blue eyes, or the shape of the nose. His chin was hidden by his beard. The pearls braided into it were large and perfect.

Then the image faded. The bowl was empty and dry.

"He is bespelled, NordornKing," Askepott said. A fresh murmur arose in the room. "Yes," she went on, "it is a spell laid on him by a woman of the Wykenigs, though not Wykenig herself. I don't think she knew or cared about the damage to your son. Before I left Holger den Forferdelig's steading, I was aware that he was growing at an unnatural rate. Now I know that he was aging as well."

"And—and is he still aging at this terrible rate?" Gaurin tried and almost succeeded in keeping his voice steady.

"I do not know, NordornKing. Perhaps now that he is out of Gunnora the Golden's sight, the aging will slow down."

"You said the woman Gunnora was not Wykenig. Do you know aught of her?" asked Duke Einaar. His voice was not much steadier than his brother's.

"I do."

The women invoked the ritual again. With quick, economical phrases, Askepott described Gunnora's heritage, ignoring the gasps of dismay at the news of the woman's origins. And all the while, the image of what Mikkel had become dominated the attention of those in the Council Chamber. At one point, Mikkel could be detected consulting with the white-clad Rock-Maiden. And, again, she glanced around as if aware of something yet unseen.

"It's clear what to do now," Tordenskjold announced. "He is on a ship, and so we will take *Ice Princess* out, intercept him, and bring him back home."

"You forget Holger den Forferdelig," Askepott said. "I believe that he, too, will be seeking Mikkel, and even that Mikkel will be seeking him in turn."

"Wait," Ysa said. She held out her shapely hands and Askepott and Zazar clasped them. Then she said the words that allowed all to hear as well as see.

The figure of Mikkel was speaking in a tinny, but audible voice. "Our sea trial has gone well, much better than I expected," he was telling the Rock-Maiden by his side. "Let us return to the City 'Neath the Waves before we encounter a floating island of ice that will put all our efforts at salvaging the *Snow Gem* for naught."

"As you say, Ridder Rødskjegg."

Mikkel laughed. "My father, Holger, called me Ridder Red Fox."

"That was when you were still a boy," the Rock-Maiden said. Zazar was now convinced; the Rock-Maiden definitely seemed to be speaking for another's benefit. "You are more than that now. You are the Knight of the Red Beard who will defeat Holger den Forferdelig and free my people and many others from his cruel and thoughtless oppression."

Mikkel laughed again. He might have drawn the Rock-Maiden into an embrace, but the small figures dissolved into the mist before the onlookers could see.

"He called Holger his father?" Ashen asked. "I was not aware of that earlier."

"It would seem that he thinks so," Askepott told her. "I have no way of knowing how Gunnora's spell has affected his mind in addition to aging him unnaturally."

"I should be grateful that he is still alive, even so altered," she said.

The NordornKing arose from his chair and bowed. "We thank you, noble ladies all," he said. "Now that we have at least an inkling of what we face when our brave Admiral-General finally does go out searching for . . . for Ridder Rødskjegg, we can begin to make our plans."

Tjórvi Sea-Rover, who had found a spot close to Ashen's chair, now moved forward and took her hand. "Please don't cry," he said. "Maybe you have lost Mikkel. Maybe not. We don't know yet." He swallowed hard and then went on manfully. "But you have me."

Ashen folded the boy in her embrace.

"I—I was sore afraid that when Mikkel came back, when Uncle Tordenskjold rescued him and put an end to Holger den Forferdelig,

Andre Norton & Sasha Miller

you wouldn't want me anymore," the youngster said, his voice breaking a little. "You'd turn me out to go back to New Vold, and they wouldn't want me, either. I'd be too Nordorn for them. But now—"

"Now," Ashen finished for him, "you're all the boy I've got. Bjaudin is a man, a young man, but he is a man. And Mikkel does not know me or his father." She hugged him even closer, tears running down her cheeks.

Most of the men in the room were weeping as well by now and even Tordenskjold found it necessary to clear his throat and rub his nose.

"Well, Duchess Ysa, I thank you as well, and Zazar and—whatever your name is." Tordenskjold cleared his throat again.

"Askepott."

"Yes. You've given us something to go on whereas before we had nothing." The Admiral-General glanced at Gaurin, who nodded.

"Our kinsman Rohan will be sorely offended if he does not go with you on your quest," the NordornKing said.

"I will send a messenger to bring him hence."

"Yes, and while we await his arrival, let us all think about what we have learned this day," the NordornKing said.

Nineteen

Gunnora the Golden huld calmed herself from the fit of fury that had threatened to unhinge her reason when she discovered that not only had the young Nordorner hostage and the cracked-brain girl disappeared from the steading, but so had Askepott, taking with her who knew what magical secrets.

Well, I have secrets of my own, Gunnora thought with a certain savage satisfaction. *Many secrets, and important ones, too.* First making sure the door to the room she shared with Holger was firmly locked, she set a bowl of snow on the floor near the hearth. Then she opened her jewel box and pressed a certain spot on the interior design. The false bottom of the chest in the lower right-hand corner popped up enough so she could remove it from the niche.

Inside were three little dragon shell-teeth, all that now remained of the Mother Ice Dragon's broods. Useful, of course, as all dragons were, but not the same as the fabled Jewel Dragons of the Bracelet of the Nine.

How she wished she could have seen the Ice Dragons in flight, and to have seen Flavielle the Sorceress, leading them. But Mother wouldn't let her go near the beasts without very strict supervision, and there never seemed to be any time she could spare to satisfy a child's curiosity.

Mother. And the entity she had chose as her—her mate, bizarre as the notion was. Whatever had she seen in that altogether weird creature from another world? And, of course, the answer came as it always did when she contemplated this question. It was power, power, and more power—not entirely the magical kind.

She remembered looking at Flavielle's body preserved on the icy bier under the crystal dome that covered her, untouched by any hint of decay. Well hidden it was, deep in the Maze that was the home of the Great One Whom All Served. But she found it, she, Flavielle's daughter.

Who her actual father was, she could only speculate but she believed it was Farod, the Great One's lieutenant. Once, Farod told her, his hair had been golden, like hers. Also, there were other resemblances in the shape of her face and features. It was Farod who had lived on the crumbs of Flavielle's favor, and then, after her death, lived for the child he had undoubtedly sired on her. Why else would he have crept back to the Maze, sorely wounded, and cared for her until Holger's father had found them?

He had told young Gunnora many stories of Flavielle and of the great ones in Rendel and the NordornLand, stories that she stored in her memory to be taken out and thought on later.

It was very like the puzzles that formed little carved animals when put together properly, of which some Wykenigs were fond. With the appearance of the boy, Mikkel Red Fox, in the steading, a few more bits of the puzzle became apparent.

Flavielle had been killed in battle by the NordornKing, the title then held by a man called Hynnel. This, Farod had told her. By listening when she appeared to be occupied with nothing more important than the proper setting of her table, she learned that Mikkel was the youngest son of a different NordornKing, Gaurin. *Of course*, she said to herself. *It has to be, because Mother had slain the other NordornKing with Dragon's Breath from the Rime Rod and Farod had taken it to use in her memory*. It did not lie in the jewel chest, but now hung from a cord attached to her girdle. She fingered the slender silver rod, one of the few artifacts remaining from Flavielle's existence. Now she wished she had used it on Mikkel Red Fox instead of the aging spell.

But if she had, she would have had no access to the treasure she knew lay in the NordornKing's castle, perhaps in another jewel box—the Bracelet of the Nine.

This potent article of Power had been in the steading, that she knew, but did not yet know how or by whom it had been brought. Obviously, it had been a fool with no idea of its value and, furthermore, someone who consorted easily with another fool, Old Askepott.

It took no magical ability to reason that no one would have reason to transport to Holger den Forferdelig's steading except to learn of Mikkel's well-being. Therefore, the visitor, doubtless another crone convinced that she wielded Power, had come from the NordornLand.

Objects imbued with as much Power as this bracelet possessed gave off an aura plainly discernible to those who had the ability to perceive it. She had literally *smelled* its presence while it was so close. And then, it was gone. Where? Where else but back to the NordornLand? Twice over proved beyond any doubt that the fool who had brought it for Askepott's inspection was also from the NordornLand, and that meant in turn that Askepott herself now resided there.

Gunnora's world was one in which twists and tangles of meaning were commonplace, but this was simple and easily read.

She had miscalculated, for once, had done what she had always promised herself she would not do—repeat Mother's flaw of arrogance born of the knowledge of the Power she possessed. Gunnora had thought Holger would speed up negotiations with the NordornKing for the boy's return before he fell into the decrepitude of old age and died, thereby giving her access to the place where the Bracelet of the Nine lay. Now she might know where Askepott had vanished, but she had no idea as to the Red Fox's whereabouts.

Therefore, she needed the fools from the NordornLand to

come and find him for her. That, she thought, presented a problem for she could not reliably force them to go anywhere but at their choosing, not hers.

There was one thing she could do, though, and would. Lest all be lost with a boy's death from old age, she could freeze the spell so Mikkel stayed permanently as he was now. Later, perhaps, she would amend it again. This she would do not from any sense of pity for the boy, but rather to buy the time she needed to discover the best way to obtain the precious bracelet.

Then— She smiled.

Some years back, Holger had acquired a wealthy woman captive. Lady Acindia, she called herself, claiming that she was a baroness. Nobility or not, she was someone Gunnora knew instinctively was a wielder of Power, if on a minor scale. Her ransom was quickly paid and she departed forthwith, but Holger, at Gunnora's insistence, made her leave all her belongings. She departed with only the clothes on her back; Gunnora immediately took the jewels and other finery for herself.

Lady Acindia, oddly, had formed a friendship with Askepott and when Acindia left the steading, Askepott managed to filch a bundle of the woman's writings that otherwise would have gone to the fire. This troubled Gunnora not at all, for one of the first things she had done was to make a fair copy of everything before Askepott could get her hands on it. One page in particular had proved very useful.

As soon as Gunnora had completed the counter spell that stopped Mikkel's unnatural aging, she brought the bowl of snow, now melted into pure water, to a table lit by a single candle. She wanted to see the results for herself. She spoke the words over the water, and then said one word more: "Mikkel."

"You—you *what?*" Admiral-General Tordenskjold shouted at the three women standing at the table in the Council Chamber of Cyornas Castle.

All those nobles still in the city again occupied their accustomed places, this time accompanied by as many retainers and hangers-on as could fit inside the room. Those inside relayed what was happening to those crowding the corridor outside.

Count Mjødulf allowed a slight frown to disturb his brow; Duke Einaar scowled outright. Lord High Marshal Svarteper shook his snowy head as if he could not believe what he had just heard. Bjaudin NordornPrince uttered a barely muffled, "No." Even Gaurin NordornKing seemed more than a little taken aback. But the Duchess Ysa remained unruffled in the face of the nearly universal disapproval of the nobles.

"Since you seem not to have understood me, I will repeat my statement. When you depart on the search for what has become of Prince Mikkel, Zazar, Askepott, and I must accompany you."

"Nonsense," Svarteper declared. "This isn't any pleasure jaunt."

"Nor do we expect it to be," Ysa returned calmly. "Nevertheless, we three"—she indicated Askepott and Zazar—"may well hold the key to finding what has become of young Mikkel and returning him safely to his family."

"How so?" Tordenskjold asked truculently.

"Would you sail aimlessly, seeking that which might not want to be found?"

Tordenskjold's frown deepened but he did not dispute the Duchess's point.

"Only we three can guide you and Rohan on your way. Not even his Wave Reader can do so as well as we. And furthermore, you know it."

"I am against it. Only if I am ordered, will I allow three women on a ship of war." He looked to Gaurin, but it was Ashen who spoke.

"Then I so order." Ashen turned to Ysa. "Madame Mother," she said, her voice shaky but her expression resolute, "go with the two Wysen-wyves and help our brave Admiral-General and our equally brave ally and foster son, Rohan of the Sea-Rovers, in their quest to find and return Mikkel to us."

"Then, barring objection from Gaurin NordornKing, I must obey," Tordenskjold said.

Gaurin said nothing, but nodded his assent.

"Good," the Duchess Ysa said. "Now I must go and write a letter to my granddaughter informing her that she must rule Iselin in my name a while longer."

Contrary to her usual choice of pink or peach or yellow, this night Princess Elin of the NordornLand had donned spring green, her father's color. A certain softness in the air bespoke of the coming end to winter's grip on Iselin. Twi-night—the time halfway between day and night—was shorter now, and the lights in the northern sky less brilliant.

With a clear and untroubled mind, she was enjoying the entertainment Tinka-Lillfot and her dog were presenting to the Court. Really, Elin thought, the diminutive woman had trained the animal to an amazing degree. At her command, the dog, which she had named Hagbart, turned somersaults in midair, jumped through hoops, and as a grand finale, spun and twirled as if dancing with his mistress.

Elin was so entertained she didn't even mind that both dog and fool were wearing green as well, though nearer the dark emerald shade so favored by Granddam Ysa. She laughed and clapped her hands as Tinka-Lillfot, with a tap on his shoulder, caused Hagbart to mimic her bow before leaving the Hall.

Baron Gustav leaned forward. "Your Highness seems in good humor this evening," he said.

"I am," Elin told him.

A wrestling match was now in progress between two of the younger men of the household, with much shouting, laughter, and placing of bets.

"I would speak with you and also with Caspar and Isak, but I cannot hear myself think. Anyway, it is a private matter."

"Then we shall adjourn to Your Highness's audience chamber."

He caught the eye of both Isak and Caspar and indicated that they should come with Elin and him. Isak complied a little reluctantly; his man looked likely to win the match.

Presently, the four were seated in the outer room of Elin's apartment that served as her audience chamber. A servant brought the customary heated snowberry juice mingled with wine.

Elin drew a folded piece of paper from the pocket in her sleeve and spread it out on the table. "I have had a letter from the Duchess Ysa, telling me that she will not be returning to Iselin as quickly as she had thought when she departed."

"Is she well?" asked Baron Isak.

"Oh, quite well. In fact, she is going on a sea voyage."

"Then we will have the pleasure of your continued rule over us in her absence," Gustav said diplomatically.

"So it would appear." Elin took a deep breath. "My good lords, I confess that I have not fulfilled my duties as best I may, up until now." She held up her hands to forestall the expected—and false—denials. "My Granddam Ysa was to return very shortly, or so I thought and so did she, I'll warrant. Also, during the quiet of deep winter no great matters need be solved that cannot wait until the stirring of spring. But now spring is close upon us and, like the earth, I must also bestir myself from winter's grip. I must go out among my granddam's people. And you, my lords, must teach me how to govern them."

As one, the three barons arose and bowed low to her.

"I know that I speak for my fellow Council members," said Gustav, "when I say that it would be both an honor and a privilege."

Elin smiled. "Then please, when the weather permits, let us go a-progress through Iselin. I would get to know its people, and them me."

Pleading fatigue, she dismissed them to return to the entertainment in the Hall while she retired to her bedchamber. Once her ladies had made her ready for bed, however, and tucked her in, she lay long thinking, staring up at the canopy embroidered, oddly, with bears standing erect on a background of oak leaves.

Andre Norton & Sasha Miller

Yes, Granddam Ysa was right—again—and it was fortunate for both of them that Elin was established safely in Iselin to learn the art of ruling, thus leaving the Duchess free to lead the search for Mikkel.

She hoped her little brother was making as good use of his time away from the Nordorn Court as she, Elin thought. And then she fell asleep.

Twenty

With Ysa in the lead, Zazar carrying the bowl and Aske-pott the bucket, the three women entered Ysa's apartment. Little Alfonse immediately began barking and pawing at Ysa's skirts.

"Poor darling, I've been neglecting you," she told him. Her ladies came bustling in, a bit belatedly. "Grisella, send for heated wine. Ingrid, bring us some meat pies and a dish for Alfonse. Gertrude, pull three chairs around that table. Then, the three of you, leave us in private."

"Yes, Your Grace," they said, almost in unison. Then each lady went to do as she was bid.

Without being told, Askepott left the apartment to gather more snow. Zazar set the bowl on the table, and seated herself in one of the chairs. "I take it that we will be doing the Ritual of Seeing again," she said. "This time directed at the woman who seems to have caught Mikkel's fancy."

"I cannot shake off the feeling that she is aware of us, if not what we are about, and I think this is something shared by Aske-pott."

Andre Norton & Sasha Miller

"If not, she will surely find no objection to our investigating," said Zazar.

Askepott entered, bearing the bucket of snow. She set it down and blew on her fingers to warm them. "Spring may be upon us but winter has lost none of its grip," she commented. "Very well, now are we to look in on Petra?"

Zazar handed her a steaming goblet. "Yes. I confess myself curious about these Rock-Maidens and how one of them has Mikkel in thrall. Now eat, before the food is all gone."

Alfonse was greedily snuffling over one of the meat pies. Weyse appeared out of nowhere and helped herself to one as well. Askepott took the last one from the platter.

"A person has to be quick around these two," she commented.

Zazar was already ladling the snow into the bowl, adding more as it melted. By the time Askepott licked the crumbs from her fingers, preparations were complete.

Doing the ritual was becoming easier with practice, Zazar thought. The image of the Rock-Maiden they had seen in Mikkel's company appeared. She was alone, in what seemed to be her bed-chamber, sitting at a table where she was stringing pearlescent shells onto a silken cord. She raised her head as if seeking the source of the magical stirring she felt.

"So you grasped that I was aware of you and so have come to me directly," she said. "Well, then, who is it that seeks me out? Speak to me. I will hear you."

"You do it," Ysa told Askepott in a whisper. "She knows your voice. Zazar and I are but strangers."

"Do you recognize me, Petra?" Askepott said.

"You're Askepott, the woman from Holger's steading. Did you flee from his wrath when he discovered that both Ridder Red Fox and I were missing?"

"Something like that."

"Are you the one who has been watching him then? For what purpose? Do you wish to return him to Holger, to buy back his good favor?"

"I have sought him, yes, and others as well, but not to return him to Holger's keeping. His mother has been in a decline since he disappeared. Now she is better, knowing that he lives."

"His mother. Ah, yes, I forget that the people outside bear young and are fond of them. But why do you come to me now?"

With Ysa and Zazar's help, Askepott related the Nordorners' plans to apprehend Holger and also to find Mikkel and bring him back to the NordornLand, where what calamity that had befallen him could be reversed.

Petra digested this in silence. "And what would you have me do?" she asked finally.

"Your help in seeing to Mikkel's well-being," Zazar said.

"Ridder Rødskjegg needs not my help, nor yours for all that he is but a human. He will go where he list."

"You love him." That was Ysa.

"Love? You would think so. 'Love' among the Rock-Folk is a dangerous undertaking. When a Rock-Man captures one of us, his embrace causes young to form from her body until nothing is left of her but a pile of dust. We are different in every way imaginable, including the ability to sense your spell-casting and to speak through it. But this one thing causes me to consider your words and not reject you out of hand, that you would remove Holger den Forferdelig from his current seat of power so that he ceases to be a scourge to all at sea or on land."

"That is a worthy reason for soliciting your aid," said Ysa diplomatically.

"You say that you three will be on the ship seeking Holger?"

"Yes. We hope to find both him and Mikkel on the trackless sea in that fashion."

"Well, then. I know Askepott. I must meet the other two face to face so that I might judge you better. Then, I will decide whether to tell him of you so that he can make his own decision as to his fate."

Ysa glanced at the Wysen-wyves. "I sense that we can do no better at this time," she said.

Then Petra gave them instructions as how best to preserve the pure water they would need when they were too far from land to go gathering snow. They would need silver ewers, stoppered with silver, and kept under close guard from seamen who might think they were only water vessels for the use of delicate women too good to dip from the common barrel and so contaminate or even steal them for the silver.

"There is a spot on the coast, north to you but southerly to those who live in Wykenig country, where a fresh stream flows from snowmelt and seafarers go to fill their water casks. There I will meet you when conditions permit. Good-bye until then."

The figure of the Rock-Maiden winked out. To Zazar's surprise, despite the length of contact, there were still a few drops of moisture remaining in the bowl. That must be, she thought, yet another ability of the Rock-Folk. She wondered why she had never heard of them ere now.

If Admiral-General Tordenskjold had been truculent about the notion of women being aboard his warship, he was downright mutinous now.

"How dare you propose to take over my quarters!" he shouted. His face was developing a purplish tinge.

Ysa drew herself up to her full height. "I am the Duchess of Iselin, formerly Dowager Queen of Rendel, First Priestess of Santize, holder of more titles than you can dream of, foster mother of Ashen NordornQueen, and through her, kindred of Gaurin NordornKing. Consider yourself lucky to be sharing the third mate's quarters and not relegated to the crew's quarters where you would no doubt be pleased to relegate me and the ladies with me."

"Th—third mate's quarters?"

"Of course. Zazar and Askepott are no more to be expected to fight for a bunk with some seaman than I. They will have the first and second mate's cabins."

After some more spirited discussion, Ysa and Tordenskjold

reached an agreement whereby the three women would occupy the Admiral-General's spacious cabin and he would share quarters with First Mate Sigurd.

Later, Ysa sat at the Admiral-General's desk and supervised while sailors carried Tordenskjold's belongings out of his cabin and other men carried Ysa's luggage in and piled it in the middle of the floor; Zazar and Askepott had one carry-sack each. Efficiently, the men set up temporary beds for the Wysen-wyves' use. Then they returned to their usual duties.

"Ah, these are much better accommodations than we would have had on *Spume Maiden*," the Duchess commented to Zazar and Askepott as they retrieved their belongings and began putting bedclothes on their cots, "for all that I could have made Rohan give up three cabins for us. I never really expected it of Tordenskjold but demanding allowed him to back down a little and still save his dignity. This way, we are uncrowded, and on the best and fastest ship to be had either in Rendel or the NordornLand—at least until the shipwrights build another."

"*NordornQueen's Own*, it will be called," Zazar told her.

"Of course," Ysa said absently. She arose from her chair and picked up a silver ewer, filled with clean snow water and carefully stoppered with a wax seal. "Fine silver," she commented.

"We managed to get six of these," Zazar said. "Ashen will have to make do with pottery at her tables for a while."

"Six will do," Ysa said. "For the time, at least. We will replenish when and where we can. Where is the bowl?"

"I have it." Askepott dug the article out of a pile of Ysa's clothing. "I do hope you don't think Zazar and I are going to act as your maids."

"Of course not." Ysa glanced around. "Here. This cabinet will do to keep the ewers and bowl in while we're not using them. It has a latch on the door."

The cabinet proved to be spacious enough to hold not only the supplies for the Ritual of Seeing, but also most of Ysa's clothing, carefully and neatly folded by the Wysen-wyves.

"I made do with pegs on the wall," Askepott commented, "like these. But then I never dreamed I'd be sailing on the seas in a ship from a country Holger always thought of as an enemy."

"We must keep track of Holger, as we go," Ysa said. "Tordenskjold will have the services of one of Rohan's Sea-Rover Wave Readers, but there is no doubt at all that we three can be of more use—if he ever comes off his fit of temper over being evicted from his comfortable quarters."

"Oh, he will," Zazar assured her. "For a man, he's more practical than most. He'll come around soon enough when he sees how very useful we can be."

"Especially when we are successful in allying ourselves with the Rock-Maiden Petra."

"She called herself a princess," Askepott said thoughtfully. "Perhaps she is. She wore the sea-green glass badge Holger took from her when she was captured. Also, she seemed to have a commanding presence whenever we saw her through the ritual. And now that I think back, she always held herself a little apart from the rest of the younkers, as if she thought she was somehow better than they were."

"Does Tordenskjold know that part of our errand lies in meeting this Rock-Maiden?" Zazar asked. "Princess or no."

"I have not yet informed him," Ysa said. She began to smile.

Zazar stared at her. "This is the first time I have ever seen you playing a joke on someone," she declared. "A harmless joke, that is."

"Oh, sea air does wonders for me, I have discovered," Ysa replied. Her smile turned into laughter. "When the sea is calm, that is."

"Speaking of sea air, I think we are underway," Askepott said.

The three women, muffled in warm cloaks, emerged from the Admiral-General's quarters directly onto the top deck of the *Ice Princess*, from where they could immediately see that the ropes mooring the vessel to one of the buoys in Cyornas Fjord had, indeed, been cast off. Under a rag of sail the ship was heading for the mouth of the sound where Rohan, on *Spume Maiden*, was already hove to, waiting for them.

By squinting and straining her eyes a little, Zazar could make out both Rohan and young Obern on deck. Either Obern had mended his ways, she thought, or Rohan didn't trust the silly noddle-noodle out of his sight. In her opinion, young Obern was so worthless it made her wonder if someone else had had a hand in his begetting.

But no. Rohan had been utterly faithful to Anamara since the moment the two had met, and she to him, even during that time when the poor thing was addle-headed from the Sorceress's spell and thought she was a bird.

That must be where Obern's conspicuous lack had come from. Spells like that had a way of lingering, and even close exposure to magic could influence a child in the womb. Just look at Bjaudin, gravely serious and old for his years from his first breath. Elin— well, she was still forming. Perhaps her character had not taken as much harm from Ashen's encounter with the Mother Ice Dragon as Zazar feared. Firmly, she shut off thoughts and worries about the Princess of the Nordorners. She would consider Elin later.

Rohan's other children seemed bright enough. Elgar, what little she had seen of him, was friendly, talkative and engaging. Amilia, Rohan's older daughter, she knew little about, and little Naeve was still too young to judge. Tjórvi would be all right as soon as he got over feeling guilty because he emerged virtually unscathed from *GorGull*'s deadly encounter with the Wykenigs, whereas Mikkel had fallen captive.

Disappointing though Obern must be to the man Rohan had become, Zazar thought he could be grateful that only the one child had suffered the lingering aftereffects of the spell laid on Anamara that had removed her humanity and given her the limited intelligence of a bird. Probably he had no such gratitude, however. People were like that, especially men.

The breeze freshened, filling the newly raised sails of both ships. A cry went up from the crew of *Ice Princess*, manned by Nordorners but carrying a complement of Sea-Rover Marines, and quickly echoed by those aboard *Spume Maiden*: "Let us go with wind in the sails and waves favoring!"

Andre Norton & Sasha Miller

It was the traditional call upon the Ruler of Waves. Zazar hoped it would bring them luck.

Then, before the cold wind reached her bones, she returned to the once-spacious cabin, now cluttered with the belongings of a spoiled noblewoman. At least, Zazar thought with a flash of amusement, she had not insisted on bringing Alfonse along.

Twenty-one

*A*dmiral-General Tordenskjold *was even* less happy when he found that his high-born passenger insisted on being taken to a specific location where, as she put it, she could refresh herself with the water from a particular spring.

"And also," she added, "you may refresh *Ice Princess's* water barrels."

"Madame," he said, fuming, "I can manage my own ship. Even the water barrels."

"Nevertheless, I insist," Ysa told him.

Zazar and Askepott, unbidden to this meeting and yet unwilling to miss it, hovered in the background. Zazar stroked Weyse, who had mysteriously appeared out of nowhere, as was her wont.

Tordenskjold's florid facial coloring deepened. "Women!" he finally expostulated. "No women on my ship again, ever!"

"That's as may be," Ysa returned. "For now, you have not just one but three powerful women on your ship—which is not, strictly speaking, your ship at all, but belongs to the NordornKing and NordornQueen. My close kindred."

Zazar thought the Admiral-General was surely going to have a seizure. She and Askepott exchanged glances and raised eyebrows.

"We should leave him," Askepott whispered behind Ysa's back.

Zazar nodded. "Come, Ysa," she said, "let us retire and let our good Admiral-General think over your request." *And regain his temper*, she thought. "I am certain that on consideration he will find it not to be unreasonable at all."

"Very well," Ysa said, apparently unruffled by the force of Tordenskjold's annoyance and irritation that sent waves of anger crashing against the bulkhead of his former cabin so strongly that Zazar expected cloaks to fall off pegs. "Go over to *Spume Maiden*. Talk to Rohan. You always feel better after you do this."

"I am not to be ordered about on my own ship," Tordenskjold muttered.

Nevertheless, he left his former cabin without further objection and, a few minutes later, the women could hear the sound of davits and pulleys as the captain's boat was being lowered.

"He is a very difficult man," Ysa commented. "I expect that the Countess Gyda is happiest when he's out at sea."

"It's been hard enough for me to endure living on this ship the last two days," Askepott declared. "If we make it through this voyage without him casting us adrift in one of those little boats it will be a miracle," she added. "At sea, a captain's word is absolute law and you, Duchess, are pushing him beyond his limits."

Ysa shrugged. "He does not intimidate me."

"Well, perhaps not, but you could at least refrain from antagonizing him," Zazar said. "I for one have no desire to row back home. Or swim."

Ysa merely shrugged again. "We sail under a good breeze with a relatively calm sea. Let us perform the Ritual of Seeing and contact the Rock-Princess. And also find out, if we can, where Holger den Forferdelig is."

She set the silver bowl on Tordenskjold's desk. Askepott broke the wax seal and poured the first ewer's contents into the bowl.

Then she unstoppered the second and added most of the water it held as well.

"We really are going to have to stop and replenish," she observed, "if it takes almost two of the vessels we brought with us to fill the bowl properly."

Ysa was already intent on the ritual. "If he asks, I might inform him. Now, let us begin."

With the invocation of her name, the image of the Princess of the Rock-Maidens coalesced. "I was wondering if you'd ever contact me again," she said by way of greeting. "Or if you had decided to leave Ridder Rødskjegg and me alone to find our fates for ourselves."

"We contacted you as soon as we could," Ysa told her. "Please don't be impatient."

That got a laugh from the Rock-Maiden. "I have the patience of a stone, Madame! You know nothing of Rock-Folk. However, others do not. Ridder Rødskjegg is already asea, and I with him. Look around." She indicated her surroundings—dimly seen in the mist of the spell, but apparently she was in the cabin of a ship, just as they were.

"Where does he sail?" Zazar asked.

"He searches for Holger den Forferdelig, of course," Petra said carelessly. "At the present, *Snow Gem* stays close to the shore. There is still ice, which is only to be expected, but there is also an open lane where Holger might go. In fact, we are fairly close to the place where I said we should meet."

"And we draw nearer as well. Can you persuade Mikkel to stop there?"

"Perhaps. If not, I can always walk."

"Walk!" exclaimed Ysa. "Rock-Maidens can walk on water?"

Petra laughed again. "Not on, under. We do not drown. I can slip over the side and make my way along the bottom. The stream makes a path there where it joins the Icy Sea. I have explored it before. Later, I can signal to be picked up again."

"Or we can take you back with us when we meet up with Mikkel at last."

"Perhaps," the Rock-Maiden princess said again. "Much remains to be determined."

"Is Mikkel well?" asked Zazar.

"Of course he is well! He is eager to join battle with Holger and so am I and my Warrior-Maidens. But I think I will meet you first."

"I think that is the wise course to take. Shall we meet two days hence?"

"Yes. I will be there at the stream."

"Until then."

The image winked out. Ysa stretched as if relieving kinks in her back. "We must do a ritual for Tordenskjold and Rohan. The Admiral-General has seen it before, true enough, but Rohan has not. I think he might be a good voice to add to our own."

"I'll go have someone signal that the two should return to *Ice Princess.*" Zazar arose from her chair and went to take her cloak off its peg.

"Could you find something warm to eat and drink?" Ysa asked Askepott. "This ritual can be very draining."

"Yes, I know. I feel it and I daresay Zazar does, too. I'll see what can be found."

By the time Rohan and Tordenskjold returned to *Ice Princess* and the Admiral-General's old cabin, the three women had fortified themselves with stewed salt pork and mugs of diluted spirits, a beverage much loved by sailors.

"Tell us whom you want to see," Ysa said to Tordenskjold.

"Holger, of course."

The Duchess began the ritual, and spoke the name. The mists cleared and the image of Holger den Forferdelig appeared. The Wykenig leader was on the deck of his ship and, at Tordenskjold's request, Ysa widened the viewing area so that they could all see that the ship, *Dragon Blood*, was under good but not full sail. There was ice in the water, but not of a dangerous size.

"She heads south," Rohan observed.

Then Ysa switched to Mikkel on board his white ship, *Snow Gem*. The Rock-Maiden Princess, Petra, stood close by him.

"What a wonderful way you have discovered, Granddam Ysa, to learn so much concerning those we seek!" Rohan exclaimed. "I would have you teach my Wave Reader Saugle this magic if possible. Admiral-General, we are lucky beyond measure to have this advantage available to us."

"Yes, well," Tordenskjold said. He settled his cloak about his shoulders. "It was my pleasure to bring these fine women along with us so that they might show us the best direction to find the Wykenig."

To Zazar's mixed amusement and exasperation, Ysa chose not to call Tordenskjold on his abrupt change of course. Sooner or later, though, she would make certain the Admiral-General smarted for his previous treatment of them—of that Zazar was certain.

"Is there someone you would look in on, Grandson?" Ysa inquired.

"My wife. My family."

The Duchess murmured the words and the image of Anamara appeared. She was working at a loom, and nearby her daughter Amilia plied her needle in embroidery. Anamara's pregnancy was obvious and she smiled as she worked.

"And Elgar?" Rohan said.

Elgar's image appeared a few seconds before spluttering out, the bowl empty. He was well wrapped against the cold, in a wooded area still leafless, obviously out hunting with a band of companions.

"All is well," Rohan said. "That alone is worth your presence, Granddam."

"Our supply of clean snow water is low," Ysa replied. "We could bring only a small amount, but hoped to replenish it along the way."

"Of course you shall!" Rohan exclaimed. He turned to Tordenskjold. "Look you. You have a good idea now of where to go to

engage Holger. Likewise, with Granddam Ysa and Granddam Zaz
and Askepott working this magic, I should be able to locate Mikkel
on this white ship of his and they can teach Saugle as we go.
Therefore, I propose that we split our forces. I will take the women
on board *Spume Maiden* and continue to sail up the coast, stopping to replenish the clean water they need for their magic-
making while you go after Holger. What say you?"

Zazar could fairly hear Tordenskjold's thoughts: *And I can
have my quarters back.*

"I agree," he said aloud. "Let us begin the transfer of the ladies
and their belongings at once."

Ice Princess was no longer even a smudge on the horizon. *Spume
Maiden's* new passengers had barely begun to get settled in their
quarters—not quite as Ysa had predicted, for Zazar and Askepott
shared First Mate Finrod Felagund's cabin—when the rendezvous
spot appeared ahead of them. Rohan ordered the sails furled and
the anchor dropped.

"Let two of your men row us ashore," Ysa instructed Rohan,
"and then let them stay out of sight. We have that to perform that
will not tolerate the gaze of untrained eyes."

"So shall it be done, Granddam."

Presently, with Ysa's belongings not yet stowed neatly in Rohan's cabin and Zazar's and Askepott's carry-sacks tossed into the
cabin assigned to them, the three women carrying four silver ewers
among them climbed into the little boat and, with the two Sea-
Rovers skillfully manning the oars, began the trip to the shore.

"The stream you seek is just beyond yonder headland," one of
the sailors told them, pointing north. "We'll snark down here and
wait. You'll need help getting them silver jugs back with them full
and all."

"We thank you," Askepott said. She turned to the others. "I
think I should take the lead in this if you don't mind."

"I'm content to follow you," Zazar told her.

"And I," said Ysa, a little reluctantly it seemed to Zazar. But then the Duchess was much too accustomed to being in command to step back easily.

The ewers were now equipped with leather shoulder straps. Askepott slung two of them on her back and started off north, on the rocky beach still treacherous in spots from ice on the stones. Zazar picked up one of the remaining silver vessels, leaving the last one for Ysa.

"I thought surely you could carry two empty ewers," the Duchess grumbled as she slung her burden over her shoulder. "Of course, once they are full—"

"Oh, do give up your fancy airs," Zazar snapped. "Take your fair share of the burden."

Without any more complaint from Ysa—at least aloud—the three women trudged past the headland pointed out by the sailors and discovered that the stream had found a cut through the rock and formed a sheltered miniature cove, covered with fine white sand. The stream did not pour directly into the Icy Seas, but dropped into a stone-rimmed pool from a musical waterfall. This pool, actually a catch basin, owed much to the touch of hands, human or otherwise. A thin thread of water spilled over the side of the basin and snaked its way across the sand and into the sea itself. Judging by the line of wrack, high tide would not quite reach the rim of the basin.

Prudence directed that they climb up to make certain the clean water had not become contaminated along its journey. A series of stone ledges that might have been set as stairs by the same hands that had fashioned the catch basin wound up one side of the waterfall.

"Well, up we go, ladies," Askepott said. Without much ado, she girded her skirt under her belt to knee-height, revealing sturdy shoes and knitted snow-thistle silk and wool hosen. Zazar promptly did likewise and, after some hesitation and a sigh she did not bother to hide, so did Ysa.

Before they could begin their climb, however, a slim white figure appeared over the northern side of the rock cut. "You needn't be concerned," Petra told them. "All is well. In fact, you can fill your jugs from the pool, if you like." She gazed at the women. "Welcome, Askepott. It's quite a change from Holger's kitchen, isn't it?" She leaped lightly down the rocky face to land on the sand. "And you are?"

"Zazar," the Wysen-wyf said. "I suppose you could call me Askepott's sister, after a fashion."

"And I am Ysa, Duchess of Iselin and Mikkel's granddam. We all have great interest in his well-being, me perhaps most of all."

"Of course," Petra returned coolly.

Zazar couldn't help staring, this being her first real look at a Rock-Maiden. As in the conjured pictures, she wore a short white tunic though she had laid aside her bow in favor of two throwing-spears. Slung on her back was a buckler that seemed made of flat, iridescent white shells. Around her neck was the silver chain set with a large green gem and on her upper arm a circlet that looked very like the white stone bracelet Ashen treasured so much, Gaurin's gift. Her feet were bare, ornamented with pearl rings on her toes. "Did you walk?" Zazar asked.

Petra laughed. "Not far, this time. I asked Ridder Rødskjegg, Mikkel, to anchor offshore nearby, so that I could visit this place that might be the remains of a Rock-Maiden stronghold." She surveyed the stonework of the pool and the face of the stony cliff from which the stream fell. "And so it might be. Some other time, I will investigate. Now, we have other matters more pressing."

"And do we pass muster for you?" Zazar asked.

The Rock-Maiden turned her scrutiny from the cliff to two of the women. "Perhaps. Enough, anyway. I believe that you care about Ridder Red Fox. But know this. He does not remember you. Would you be doing him a service, pulling him from a life that he did not choose, but which has chosen him? Think on this."

"We could, the three of us, work to restore his memory," Ysa told the Rock-Maiden. "We would return him to the family that loves him."

"Their Maimed Majesties," Petra returned. "Yes, I have heard of them. In so doing, you would take him from me."

"Their hearts are heavy with the loss of their youngest child," Ysa said, "for all that he has unnaturally grown into a man."

"Gunnora's work."

"I feel that Gunnora is dangerous in her own way, as is Holger den Forferdelig," Zazar said.

As if in answer to her name, and to the utter astonishment of the four in the sandy cove, Gunnora herself rose into view, seated in the natural saddle behind the head of an Ice Dragon. She was clad in a skintight garment that might have been made of scales, and she glowed in the pale light.

"And so I am dangerous!" she cried. "Even more so than Holger! Cower back, you fools, for all the good it will do you, for you will die this day."

To Zazar's astonishment, Ysa gathered courage from some unknown place and stepped forward. "You will not kill us," she declared, her voice strong and firm.

"And why not?"

"You need us too much. I see that you have now become a Dragon-Rider. Where did it come from?"

"You don't need to know, but I will tell you. I have a few shell-teeth from the last brood. With one of the teeth, I summoned this one to life."

"I see."

Zazar caught her breath, wondering how Ysa could remain so calm. Now it was plain why Gunnora coveted the Dragon Bracelet! With that in her possession, she could mount a force unknown in modern times—six different dragons with differing attributes and abilities, and three mighty humans returned from long ago to follow her in whatever direction her ambitions took her.

"And how did you know to come here, at this time?" Ysa asked.

For an answer, Gunnora let out a derisive laugh. "Do you think you are the only one who knows the Ritual of Seeing? Your every move has been known to me right from the start. As for you," she said to the Rock-Maiden, "it was easy to disguise my presence as just more of their prying."

"I had not thought to kill you," Petra replied, "until now."

"Let me think," Gunnora said. She pulled on the Ice Dragon's reins and it came to rest on the edge of the rocky crest and folded its wings. She did not dismount.

"Very well," she said. "I will not kill all of you. Just you, you unnatural stone creature, and Askepott. The pretentious snobbish fool and the old woman-thing with her I will take back with me, to ransom for that—that certain item that you know about."

"You cannot kill me!" Petra cried. "But you cannot say as much for yourself." She hefted one of the alabaster-tipped spears, and let fly.

The Ice Dragon reared its head, causing the spear to miss its target and lodge in the dragon's jaw instead. With a roar of pain and outrage, the dragon raked the spear loose with its forepaw to go clattering down the cliff to the sand. It would have launched itself at its tormentor if Gunnora had not pulled back on the reins.

She aimed a silver rod at the Rock-Maiden. A spray of what looked like ice crystals enveloped her and her movements slowed to a near halt.

"I've long known that you wanted to kill me," Askepott said. "My kettle showed it to me."

"You let Mikkel and this . . . this creature escape. That is tantamount to stealing my property. Also, you hid the presence of the Dragon Bracelet from me when it was in Holger's steading." Gunnora turned the silver cylinder toward Askepott. "Breathe deep of the Rime Rod's vapors and it will go easier for you."

"Never!" Zazar cried. As the stream of ice crystals flew toward Askepott, she yanked the other Wysen-wyf out of its path. A portion of the rock wall behind them suddenly glittered with a thin layer of ice.

"You have now become a target as well," Gunnora got out from between clenched teeth. She leveled the Rime Rod at Zazar. When she pressed the button, however, nothing happened. It seemed to have depleted its store of deadly vapor, if only for the moment. With a scream of fury, Gunnora held her hand aloft and gathered twinkling sparks that appeared out of nowhere. She hurled them at Zazar just as a rocket came roaring at the cove toward the Ice Dragon.

"Returning the favor," Askepott said as she stepped in front of Zazar. The sparks enveloped her body and she dropped to the sand.

The rocket ricocheted off the dragon's shoulder, hit the rock wall behind where the three women were standing, and struck Petra as it exploded. With another scream, this time of frustration, Gunnora clung tightly to the Ice Dragon's reins lest she be thrown off as it leaped aloft. As suddenly as she'd appeared, she was gone.

Petra, released from her icy prison, rushed across the stream. Zazar was already kneeling beside Askepott, lifting the other Wysen-wyf's head onto her lap.

"How does she?" Ysa asked. She knelt on Askepott's other side, and took her hand into both of hers.

"Not well. I don't know what spell it was that Gunnora used, but we will have to work hard to keep it from doing its mischief."

"You mean keep it from killing me?" Askepott asked feebly. She coughed and managed to open her eyes a little.

"You can't die!"

Askepott regained a little of her spirit. "I most certainly can," she said with some asperity. Then she closed her eyes again and took a breath as her head fell back.

Petra all but shoved Ysa and Zazar aside as she flung herself down next to where Askepott lay. "Do not hinder me!" the Rock-Maiden cried. "The spell still envelopes her and she hasn't let out her last breath yet."

Faster than thought, white sand geysered upward between the Rock-Maiden's fingers as she formed it into a casket of the purest crystal to shelter the old Wysen-wyf.

At her gesture, the casket lifted from the sand of which it was formed, coming to rest on a plinth of stone that arose from the surface of the cove. Now Askepott, occasional sparks from the spell still glittering like random fireflies, lay on a crystal bed, her head on a pillow and a warkat at her feet. On the side of the casket, Petra formed a plaque in the crystal spelling out the name *Askepott* in raised letters.

"There," she said. "She will sleep undisturbed until you can find a cure for the spell that has almost killed her."

"But you were frozen—" Zazar said. The events of the past few moments had happened too rapidly for her to grasp at once.

"The rocket," Petra explained. "Its fire thawed me."

"But why did you do this—how—? I thought you had no reason to love Askepott."

The Rock-Maiden gazed at the casket. "Askepott was kind to me, in her fashion. And kind to Mikkel as well."

Ysa spoke truly, Zazar realized, when she guessed that Petra loves Mikkel. *Different as our two species are, nevertheless, she loves him. What a world.*

A white vessel hove into view, its sails brilliant in the morning light. Petra looked up and pointed at it proudly. "Look you, out to sea. It is Ridder Rødskjegg, Knight of the Red Beard, come to my rescue and that of you others as well, though he came almost too late for Askepott."

Just then, the sailors from *Spume Maiden* came pounding around the headland, one with sword drawn and the other with arrow nocked. Petra immediately gripped her remaining spear and shifted the buckler to her left hand. She moved toward where her other spear had fallen.

"Neither arrow nor sword can harm me," she said, her voice full of challenge. "Come ahead and do your worst."

"Stay!" Ysa ordered. "Put up your weapons. We are all friends here." She turned to Petra. "We have a boat. Can we all go out to your beautiful white ship, so that we may talk with—with your red-bearded knight? My grandson? Yes, and Zazar's also?"

The Rock-Maiden's brows pulled together. Reluctantly she lowered her spear as the Sea Rover sailor released the tension on his bowstring. The other man sheathed his sword though his hand stayed close to the hilt.

"Let me go first," she said at last. "Explain the situation. I'm sure that Ridder Red Fox will be interested, but do not expect your presence or the tales you tell to restore his memory. Then, it will be his decision as to how many of you will go to his ship and how many will return to your own."

"*Spume Maiden* was at anchor not far from here," Zazar said, "though I expect Rohan is even now making for this spot. He can spot a flying Ice Dragon as well as the next one."

"Then there is no time to lose."

"Here," Ysa said, loosening a scarf and handing it to the Rock-Maiden. "This bears my colors and insignia. Let Mikkel fly it as a banner and it will inform Rohan that he is to remain neutral, at least for the present."

"I hope he is bright enough to figure it out," Zazar muttered. "If not, there's apt to be a fight he won't want to have."

"Then we will not waste time. You," Petra said, addressing the two men. "I presume you rowed here."

"Yes, Lady, we did."

"Then put us all into the boat, save Askepott, of course, and take us out to *Snow Gem* at once." She turned to the other two women. "Askepott will be safe here."

"But not left here permanently," Zazar said.

"No. Not permanently."

Twenty-two

In the Council Chamber at the Castle of Fire and Ice, Gaurin NordornKing called a conference with his nobles. Tordenskjold was absent, of course, but Svarteper and Mjødulf occupied their accustomed seats. Baldrian of Westerblad was absent, as was Baron Arngrim. Håkon of Erlend was present, however, and, for a wonder, so was Gangerolf of Guttorm.

"Here," the NordornKing said, indicating a letter bearing a red wax seal, "is disturbing news from our friend, kinsman, and guardian of our southern border, Earl Royance."

He handed the letter to Einaar who took it from him and began to read:

> Greetings, my liege lord, friend and ally, from your vassal, Royance of Grattenbor and of Åskar.
>
> It is reluctantly that I must report unrest on your borders and, yea, throughout the land if rumor is to be believed. The good and able Baldrian the Fair is abroad with a troop of men, putting down outbreaks of violence

where he finds them. My kinsman Nikolos and I would go
forth as well save for his old injury in a tournament. Also,
my beloved Countess Mjaurita, having lived as a wealthy
widow for some years, has expressed herself unwilling to
repeat the experience. We had quite a spirited discussion
about it. Therefore, I have sent for aid from the Lord High
Marshal of Rendel. He has promised to send a young offi-
cer, Cebastian, your cousin, and a company of soldiers to
aid Baldrian and I expect them daily.

I have no doubt that this unpleasantness will soon be
resolved, so you may have no fear either for your safety,
that of your beautiful NordornQueen, nor of the NordornLand itself. When all is secure once more I will come
to Cyornas and report in person.

"He does not mention Iselin," Ashen said.

"No, Madame, he does not," Einaar said. "But I am sure that if
Princess Elin were in the least peril, he would have found soldiers
to go and reinforce the manor and even have ridden out himself
regardless of his wife's frowns."

A ripple of laughter went around the table.

"There will be no need," Bjaudin declared. "I will take some
men and go to Iselin myself."

"It is a brave thought," Gaurin said, "but I believe that a better
way to quell any unrest that seems to have arisen in our land during the winter is to take the path of peace. I will go a-progress
through our land, seeing the people and having them see me, and
talking with them and listening to their grievances. Time enough
for soldiers and drums and warfare."

"I will go with you, then, Father."

"No, I will need you and Einaar to see to the governance of
our land in my absence. Obey me in this."

"As in all things, Father, but I would rather be with you. Is it
not important for the people to see me as well?"

"It is, but now is not the time. Obey your father, my son," Ashen said. "In the event that Tordenskjold and Rohan are successful in returning Mikkel to us, you and Duke Einaar will be needed here to make him properly welcome." She turned to Gaurin. "I will go with you in Bjaudin's stead. Surely if the people see me, they will know that our purpose is peace and they will be soothed thereby."

"Are you well enough for such a journey?"

"Of course I am!" she exclaimed. "It is for the good of our kingdom. It would be a disgrace if I stayed behind."

"Good thoughts all," Einaar said. "May I make a further suggestion?"

"Of course, my brother," Gaurin replied.

"Bring back the custom of the King's Penny, as it was in the days of Cyornas of noble memory."

Gaurin pondered a moment. "Share the benefits of NordornLand peace. Yes, that we will do. We will grant a silver penny to each farmer, townsman, and shareholder, and a gold penny to the mayor or other magistrate of every village."

"I will give orders that treasure boxes be filled." Einaar smiled with a trace of his old mischievousness. "It will give the guards something to do, looking after the boxes."

"Then it is settled. The NordornKing and the NordornQueen will both go a-progress through the NordornLand. Let heralds ride forth and so proclaim."

The nobles arose from their chairs and bowed deeply to their sovereigns. Mjødulf spoke for all: "Earl Royance is a man of great experience but unlearned in the ways of our Land of Ever Snow. We have experienced this sort of thing before, and from what I believe are the same reasons. These problems arise from the annoyances of a hard winter and living too closely together and, as such, will be easily and quickly resolved. May your journey and your generosity bring with it the fruits of peace to our land once more." Then, with a smile, he added, "And when you see my aunt and uncle, please give them my best regards. It would seem that each have found a match in the other."

"Yes, I am going with you, and that's final," Ayfare said firmly. "And Nalren will be attending your lord husband. Someone has to look after you."

"But what about Cyornas Castle?" Ashen asked, amused.

"Huldra is perfectly capable of managing in my absence. And Nalren has been training Rols as his second. The place will survive without us."

"The entourage is growing even as we speak."

"You must put on a brave, fine show, and well you know it. Your ladies, your House Troops, Gaurin NordornKing's House Troops, servants to handle the wagons and baggage—yes, it will be a sizable entourage. But think, my lady. How long has it been since you and the NordornKing have gone out and seen your people, and even more important, let them see you?"

It was a fair question. Ashen pondered several minutes. "Years, I think. We have not ventured far from the city walls since we returned from our encounter with the Mother Ice Dragon. We were both sorely hurt, and lay abed for quite a while. And then, it seemed that the people were content to come to us, to glimpse us from the streets of Cyornasberg and we grew content to have it so."

"Well, now unrest has sprung up from somewhere—and never mind what I think of the source—"

"Now, Ayfare, Madame Ysa is out at sea, searching for Mikkel. Unless she took messenger birds with her I'm sure she could have had nothing to do with the present uneasiness among the people."

"Be that as it may, unrest exists and no one can put all to rights but you and Gaurin NordornKing. And both of you will need special care, such as your ladies and his gentlemen cannot provide. So we are going with you and there's an end to it."

Ashen smiled, happy in spite of her protestations, for Ayfare's loving bullying. "Then let us pack fine garments to show us off to our best advantage."

"Already being done," Ayfare returned, smiling as well. "You need to select gifts for Princess Elin. Iselin will be your first major destination."

"And then on to Åskar, the center of the unrest. I am a little uneasy about taking all the House Troops. Don't you think it looks too, well, aggressive?"

"Eighteen armed men to guard the NordornKing and NordornQueen and to see to the safety of their servants and belongings, not to mention protecting the King's Penny? There are those who would say they are not nearly enough. I daresay Count Baldrian will be glad of their presence. Gossip has it that he is guarding Åskar and, through it, both Rendel and the Nordorn-Land though he has only a handful of soldiers."

"I wonder what Rohan and Tordenskjold have found by now."

"Well, if these things go as they usually do, one or the other of them will have found Prince Mikkel and are bringing him back home, and they will arrive just as you and the NordornKing are halfway to Åskar."

At that, Ashen laughed aloud. "I hope your predictions are correct! That will give Bjaudin NordornPrince something to keep him occupied, mending young Mikkel's manners after such a long sojourn with untamed Wykenigs. We will keep messengers busy, going back and forth, while we are gone. I wouldn't want to miss this news for any reason."

"And you say you are my uncle?" asked the red-bearded man, for what Zazar thought must surely be the dozenth time.

"In a manner of speaking," Rohan replied patiently. "I am the foster son of your mother, Ashen NordornQueen and but a few years younger than she. I have functioned as uncle to all of her children, you included."

"My mother is a queen. That would make my father a king."

"Gaurin NordornKing. Both your parents have been sick with worry over you, since you were taken captive by Holger den Forferdelig."

Mikkel shook his head, clearly not understanding. "But Holger is my father, though we have a blood quarrel between us."

"Let me speak," said the Duchess Ysa. "Grandson, it is clear to me that you are bespelled. Until we find a way to lift this cloud from your mind, we must ask that you believe what we tell you, for it is the truth and also it is for your long term benefit."

Petra, standing behind Mikkel's chair, put her hand on his shoulder. "I think this lady, and the other one as well, speak the truth as they know it."

He turned and looked up at her. "And do you also think I am bespelled?"

"I have thought it for a long time, ever since you came to live with me in the City 'Neath the Waves."

Zazar noticed Ysa flinching visibly at this; it was obvious to the old Wysen-wyf that the Duchess was having trouble with the idea that the Princess of the Rock-Maidens loved Mikkel in the way that a woman loves a man and, furthermore, that he returned it. For all his grown-up appearance, however, Zazar could tell that emotionally he was still a child, and could not yet understand what it meant when a man and woman loved each other.

"Then you do advise me to believe my . . . my uncle and my granddam and— Who did you say you were?"

"Zazar," she replied a little snappishly. "Also your granddam because I reared your mother from the moment she was born."

"Granddam Ysa. Granddam Zazar. And Uncle Rohan?" Mikkel said, a little hesitantly.

"That is correct," answered the Sea-Rover. "And we have come to take you back to your NordornLand home, if you will go."

"I confess I am intrigued by your stories," Mikkel said. He turned to Petra again. "Would you want to go as well?"

"I will follow you."

Rock-Maidens, the crew and warriors of the snow-white ship, crowded at the door, intent on finding out what their Princess and the human man she had brought to live in their city were going to do. They murmured among themselves at the declaration that she was willing to go with him to the unknown lands whence he came, but Zazar could detect only curiosity, not protest.

"Admiral-General Tordenskjold—do you remember him?— even now searches for Holger den Forferdelig," Rohan said. "There is some score to settle for he was most insolent when we first encountered him. Therefore, we can be reasonably confident that he will not fall upon our ships without warning, while we sail south."

"May I suggest that you take the crystal casket that holds Askepott aboard *Spume Maiden*, and carry it back with us?" Ysa asked.

"Of course, it will be done, for it is unthinkable that it be left behind, at the mercy of wind and water. I think I might need the services of Princess Petra to help us remove it from its plinth."

"Oh, any of us can do that," Petra replied with a careless shrug. "Hild, please come forward. To you I give the task of overseeing this delicate project." She turned to Rohan. "She is my body-sib and ruled the city in my absence."

" 'Body-sib.' What does that mean?"

"It means that she was formed as I was, from the body of a Rock-Maiden who had been captured and ravished by a Rock-Man. She was Princess of the Rock-Maidens, even as I am. I emerged from the rubble of her corpse first and so inherited her title."

"I see," Rohan said, clearly not seeing at all.

One of the Rock-Maidens squeezed past the crowd and through the door into the cabin. She bowed. "I accept the task gladly, my Princess."

"And I will assign six men to assist her," Rohan said. He turned to the Rock-Maiden Princess. "I would suggest that you join the Duchess and Granddam Zazar on *Spume Maiden* rather than remain on the white ship."

"*Snow Gem*," Mikkel said. "Why do you want to separate us?

"It is only for a short time," Rohan said. "I will stay on board *Snow Gem*."

"I see what Rohan Sea-Rover is about," Petra said, smiling. The light glinted off the planes of her face. "We make an exchange, me

for him. He wants to make sure that we do not decide to sail away
into a fog bank and lose him in the trackless ocean. Nor can the
women search for us with the Ritual of Seeing, now that Gunnora
claims to be aware of every time the ritual is invoked."

Rohan smiled in return. "Also, perhaps I could even show my
nephew a few tricks when it comes to managing the vessel."

For the first time Mikkel's face lit up with enthusiasm. "That
would be wonderful! The ship fairly sails herself, but I admit there
is a lot I do not know about maneuvering."

"It is settled, then," Ysa declared. "Please have Askepott's crystal casket placed in my cabin, Rohan. I wish to study and think on
how to release her from the spell she is currently under."

"That may come before we release Mikkel from his spell, if it
can be done," Zazar commented. "Both enchantments were laid by
a sorceress whose Power we do not yet know, except that she is exceptionally strong. However, I will lend such help as I may in both
endeavors."

"So let it be done," Petra declared. "I will go now to the Sea-
Rover vessel. When Hild has brought Askepott from the shore,
both ships will set their sails and their course southward. There, in
a strange country among strange people, Ridder Rødskjegg, we
will be together once more."

She reached out and touched Mikkel's cheek. Zazar had the
feeling that if they had been alone, she would have kissed him.

Mikkel didn't seem to notice. He appeared more interested in
the prospect of learning more about how to sail his ship. That, and
in being around a man who wasn't trying to kill him.

"Do you know the game of *Hnefa-Tafl*, Uncle?" he asked. "We
played it often in Holger's steading. I have made a board but none
of the Rock-Maidens care to learn. Perhaps we could have a game
or two on our way to Cyornas Fjord."

Ysa, Zazar, and Petra watched from the deck of *Spume Maiden*
while Hild and the Sea-Rovers rigged a woven rope sling and used

pulleys to haul the crystal casket aboard. It seemed curiously light. Then, with it still swathed in ropes, they carried it to the cabin customarily occupied by Rohan and lashed it down securely lest it shift during the voyage and come to grief. When all was secure, the Rock-Maiden Hild returned to *Snow Gem*.

"I confess, my heart was in my throat during the transfer," Ysa declared. "These men can be so rough."

"Hild made sure they could handle their burden well enough," Petra said. "However, even if they had been clumsy, the crystal is tough enough to survive all but a deliberate attack with a hammer or maul."

Zazar gazed at the occupant of the casket. She lay on her transparent bed as softly as if on the finest snow-thistle silk mattress. Sparks still glittered inside the crystal from time to time, like so many fireflies that had been trapped within. Far from the pallor of death, her face was of good color. Truly, she looked as if she were merely sleeping and would waken at a word or a touch on her shoulder.

"They will be raising the anchor soon," Ysa said. "I will go out on deck for the fresh air until we get well and truly under way, for I do not expect to do so very often on our voyage. I have much thinking and meditating to do and watching the horizon rise and fall can affect my digestion. This is not conducive to clear thinking." She wrapped her cloak around her shoulders. "Zazar, I suggest that you do the same, unless you are untroubled by the motion of the ship."

"If Askepott were—well, I started to say *alive*—I daresay she would join you. But I will stay where I am," Zazar replied. "I have thinking of my own to do."

"And a good portion of that thinking is about me," Petra said, once the cabin door had closed behind the Duchess.

"Indeed, it is."

"It doesn't take any extraordinary effort to understand. It is part of why I am here, on this ship, rather than on *Snow Gem*. Well, make the most of your opportunity. What do you wish to know of me?"

"First, how did Holger den Forferdelig come to take you prisoner? And how did he keep you in such a state?"

Petra shrugged. "I was careless and not properly wary, and fell into a trap intended to catch an animal for Holger's table. I have learned better since. As for how he kept me prisoner, it was the iron. My people cannot endure the touch of cold iron and all the captives in Holger's steading wore iron torques. Iron burns us, makes us weak, and takes away many of our powers unless we drink a special potion made from a very rare plant, and I had none with me. I had to wrap my torque in a scrap of cloth to keep it from burning me. When Mikkel removed it, it was as if I had awakened from a long and none too pleasant sleep. Mikkel did not seem to be similarly affected; he was under a different bespelling."

"You spoke of a special elixir. Is that how you are enduring the iron around you on this ship?"

"It is." The Rock-Maiden held up her arm. Dangling from one of her bracelets was a tiny stone flask. "This is all I have until I can find the special plant and make more."

"I have some skill in herb lore. Let me have but a drop of it, and I will try to duplicate it for you."

"You are very kind. If you can do this, you will put me in your debt."

"You do not seem overly concerned that Mikkel will remember all his past and return to live in the place where he was born."

"No, Madame, I am not. I think his memory is locked away so securely that even your Duchess with all her books and all her spells cannot retrieve it."

"When you set sail, you had no intention of actually allowing Mikkel's ship within ten leagues of Holger's vessel, did you." It was not a question.

Petra laughed and stretched, rubbing her smooth arms. "Of course not! *Snow Gem* is a tiny ship, smaller even than the least of Holger's fleet. Red Fox might be able to stand off the *Marmel*, but he would not last an hourglass turning if he should encounter Holger and *Dragon Blood*!"

"Perhaps Mikkel's fate is tied to Gunnora's, and if she dies so will he. I do not know how to predict this."

"Perhaps. I do not know."

"I knew that his future was clouded well before he ran away on his harebrained adventure. So did the Wave Reader Jens on the ill-fated *GorGull*, and he told him so. I will do a Ritual of Asking once we arrive at our destination."

"I have heard of such."

"It is one of our few ways of scrying the future, and of interpreting the present."

"I have seen that you are a holder of Power, even as I hold some Power of my own. So was—so is Askepott."

"I could wish that Askepott were able to add her store to the mix. Among us, surely we could fathom a way to thwart the Sorceress's daughter, Gunnora, and to restore Mikkel to his rightful place in life. Even if it turns out not to be in the NordornLand but with you."

Petra shrugged. "Which would be my preference, as you know. Well, all is not yet beyond reckoning or repair. Askepott is not irretrievably lost. I filled the casket with a special kind of air my people use to preserve those who are not yet dead. Askepott will lie safely until we find a way to bring her back from the edge of the Void."

"This has been a very enlightening discussion, Princess. I believe that the Duchess Ysa need not know all of what we have been talking of," Zazar said thoughtfully. "I think you know more than you are telling about Mikkel, and I suspect you will tell me nothing more until we have consulted my kettle and possibly not then. Let Ysa concentrate on releasing Askepott from the spell that has almost killed her and let me work on the problem of my grandson's bespelling."

"You mean to withhold information from her?"

" 'Postpone informing' her is more accurate. Let me give you some good advice. You have not been entirely open with me, but you have not lied, either. You are skilled in the art of saying one thing and concealing another, but Ysa is even more so. It is no mean feat to outmaneuver Ysa. If she gets the least inkling that you have done so, you can be sure that she will become a smiling enemy."

"Thank you for the warning. I will be doubly careful in my dealings with her."

"She is sincere in one thing, though, and that is her desire to release Askepott from her slumber."

"I believe Askepott will sleep long before that riddle is solved." Petra gazed at the crystal casket, beautiful even though swathed in ropes. "Perhaps both you and the Duchess will live to see her with us once more."

"Hark. She returns."

The lady in question entered the cabin and pulled the door closed behind her. "The breeze is freshening, which is the same as saying it's enough to freeze an ordinary person out on deck. The lights in the sky are brilliant but not enough that I want to stay out there and look at them. I have sent for hot food and drink—you do eat and drink, Petra? Good. I have a few ideas regarding Askepott that I would like to discuss with you both."

"We stand ready to profit by your wisdom and learning," the Rock-Maiden responded demurely.

Zazar snorted, and managed to turn it into a fit of coughing. "By all means," she said, when she could speak, "let us pool our knowledge, such as it is. It may yield no results before we can get to Cyornas Castle and your books, but it may give us a general direction in which to go."

"I think that this time Esander will not grudge me the loan of the books. Not grudge it at all."

Twenty-three

C ount Tordenskjold of Grynet, Admiral-General of the NordornLand's growing fleet, was never happier than when at
sea. That he was in command of the finest, newest ship in the
fleet, and furthermore in pursuit of an enemy who was unaware
he was being tracked, sweetened his mood to the point that he
was actually amiable when a sailor let a line slip.

"Sorry, sir," the man said, cringing a little.

Tordenskjold could tell he was expecting of one of the
Admiral-General's famous explosions of temper at the slightest
mishap. But he was feeling far too content for that.

"Give it a turn around that cleat, boy," Tordenskjold told him.
"That'll secure it."

"Aye, Admiral-General." The sailor quickly did as he was told
and vanished, perhaps in anticipation of Tordenskjold's good temper evaporating like morning fog.

Fog. Tordenskjold scanned the horizon. No sign of sail, yet.
There was definitely a bank of fog lying a league or so distant.
Holger, if he were out there, could not see him, but contrariwise,
neither could he see Holger. Furthermore, in such a fog, a ship

would be vulnerable to running up against floating ice. No captain worth the salt spray that rimed his beard would risk that. Therefore, he would remain out in the open, every man on full alert, and ready to rush into action at a moment's notice.

Do not attack at once, he told himself, mindful of the instructions given him by Gaurin NordornKing. Prince Mikkel's whereabouts may have been discovered, but Holger still might have information that would be useful. No sense in sending him down to the Sea-terror Draig's lair before learning all that he knew.

Contentedly, he watched Jens, lately Spirit Drummer and Wave Reader on the *GorGull*, at his duty. Sea-Rovers did not hold with such as magical bowls and water that formed little people who spoke and, Tordenskjold discovered, neither did he. The old ways not only sufficed, they were also better in his estimation.

Jens, busy stroking his drum and scanning the waters ahead, signaled the helmsman who gave the wheel a turn. Presently, *Ice Princess* glided past a large chunk of pack ice, newly broken free to float where the currents took it.

So deftly had Jens estimated the size of the ice and its location, Tordenskjold felt the tiny vibration as the ship's hull kissed the hidden underwater floe. Nothing, he knew, had been harmed; not even the paint covering the planks would need to be touched up. Jens looked back at the Admiral-General from his station at the prow of the vessel and grinned.

Showing off, Tordenskjold thought, as he grinned back. And well entitled. Holger might know these waters like he knew the hairs on his head, but he did not have a talented Wave Reader to make the way smooth for him, nor one who was also a Spirit Drummer who could foretell all sorts of other matters as well.

Tordenskjold made a note to have Jens see into his future. Not, of course, that he had any doubt as to the outcome when he and Holger should meet, but it never hurt to have a little foreknowledge as well.

Holger den Forferdelig's third ship, *Marmel*, never left the steading via the secret way. By tradition, the three-ship fleet sailed out through Forferdelig Sound, blood-red banners flying. Later, once they had cleared the headland, these would be furled and set back for use when Holger decided to declare his identity.

Even if the Wykenigs had wanted to use the secret way, *Dragon Blood* was too big to fit through the channel, as was *Ice Rider*. Only *Marmel* was small enough. Then little *Marmel* came into its own, running from a larger foe. The entrance to the narrow fjord had trapped more than one vessel whose rash, unwary captain found himself unable to come about and escape when the *Marmel*'s captain, Ridder Shraig, turned to fight.

Later, when the ship had been vanquished, it was either towed out of the fjord with a greatly lightened cargo hold and let go with much merriment at the expense of the captain who had been taken so easily, or the hulk removed to be scuttled where it would not be a peril to Wykenig navigation. The bottom of an inlet some two or three leagues distant was littered with the corpses of ships taken and destroyed.

Therefore, this day, Holger's three ships sailed proudly from the sheltered entrance to Forferdelig Sound, scarlet banners floating in the breeze. They made a brave show; Ridder Holger was the only Wykenig who could boast of commanding three fine ships. His pride in his fleet was dimmed only by Gunnora's absence. Surely the Knight-King of the Upplands should be graced by the presence of his lady wife when he went out a-venturing. But Gunnora was absent on some unnamed errand and he knew from experience that trying to find out what she did not want to divulge was an exercise that would yield him nothing but domestic disharmony. So, wisely, he said nothing.

After all, she had counseled him that a rich prize was his for the taking, if he so chose: two NordornLand ships were plying the waters close to Holger's haunts. Also, she hinted at a mystery ship that needed investigating. Then she had left.

The NordornLand ship he craved as his own, Holger knew,

was as good as lost to him with young Ridder Red Fox's disappearance, for he had nothing with which to barter. Now he wished he had come to some kind of agreement back during the winter rather than teasing Red Fox's parents with hints of how well he was doing.

But no matter. If there were three ships to contend with, he also had three ships and they were filled with Wykenig warriors, all on edge with battle spirit after the forced idleness of winter.

Dragon Blood led the flotilla by a league and a half—far enough distant that *Ice Rider* and *Marmel* could come upon a quarry almost unremarked and flank the ship under attack. It was a maneuver Holger had employed many times. If, however, there really were three NordornLand ships, each of his would have its target laid out plain.

Gunnora had been vague about that third ship, hinting only that it was, somehow, different from the others. A white ship, she said, and gave no further details. As usual, Holger did not question her about how she came by her information. She was a woman of mystery, and she employed mysterious ways.

A lookout high on the main mast called out. "Sail on the horizon!"

"How many?" Holger shouted back.

"One."

One. Holger frowned, thinking. That might mean that the Nordorn flotilla had separated, or it might also mean that the man to whom he had spoken months ago who identified himself as Admiral-General Tordenskjold of the NordornLand, the one he observed to be capable of being very unpleasant if the mood took him, was canny enough to have blundered onto Holger's own tactics.

It deserved investigating. He gave orders that the other two ships hide in a fog bank and the parley flag be run up.

"No, surely," said Asbjørn, first mate on *Dragon Blood*.

"Learn patience," Holger rejoined. "We have nothing to lose by negotiating first."

"The men will mutter at the delay in fighting."

"Let them. I'm in command here, and there will be fighting enough for all before we return to Forferdelig Sound. Now, obey me."

"Aye, sir."

Presently, the parley flag—white with a branch of greenery and a talking-stick in gold—floated out in the slight wind as the two ships neared each other. After some delay, the NordornLand ship ran up its parley flag as well.

"Now," said Holger, "we will see what we are about."

The NordornKing and NordornQueen, mounted on palfreys, rode at the head of their procession, out through the gate of the Castle of Fire and Ice, through the town, passing through the barbican where Count Svarteper, Lord High Marshal of the NordornLand, waited to bid the sovereigns farewell. He was formally clad in armor, as befitted his office, and over it wore a jupon of black embroidered with a silver devil-tree, his device. Once his hair had been as black as his jupon; now it rivaled the silver of the embroidered devil-tree. He was accompanied by Hod, a young trumpeter who had distinguished himself in the Battle of Pettervil. Now he bore the rank of lieutenant and had become Svarteper's chief aide. Out of pride, perhaps, the Lord High Marshal refused to have a second in command.

By custom, Svarteper presented the monarchs with new banners—Gaurin's was of spring green bearing a silver snowcat, chained with a silver collar, and Ashen's, flame rising from a blue vessel on a white ground. Two guards riding behind the king and queen accepted the banners Hod handed them, unfurled them, and inserted the thin rods that would hold them out even if the air were too still to let them flutter bravely.

"Good fortune to you, Sir and Madame," Svarteper told them. "Have no fear for the safety of the realm in your absence."

"You stand like a bulwark against anyone who would disturb the peace of our country," Gaurin replied.

"Farewell," Ashen said. "Look for our return when we have seen to the welfare of our kingdom."

Then, spurs and harness jingling and wagon wheels creaking, the entourage made its way out through the north gate of the city and onto the road leading to Iselin, their first stop in their journey. To Ashen's acute embarrassment, her House Troops struck up the verses of "The Song" that had first been composed when she had followed after Gaurin to aid him in the battle against the Mother Ice Dragon. In moments, the other Troops took up the melody as well, and everyone else who knew the words:

> *Stalwart Gaurin, praiseworthy NordornKing,*
> *Faces unflinching the danger unknown.*
> *His greatest weapon, steel-slender NordornQueen,*
> *They live forever in story and song.*

Gaurin reached out and took her gloved hand in his. "You are well loved by everyone, my dear," he said, eyes twinkling, "and not just by me."

Nevertheless, her cheeks burned even though she rejoiced at Gaurin's good humor and obvious pleasure at this undertaking. He seemed to be feeling a resurgence of his old strength and resilience and if it took being disconcerted by the singing of a song, she would gladly endure it for his sake.

One of Gaurin's projects, early in his kingship, had been to order all main roads to be paved with stone if possible, and if not, to have a bed of pebbles laid to keep them from becoming impassable morasses in foul weather. Thus had the Duchess Ysa been able to travel between Iselin and Cyornasberg in weather that, in another time, would have had her coach bogged down to the axles.

Now the monarchs and their entourage rode through slowly melting snow, reaching their destination late in the same day on which they set out.

Princess Elin, wrapped in a fur-lined cloak and flanked by such dignitaries as Iselin boasted, waited for them at the manor house.

Andre Norton & Sasha Miller

"Welcome, Father, welcome, Mother!" she said. "Your message announcing your progress came just in time to delay my own through Iselin. Now we can go together."

"A pleasant thought." Gaurin dismounted, accepting only minimal help from Nalren. He did, however, take the staff Nalren offered. "I am stiff. Unused to the saddle, it would seem," he said a trifle wryly. "Perhaps this outing will get me back in trim once more."

Ashen also allowed Hensel, one of her Troopers, to lift her from her saddle. She smiled a little, remembering how Goliat had used to render her this service, and how his big hands had almost met around her waist. Brave Goliat, fallen protecting her from one of the Mother Ice Dragon's spawn. A memorial to him stood in the public square in Cyornasberg.

"I am almost as stiff as you," Ashen told her husband. "We will be glad of hot food."

"All should be in readiness, both for you and those with you," Elin said. She turned to the seneschal, identified by the pewter cup on the necklace he wore. "Harald?"

"Good comfort awaits within, Your Majesties," he said, bowing.

"And where do you go when you leave Iselin?" Elin asked when they were all seated and the meal served.

"We have heard of unrest and rebellion in Åskar. Earl Royance has sent a letter requesting assistance."

"The House Troops are hardly up to the task of quelling a rebellion," Elin observed.

"Lord High Marshal Lathrom of Rendel has already dispatched my cousin, Cebastian, with a troop of men," Gaurin said. "He is an able commander, and I look forward to seeing him again. I have no doubt that the rebellion will be well and truly over by the time we reach Åskar."

"May it be so. Now, please, enjoy yourselves in such hospitality as I am honored to offer my esteemed parents."

Ashen quirked an eyebrow at this unexpected courtesy on her daughter's part, and then told herself that Elin was, at last, growing up. Tinka-Lillfot had begun her entertainment, and Ashen turned her attention to the little woman, curious about her. She was truly clever, as were the tricks she had taught her little dog—Ashen found herself laughing out loud and applauding with unfeigned enthusiasm. Perhaps she could persuade someone like Tinka-Lillfot to take up permanent residence in Cyornas Castle. That way, Lady Pernille could rest at times in the evenings.

Though it strained the resources of Iselin's manor house and its surroundings, somehow space was found for all of Gaurin and Ashen's people and nobody but the jarls who drove the wagons had to sleep in the stable. This was no great hardship for them, as the beasts gave off much heat and so they rested as comfortably as Gaurin and Ashen in the big house.

The next day, the NordornKing and NordornQueen began distribution of the King's Penny to the farmers and herders and other good people of Iselin who had come to crowd beside the road in hopes of getting a glimpse of the fabled Maimed Majesties.

One farmer spoke for all. "Thank'ee, Queen," he said as he doffed his cap. "You're a good 'un, so they all say and yon King, too, and I think you oughter call it the 'King and Queen's Penny.'"

He bowed as Ashen laughed with pleasure. "Perhaps next time," she said. "For now, we follow the old custom."

Elin obviously basked in the goodwill shown to her parents. She distributed no coins, but accepted the praise and adulation of the people of Iselin with gracious smiles.

She is hoping that Iselin will be hers, Ashen thought, *and is practicing for that time. Well, it does no harm. Who knows when Ysa will return.* At that, a fresh pang struck her, at the prospect of being absent when Mikkel came back home.

Resolutely, she put the thought aside. For now, they were on the road to Åskar, the trouble spot of the NordornLand, and where she and Gaurin would be most needed.

Signs of the near-rebellion were visible along the road—a crofter's steading burnt, winter grain left unharvested.

"Our good Earl may not have told us the full story," Gaurin observed. "I think matters may have stood worse for him here in Åskar than he let us know."

"Let us hasten to his capital," Ashen said. "I hope that he and the Countess have suffered no harm."

"With Cebastian and his men coming to his aid, I doubt that he has been in great peril. Don't forget, my Ashen, that Royance can command respect and obedience by a look. Still, it is a measure of how things stand that he sent what word to us that he did."

At that moment, they espied a rider, accompanied by a troop of armed men, approaching. Two of the soldiers carried banners, one bearing a silver burhawk on a red ground, the other four trees, quartered, on a blue ground.

"That is Royance, with the troops sent by Lathrom!" Gaurin exclaimed. "I recognize the Rendelian banner!"

Both parties picked up speed and in a few moments, they had caught up with each other.

"Well met, Sir!" Royance cried, tactfully extending his left hand so that the NordornKing would not have to use his withered one. "Well met, indeed!"

Gaurin grasped the proffered hand. "I rejoice to see you in health. And who is this? Can it really be my kinsman?"

The man addressed grinned and moved his horse closer. "It is Cebastian, Sir, in the flesh."

"You've grown into a real warrior who would be an asset to any kingdom. How can I persuade you to come to the Nordorn-Land?"

"You would have to speak to the Lord High Marshal, Count Lathrom. He regards Steuart as his right arm, and me as his left."

"I remember Steuart. Able man. Count Lathrom, is it? Well, he's deserved elevation to the peerage for a long time. And I do believe I will speak to him. Our own Lord High Marshal is accumulating years, and he has no real second. Surely Lathrom can spare you."

"Sir."

"And who is this?"

"Nikolos, once of Grattenbor, now of Åskar. Earl Royance's King-at-Arms." His left sleeve hung empty.

"This is a gratifying display of old friends' meeting," Royance said, "but it can be conducted in greater comfort—not to mention safety—inside Åskar Manor."

"So shall it be."

"Stay you in the midst of guards, my Ashen."

She nodded. Gaurin guided his horse so that he rode beside Royance and the two men could talk. Typically, as the warriors they were, they rode in the van.

"I see that Cebastian's men have seen service here," the Nordorn King observed.

"That they have, Sir, and recently. I would have been with them—"

"Except that your good lady wife objected," Gaurin finished for him, smiling.

"She is quite formidable. I thought about unleashing her on the rebels. She would have sent them all packing inside an hour."

At that, Gaurin laughed outright.

"Your husband, the NordornKing, is in good humor," Cebastian said to Ashen. He had fallen back so that he rode beside her.

Where he can best guard me, Ashen thought. *Things here must not be as tranquil as they appear on the surface.* "The last time either of us saw you, you were a cadet, just past boyhood," Ashen said. "Now you are a grown man, even as Rohan is."

"And how does Rohan, Madame?" Cebastian asked. "For such close friends as we have always been, I hear from him seldom."

"I am his foster mother, and I hear from him no more often than you," Ashen rejoined.

They continued to converse amiably, as did Gaurin and Royance, until Åskar Manor came into view.

"Ah, I see that the handsome Mjaurita has come out to greet us," Royance observed. "She will have a feast already prepared if I know my wife—and I believe I do."

Presently, the greetings having been given and the royal entourage shown to the places where they would stay while in Åskar, the Nordorners were called in to dinner by Jervin, Earl Royance's Seneschal. There was plenty of room for all, as Royance's Great Hall was large enough and ornate enough to rival that in the Castle of Fire and Ice.

"You are virtually a king in your own land," Ashen noted as she washed her fingertips in the bowl of warm perfumed water and dried them on a linen napkin. "And the Countess Mjaurita a queen."

Royance shrugged. "Just a few comforts for my old age," he said. "And, of course, for my eternally youthful Countess."

Mjaurita laughed. "My lord husband has a wily tongue. He flatters me incessantly."

"No flattery, my dear," Royance said, taking Mjaurita's hand and kissing it. "Truth never is."

"Fie," Mjaurita rejoined, but laughingly.

"When shall we ride out and begin meeting the people of Åskar?" Gaurin asked. "I wish to show myself and the Nordorn-Queen to them, and also to begin distributing the King's Penny."

"Tomorrow, if you are not too tired," Royance said.

"So shall it be."

Then the diners gave themselves up to the pleasures of the feast. Royance and Mjaurita kept no permanent entertainer such as Tinka-Lillfot, but there was a troupe of jongleurs and acrobats early out on the road who performed dazzling feats of skill to the delight of all watching. In addition to having their share of the feast, as they were accustomed to do, the entertainers also received a purse heavy with coin and so they left to find beds in the stables, well satisfied.

Dragon Blood drew close enough to *Ice Princess* that the two captains could converse with another without having to shout.

"And what brings you to my part of the Icy Sea?" Holger inquired.

"I think you know," Tordenskjold replied. "We came seeking Prince Mikkel, but I think you have misplaced him."

"Perhaps, if you give me your fine ship, I can find where I put him."

"You cannot even keep track of that necklace with the big green stone in it you were wearing when last we met," Tordenskjold retorted. "What makes me think you know where our Prince is?"

Holger's face darkened with a scowl. "You had best watch your tongue, if you want to have civil discourse with me."

"Or what?"

"Or I will attack and seize your ship and send you and your men down to the Sea-terror's lair."

"An idle boast. I think you'd have a hard time following through on it." Tordenskjold turned to Sigurd. "Show Captain Holger what he would be facing."

The first mate grinned, and called, "Sea-Rover Marines! Step out!"

As if materializing out of thin air, men armed not only with arrows but also with short, sturdy swords and throwing-spears filled the deck.

"Now," Tordenskjold said, his voice almost a coo, "what was that you were saying about Draig the Sea-terror?"

"Why do you want to attack me?" Holger said, all innocence. "We have shown you no hostility. Just words."

"True enough. So we have another impasse. You cannot produce Prince Mikkel, and I will not give up *Ice Princess*. Oh, what to do, what to do."

For answer, Holger turned to his first mate and said something Tordenskjold could not hear. The order became clear only a moment later, when a signal rocket roared aloft.

"I suggest you surrender now," Holger said, "while I am still in a good mood. Here's what I offer. I won't send you down to Draig's lair, but will allow you to take your boats and as many men will fit into them even though the boats are valuable and I will have some pains to replace them. But I like you, Admiral-General. Not many men would parley with me with such spirit as you have shown. You deserve to be rewarded."

"And you deserve to be boarded and vanquished!" Tordenskjold shouted. He turned to the eager Sea-Rovers. "Make ready!"

The lookout above cupped his hands and shouted, "Sails!"

"Where away?" shouted Sigurd.

"Yonder, coming out of that fog bank!"

Tordenskjold immediately rushed forward, where he could get an unobstructed view in the direction the lookout indicated. He squinted and put the far-see glass to his eye. Then he swore.

Holger waited where he was, grinning, as Tordenskjold returned to his former spot.

"Two more ships," the Admiral-General said disgustedly. "What is it? You couldn't fight me fairly, but had to bring numbers that even I could not best?"

Holger shrugged. "I don't take chances, Nordorner. You also have three ships, so send up your own signal."

Tordenskjold glared at the Wykenig. "I have no other ships."

"Then that will make it that much easier for me." He turned again to his first mate. "Take down the parley flag and run up my personal banner. Now we fight."

The two ships were drawing nearer, close enough to see their battle flags flying.

"There is another fog bank, closer than the one they came out of," Sigurd said.

Tordenskjold scowled fiercely. "These are not odds to my liking," he told the first mate. "Nor is it to my liking to run from a fight."

"Even less to your liking to lose a fight you cannot win, no matter how brave you and all our men are," Sigurd rejoined. "Hide now, and fight another day."

Tordenskjold took only a moment to think. Sigurd was right. He could not let pride be his undoing. "Make it so."

Immediately Sigurd began issuing orders as quietly as possible.

"Every rag of sail you can find," he told the men. "Helmsman, make for that bank of fog. Jens, speak to that drum of yours. Fill our sails and empty his. Make the way smooth for us, and let the Icy Sea be so rough the enemy cannot follow."

A shout began to go up on *Dragon Blood* as the Wykenigs realized what Tordenskjold was about. But by the time they, too, raised sail, the *Ice Princess* was well away, dashing under a freshening breeze to the safety of the concealing fog.

Twenty-four

Spume Maiden and *Snow Gem* sailed in a leisurely fashion southward, following the jagged Nordorn coastline. Rohan was at the white vessel's helm, Mikkel beside him, ostensibly having another sailing lesson. His attention had flagged, however.

"Is it far?" Mikkel asked. "I hope so, because I would learn even more about my ship with you to teach me."

"Not so far as New Vold, where I live," Rohan told him.

Mikkel shook his head. "And I know nothing of it. Have I ever been there?"

"I don't think so. Your mother and father—"

"Their Maimed Majesties."

"Just so. Your mother and father have not left Cyornasberg where they live since the battle they fought with the Mother Ice Dragon."

"Do they live in a big house?"

"You might say so. It is a castle, made of stone, atop a high cliff on the north side of Cyornas Fjord. There is an ice-river on the other side."

"It sounds nice."

"You used to think so. At least Tjórvi indicated that you did."

"Who is Tjórvi?"

"He is—he was your best friend. He is my son. Now he lives in Cyornas Castle."

"Why?"

"He is there in your place."

Mikkel digested this in silence. Rohan wondered if he truly understood what he had been told. He is still a boy in a man's body, Rohan told himself, though at times he seemed as mature as his physical appearance. The spell he was under had a very uneven effect. Also, Rohan noted, the farther south they sailed, the "younger" Mikkel became.

"Do you think Tjórvi will know me, when we get there?"

"I don't know. We will have to see."

"I'll teach him to play *Hnefa-Tafl*," Mikkel said happily. "Would you play a game with me now?"

"Yes, if you like."

Rohan glanced at Hild, who nodded. Without a word, she took his place at the helm and Rohan followed his nephew, the boy-man Mikkel, Ridder Red Fox, Ridder Rødskjegg, the Knight of the Red Beard, to his cabin where a game board was always set up.

Despite the jongleurs and acrobats, Ashen could tell that Åskar Manor was a house under siege. Many of the weapons that customarily were kept on the walls of a Great Room had been taken down, presumably to be put to active use.

The remains of the dinner had been removed and now Gaurin, Royance, and Cebastian were talking animatedly over the customary wine mixed with snowberry juice. Though they were oblivious to any but themselves, Countess Mjaurita leaned closer to Ashen so she would not be overheard.

"Forgive me, Madame, if I offend, but my Lord Royance has long thought of you as his niece and so perforce do I. Therefore, I will speak plainly: it seems to me that your lord husband looks—tired."

Andre Norton & Sasha Miller

Ashen glanced involuntarily at the three. Even if she had wished to deny the Countess's observation, the truth of it was obvious. Cebastian, in the full flower of his manhood and strength, was holding forth on how best to curb the unrest and deal with the leaders. Royance's hair was snowy and his skin beginning to thin—his eyelids were almost transparent—but he was no less engrossed. Dark smudges under Gaurin's eyes emphasized the gauntness of his cheeks and he leaned his head on one hand. He was perhaps a decade older than Cebastian, more than a decade younger than Royance, and yet he appeared the most aged of the three.

"Indeed," Ashen told Mjaurita, "Gaurin does look fatigued. Both of us have grown soft in our ways, castle-bound, and this progress demonstrates to us what a poor policy it has been."

"Then you are not angered by my words."

"Of course not. I had not thought of Royance as my uncle, but it is a fair assessment. It was he who championed and supported me when first I came to the Rendelian court. It was he who accompanied me to the Snow Fortress when I journeyed there with news of a certain matter that would have meant the end of our world and its domination by the unearthly creature known as the Great Foulness. In short, whenever there was need, there my Lord Royance was." She reached out and touched Mjaurita's hand. "Could I feel any less well disposed toward the woman who finally won his heart? Whom I must regard as my aunt?"

"Madame." Mjaurita bowed her head. Then she looked at Ashen squarely once more. "Now, what shall we do to conserve Gaurin NordornKing's limited strength?"

"I will interrupt their pleasant, bloodthirsty converse and insist that he go to bed," Ashen said.

Both women laughed softly.

"And so shall I bid my lord husband. I daresay that if Cebastian's lady, Alfhild, were here, she would do the same."

"Men were ever an impractical breed," Ashen observed. "And it is we women who must ultimately maintain order."

So saying, the two arose from the table, making enough stir about it that the men paused in their conversation.

"I believe that my lady wife is bidding me call the evening to a close," Royance said. "And, as usual, she is right. We must be rested and ready for whatever tomorrow brings."

"Good night, my good Earl Royance," Gaurin said. "And to you, kinsman. I do believe I will have to insist that Lathrom give you up for the betterment of his staunchest ally, the NordornLand."

Cebastian's eyes twinkled. "It will be as it may, Sir." He bowed to the women, and to Royance and Gaurin. "We will ride out early tomorrow morning among the people of Åskar and see if hope holds true and your presence brings peace once more."

The next morning, Gaurin looked much better, particularly after Nalren's attentions with massage and rouge, but Ashen could tell that there was a deep reservoir of fatigue in her husband. That, she feared, nothing externally applied could remedy, nor could anything daunt his spirit. He mounted his palfrey unaided and waited for the entourage to form.

"Sir, you wear no armor," Cebastian objected. "We are in dangerous country."

"I am here on a mission of peace," Gaurin replied. "It would look ill if I came in full harness astride Marigold even if my charger hadn't been turned out to pasture long since."

"Then at least have your Rinbell sword close."

"That," Gaurin conceded, "I will agree to."

Once the weapon had been secured to his saddle where he could reach it with his left hand, he headed the procession to Åskar Village, the small town that had sprung up about half a league from the manor, begun around a mill at a stream nearby. Ashen followed close behind beside Earl Royance. Cebastian, and a troop of his warriors, rode guard for all. One of the troopers carried a small chest full of coins, ready to be distributed.

The village itself was formed around a central square. Here dwelt artisans and merchants. Farmers brought their grain to be ground at the mill, and bakers in turn came to buy the flour to make bread not only for the manor but also for ordinary people. Some shops had signs to show those who could not read what wares could be found within. Here was the fuller, next to the tailor. A little farther a very new sign proclaimed a shoemaker—possibly a customer for the leather from the cattle. A sign painted with a loom identified the weaver, which in turn meant that somewhere sheep were being raised.

Outside the village, pens held milk cattle and within easy walking distance there was a shop where cheese and butter were sold.

"It is a fine, enterprising place," Gaurin commented as they drew near, "and many people have come out to greet us."

"So they have, Sir," Cebastian told him. "But be on your guard. Not two days past, there were angry mobs in the village square."

"But today all is quiet and serene." Gaurin gestured to Ashen to move closer. "Come, my beloved. Let us go among our people, and distribute the King's Penny."

Close by the community fountain stood the usual raised wooden platform. Here news was proclaimed; here also malefactors of various sorts were brought for punishment. Stocks stood empty, and on the far side of the platform a gallows reared. The soldiers brought out the chest containing coins and placed it on the platform, and one of Gaurin's Troopers, Dain, took his place beside the chest. The NordornKing and NordornQueen remained seated on horseback, so they could see and be seen.

"Good people of Åskar Village!" Dain cried. He had a good, loud voice that carried to the farthest parts of the village. "I am come with Gaurin NordornKing and Ashen NordornQueen to distribute the King's Penny—one silver penny to each citizen, and a gold penny to the mayor! Who might he be? Step forward, and receive the bounty from our gracious Majesties!"

"I'm Torfinn," said a burly man wearing a blacksmith's apron and carrying a hammer. "I reckon you might call me the mayor."

"Then receive the King's Penny and let your people step forward to receive theirs."

Torfinn bit the coin, judged it genuine, and juggled it on his palm. Then he slipped it into his belt pouch. "Gold for me, and silver for everybody else. We doesn't see much coin here besides copper bits. Mostly we trades. A silver penny is a year's wages and a gold is—"

"Ten times that," Dain told him.

The blacksmith gazed at him keenly. "Mighty generous." He turned his attention to Gaurin and Ashen. "And where was you when crops failed and cattle died and we went hungry?"

"We were unaware of your plight, citizen," Gaurin told him. "But now we pray you to let us make up for our oversight."

"Yon chest," Torfinn said, gesturing toward it. "I expect it contains a power of treasure."

"Enough coins to distribute the King's Penny to all," Gaurin told him.

"And more besides, I'll warrant. We hasn't got that many folk here in Åskar Village."

Cebastian scowled. "This fellow was in the forefront of the unpleasantness two days past," he murmured to Ashen. "He's got something in mind, you can count on that."

"There's word you have dragon's treasure, red gems laid up in heaps back in Cyornasberg. And you come to us with pennies."

"We'll take it all!" came a loud, angry voice from the rear of the crowd, "and then we takes the dragon's gems!"

A shout went up and villagers—men and women alike— began to surge forward. In the blink of an eye the situation had turned ugly and threatened to turn uglier still as the crowd surrounded the King and Queen. Torfinn hefted his hammer.

At once Cebastian nudged his horse close and leaned down enough to speak to the man. "Make one move with that thing toward the NordornKing and you will lose your arm at the elbow."

He did not raise his voice, nor brandish the sword he had at his hand. He actually smiled. But the blacksmith grew pale and backed away.

"Leave off!" the man shouted. "Let 'em be!"

But once begun, events like these could not easily be stopped. Weapons—scythes, kitchen knives, cudgels—appeared in villagers' hands.

"Get back, Ashen!" Gaurin shouted. "You, Fritz, guard the Queen!"

With one motion he drew the Rinbell sword, wrapped the reins around his withered hand, and yanked on them, causing his palfrey to rear. The crowd halted and backed up a little, but only for a moment.

Royance also drew steel. "If you won't obey your sovereign King, then obey me!" he roared.

He and Gaurin looked at one another, nodded, and rode forward into battle. They laid about briskly with the flat of their weapons, unwilling to draw blood unnecessarily. From somewhere in the crowd, clumps of rotten vegetables began flying at the soldiers. A Rendelian Trooper ducked, and men immediately tried to pull him off his horse.

Then, as Ashen watched in dismay, a villager picked up a stone and threw it. The sound of it striking Gaurin's head—the head that wore only a tiara and no helmet, the head of the King who loved his people and went unarmed among them—echoed shockingly through the square.

The riot, if riot it was, stopped immediately. Villagers watched in horror as their King slumped in his saddle, dazed and reeling. Cebastian was the first to leap from his horse to help ease him to the ground. Ashen screamed and would have flung herself from her horse likewise, except that she was restrained by her guard.

"Make a cushion for the King's head," Cebastian ordered to no one in particular.

"Use my cloak." Earl Royance handed the garment to Cebastian and then turned to face the villagers. "You are all guilty, one and all, of violence toward the King's Majesty, and you will suffer for it."

"Please, my lord," said one of the villagers. He and a companion grasped the arms of a large, gangling youth, just the sort to act first and think later if at all, and dragged him forward. "He done it. Nobody else. Don't burn the village. Don't kill everybody."

Royance stared at the youth, scowling. "And you are—?"

"Omer. Blacksmith's 'prentice. I didn't mean to hit King, I just throwed the rock." He looked down shamefacedly.

Royance did not move. "Torfinn."

"Aye, my lord?" The man seemed as subdued as he had been aggressive only a moment before.

"You're supposed to be the head man here. Act like it. Take this—this creature of yours into custody and bring him to Åskar Manor where I will put him under lock and key until I decide what to do with him." He gazed around. "None of you is innocent. Go home. Close your doors. Think on what you have done this day. I will decide on your punishment later."

"That is not enough!" Ashen protested despairingly.

"And what would you have me do, Madame?"

"I—I don't know!" Abruptly, she stepped into that strange kind of time where everything seemed to move slowly, if at all. "Let his fate be that of the NordornKing!" Her words were drawn out and hollow-sounding, as if coming from a distance.

I have done this before, she thought, *when Gaurin was under attack. I will do it again, though tardy.* She raised her arms and grasped in both hands the ball of pure Power waiting for her. With all her strength she hurled it at the gangling youth who had brought down her husband. Time abruptly snapped back to its accustomed pace again.

Those standing nearby scattered, terrified, as the ball thundered toward Omer and engulfed him. He staggered back and fell to the ground, his clothing smoldering.

"Now, my lord Royance," Ashen said with unnatural calm, "you may take him and do as you will."

Then the world went black and the last thing she remembered was slipping from her saddle.

Twenty-five

og enveloped Ice Princess, so thick that Tordenskjold couldn't see the bow from his station on the stern.

"I think we've given them the slip," Sigurd told him.

The Admiral-General scowled. "I don't like having to run," he said, not for the first time.

"Nor I, sir, but I'd hate even more nudging elbows with the Sea-terror Draig."

"We should make for home," Tordenskjold said gloomily. "I see nothing to be gained by sailing hither and yon, just waiting to be set upon by a Wykenig fleet. Inform Jens to get that drum of his going and roil the waters for anybody who thinks about chasing us."

"Aye, Admiral-General."

"Maybe," Tordenskjold said, brightening a trifle, "*Nordorn-Queen's Own* will be completed by the time we get back. With another like *Ice Princess* we could take on Holger den Forferdelig and his friends, too. If he has any."

The sea had turned choppy, though no storm lay on the horizon. On the deck of *Spume Maiden*, Zazar suddenly sat bolt upright from where she had been dozing in the fitful sunlight. "Ysa!"

"She is not here," Petra said. "I think she is sick and lying abed in the Sea-Rover Captain's cabin. Shall I go with you to find her?"

"Suit yourself." Zazar, followed by the Rock-Maiden Princess, hurried aft and opened the door. Ysa was lying down, a damp cloth on her forehead.

"What is it?" the Duchess said, obviously irritated. "I am ill."

"Get the water from the ewers."

"Water?"

"*Water*. Surely you remember the word. The ewers are in the cabinet. Get them, and the basin."

"But we used the basin twice, and it took almost all of what we brought—"

Petra laughed. "And while the men were loading the crystal casket on the longboat, my body-sib, Hild, filled them again."

Zazar glanced at Petra. *Who knew she had been so foresighted*, she thought approvingly. "Get the water. There is that I must see."

"I am too ill to be disturbed for this," Ysa said, but nonetheless she opened the cabinet and got down the silver vessels. Then she set up the basin on the table. "What is so important?"

"Maybe nothing. Maybe everything."

Weyse appeared out of nowhere, as was her wont. Zazar picked up the unearthly little creature, who clung to her neck while Ysa began the Ritual of Seeing.

"Who do you wish to see?"

"Ashen first. Then Gaurin."

The image formed quickly. Ashen NordornQueen lay in a litter. It was being carried somewhere, but Zazar could not determine where.

"Can you make the view larger?" Petra asked, interested.

"I will try."

"Gaurin," Zazar breathed. As his image appeared, Weyse whimpered a little.

The NordornKing likewise lay in a moving litter. A bandage, stained with blood, was wrapped around his head. Just within the range of the vision Zazar could see Earl Royance, his face like a thundercloud. A Trooper rode by his side, and a host of others, too blurry to make out their identities, followed.

"So those are the famous Maimed Majesties," Petra murmured.

"And badly hurt," Zazar told her. "Oh, let them speak," she whispered to the basin.

As if he could hear her, the warrior asked Royance, "How long until we reach Cyornasberg? Remember, it has been a long time since I have been in the NordornLand, and I have no clear grasp of how far Åskar Manor is from the city."

"We should be there tomorrow," Royance replied. "We must pause at Iselin to let Princess Elin know how gravely matters stand with her parents. Then we will depart and she will follow after. I have sent Nikolos ahead, bearing the news."

"If only I had been quicker—"

"Do not reproach yourself, Cebastian. You were not to blame for the wild tales that inflamed the people of Åskar."

Ysa started, jostling the basin, and the image winked out. She muttered something under her breath and then, aloud, "A movement of the ship. But how? What has happened?"

Zazar stared at the Duchess keenly. "Is this the result of some of your scheming? I think you know more than you are telling," she said.

"As do I," Petra said. "The ship made no untoward move."

"Well, there's no time to pry it out of you just now," Zazar declared. "It's plain to see that both Ashen and Gaurin are in a bad way, perhaps at the very doorstep of death. We must make all haste to arrive at Cyornas Castle before them so that we may prepare the way for their arrival there. Perhaps there is something we can do, and perhaps not. But I, at any rate, shall try."

With that, Zazar went back on deck and sought out Finrod Felagund. Young Obern was nowhere in sight; Rohan, though allowing him to sail, had reduced him in rank to little better than a common sailor, apprentice to the third mate, Gand.

"We must make all haste back to Cyornasberg," she told the acting captain. "Leave the white ship in your wake if you must, but put up every rag of sail you can find, even your pocket handkerchiefs. There is need."

As the Chieftain's granddam, Zazar's authority carried considerable weight with the Sea-Rovers.

"Aye, Madame Zazar," Finrod said, saluting. He then turned and began shouting orders.

As sails snapped up, the ship began to leap forward in the water. *Let Ysa be sick as she may,* Zazar thought, clutching Weyse more closely, *if only I can get back home in time to forestall what I read on their pale countenances. If only.*

On *Snow Gem*, Rohan noticed at once the raising of *Spume Maiden's* sails. *Something has happened,* he thought, *to make a swift return necessary. Fortunately, we are not far from Cyornas Fjord.*

He turned to Hild. "Raise sails likewise," he told her. "We cannot keep up with her, I fear, but let us not lag far behind."

"You'll see how *Snow Gem* can fly through the water," Hild replied.

And truly, the small ship was exceptionally neat, cutting through the chop as if it scarcely existed. Nevertheless, *Spume Maiden* was but a smudge on the horizon by the time she lowered sails once more and prepared to enter the fjord.

By the time the white ship came into view of the castle and the ice-river *Spume Maiden* had reached the freight dock, some distance farther up the fjord than the buoys where ships customarily tied up.

Hild looked at Rohan, a question in her eyes.

"I daresay Finrod Felagund wants to get the crystal casket off the ship first. Then they must carry it up the cliff to the castle."

"The Rock-Maidens can do that," Hild said.

"Then I will make for the freight dock as well."

The freight dock, now completed, had been built to accommodate the unloading of trade goods. Like the buoys, it was not rooted in a firm anchorage, but was a kind of raft instead. The dock, however, had the advantage of being lashed to stanchions hammered into the rock. There was some talk, Rohan recalled vaguely, of expanding the dock so it could be used for unloading passengers as well as trade goods.

Mikkel had come up behind him. "I thought we were going to visit the castle!" he said fretfully.

"In a while," Rohan assured him.

"I want to go there now!"

"As soon as possible."

"No, now."

"If you are patient, you can go with Petra. Would you like that?"

"Petra! My friend! I love Petra. Where is she?"

"On *Spume Maiden*. She will be with you as soon as she can."

Mikkel was getting worse, Rohan thought. His speech and behavior was now that of a very young child. He had a feeling that if Mikkel stayed long in Cyornas Castle, he might well revert even to infancy. He resolved to consult with Petra. Alien the Rock-Maiden might be, but she had proven helpful in many ways, and she was undeniably fond of Mikkel. When she saw with her own eyes what was happening to him, she would quickly find a way to remedy it. Or, at least, to try.

Zazar waited at the wharf to speak to Rohan as soon as he had disembarked.

"Something has happened," she told him. "We don't know just what yet, but I don't think it's good."

Quickly, she filled him in on what the silver bowl had showed them. "Ysa has gone ahead to the castle to notify Einaar and Bjaudin and the other nobles so they can make all ready not only for Askepott's casket but also for when Ashen and Gaurin arrive. I wanted to stay behind and speak to you."

Likewise, he told her of what he had observed in Mikkel's behavior. "I think he should leave Cyornas Fjord at once, without waiting for Ashen and Gaurin. They will all be disappointed, but I feel he may take permanent harm—besides what he has already suffered—by his presence here."

Zazar scowled, thinking. "I believe you are right. We must notify Petra."

"When we have done that, what can I do, other than wait?"

For answer, Zazar pinched him, hard. "You may yet have a more active role to play, Rohan. Do not be so impatient. Now, send Petra to me."

"Yes, Granddam," Rohan said, rubbing his arm.

Presently, the Rock-Maiden Princess joined Zazar at the wharf-side. She agreed at once that Mikkel should leave the area as soon as possible. "I have seen him. We do not know the full effects of that horrid spell Gunnora put him under but it will do no one good if he stays. I will take him back to the City 'Neath the Waves."

"Rohan said he wanted to see the castle."

"Small boys, I am told, like that sort of thing. Leave it to me, Madame Zazar. Come up to the castle and show my women where to place the casket. They must move quickly, as they do not possess any of the elixir."

"It's not going indoors so they don't have to worry about wrestling it up the stairs to my tower room. I want it put where Askepott is looking north. She should like that, when she wakes up."

Petra smiled. The planes of her face glinted in the wan light. "Indeed she would like that, if she knew. You are a good woman, Madame Zazar, though you might not like my saying so."

"No, I don't," Zazar told her snappishly. Then she softened a trifle. "Look you. We can still communicate by means of the silver bowl. I think I know how to use it even without Ysa's help and she doesn't need to know everything we might discuss."

"Such as?"

"It may be possible, later, if all goes well, that Mikkel may yet be with his parents if we meet, say, at the waterfall. If all goes well."

"There is water running down your face," Petra said.

"That is neither here nor there," Zazar said, dashing away the tears. "It's just that I might— There might be need for your skills with stone-working later."

"I am at your command."

"Thank you."

Petra removed the bracelet from which dangled the small bottle containing the scant remains of the important elixir, and handed it to Zazar. She then went to join her people and led the Rock-Maidens as they guided, rather than carried, the crystal casket up the slope from the wharf and through the castle gate. By the time they arrived, a sizable crowd had gathered, including Bjaudin, Einaar, and as many nobles as were currently in the city. As they watched, the Rock-Maidens created a platform for the casket containing Askepott at one end of the ward, close by the barbican gate, and placed it thereon. Then they all returned to their beautiful little white ship.

Presently, a sobbing wail as from a frustrated child echoed from the fjord walls as the *Snow Gem* raised sail and began its journey back whence it came.

Gaurin's chair at the Council table stood empty. Bjaudin Nordorn-Prince occupied the chair to the right of his father's and Duke Einaar sat on the other side. The carving on the NordornKing's chair caught the light, a fine representation of Gaurin's coat of arms, the silver snowcat, chained and wearing a silver collar, on a green ground surrounded by his motto, *Serve I all*. At the opposite end of the table, Ashen's empty chair was likewise decorated with her arms, a blue vessel on a white ground, with flames rising from it. A border proclaimed the canting pun of her family motto—*Without flame, there can be no Ash*—and a pendant beneath the lozenge-shaped shield bore the ancient Ash motto, *Loyalty ever binds me*. Both of the monarchs' cognizances were surmounted by crowned royal helms and their mantling, in the dominant colors of their shields, was lined with ermine.

"Lord Royance's King-at-Arms, Nikolos, has arrived at Cyornas Castle," Bjaudin told those at the table. "Bid him come in and tell us all."

Nikolos, followed by Zazar and the Duchess Ysa, entered the Council Chamber, ushered in by Rols, acting as Seneschal in Nalren's absence. Nikolos laid Gaurin's treasured Rinbell sword on the table. No other gesture could better describe the gravity of the circumstances. In concise, terse terms Nikolos described what had befallen the NordornKing and NordornQueen. "My master Royance bade me inform you so that healers may make ready for them."

"All that can be done will be done," Bjaudin said. His hands shook, though his voice was firm enough.

"I did inform Count Svarteper, Lord High Marshal, as I entered Cyornas Castle. Even now he is riding out to provide additional escort for . . ."

For the fallen monarchs, Zazar supplied silently.

Duke Einaar spoke up. "And you, Madame Zazar and Your Grace. Did you know aught of this?"

"We did," Ysa replied. "Had not Royance's herald been so swift, we would have told you. Now we can only say, to our sorrow, that we know the story to be true."

"And were you there?" Count Mjødulf inquired.

"No," Zazar answered. "But we saw it right enough, in the pictures conjured by the silver basin you yourself have observed."

The others at the table—Baron Håkon, Baron Arngrim and Count Mjødulf—exchanged stunned glances. Tordenskjold was on his way. Gangerolf, of course, was absent and Baldrian might or might not be with those accompanying the King and Queen. He might just as likely have remained at Åskar in case civil unrest arose again.

Bjaudin slammed his hand down on the polished table. "I am heartily sick of Gangerolf and his infernal tardiness!" he cried. "Someone, go and drag him in here, by the ears if necessary. If he's to be one of the nobility, let him act like it or suffer removal of his title and privileges."

"At once, Your Highness," Rols said. He left the room.

"Well then, my good sirs and ladies," Einaar said in the echoing silence, "there is nothing left for us to do save wait our Sovereigns' return. And Gangerolf's arrival."

A little bitter laughter greeted those words; apparently Bjaudin's outburst had echoed the others' opinions.

"I am going to consult with our Court physician Birger," Zazar said. "Not until the King and Queen arrive will we have an idea how to treat their wounds."

"If then," Einaar said grimly. "Now I do regret me of my complaisance in that scheme of Gaurin's to go out among the people. Not without a much larger armed guard than he had."

"But that would have put all his efforts to naught," Mjødulf commented. "His was a peaceful mission."

"Aye, and see what it got him."

"Gentlemen, we must not argue," said Bjaudin. "Instead, we must seek counsel and wisdom where we might find it, for it is certain that the King and Queen—my father and mother—are in grave straits. For me, I will go to the Fane and talk with Esander the Good." He arose to his feet. "Then I will consult with Duke Einaar."

"Yes, Your Highness," the others at the table said, as they likewise stood up.

Only Ysa had remained silent. Again, Zazar wondered what was going through the Duchess's mind. She suspected she knew, but had no proof. *Well, sooner or later I'll have the story out of her—and then we'll see,* the Wysen-wyf thought.

Twenty-six

ith tender care, Gaurin's attendants laid him on his bed and, with equal tenderness, put Ashen on another bed, in the room outside the royal bedchamber.

Physician Birger unwrapped the bandage around Gaurin's head and examined the wound. "Not good," he murmured to Zazar, who hovered close by his side. "See? There is a depression there, just behind the right ear. I fear the skull is broken and pressing on the brain, which is why he does not regain consciousness." He began replacing the bandage with a fresh one.

"Is there nothing you can do?"

"I have not the skill nor the courage to open the skull and try to relieve the pressure. I might kill him instead. Not that I think he has much chance anyway. Wounds like this—"

"What about Ashen?"

Birger straightened up, dipped his hands in a basin of scented water, and dried them on a towel. "The NordornQueen's malady is from a different cause entirely. I do not know what is causing it and I cannot rouse her, even by burning feathers under her nose.

Thus, I will have to rely on you, Madame Zazar, if you will undertake to discern the reason for her continued faint."

"I caught Ashen as she was being born," Zazar replied. "I will tend her even if she—"

"Do not say it, lest it come true."

Zazar nodded, acknowledging the doctor's words. No sense in summoning the dark-robed shadows that took someone's life away by mentioning them aloud.

"She is sleeping peacefully now," she told Birger, "and there is no task presently for my hands and Ashen's ladies will look after her. I want to go up to my chamber in the northeast tower where I might find something among my collection of herbs and other remedies that might be of use. If anything changes before I return, send for me."

"I will," Birger said, bowing. "May your search be fruitful."

It took only a few minutes to gather healing herbs and elixirs. The real reason Zazar wanted to get to her tower was that there she was not apt to be interrupted, particularly by Ysa, in what she was proposing to do.

The silver basin sat on her worktable, as she had directed. Beside it, stood the ewers she had confiscated from Ashen's table goods—it seemed like years ago—still filled with clean water from the Rock-Maidens' waterfall.

Carefully, she poured water into the basin and, relying on her memory, began to intone the syllables of the ritual Ysa had employed so many times. At worst, the experiment would fail and Zazar would be unsuccessful; at best, she would be able to duplicate what Ysa obviously thought her area alone.

Unexpectedly, in midword, Zazar experienced a draining away of her strength. She tottered and would have fallen except that Weyse appeared out of nowhere and laid her clever paws on Zazar's arm.

New strength flowed into her from the source that had been

tapped into by the benevolent summit, and she resumed her recitation. As before, when Ysa had been in command, a mist began to form above the water.

Zazar had not believed Gunnora's assertion that she knew each time the Ritual of Seeing was invoked. Only Petra had so claimed, and her reaction when she happened to be with Mikkel, as the three women observed him, gave proof. No such reaction from Gunnora. Therefore, she was certain the woman was bluffing. And even if she were not, the possibility of learning more about this person made the risk worth taking.

"Gunnora," she said.

The mist immediately formed, revealing an interesting tableau. The woman Zazar had last seen riding an Ice Dragon was coming from a cavern, its blackness plain against the snow. She wore a tunic with a hood rimmed with wolvine fur, and showed no sign of being aware that she was being observed. While the Wysen-wyf watched, she mounted a sled without dogs to pull it. Instead, she kicked the sled's side, and it sputtered into life.

That is an ice sleigh, Zazar thought. *Askepott told me of such, and how she escaped Holger's steading on one. But where is she going, and where has she come from?* There were no answers, yet.

She spoke aloud. "Petra."

The image shifted. The Rock-Maiden Princess was on the deck of the *Snow Gem.* With a nod of her head she acknowledged Zazar's spell-making, and hurried to her cabin so that they could converse in private.

"I have seen Gunnora," Zazar told her. "I don't think she was aware of me. She was busy." Quickly, she told Petra of what she had seen.

"I do not know where she might have been," Petra said. "But she would occasionally leave the holding for a day or two and then, without a word of explanation, return once more. A cavern mouth, you say?"

"It looked like it."

"I will see what I can learn."

"Thank you."

The image winked out. Zazar sat staring at the silver basin for several minutes, frowning with thought. Then an idea took her. She filled the basin with water again, and, with Weyse supplying energy from whatever mystical source the little creature had access to, repeated the ritual.

"Now let us see if my idea has any degree of soundness," Zazar muttered to herself. "Flavielle."

The image cleared at once; Zazar was peering into a chamber of ice. More than that. To her astonishment, Zazar found herself gazing at the body of the Sorceress, clad in a thin, snow-white dress. Her limbs were composed—but what magic had allowed her to have remained unchanged during the years since her death?

The woman lay on an icy bier beneath a dome of the clearest crystal. Occasional sparks glinted, like fireflies. If Zazar had not known better, she looked as if she would awaken at a touch.

The floor, also of ice, bore marks indicating that someone living had recently been in this . . . this tomb, for such it surely must be.

Gunnora has been here, Zazar realized. But for what purpose?

The body of a man, dried to a husk by the cold and lacking the crystal protective dome, lay close by. Despite the sunken cheeks and leathery skin, Zazar recognized him. Farod, the Dragon Rider. Her stomach lurched as she realized the man's head had been cut off, and then sewn back on with large, clumsy stitches.

She remembered Farod well. She, Ysa, and Ashen had stood atop a promontory, invoking such force as they might, while an Ice Dragon floated down, bearing Farod and his master, the Great Foulness.

Summoned by the iridescent bracelet Ashen wore, Gaurin had come rushing into danger and he and Farod had fought hand to hand on the plain at the base of the promontory while the Great Foulness watched, amused, from atop a pillar of ice he had caused to arise.

His amusement turned to anger when Gaurin killed Farod, running him through, and he himself was vanquished by a magical flame brought forth by the three women.

"But obviously his lieutenant, Farod, didn't die," Zazar murmured. "Not then, at any rate. He found his way back here, back to Flavielle his lover. Back to their child, I surmise. At least, that will do until a better theory comes along."

The image vanished, leaving Zazar bone-weary. She dragged herself up from the table and, trembling in all her limbs, found the bottle of *brandewijn* and poured herself a generous dose. It had the welcome effect of strengthening her rather than muddling her senses.

She quickly scrambled the jars and bottles she had selected earlier into a carry-sack. Almost as an afterthought, she picked up the bottle of *brandewijn* and added it to the collection. Then she returned down the stairs to the chambers where Gaurin and Ashen lay.

When she arrived, she learned that Tordenskjold had returned.

"He was in a marvelous foul humor," Lady Esmiralda, one of Ashen's ladies, told her. "But that vanished quickly when he discovered how things stood with Their Majesties."

"I take it that he was not successful against Holger den Forferdelig."

"He was forced to run. Holger put three ships against him."

"No wonder his temper was foul," Zazar commented. "Well, he'll recover and fight Holger another day. Now, how is Ashen?"

"I think she might rouse before long."

"Then I must be with her." A sudden suspicion hit Zazar. "Where is the Duchess Ysa?"

"I think she has confined herself to her apartment with her little dog. She said she would be no help here in the sickroom, and didn't want to be a hindrance."

A likely tale. Zazar started to go in to Ashen.

"Madame—"

"What is it? Is it Gaurin?"

"Yes, Madame."

"He is worse?"

"His breathing, Madame. It is loud, and labored."

A bad sign. Torn between going to Ashen and seeing if there was anything at all she could do for Gaurin, Zazar chose the latter. At least Ashen hadn't had her head bashed in by a rock thrown by a witless oaf.

It was as Esmiralda had said. Gaurin drew breath with the greatest of efforts, and the sound of it filled the chamber. Birger hovered over the NordornKing and looked up as Zazar approached. A wordless communication passed between them; Gaurin was dying.

"I will send messengers to gather family and nobility," Birger told her. "It is time."

"Yes."

Zazar took his place by Gaurin's bedside. "Esmiralda," she said. "Lady Esmiralda, I mean."

The lady-in-waiting appeared at Zazar's summons. "I am here, Madame."

"If Ashen can summon the least bit of consciousness, she must be here as well when the NordornKing breathes his last," Zazar told her. "Support her, carry her in a chair, if need be."

"It will be done, Madame."

The Nordorn Court must have been assembled outside, awaiting the news, and they now filed into the room. Even Ysa ventured out of the safety of her apartment and joined those standing about the death chamber.

Ashen, propped up in the chair in which she had been carried, seemed not entirely aware of what was transpiring. "I am so tired," she whispered to Zazar. "I gathered a ball of Power. I had done it before. It drained me."

"Yes, I know," Zazar said soothingly. She took the bottle of *brandewijn*, opened it, and poured a dose into a cup one of Ashen's ladies handed her. "Drink this," she urged, holding the cup to Ashen's lips.

Though she coughed when she swallowed the dose, a little

color returned to Ashen's cheeks. She gazed somberly at her husband. "He is dying, isn't he."

"Yes, I fear so."

"He fell in battle," Ashen said. "And so inform them all."

Svarteper was standing nearby. "It is the proper way for a warrior to die, Madame," he said. "The only way for one such as Gaurin NordornKing." He glanced at Zazar and motioned for her to move aside a pace.

"Her Majesty seems to be dazed," he whispered. "She doesn't appear to know what is happening. Have you, well, have you given her something to dull her senses?"

"Only a tot of *brandewijn* just now," Zazar whispered in return. "It seemed to strengthen her."

Svarteper shook his head sadly. "Then it is graver than I suspected. I have seen such before, in soldiers who were mortally wounded. They could watch their closest friend die with no more outward emotion than she is showing now."

"But she was untouched in the incident at Åskar Village."

Cebastian had joined them. "I saw— Well, I saw something."

"She did mention a ball of Power. I thought her mind was wandering."

"Not so, Madame. I witnessed it myself. It formed in response to her summons. Then she hurled it with all her might, and I saw what it did to the man who brought the NordornKing down."

Zazar could no longer deny the obvious. Ashen, too, is dying, she thought. Her heart sank at the thought. "She has given the last of her life force on behalf of the man she has loved ever since the first moment she saw him," she said aloud.

"And he her, Madame," Svarteper said. "It is a story the poets make songs of."

"Put her on the bed beside him," Zazar ordered. "Do not make her spend the few sparks that remain in her, trying to sit upright. In life they were not separated save at great need, and they shall not be separated now."

Ayfare sprang forward, ahead of Ashen's ladies, and quickly

obeyed. Tenderly, the Chatelaine laid Ashen by Gaurin's side. She touched him, and it seemed to Zazar that for a moment he breathed easier.

If anyone took hope from this, that hope vanished almost immediately. While the people crowded into the bedchamber wept loudly or softly according to their natures, Gaurin NordornKing took a last breath, released it, and breathed no more. Ashen NordornQueen smiled on him, lifted her hand, and touched his lips. Then she, too, closed her eyes and her breathing ceased.

Twenty-seven

The *people of the* NordornLand and particularly of Cyornas-berg went into deep, shocked mourning for their lost King and Queen. Black banners flew from every tower, and it seemed that every doorway was hung with black crepe.

Reality dictated that the funerals be held before the new Nor-dornKing could be crowned. Early on the chosen day Zazar and Ayfare, followed by Nalren, Gaurin's gentlemen, and Ashen's ladies, proceeded to the room where the late NordornKing and NordornQueen lay on two biers, passing guards who saluted as they approached. Only the women went in. Until the bodies had been washed and dressed at least partially, the men would remain outside.

The room was cold, kept so with blocks of ice laid around the walls. The women's breath puffed out white and frosty.

For the last time, Ayfare washed Ashen's hair, while Zazar and Lady Ragna performed that service for Gaurin. They removed the bandage that still covered his head and carefully sponged away all the blood that matted the area behind his ear. Then they dried it and combed it out neatly to hide the depressed spot in his skull. When they had finished, Gaurin's hair lay loose and clean, lightly curling. Ayfare began braiding Ashen's silvery locks.

"No one could ever arrange my lady's hair like I could," Ayfare said, her voice breaking.

"She was always beautiful, and you made her more so," Zazar told her. She glanced at Ashen's ladies, several of whom were practically useless with weeping. "Here, you women. Compose yourselves. We must array them in their finest. Go and fetch the appropriate clothing."

"We would have brought it, but we did not know what to choose," Lady Frida said, wiping her nose.

"That would be the white snow-thistle silk, their best," Ayfare said. "These are the ones Their Majesties wore last at the welcome feast when the Duchess Ysa returned to Cyornasberg."

"Yes," Lady Frida said. "I know the ones. Esmiralda, Karina, come with me. And you, too, Amanda."

Presently the ladies returned with the required garments. *Yes,* Zazar thought, *these will do, to send them bravely off into the world beyond.* The clothing was very rich. The finest embroiderers had worked the Ash badge on Ashen's skirt and the silver-collared silver snowcat on Gaurin's doublet. Embroidered silver snowflakes glittered on dress and doublet.

"Call Nalren once we have dressed the NordornQueen so she is not exposed," Zazar told Lady Karina.

"Aye, Madame Zazar. I know he would feel slighted if he were not allowed to do this last service for his lord."

"And bring jewels."

"The State necklaces," Lady Frida said.

"And their crowns," added Lady Amanda.

"No, not the crowns," Ayfare said. "They wore tiaras when the occasion demanded. Who knows where they are kept?"

"I do," said Lady Frida. She left the room where the monarchs' bodies had been laid to go and fetch them.

Good, Zazar thought. *Give them tasks to do, keep them busy, and they will not be so prone to fall into useless tears. That goes for me also,* she added honestly.

When Ashen's dress had been put on her, Nalren entered the room with a box of cosmetics tucked under his arm. He set the box on a table and Ayfare opened it to extract what she needed. While the ladies and Zazar watched, they began applying creams and tinted lotions, and a dusting of rouge. Under their skillful hands, the waxy look of death receded until Ashen and Gaurin appeared to be merely sleeping.

Then Gaurin's gentlemen joined those who were preparing the monarchs for their last journey. Gently, the men lifted the bodies while the ladies slipped fur-lined crimson sleeveless coats on them, and fastened crimson mantles about their shoulders. Then, as finishing touches, they placed the State necklaces around their necks, and settled the tiaras in place on their heads.

Zazar took a deep breath. Now came perhaps the hardest part. "Nalren, please go and inform—inform them."

"Yes, Madame Zazar," the Seneschal said. He bowed and left the room.

Presently, the nobility of the NordornLand filed into the room. Einaar of Åsåfin and the NordornLand, Baron of Asbjørg, led them, closely followed by Earl Royance of Grattenbor and of Åskar. Then came Count Tordenskjold of Grynet, Count Mjødulf of Mithlond, Count Svarteper of Råttnos, Baron Arngrim of Rimaxe, Baron Håkon of Erlend, and Baron Gangerolf of Guttorm. Only Baldrian the Fair, Count of Westerblad, was absent, still on duty in Åskar where the uprising had begun.

The eight men lifted the biers to carry them on their shoulders to the inner ward and the Fane where Esander the Good would conduct the funeral service. As Gaurin NordornKing's half-brother, Einaar claimed the spot of honor, at Gaurin's right shoulder. Likewise, as a lifelong friend, champion and ally, Royance took that position with Ashen's bier. The monarchs' ladies and gentlemen followed, giving place to wives and children as the cortege passed through the Castle of Fire and Ice.

Wives and children of the nobles, castle staff, townspeople, tradesmen, crowded in to the castle grounds, filling every spare space, as if drinking in all the memories they could.

The monarchs' ending had been swift, allowing no time to send word for representatives of the NordornLand's allies to come. Even Hegrin, perforce, must miss the laying to rest of her father and mother. Bjaudin, NordornPrince and soon to be crowned NordornKing, stood stony-faced throughout his parents' funeral. He would not look at his sister Elin, who stood with the Duchess Ysa, both weeping copiously.

Perhaps, thought Zazar from her spot far to the back of the nobility, he had heard a bit of the quarrel these two had had upon Elin's arrival back in Cyornasberg.

"You killed them!" Elin cried, her voice so choked with tears that it was scarcely audible.

"Hush, child! I did no such thing."

"You told me yourself. You started rumors about how Mother and Father were hoarding wealth, and how the people were being oppressed. You stirred up trouble between Prince Karl of Writham and Duke Bernhard of Yuland in hopes that they would go to war with one another." Her voice grew stronger. "You are responsible for the outbreak of rioting, and just look what happened. They are dead, and you are responsible. You killed them."

"Now see here, you little upstart," Ysa said, pulling herself up to her full, formidable height. "It was mischief only, meant only to amuse, and you were a willing participant in it."

"I never thought anything like this would happen."

"Nobody did. You were in it fully as deeply as I, and share the blame. But it can't be helped now. All that we can do is salvage what we can from the tragedy."

"Like what?"

"Well, you will need my guidance now even more than before.

We are much better off allied than separated. Therefore, you will return home with me. You do hope to inherit Iselin from me, don't you."

"Granddam—"

"Don't bother to dissemble. There's no shame in ambition. The shame comes if dishonest methods are employed to make those ambitions into reality. Remember that."

"Yes, Granddam."

No one knew who had been lurking near the door, listening, but the story went through the castle like the wind. Perhaps it reached the ears of Bjaudin NordornPrince. Perhaps not. Perhaps most people dismissed it as idle gossip. Zazar, however, believed every word.

When the funeral ceremonies conducted by Esander the Good were concluded, Bjaudin ascended to a platform that had been set up for him in the castle ward. He was dry-eyed and composed, but his shoulders sagged under the weight of his new responsibility.

"We have come together to mourn your King and Queen, and our beloved father and mother," he said to the people gathered, "and also to celebrate the wondrous things they accomplished. The NordornLand lay in rubble, almost destroyed by a terrible foe. The last direct heir of Cyornas NordornKing of honored memory, was killed in battle with none to survive him. With his last breath he passed his kingship to his cousin Gaurin. Together he and Ashen rebuilt the NordornLand with their own toil, through their own great efforts. All that they did was for the ultimate good of their country. They ruled in peace and justice, and when unrest touched the land it was only fitting that they gave their lives in defense of the kingdom they had worked so hard to create.

"It is fitting likewise that I carry on to the best of my ability. I will never be the great warrior Gaurin NordornKing was, but I can strive to be as good, as fair, and as just. To settle any unrest or un-easiness, this day I vow to all here that I will finish his progress through the land, distributing the King's Penny, so that the people can see that the kingdom is secure and he lives on in me."

All the nobles gathered and the townspeople as well nodded in agreement, and with one voice, said, "Aye."

Then Bjaudin NordornKing gestured and the best stonemason in all the NordornLand stepped forward. In front of all the people gathered, Bjaudin addressed him. "Make for Gaurin and Ashen the finest tomb you can devise. Make it of pure white stone. It will be a monument to them, here in the castle ward. Later, we will place atop this tomb a fair likeness carved with them lying side by side, as they lived and as they died. Their withered right hands, sacrificed in the service of the land they loved and ruled, will be made whole once more. These fair hands shall be clasped in memory of the love they had for each other."

"I will make the tomb, Sir," the man said, bowing. "Though I feel unequal to the task, I will try."

"There is a funeral feast within," Bjaudin announced to the people, "for those who desire it."

Then the nobles bore the bodies to a temporary tomb outside the castle walls, and returned to the Great Hall where the feast had been laid out. Bjaudin would occupy the central seat at the High Table with Princess Elin beside him. Everyone waited to en-ter until they were seated. The nobles and those who had had part in putting down the late uprising were to be grouped at tables to the Prince's right, to honor them. The ladies were likewise seated at tables set to Bjaudin's left.

Cebastian sought out Svarteper as they waited in the vestibule. "Sir," he said, "I would ask something of you."

The High Marshal of the NordornLand stared at the Ren-delian warrior. "Say on."

"Well, my lord Gaurin NordornKing asked me—that is, he mentioned, if you would be agreeable—"

"Oh, spit it out, man."

"He wanted me to come to Cyornas Castle and be your second, an it please you, sir."

"An it please me." Svarteper glowered, his face becoming red. "And did my lord NordornKing then think me in my dotage?"

"No, sir. He but thought you might appreciate having a little of your burden of duty lifted from your shoulders."

"Hmmm. I will think on it," Svarteper said grudgingly. "Seeing as it was practically his last wish and all."

Zazar had been watching this exchange almost with amusement. "Well," she said to Ysa. "That's settled. Now, what do you propose to do?"

The Duchess dabbed at her eyes with a handkerchief. "I will return to Iselin, and Elin with me, to see to her upbringing."

"That's very noble of you, considering . . . well, considering what I think you did but cannot now prove."

"I had nothing to do with the way those ungrateful peasants rose up against their rightful lord!" Ysa exclaimed.

"I do not remember suggesting that you did," Zazar returned. "Will you never learn to stop your idle meddling? This time the consequences were more dreadful than you could even imagine."

"It was done in all innocence," Ysa protested. She dabbed at her eyes again. "It was a frivolous pastime, nothing more, making suitors jealous to entertain Princess Elin—"

"—who does not need to learn such games. Nor do I think that is the whole of it, but let it go." Zazar sighed. "Think on this. Next time you decide to amuse yourself in such a fashion, I will be waiting to turn it back on you. And so remember."

"I will be true," Ysa said fervently. "And so I swear."

"Oh, go, go, before you start twisting words again to change the meaning of your oath."

Duke Einaar approached. "The Prince has taken his place at the High Table. Shall you go in to supper?" he asked.

"I couldn't eat a bite, but I will go in," Zazar said. She took the Duke's proffered arm before Ysa could, relishing the startled look on her face.

And so, she thought, as she picked at the plate of delicacies Duchess Elibit insisted on preparing for her, I remain here while Ysa escapes to the safety of her duchy.

As the meal neared its end, Rols approached and leaned down to whisper in Zazar's ear. "Bjaudin NordornPrince would have a private conference with you, when everyone has gone."

"Tell my grandson that I will await his pleasure."

To her surprise, Bjaudin did not wish this discussion to take place in his apartment or even the apartment the late King and Queen had shared and which, by right, was now his. "Let us go up to your private quarters, Granddam. There is that I wish to talk with you about and it does not need anyone else around to overhear."

"It's a long climb," Zazar said, but nevertheless she led the way.

To her further surprise she found the silver ewers neatly lined up outside her door along with the silver basin.

"The ewers are all filled with clean water," Bjaudin told her. "I would have you perform the Ritual of Seeing for me."

It was on the tip of Zazar's tongue to tell him that it was far too late at night to be peering in on anybody, but nevertheless she led him into the tower apartment and lighted the candles. She then laid out the basin and filled it from two of the ewers.

"I have never been in your quarters before," Bjaudin commented. "You could have more comfortable accommodations down in the main house."

"This suits me well," Zazar told him. "And it is private. I think you said that this Seeing was to be a private matter."

"So I did."

Weyse appeared at Zazar's side, and she began the Ritual. "Speaking of privacy, whose are we invading at this time of night?"

Bjaudin answered with another question. "Can you beg a favor of the Rock-Maiden Princess Petra?"

Zazar's eyebrows rose. "You could say that she owes me something. Or will. I have located the source of a particular root from which an elixir can be made that lets Rock-Maidens endure the presence of iron for a time," she said. "It grows, rarely, in the Lowlands."

"Good. Then please proceed."

She continued the ceremony without further comment. When she spoke Petra's name, the image of the Rock-Maiden materialized in the mist. She seemed to be asleep, in a bed that looked like a giant white shell. Zazar noted that she was alone.

"Petra," she said again. "Petra, please wake up."

The Rock-Maiden roused and sat up, her white silken bedclothes falling around her waist. She slept nude. "Who calls?"

"It is I, Zazar," the Wysen-wyf replied. "Sorry about the lateness of the hour."

"It must be important."

"Yes, it is. There are several matters. First, Gaurin Nordorn-King and Ashen NordornQueen have died," she said, trying to keep her voice steady. "Their funeral was today. It is too late to tell them how young Prince Mikkel fares, but I want to know. As does someone else here with me."

"I am sorry for your loss," Petra said, and, indeed, she did looked saddened at the news. She arose from her bed and donned a white silk robe. "You may set your mind at peace about Ridder Red Fox. The farther north we sailed, the more he came back to himself—well, himself as he was before we set off on our journey but not as you knew him. He is content, and happy with me."

"That is good news among all the bad," Zazar said. "His future, though—"

"He is safe and secure as long as he is with me," Petra said. "Mikkel is as one who has been frozen in time. His body grew, while his memory diminished. Since his body cannot ungrow, so shall his memory of his early years remain a mystery. He is caught in a niche in time. He does not further age, nor does he decline. He is, in a way, almost as immortal as I am. Barring an unfortunate accident—which I am fully prepared to avoid on his account—he will live forever."

Andre Norton & Sasha Miller

Zazar digested this in silence. Try as she might, she could find no flaw in the Rock-Maiden Princess's logic. "That is very interesting." She exchanged glances with Bjaudin.

"You said there were several reasons you have roused me from my sleep."

"Bjaudin NordornPrince is with me. He wants to speak with you."

"Let him. I would know what sort of man my Ridder Red Fox has as brother."

"I give you greetings, sovereign to sovereign," Bjaudin said. "I wish to make my parents' tomb fine, and there is no one better to ask than you to create the fair effigies that will lie atop it."

Zazar wondered why she had not thought of this herself. "Bjaudin NordornPrince speaks for me as well," she said. "I told you that I might call on your skill with stonework. And so I do."

"I would comply at once, except . . ."

"The elixir."

"Yes. My Maidens were ill most of the way home."

"I apologize. However, I believe I have unlocked its secret. I will call upon someone who is a kind of sister to me to send me all she can find of the necessary ingredient. I will have a good supply waiting for you when you return."

"Without Ridder Red Fox."

"Yes. Without Mikkel. Come at midsummer. Bjaudin NordornPrince is to be married then and crowned NordornKing."

"What finer wedding gift could there be to give the brother of my Red Fox. I will be there, bringing my most skilled artisans."

"One more thing. If the little warkat and his mate show up at the door to your underwater city, let them in."

The Rock-Maiden smiled just as her image winked out.

"My mind is now at ease about my brother's welfare even though his fate is not one he sought," Bjaudin said. "He is safe with one who, I believe, will die before harm comes to him. The amulet he filched from Mother's jewel box brought him luck after all."

"That seems cold," Zazar said, "as if you didn't care."

"I care deeply, Granddam. I am not abandoning him. I plan to send an envoy to the City 'Neath the Waves, someone Mikkel once knew. Tjórvi, his friend. Do you think he might help Mikkel regain his memory?"

"I have heard worse ideas," Zazar admitted. "Not sure if Petra would relish losing her Red Fox, though."

"It is possible he will ever be as he is, and if so, he will be happy with her. I am at ease about my parents' tomb also. The jewels and tiaras worn by the NordornKing and NordornQueen will go into the Nordorn treasury. In stone, however, they will wear their crowns, and their heads will lie on tasseled pillows. Their feet will rest on subdued Ice Dragons." He seated himself in one of the chairs beside the fire. "Now, Granddam Zazar, may I have a cup of tea? There is yet that which I wish to discuss with you."

"Of course."

Zazar filled her teakettle, added leaves to it, and set it over the fire to heat. As she prodded the coals into flame, light glinted on a ring that Bjaudin wore on the forefinger of his right hand. The last time she had seen this ring, Ashen had been wearing it.

"Yes," Bjaudin said, "this is the Great Signet of Ash." He leaned forward in his chair, clasping his hands in front of him. "You have been very tight-lipped about your worries, but others have not been so discreet."

"Ysa."

The NordornPrince smiled. "Yes. Granddam Ysa. I know that the near-death of the other Wysen-wyf weighs heavily on you, with the question of how to revive her, or even if she can be brought back."

Zazar gave the mixture in the kettle a stir, and poured out two mugs of tea. She handed one to Bjaudin. "Say on."

"You worry also about the Bracelet of the Nine and the Sorceress's daughter, Gunnora."

Zazar stared at him in frank astonishment. "Is there nothing you don't know about?"

He smiled. "I try to know as much as possible about what goes on concerning people I care about."

"I had long since decided to hide the bracelet where Ysa could not 'accidentally' find it and take it back to Iselin with her."

"Granddam Ysa will remain in Cyornas for a while. Elin will return to Iselin in her stead."

"And why, I would like to know?"

"We will need her. Gunnora is a great danger to the NordornLand—indeed, to the world." Bjaudin sipped at his tea, and then seemed to change the subject. "Do you remember the Arikarin? No, I suppose you do not, but it threatened Cyornas Castle while you and Mother were traveling north to the aid of my father."

"I remember the horrible smell of the thing, when we returned."

"Uncle Einaar had knowledge of trolls and the wit to gather all four of the Great Rings. With them, we fought the troll-slug. I held Mother's ring."

She did some quick calculations. "You were just a baby at the time."

"That is correct. Beatha carried me to the platform where Aunt Rannore, my brother-in-law King Peres, and Granddam Ysa waited. I took the ring in two fingers and clutched it in my fist. And then we subdued the Arikarin."

"And you truly remember all this? Not just think you do because you were told later?"

"I truly remember it. I was teething, and chewing on the sapphire felt cool and soothing to me. Uncle Einaar has suggested that we could use the Great Signets again in these current difficulties, and I agreed."

Zazar could have slapped herself as sharply as she had once chastised the slow-witted in her charge. She had completely forgotten the Great Rings and the Power they could command. But then, she had had a lot on her mind, and had not actually seen the might of the Rings. Also, she had always thought of Bjaudin as a

olemn, scholarly boy, older than his years, but very much in the
hadow of his illustrious father. Now, it was apparent, he was com-
ng into his own, and brilliantly, if this converse with him was any
ndication. A great weight lifted from her shoulders. "I have been
eeling very alone, as if I were the main—the only—bulwark against
he Sorceress's daughter."

Bjaudin smiled and set his mug down on the hearth. "You are
ot alone, and never have been."

"Your mother was carrying you when she and Ysa and I sub-
ued the Great Foulness. I knew from the time you were born
hat—possibly as a result—you commanded Power but I didn't
now what form it would take."

"And she was carrying Elin when she killed the Mother Ice
Dragon. Elin has Power also."

Zazar did not comment on this observation. She knew there
vas no need to, for both knew that Elin's store of Power was sure
o become a trial for the young King in days to come.

"Tordenskjold and Uncle Rohan," Bjaudin continued, "will be
oing after Holger once *Nordorn Queen's Own* has been com-
leted and the odds shortened in Nordorn favor. If anyone can
ring a halt to Holger's heretofore undisputed monarchy of the
orthern seas, it will be those two. They will enjoy it enormously
nd will need no help from me. From us."

"Us?"

"Of course, Granddam. I will never cease to need your wise
ounsel."

To her astonishment, Zazar burst into tears. "Since Ashen and
aurin died, I have been numb, not yet feeling grief or sorrow,"
he confessed brokenly. "Too much to do. Now you have made it
ossible for me to mourn. They are gone, irretrievably gone, their
asks complete, their lives finished. But they left a worthy succes-
or whom I greatly underestimated until now." She swallowed
ard and wiped her eyes on her petticoat.

Weyse jumped up into her lap. Zazar hugged her close and
oke into her fur. "Hope remains, and life continues. Ah, Ashen,"

she murmured, her voice still thick with tears, "what marvels you
and your Gaurin have set in motion. I hope to live long enough to
see them spun out to completion."

In the bustle of tardy guests arriving to express their condolences,
Earl Royance and his Countess traveling back to Åskar, and a very
sullen Princess Elin returning alone to Iselin in a flurry of carriage
and boxes and new clothing, the disappearance of the four
warkats went almost unremarked.

If it hadn't been for Weyse, even Zazar might not have noticed.
But the little creature clung to the Wysen-wyf, disconsolate, until
she went in search of the warkat Finola, with whom Weyse had always had a loving relationship. But the warkats were gone.

"What does this mean?" she asked Einaar.

"Warkats come and go as they please, you know that," he
replied. "They have ever allied themselves with men when it suited
them, as they did with my brother and also with Ashen. There is
no longer need for them, and so they have returned to their home
somewhere in the far northern reaches."

"Well, they might have notified me," Zazar said grumpily.
"Weyse is heartbroken over Finola's absence."

"She will figure out where her friend has gone. She will visit
from time to time, and all will be well."

"Bjaudin NordornKing is lucky to have you as his most trusted
friend and adviser," Zazar said.

"Thank you, Madame."

She turned somber. "They had a full life, didn't they."

For a moment, Einaar seemed at a loss as to her meaning. "Oh,
Gaurin and Ashen. Yes, they did."

"I only wish— Well, I wish I could have told them that I . . .
that I loved them."

"I think they knew, Madame Zazar. I think they knew."

TOR

Voted
#1 Science Fiction Publisher
20 Years in a Row
by the *Locus* Readers' Poll

———•———

Please join us at the website below
for more information about this
author and other science fiction,
fantasy, and horror selections, and to
sign up for our monthly newsletter!